T0271530

WINTER LOST

WINTER LOST

PATRICIA BRIGGS

orbit-books.co.uk

ORBIT

First published in hardback in Great Britain in 2024 by Orbit

1 3 5 7 9 10 8 6 4 2

Copyright © 2024 Patricia Biggs

The moral right of the author has been asserted.

A CIP catalogue record for this book is available from the British Library.

HB 978-0-356-1833-6
C format 978-0-356-51832-9

Printed and bound in Great Britain by Clays Ltd, Elcograf S.p.A.

Papers used by Orbit are from well-managed forests and other responsible sources.

MIX
Paper | Supporting
responsible forestry
FSC® C104740

Orbit
An imprint of
Little, Brown Book Group
Carmelite House
50 Victoria Embankment
London EC4Y 0DZ

An Hachette UK Company
www.hachette.co.uk

www.littlebrown.co.uk

To my partner in crime—Dan dos Santos, who understands that a picture paints a thousand words. Thank you, my friend.

PROLOGUE

MERCY

AN ARTIFACT IS AN OBJECT THAT EITHER HAS A MAGI-
cal effect or can be used to create a magical effect. Most of these
are minor things—a lucky penny or a staff that helps you find
your way home when you are lost. But magic is unpredictable,
and some artifacts change in purpose and power.

Most artifacts are intentionally made, usually by the fae,
though witches, warlocks, and wizards have also made their fair
share. Some artifacts just happen. My friend Warren has a car,
given to him by his lover with the intent of making him safer, that
magicked itself spontaneously. That car tries to take care of him.
Annoying, but also sweet.

The Soul Taker was an artifact like Warren's car, in that it just
happened. But it was the furthest thing from sweet. It was old, a
sickle used to harvest the blood of sacrifices in service of some
unknown and long-forgotten god. By the time I encountered it, it

had become sentient and fixed in its purpose of bringing its god back on a bridge of the dead.

It did something to me, to my magic and to my soul. I thought that those effects would go away when I had it destroyed.

I was wrong.

INTERLUDE

June
Montana

SUMMER WASN'T HIS SEASON, BUT THE CREATURE known to the locals as John Hunter still liked the storms. This one came with lightning and thunder, making the interior of his cabin feel like a refuge and adding unexpected percussion to the music filling the room.

It was chilly so he'd lit the fire, and the smell of the burning wood was as warming as the flames. Not that the cold bothered *him*.

He closed his eyes, stretching his legs out. His dog grumbled and scooted around until his great muzzle weighed down John's right foot again.

They both listened to the music—but the dog didn't wince when their musician hit a flurry of wrong notes.

"I told you, harp or guitar I can do. But this is not like either one of them to an amazing degree." Pause. "It probably would have helped if the person who created this thing actually knew how to play it."

Amused, John Hunter opened his eyes and turned his head to look at his entertainment.

The clever and graceful, if work-begrimed, fingers of his guest danced over the lyre. The man, dressed in battered jeans and a torn T-shirt, looked at home in the cabin in a way that the lyre did not. Silver-covered wood inlaid with luminous blue turquoise formed the arms of the lyre, ending with elaborate carvings of wolf heads, or possibly dogs. At the base, the sound box was carved into a beautiful woman's face. The artifact would have been more appropriately housed in an art museum instead of a cabin in the mountains.

"Doesn't the magic help?" John asked.

His guest looked up, mischievous eyes alight. "Haven't you learned by now? Magic *never* helps."

1

December

MERCY

THERE WAS A 1960 BEETLE PARKED IN FRONT OF MY shop.

I eyed it warily as I let myself into the office. Having a 1960 bug parked outside was not unusual—I specialized in the old air-cooled VWs to the point where people brought them to me from other states to work on or restore. I just hadn't seen this particular one before.

I would have remembered.

I locked away my purse, draped my coat over the chair behind the counter, then walked into the garage bays. The light was already on and Zee was hard at work. He'd been here for a while because the big furnace had already heated the space to human-friendly temperatures.

Buried in the engine compartment of the car he was bitterly cursing in German, Zee looked like a wiry old man with white hair that was thinning on top and a bit of a potbelly. Thanks to fae glamour, he bore no resemblance to the Dark Smith of Drontheim, who had built many deadly weapons and used them in his time to slaughter saints, kings, and anyone else who annoyed him. Currently, he worked a little more than full-time in the garage he'd once owned, helping me repair old cars.

"Unusual paint job out there," I told him as I got into my overalls.

Zee grunted and tapped the quarter panel of the vintage Porsche 930 he'd been working on for the last three days. It was decked out in metal-flake red with extremely good pin-striping that included the word "Widowmaker" hand-lettered on the driver's side in silver. The passenger door had a fist-sized black widow just below the side-view mirror with a silver web that extended over the rest of that side.

"Okay," I said. "But the Porsche's paint job is beautiful, and everyone knows the 930 turbo is called the Widowmaker. Why in the world would you paint a giant eye on the hood of a bright purple bug?"

Zee, back to tinkering in the engine compartment, grunted.

"Not that purple is a bad color for a bug," I said. "And *two* eyes might even be cute—if they were soft and happy. But one crazytown eye on the hood is just creepy."

"Shameful thing to do to a nice old car," he agreed. "Did you see the plates?"

There was something in his voice that sent me back out into the cold to check the vanity plates on the bug.

PPLEATR

It took me a moment to work it out.

I went back into the garage and went to work. After about twenty minutes, I said, "Does it eat flying purple people? Or purple people? Or just people?"

"Now you've done it," Zee grumbled. "Be silent if you can't be useful."

I grinned and went back to work.

Zee broke first. By lunchtime, though, we were both humming the stupid song. An hour later, to change things up, I sang the first line of "Itsy Bitsy Teenie Weenie Yellow Polkadot Bikini," and our earworm grew by one.

The phone rang as Zee was fighting back with "It's a Small World," which was cheating.

"Mercy's Garage," I answered.

"It's Mary Jo. I—" She paused. "I really need to talk to someone about something and I think you are the right someone."

Mary Jo wanted to talk to me. Maybe the Purple People Eater had changed the orbit of the planet, or hell had truly frozen over.

IN DECEMBER AT SIX P.M., EVEN WITH THE STREETLIGHTS, it was dark. I was running a little late because I'd stopped at home to change.

The overhead clouds blocked the stars and left the waning but still nearly full moon a faint glow in the sky. Snow drifted down in the giant fat flakes that only happened when the temperature was just perfect, snowman-building snow. The kind, in fact, that stuck to my wipers so they both squeaked and also left water splotches on my windshield.

Mary Jo had asked me to meet her. As I drove through the accumulating snow, I had the same triumphant feeling in my belly that I did at the end of a difficult but successful hunt.

Mary Jo and I had been not friends but certainly friendly until her Alpha had pulled me into the werewolf pack as his mate. She wasn't the only wolf who had resented him bringing in someone who turned into a coyote, but Mary Jo had been the central player in the anti-coyote faction of the pack.

At first I'd tried ignoring their dislike of me. The pack was Adam's problem, and they seemed to run better when I kept my head down. He'd put a stop to any active harassment, and what various of the werewolves had *thought* about me hadn't mattered.

But things were different now. Our pack was responsible for the safety of anyone in our territory, thanks to yours truly. As an added bit of icing on the cake, we had to do it as a lone pack.

The Marrok who ruled the werewolves in this part of the world was worried that our actions could draw them all into a real war. So he'd cut us off. If we were unaffiliated (what a pedestrian word for the blood-and-flesh bonds that bound the werewolves together), then the worst that would happen is that the fae would wipe out our pack. Or the humans would kill us all. Or the witches. Or the vampires. Or some unknown nasty we hadn't run into yet. But the damage would be local and not an interspecies war.

We were on our own and in over our heads. That meant we didn't have time for petty rivalries or stupid games within our pack—we were too busy running to put out one figurative fire before another started. I *had* to fix the damage bringing me into the pack had done.

As Adam's mate, I'd taken my share of organizing the defense of our territory. I had made a point of taking on the worst of the resultant jobs myself—and I'd made sure to bring Mary Jo with me. Every time we went out, she was a little less unhappy with me. Two days ago, we fought a fishy-something-with-teeth that decided to take up residence on one of the small islands in the middle of the river.

When Mary Jo killed it, the unidentifiable giant river monster thingy had exploded into a mass of inch-long versions of the giant thing. My legs still had bite marks. But Mary Jo had given me a high five when we'd hunted the last of them down.

Mary Jo wasn't the only recalcitrant wolf I brought with me to awful jobs. She had just been the most resistant. There was nothing like shared misery to build relationships. Adam said that he'd felt the pack bonds settling in tighter since I'd started my campaign.

As I headed to the meeting with Mary Jo, I thought that just possibly I could start giving some of the worst jobs to people other than me. That would be nice.

My cell phone rang as Columbia Drive swung west on its trip to the Blue Bridge. The suspension bridge would have made the journey a lot shorter, but a troll fight had damaged it, then a fae lord demolished it. Reconstruction was set to finish, barring delays, in the spring, and in the meantime the Blue Bridge, already overcrowded, had become the main artery between Kennewick and Pasco.

I'd taken my Vanagon tonight. Built in the last century, it had a CD player but no Bluetooth. As a small business owner and the mate of the Alpha of a werewolf pack, I needed to answer my phone. I'd solved the problem with a Bluetooth earpiece.

My stepdaughter, Jesse, rolled her eyes when I first put it on.

"The time-share call center called, and they want their headset back. Get some earbuds, Mercy, you'll thank me later."

Earbuds and mechanicking weren't good partners—at least not for me. I'd lost three pairs of earbuds before I decided that my twenty-dollar Bluetooth earpiece that could go through the wash and still work was a better option.

The phone rang twice before I'd fumbled the earpiece in and tapped to activate it.

"Mercy here," I said.

No one answered.

I knew that silence. My breath hitched because my diaphragm thought it would be a really good idea to run away from whatever was scaring us. Scaring me.

I'd gotten a different number and switched carriers. Only the pack and family had this number. It wasn't listed anywhere—and my current phone was under Warren's boyfriend Kyle's name.

It could have been a misdialed number or a failed robocall. I hoped for a thickly accented voice to tell me their name was Susan and they were calling to talk to me about my credit card. But I knew who it was.

I felt my heart rate pick up as the seconds ticked slowly by. I should have disconnected, because anyone I knew would have already spoken by now. But I didn't hang up. He would only call back.

The windshield screeched again, so I turned the wipers off. Someone honked at me. To get out of traffic, I took a right-hand turn too quickly, veering briefly into the wrong lane. Rather than continuing to drive, I pulled over and parked next to a used car lot.

"So nice of you to join us," whispered Bonarata, the Lord of Night.

He wasn't here. But I pictured him in my head, looking more like Thug Number Three in an old movie about the Mafia than the vampire who ruled Europe and, from what I had been able to gather, any other vampires he cared to take over. A little less than two months ago he'd fought Adam and beaten him. He'd beaten me, too—but I'm a lightweight. In the ten years I'd known Adam, I'd never seen anyone beat him in a fight. Bonarata had made it look easy.

If Bonarata had wanted to, he could have killed us both. Instead, he chose to play a game. He'd decided to make an example of me because I'd escaped from him and made him look weak. I hoped that it would work out to being a fatal mistake—but we wouldn't know that for sure until the game ended one way or another.

The phone calls were to let me know Bonarata had not forgotten his promise.

My hands were shaking and I was hyperventilating. Bonarata scared me more than I would have thought possible. He had promised to kill everyone I loved—and I believed he could do it. But that would not be today, I reminded myself. Today, right now, I needed to control myself or Adam would notice.

I'd left Adam preparing for an online meeting with his business partners in New Mexico over some military legal snafu. I understood it was a dangerous matter, that lives had already been lost. Tightropes needed to be walked and tempers soothed. Adam was good at tightropes, but the temper thing was not his strong suit. Adam didn't need to know about this call right now.

I was supposed to get help when Bonarata called, so we could trace his call and figure out where he was. But we hadn't managed to trace the location meaningfully the last twenty or so times he'd called. I didn't think that this call would be the one to change that.

I could hear someone breathing in my earpiece now, shaky, shivery breaths like a rabbit pinned by a fox. The bunny knows it's about to die, but not when that moment is going to come. Bonarata was a vampire; he didn't need to breathe. And if he chose to, he wouldn't breathe like that. The Lord of Night had invited a guest to join us.

This was going to be one of the bad calls.

I'd hung up the first time and gotten an audio CD of what Bonarata had done over several hours after I'd disconnected. If I listened when he called, he said at the end of the CD, he'd be more merciful. If I hung up, he'd enjoy himself. The length of his victim's suffering was my choice.

If this was going to be one of those calls, I was going to have to do something more than just keep calm, or Adam would drop his important business to come save me when I was in no danger at all.

I shared two bonds with my mate—the bond that made me a part of the Columbia Basin Pack that he ruled, and the more intimate mating bond. I knew how to shut them down hard so that very little information traveled from me through them. Adam had shown me how to do that.

My mate understood that sometimes being part of a werewolf pack could be overwhelming to someone who'd spent most of her life on her own. Sometimes I desperately needed to be alone again. He knew that. He'd shown me how to find solitude when I was bound to him and to the pack—and to the vampire Stefan.

Because that was the other bond I held in my soul. Stefan was careful. Like Adam, he knew that if he tried to hold too tightly,

I'd chew my metaphorical foot off to be free. Stefan wasn't going to know about this call. I always kept that bond as closed as I could manage, and Stefan was used to that.

But after our pack and mate bonds were silenced and I was spirited off to Europe, Adam wasn't so sanguine about me closing down our bond, even though he could still sense me. We'd had to figure out something else.

Adam had been married before, but I was his first mate. That should have meant that both of us struggled through how to deal with our mating bond, but he'd been an Alpha since before I was born, and that gave him a distinct advantage. The mate bond was different from the pack bonds, but the rules they followed were written in the same language, figuratively speaking. He understood how the magical ties worked better than I did, and he'd figured out something that would give me privacy when I needed it without causing him to overreact.

Shadowing the bond, he called the new method. "Pull veils across the path until it's difficult to see through," he said. Pack magic, I'd discovered, involved negotiating through a lot of metaphors. Instead of closing it down like a faucet, I layered our bond with stretchy and filmy curtains. The metaphor gave me a method that worked as long as I didn't worry too much about what the curtains were made of.

Sitting cold and frightened in my old van, I pulled the shadows around my bonds until I was alone in the night with the vampire. On the phone, I reminded myself. He was on the phone.

There was a sharp noise that made me jump. It took me a moment to realize the sound had come from the earpiece.

Maybe it had been a slap, because it was followed by a pained squeak. Then someone started crying. It wasn't a cry for attention—

those kinds of cries are about hope. Someone will care. Someone will do something about the situation. There was no hope in the sound I heard.

Most of Bonarata's calls were voiceless, just me listening to environmental sounds—a street or woods or inside a building—until he hung up.

The last time he'd hurt someone, it had been a man. We'd had a package delivered from Romania with body parts in it a week later. Adam had traced it to the facility it had been mailed from, but no one there had remembered the package or who had mailed it.

That's when I'd gotten the new phone and the calls had stopped. It had taken eight days for him to figure out how to contact me again.

I should hang up. I knew I should. He couldn't make me answer the phone. But I couldn't leave this person—who sounded like a child—alone with the vampire.

"There, there," crooned the familiar deep voice. In my twenty-dollar earpiece it lacked the resonance it had in person. That didn't make it any less scary. I felt like I needed to hear every nuance in order to predict where the attack was coming from.

I pushed my earpiece deeper into my ear, and the sound got a fraction more clear.

"Are you scared?" he asked, a faint amusement in his voice that did not vanish when he repeated his question in French. "*Tu as peur, ma petite?*"

"*Oui.*" And now I could tell the child was a girl. A little older than I'd first thought—though that didn't make it any better.

The speed and raggedness of her breathing told me that she

was way beyond scared. Me, too. I was so scared for her—and there was not a thing I could do about it.

I put a hand over my mouth so I wouldn't make a sound. I didn't want to give him the satisfaction.

His next word was a whisper. "*Bon.*"

There was a gasp that sounded more like a noise a kitten might make, followed by a high-pitched whine. I sat frozen in my seat, listening to the wet sounds of Bonarata feeding.

I couldn't have said how long I sat there before there was a little pop of cartilage giving way followed by a dull thump of a body hitting a hard floor.

On Bonarata's orders, vampires were not allowed to kill their prey anymore. That didn't mean the humans they fed upon didn't die accidentally. They hid them in car wrecks and drownings. Sometimes they buried them in places the dead were unlikely to be found.

Evidently Bonarata did not follow his own rules. Color me not surprised.

Silence was sometimes very loud.

After a few more seconds, the caller disconnected.

I drew in a shaky breath and told myself what I'd just listened to had not been my fault. The problem was that I was well aware that might not be true. Maybe if Bonarata hadn't decided to make my life a living hell, that girl would have lived a long and happy life. Maybe she had always been destined to be the food of vampires.

Maybe it had been a performance just for me and no one had died at all.

My fault or not, there had been nothing I could have done

about it. That was truth, but cold comfort. I breathed slowly until I thought I was feeling more or less normal.

Then I got out the baby wipes I kept in all of my rigs because I never knew when I was going to get my hands covered with the mess mechanicking engenders. Baby wipes are surprisingly good at cleaning off grime. I used them now to wipe away tears and snot.

When I was sure that my face was clean—because I didn't want to know what I'd looked like directly after that call—I pulled down the visor and popped open the mirror. I looked a little flushed—but that would fade by the time I made it to Uncle Mike's. There was not much I could do about my reddened eyes. Hopefully the traffic on the Blue Bridge would be slow enough that they would clear up before I got to Uncle Mike's.

I should have called Adam. But I wasn't going to. I had things to do tonight.

I bent over and retrieved my purse. I pulled the phone out and set it screen up on the passenger seat, where I could see it. After a moment's thought, I grabbed it, put the ringer on silent, and set it back down, screen side toward the seat.

I turned the radio up to full blast and pulled a U-turn to get back onto Columbia Drive. As I drove over the river, flowing black and deep below me, Freddie Mercury asked me if I wanted to live forever.

AS SOON AS I OPENED THE DOOR OF UNCLE MIKE'S, I was met with a wall of magic that forced me back out into the parking lot before I took even one full step in.

I did some deep breathing for a few minutes, watching the

flakes come down. I'd had an incident with an ancient artifact a couple of months ago and it had left me with a few odd quirks that came and went, one of which left me overly sensitive to magic. Usually if I waited a couple of minutes, I'd be back to normal. Normalish.

When I got cold, I headed back in. This time, the magic wasn't so overwhelming. There was always magic at Uncle Mike's—it was a pub owned by a fae. There were wards to keep unaccompanied humans out. I was pretty sure there were wards that protected the building and its inhabitants, too. And there were just a lot of the kinds of beings who carried magic along with them wherever they went.

The scent of seasonal greenery outcompeted the mixed odors of alcohol and packed bodies that filled Uncle Mike's. Music spilled from hidden speakers just loud enough that, if I wanted to, I could ignore the conversations going on around me without the music being so loud it was painful. Both the smell and the sound level were perfectly judged—as were so many things, because the proprietor took great care that they would be so. The fae take their hosting duties very seriously, and none more so than Uncle Mike.

Usually this part of the pub gave off tacky cheap-bar vibes and not winter-themed-greenhouse stage-production vibes. But now it felt like at any moment Santa would stroll in with a reindeer or two and offer naughty boys and girls peppermint schnapps.

There was a lot more obvious magic involved in the decorating than Uncle Mike usually allowed. Or maybe my recently acquired sensitivity to magic was still acting up.

I gave the vines on the wall a wary look. Were there more of them than there had been just a moment ago?

The deep green vines could have been an odd variety of ivy, or some other creeping kind of plant, but they looked like holly to me. I wasn't a gardener, but even so, I was fairly certain that holly was usually found as a bush. Here, though, the thin willowlike withes covered in the distinctive spiky leaves and bright red berries wove through the vines to create a festive yet somehow oddly creepy air.

The knotted trunk of an ancient oak—which hadn't been here at all two weeks ago—occupied one corner of the room. Its winter-bare branches reached up to the ceiling of the pub, which, once my attention was drawn to it, appeared to be higher than usual. Where the branches intersected the ceiling, they transformed into a painted version, an unreal canopy of gray bark that spread out over the crowded venue. Those gray branches, both painted and real, were burdened with an infestation of mistletoe that dripped down into the room.

The oak looked so much a part of the pub that I wondered if Uncle Mike had created it as part of his holiday decor—or if it had always been there and we were only privileged to see it now as the shortest day of the year approached.

I didn't see Mary Jo in the main seating area, so I wove my way forward through the scattered tables and wandering people. Courtesy usually kept the dance floor in the back free of people who weren't dancing, which served to lessen the density of the crowd somewhat. If I could reach the dance floor, I could edge around to the back rooms.

I broke through the mass finally. A passing bump from someone else trying to get through the crowd knocked me sideways, and I put a foot on the rough old flooring, this night clear even of dancers. Through the sole of my shoe, magic sizzled my synapses in a way that was consuming, if not quite unpleasant. I momentarily forgot the phone call, my tardiness (I had not wanted to be late to this meeting), and the importance of what I hoped to build tonight.

I stood a moment, dazed by sensation, before I realized where the magic was coming from: the Christmas tree in the center of the empty dance floor. As impressive as the old oak had been, it was this second tree that held true power. Gradually, the scent of bodies, of ivy and other greenery, faded away and all I could smell was pine.

The magic that held me faded, though it still burbled joyously through me, wiping away the weariness of the day and the black stain of fear left by Bonarata's call. The euphoria wasn't real, not quite, but I couldn't help the smile that spread across my face.

Like the oak, the pine tree appeared to be part of the original structure of the pub. It erupted in the middle of the worn boards of the dance floor, rippling the nearby boards in an image of its root system. Mesmerized, *called*, I crossed the room until I stood near enough to touch it. It only occurred to me later that no one else approached it—even though the pub was tightly packed everywhere else. The dance floor usually wasn't empty.

Spiderwebs covered the branches in graceful drapes of silver and gold. Airflow in the pub tore the fine gold strands, and they dropped to rest in glittering patterns on the dark green needles. My eyes caught the movement of dozens of tiny golden spiders spinning more gold for the tree.

The silver threads were tougher. A branch moved and I saw a single spider, its body the size of an acorn and the color of the silver web it wove. I *felt* it look back at me. Felt *her* look back at me. I knew the silver spider wasn't a spider. Or maybe she wasn't *just* a spider. Once she had moved mountains and hunted dangerous prey; now she was content to weave beautiful decorations. Or possibly eat coyote shapeshifters like me.

Hidden in my sneakers, my toes flexed uneasily. I was not arachnophobic, quite, but the same recent events that allowed me to feel the thing that lurked in the shape of a spider made me uneasy around them.

A light flashed between me and the spider, and I realized the flickering bits of brightness that illuminated the tree were not small electric Christmas lights. They were tiny . . . *creatures* flitting around the branches with housewifely intent, eating the gold spiderwebs—though they left the silver ones alone. Once my eyes figured out how to see them, I could spot dozens of the bright creatures in the holly berries, mistletoe, and other greenery scattered around the pub at large.

I'd been so focused on the tree and its occupants that I'd quit paying attention to the crowd. Truthfully, ever since the pack had entered into an agreement with the fae, I'd been becoming more comfortable in Uncle Mike's. It made me less wary, knowing I was among allies. But that didn't mean we were all friends. Standing alone on the dance floor, I might as well have had a spotlight on me.

"Think it's pretty?" asked a rough voice to my left. "Like our *Christmas* tree, do you, little coyote?"

I'd subconsciously noticed that the crowd had quieted down since I'd stepped up to the tree. Now every sound except the piped-in music fell silent, giving way to the growing menace. I took a quick glance around but didn't see Uncle Mike. Not everyone in the place was looking at me, but even the ones who weren't were paying attention.

Being called a coyote wasn't an insult—I shapeshifted into a coyote. But the venom in the word "Christmas" would have dropped a full-grown bull dead if it had been of the literal rather than figurative type.

The fae conflated most of their present struggle for survival with the spread of Christianity in Europe. To the fae, Christmas was a four-letter word as foul as anything Ben, our pack's champion filthy-mouthed wolf, had ever said. Which made me wonder why they had a Christmas tree growing out of their dance floor.

"Solstice, surely," I returned, trying to sound calm—and mostly succeeding. "Here by the green man's table, the old ways are followed."

Uncle Mike was a green man—whatever that meant, because he was neither green nor, strictly speaking, a man. It didn't matter what a green man was right now. I used the term to remind them all that Uncle Mike held sway here. He didn't take kindly to fights breaking out among his guests.

"Stolen from us, your Christmas tree," growled the same voice, which I now saw belonged to a woman in a business suit who sat alone. Though the place was crowded, the other three seats at her small table were empty—meaning she was unpleasant or dangerous. Likely both. She'd been here awhile, judging by the nearly drained pitcher. Goody. Nothing I like better than interacting with a belligerent drunken fae, because that always turns out well.

Just because she had no friends with her didn't mean she couldn't inspire the fae crowded in here to wipe the floor with me. I'd survived being raised by werewolves when my superpower was changing into a thirty-five-pound coyote by being observant. Now I observed that the atmosphere was growing increasingly ugly. I looked around and saw a few familiar faces. I met the eyes of a woman who worked at my bank.

She was a troll, a different variety from the one who had damaged the suspension bridge—much more intelligent if less powerfully destructive. She gave me a small smile with a hint of anticipation, as if she could see my blood on the floor in the future.

In the far corner, a man drew my attention because he didn't seem to notice the drama coalescing in the center of the room. I could only see the back of his head, but I was pretty sure it was the human-seeming of the frost giant Ymir. He owed me—sort of. But he was the kind of being to make a situation like this worse rather than better. Hopefully he kept right on not noticing the building tide of violence.

I needed to stall. Until someone told Uncle Mike that trouble was brewing. To that end, I relaxed deliberately, settling onto the balls of my feet.

"Stolen," I agreed, nodding my head at the fae woman who had addressed me. I didn't try explaining who had stolen the idea of a Christmas tree from whom.

Zee had once told me that cutting down trees, bringing them indoors, and decorating them to celebrate Christmas had been a human thing. He had also added, "Placing Christmas near the winter solstice was clever *psychologische Politik* on the part of the early Christian church."

"Clearly it was *stolen*," said Uncle Mike from somewhere behind me, his voice dropping on the room like a heavy wet blanket dropped on open flames. "Beautiful things often are."

The scowling woman closed her mouth with an audible snap and looked at her drink as if it were suddenly interesting. I turned to see Uncle Mike walking toward me, all white-toothed smiles and commanding eyes. The ugliness rising in the crowded pub

subsided reluctantly as patrons pretended they had not been paying attention to me at all.

"Mercy, your companion is awaiting you in the silver room.
Do you know how to get there?"

I felt my eyebrows rise. The silver room was a small one located in the maze of private spaces in the back of the pub reserved
for secret meetings and expensive dates. I hadn't thought that
either I or Mary Jo—who had asked me to meet her here—was
of stature or need to rate the silver room.

"It has its own air vents," Uncle Mike said obscurely as he
cupped a solicitous hand under my elbow and pulled me gently
away from the Christmas tree.

The bright lights followed us for a moment, clustering around
Uncle Mike's face. He pursed his lips and blew them back to the
tree with far more effect than a simple puff of air could have
managed. I followed the green man out of the dance hall and into
the halls that led deeper into his domain.

Uncle Mike gave a whistle as we neared the closed door to the
silver room, tucked somewhat inelegantly in an alcove between
the men's and women's restrooms.

A server appeared from around one of the corners, bearing a
tray with a glass of water, a champagne flute filled with a violet
liquid, and one of those overly scented candles—this one smelling
of apples. Uncle Mike took it from her with a nod, then, balancing it on one hand, he opened the door.

The room was a step back in time to a more gracious and formal era. It was small, maybe ten feet by fourteen feet, but the
ceiling was high, making it feel larger than it was. The walls were
covered with delicately pink silk wallpaper embossed with pat-

terns of silver fleur-de-lys. The floor was marble, and the table where Mary Jo sat was oak carved with graceful flourishes.

Mary Jo's short blond hair was wet and plastered to her head. She was dressed in blue scrubs that fit her in the shoulders and hips but everywhere else were too big. The bottoms of the pant legs were rolled up and secured with a safety pin on the outside of each leg. Judging by the size of the roll, they were a good six inches too long. The muted blue of the scrubs made her sparkling purple toenails stand out.

I didn't see shoes anywhere, so she must have come here barefoot.

The silver room was a room where proposals of marriage took place or where two people might celebrate reaching their fiftieth year of marriage—elegant, expensive, and romantic. It was not a room that anyone would expect a pub to have, and in my jeans and T-shirt, I was definitely out of place—but not as out of place as Mary Jo.

Mary Jo looked exhausted, and the gold flash of the wolf in her eyes nearly distracted me from the smell. Despite the evidence of her freshly washed hair, an unpleasant reek had settled around her, a combination of harsh disinfectant topped with other chemical scents I couldn't quite place. I thought of Uncle Mike's earlier comment about air vents.

Uncle Mike, breathing through his mouth, pulled out the unused chair for me and put the tray on the table in the same graceful motion. He gave me the water glass and set the violet drink in front of Mary Jo, who already had a glass of water in front of her. Then he put the apple-scented candle on the table and lit it with a butane lighter he pulled from somewhere. It could have been out of a pocket—or not. There was too much magic running

around Uncle Mike's this afternoon for me to sense any separate act.

"The candle will help," he told Mary Jo with a sympathetic
smile that didn't reach his eyes. "Give it a minute or two and it
will eat the scent."

He paused before leaving, looking at me with a frown of
something that might have been concern. It *looked* like concern,
but he was the consummate host, and I never entirely trusted any
emotion Uncle Mike expressed that was in the category of useful
attributes to make a guest feel cared for.

"Are you doing well tonight, Mercy?"

I wondered if he could feel the thundering rush of magic that
rumbled under my feet. Or if that was something only I felt. For
a moment, as our eyes met, I saw—

Forests deep and old, hiding secret—

He averted his eyes and the insight died away, leaving me with
a harsher-than-usual headache. Since the Soul Taker had played
with my mind or whatever it had done, I always had a headache.
I rubbed my temple in irritation.

"I'll bring you something that will help with that," Uncle
Mike said at the same time that I said, "I'm fine."

He spoke, I noticed, a bit more quickly than usual and retreated, shutting the door firmly behind him. He left me trapped
in the room with Mary Jo. And that smell.

I inhaled a little too hard trying to figure out what I was smelling, and one of the chemicals dried the back of my throat. I
coughed. Mary Jo met my eyes, her own gold-touched, and dared
me to say something. Or possibly plug my nose.

"Disinfectant?" I asked, sitting down opposite her in the chair
Uncle Mike had pulled out. Normally he would have waited

around and pushed it in for me. I found it interesting that the odor emanating from Mary Jo apparently bothered him even more than it did me. My sense of smell is very acute.

"I wish it was just disinfectant," she said sourly. She took up the glass Uncle Mike had left her and swirled it a couple of times before she tipped it back and swallowed a good two-thirds.

I think she meant to drink it all, but she had to set it down. After she quit making funny noises and caught her breath, she said, "I heard that he had something that could give even a were-wolf a buzz for an hour or two, but George didn't say that drinking it would be the hard part."

"What happened?" I asked. From a closer distance I was beginning to smell hints of other scents underneath the chemicals. I'd expected skunk, maybe. Something like that. But it wasn't skunk.

"I hate stupid people," she told me. "I also hate that I was the smallest person on our team today when our firehouse got called to extract a fifteen-year-old from an outhouse vault."

Outhouse. Yep. That was the scent.

Mary Jo watched me out of gimlet eyes and brought the glass to her lips again. This time she didn't choke. I didn't smile. Or laugh. But it took an effort.

The only outhouses I knew of around here were in some of the parks outside of town. Most of those weren't in much use this time of year.

"In the winter?" I asked.

"It was damn cold," she said, eyeing the remainder of her drink. "It was why I had to go in without waiting for equipment. I'm not sure what equipment might have helped anyway. Hard to get to the hole because of the building covering it. By the time we got there, the kid had been half submerged in cold and wet goo for at least half an hour already."

She finished her glass, blinked at me owlishly, and then put her forehead down on the table.

She didn't say anything else—and I needed to hear the rest of the story. "So how did this person manage to find themselves trapped in the business end of an outhouse?"

She tipped her head sideways and glanced at me, then returned to her former position. Her voice was a little muffled when she asked, "Do you know where Big Flat is?"

Big Flat was a park on the Columbia River about fifteen miles out of Pasco. People went there to hunt birds and fish—but also to jog or ride horses. The pack didn't go out there on moon hunt nights because we didn't usually hunt fish or birds.

I nodded, but she couldn't see me with her head down, so I said, "I do."

"Teenagers." She slapped the table and sat up, her face a little flushed, but the wolf was out of her eyes and she was fighting down a grin. "I thought I was bad. But the things I've seen. And Renny has—"

She fell silent, running a finger around the edge of her empty glass as though she wished it weren't empty. I wondered what had happened between Mary Jo and her boyfriend to put that look in her eye. I waited for her to tell me. The longer I waited, the more worried I was.

Eventually, deciding to avoid Renny for now, I redirected her back to the story. "Mary Jo, how did someone fall into an outhouse? What were they doing at Big Flat in this weather, anyway?"

She shook off whatever mood she'd fallen into and said, "It took ingenuity. This group of kids skipped school to go hiking—

and drinking—around Big Flat because they thought no one would see them. It's pretty deserted during the weekday this time of year. Did you ever skip school?"

"I grew up under the Marrok's rule," I told her. "He was very strict." I paused. "Of course I did."

We exchanged smiles acknowledging our mutually reprehensible pasts. I had always liked Mary Jo. We had a lot in common.

"This one kid had a new cell phone," she said. "When she used the restroom, it fell out of her pocket and into the pit. They'd all been drinking a bit, just enough to take the edge off their common sense." She ran a finger over the lip of the empty glass beside her. "About like I am right now, I expect. Anyway, she was crying and her boyfriend took a couple of the guys in to assess the problem. There it was, bright and shiny and sitting right on top of the mound below."

"Like a cherry on top of an ice cream sundae," I said.

She gave me a look. "Thanks for that. Every time I see ice cream now, I'm going to think of that cell phone." She went back to her story. "Anyway, they decided that if they took the toilet stool off, they might be able to reach it."

I snickered. "They dismantled the toilet."

She nodded. "With tools they had in the car. With the stool off, they were definitely closer. But it was still out of reach. They evaluated their assets."

"No holocaust cloak," I murmured.

"Or wheelbarrow, either," she agreed. "They were doomed to fail, though they didn't know it. What they did have was a small dog on a leash."

"You didn't fish a dog out of the pit," I said.

"It's not really a pit," she said, though she'd used the word herself. "It's a vault—" She stopped herself from breaking into a technical explanation about the differences between a vault and a pit outhouse. "Never mind. No, though the dog was one of those little yappy things that bite everyone. Maybe it would have grabbed the phone if they'd dangled it down there by its leash. But no one tried that. They used the leash."

I bit my lip to keep from laughing. Failed.

She nodded. "They took the lightest-weight guy—today was *really* not a good day to be small—and attached him by the back of his jeans to the leash so they could lower him down to get the phone."

I put my hands over my eyes. "Holy wow. Tell me they didn't just attach him by his belt loops."

When I took my hands down, Mary Jo's laughing eyes met mine.

"To his belt," she said. "But the leash was meant for a teacup poodle. The guy was small but still around a hundred pounds. They were trying to hold the leash like a tug-of-war rope." She mimed with her hands together. "The end guy was supposed to put his hand in the loop, but his hands were too big. As anyone with the common sense of an avocado could have predicted, it slipped right out of their hands as soon as our sacrificial lamb leaned out for the phone."

"Headfirst?"

She nodded, her grin widening as her shoulders started to shake. "He—he had to use the phone to call us, because no one else had cell coverage out there."

She started laughing then—I thought it might be Uncle Mike's magical drink, because in between bouts of laughter she would say a word or two and then have to stop because she didn't have the breath to continue.

The words mostly didn't make too much sense. "Purple leash." "Twenty minutes to find the damned dog." "Poodle. Get it? *Poo*-dle."

She wiped her eyes and recovered herself a bit. "By the end of it the parents arrived. The girl's mom"—she had to giggle for a minute—"her mom said, 'At least this phone is waterproof.'"

"I would never use that phone again," I said sincerely. "Even if it was waterproof."

"My hiking boots were waterproof, too," she said before giggling some more. "I tossed them." She stuck her feet out and wiggled her toes. Something about that set her off again.

She was back to being face down on the table, this time laughing helplessly, when Uncle Mike came in with two bowls of stew and two frosted glasses containing some sort of amber liquid. He set my stew in front of me and put Mary Jo's near the center of the table, where it would be safer from being knocked over by the incautious moves of someone who had had a bit too much to drink.

After he'd deposited the glasses, he tapped the one in front of me and the color changed slightly.

"For your headache, Mercy," he said. "It shouldn't affect the taste."

I nodded. Not quite a thank-you, so it should be safe.

He nodded back, and then snuffed out the candle. Immediately the room filled with the scent of stew and apple cider, more strongly than I'd have expected. As if they flowed in to fill the gap in scents the candle had left behind. I hadn't noticed when the sewer-and-chemical smell had vanished, but it was gone.

"Effective," I said.

Uncle Mike gave me a professional smile, warm but without intimacy, and said, "It's done its job. No reason to ruin the meal."

He looked at my helplessly laughing companion and said, "That elixir doesn't last long with werewolves. She'll be herself again in a minute. Eating will help."

"Did she order stew?" I asked. Mary Jo was a burger kind of person who viewed any vegetables that weren't fried and salted with suspicion.

"On the house," he said. Then his eyes chilled a little. "An apology for the incident at the—" He said a word I didn't catch.

"At the what?" I asked.

He repeated himself. When I clearly didn't understand him again, he rolled his eyes and dropped the jolly innkeeper role. "The pine tree. I let someone else decorate, and she thought the tree would be funny. If it weren't for the spider, I'd take it down, but—"

"Let's not annoy the silver spider," I said.

"Indeed." He rocked back on his heels and pursed his lips as if in thought. "Larry was here earlier. Gave me a message for you. Said he'd tried calling but you hadn't picked up."

Larry was the goblin king. I'd never managed to discover if he ruled over all goblins or just the goblins in the Tri-Cities. He had a gift for seeing the future. Possible future, anyway.

I checked my phone. "It's on silent," I apologized, fixing that. Larry had called, but he hadn't left a message.

"He said he was headed out of town on business for a day or two, but he said, 'Winter roads are treacherous, but necessary to get you where you are going.'"

I waited for the rest.

Uncle Mike shrugged. "That was it."

I bit my lip, unease stirring in my stomach. "Seems like he put a lot of effort into getting a warning to me that is—"

"Inherently obvious, assuming you are going to be traveling," agreed Uncle Mike, staring at me as if I were interesting. Or about to become interesting.

It made me want to look over my shoulder, because my half brother maintained that whenever he or events around him started to become interesting, our father was likely about.

Coyote wasn't anyone's idea of a typical father. He'd once shoved me into the Columbia to see if a river monster would eat me. Not so much the kind of parent who threw their children into a lake to teach them how to swim, but one who did it to see if they would drown.

"I'm not planning on going anywhere," I said. Then thought about the trouble in New Mexico that Adam was dealing with tonight. My mate might be traveling soon. "I'll keep Larry's words in mind."

Uncle Mike gave me a half nod and, once more, closed the door behind him.

The stew was good, and the apple cider—a nonalcoholic version—complemented it. It also killed most of my headache. I was halfway through the glass when Mary Jo quit laughing into the table, sat up, and gave the empty glass that had held her lavender drink a considering look.

"Not quite like being drunk," she said. "Better in some ways, not as good in others."

"Did it help?" I asked.

She sighed. "A little. Maybe." She looked at her borrowed scrubs. "I didn't actually come here to get drunk—or to tell stories about idiots." She rocked her head from side to side to stretch her neck. "Thank you for agreeing to meet with me."

"No worries," I said.

She looked at me. "I haven't always been nice to you."

"I've been not nice to you back," I said. "Miniature zombie goats."

"Someone had to collect them, I suppose. Miserable little demon escape artists." She flashed me a sudden grin. "I like the way your mind works," she said.

"Don't get mad, get even," I deadpanned.

She raised her empty glass, hesitated, and set it aside to replace it with the apple cider and sipped from that. "Imagine my surprise when I ran into a personal problem and the only one I could imagine taking it to was you."

I waited.

"If it hadn't been you, I'd have canceled this meeting after I had to climb into that toilet." She looked as though that was some sort of revelation. After a minute she said, "You aren't a very judgmental sort of person."

"Thank you?" I wasn't sure it was a compliment.

She gave me a quick grin and used the flats of her hands to play out a quick beat on the tabletop.

"Here goes nothing," she said. "Why did you marry Adam?"

INTERLUDE

December
Chicago

ZANE

WHEN ZANE OPENED HIS EYES, DAWN HAD ALREADY
claimed the room. He'd slept in, then. It was becoming an unexpected habit, this sleeping in, when sleep had always been a fitful
thing that happened when he could not keep going. High anxiety,
the doctors his father had sent him to had said. Too much magic,
his mother had said with an envious sigh.

Tammy soothed his inner demons in a way medicine had never
been able to. Maybe she was magic as well, he thought whimsi-
cally, when whimsy had once been rarer than sleep in his life.

She stood looking out of the big north-facing window that
gave the best view of the frozen field that was Lake Michigan, her
body side-lit by the morning sunlight coming from the east window.

The windows were the only way he could sleep indoors at all.
That the floor-to-ceiling walls of windows in his condo gave him
magnificent 360-degree views of the lake and Chicago was a
bonus.

Watching the light play over Tammy's ash-blond hair made him think of afternoons wandering the art galleries of Chicagoland— where he'd seen nothing that appealed to him as much as she did. It didn't hurt that her rock-climbing hobby had left her body muscled in a way a weight lifter would envy. He loved to look at his fiancée.

Fiancée.

She was. She'd said yes when he was sure, so sure, after he'd explained everything to her, that she would say no. Who could blame her? Social-working daughter of a police officer, she had no background to face his fate, steeped in ancient spells and magic as it was. She didn't remember it, of course, and would not until after they were married, when it was too late. That was the nature of the magic that had made his life a living hell from the moment he was born, but he'd been careful that she understood everything that he understood. Understood and believed. Consent wasn't enough. Informed consent was precious.

She'd said yes.

He loved her hair, her body, her clear eyes that saw right through people and cared about them anyway. Her endless compassion, which was a fitting curb to his honed ruthlessness. She allowed him to be softer. Kinder. She allowed him to sleep. And she'd said *yes*.

She turned to him, though he hadn't moved other than opening his eyes.

"Good morning, sunshine," she said. "It's a bright day out today." She paused and her smile dimmed. "Means it's going to be cold."

He knew she worried about the people who weren't living in a high-rise condo. Her charges slept in alleyways and parks. Shelters were all well and good—and he funded a couple—but there were people who couldn't abide four walls and a roof, especially when they came with rules. He could understand that.

"What time are you leaving?" he asked.

The wedding was in Montana. He'd looked for something more accessible, but he was probably lucky he'd found the place in Montana. Fate, his mother said with an airy smile. He needed an isolated place—a holy place—and the old sanatorium in Montana had presented itself.

"Dad said Jimmy doesn't get off shift until eleven p.m. We're going to drive straight through, so it doesn't matter when we start."

"It's not too late for me to fly you all out," he said.

She smiled. "Auntie Elyna doesn't fly, and Dad wants one last family vacation."

"Five cops, you, and your unrelated auntie," he said.

"Hey," she said, "family is where you find it."

He sat up and put his feet on the floor, resigned to getting up. "I like yours better than mine," he admitted. "Though I still haven't met your auntie Elyna."

She was a writer, he'd been informed. She kept odd hours and she'd been finishing a book the past six months while he and Tammy had been falling in love. He'd bought a couple of Elyna's books; she wrote horror good enough that he'd had to turn on every light in the condo—and laughed at himself while he did so. Tammy said Elyna wrote romances, too, but no one could get her pen name out of her.

He stood up and stretched.

Tammy watched him, her eyes appreciating what they saw.

She let the oversized T-shirt—one of his—that she'd been wearing slip to the ground. "Done sleeping?" she asked.

2

ADAM

ADAM ENTERED THE VIRTUAL MEETING ROOM, AND four faces, including his own, filled his computer screen.

He wished he were doing this in person. He could tell a lot more when his wolf could use his senses. He could, for instance, tell if someone was lying to him. Not that he had any reason to suspect the people in this meeting of being liars. But it might be nice to be certain. Relying on virtual communications made him uneasy.

"Welcome, gentlemen," said the man running the show. His fair hair was a faint memory, trimmed short where it still traced a circle around his head, just above his ears. He wore black-rimmed glasses like the ones that Adam's own father had worn more than half a century ago. He looked like a mild-mannered bank clerk and had spent twenty years as a Special Forces sniper. And despite the glasses, Don Orson could still put a bullet anywhere he wanted it to go—both literally and figuratively.

Don ran the New Mexico branch of Adam's security company, and had done so for over a decade, since Adam had moved his main operations up to the Tri-Cities. They'd worked together for five or six years before that. Don was smart and resourceful and had a reputation for honesty and forthrightness that was almost as useful as the fact that he actually was both honest and forthright. He was also better than Adam at keeping a cool head in rough waters. The fire in his eye told Adam that Don's cool head was deserting him now.

Don didn't like losing people any more than Adam did. They'd both lost a lot of them in war—though their wars were in different centuries. It was not acceptable to lose them here and now.

"I want explanations," said the third of the four people in the virtual meeting.

They'd been told they would be talking to someone in the Pentagon, but Adam didn't recognize this person, a Black man with flawless skin that would have made him look a decade younger than Don except for the strain in his eyes. He was wearing a dress shirt, sleeves rolled up mid-forearm. The small buttons of his collar were undone, so he'd probably started today with a tie.

"We are going to have to go to the press," he said. "I don't want to do that without more information." He showed no signs of introducing himself.

Adam rubbed his ear as though it itched. Don's eyes widened slightly at the signal—Adam was usually better than Don at identifying random high-ranked political appointees.

A text announced its arrival quietly, and Adam glanced down at his phone to see that Orson had sent him information. **SecDef.** A name might have been good, too, but the position he held was more important.

Adam examined the man currently expressing his opinion of the recent events. At some point, Adam had lost track of who held the office of Secretary of Defense. The last few years had left him disliking politics even more than usual—he hadn't approved of any politician since John McCain died. Maybe because he and McCain had been from the same era, born to the same values, and refined in the crucible of the same war. That was a reason, but not an excuse. Adam's job was to keep his people—pack and employees—safe. To do that, he needed to keep track of the political climate.

Technically, the national laboratories at Los Alamos were, like the ones in the Tri-Cities, under the Department of Energy, even the secret labs like the one in question. That was why Adam's security company was employed rather than the military. Adam wasn't sure why they were talking to the SecDef instead of the Secretary of Energy. It might be important.

The SecDef demonstrated that he'd been a general at some point with a five-minute screed designed to make all of them sit up and pay attention. Orson looked serious but not worried, Adam's own face was blank, and so—Adam noted with interest—was the face of their fourth member.

The young Hispanic man wore his Hauptman Security uniform with the same smartness he'd have worn his marine uniform. His straight back was obvious even in the limited screen view. His skin bore shadows that spoke of fatigue, and his eyes looked a little reddened. He'd been awake since he'd gone on shift last night, Adam knew. He'd refused to go home until after this meeting. He was their man on the ground.

Ortega had been patrolling with another guard when they'd been ambushed. His partner had been killed immediately. By

Ortega's account, Ortega had killed two people and wounded a third before the enemy withdrew, leaving only his dead comrade to verify his story. The enemy had taken their dead and wounded—and inexplicably (for now), the cameras in that area had been off.

That lack of corroborative evidence apparently bothered the SecDef, too. Eventually, he turned his considerable ire on the former marine corporal, Ortega.

Adam would have interfered then, but Ortega wasn't flinching. If he could hold up under the barrage, it would do the whole situation a lot of good. If the SecDef learned a little respect for their witness, matters would be considerably cleaner. Adam caught Don's eye and shook his head, telling him to stand down, too.

Adam wished they were all in a room together. It would be a lot easier to make these calls.

"And furthermore, *girl*," said the SecDef—and that was when Ortega had had enough.

"My pronouns are 'he,' 'him,' and 'his,'" he said in a flat voice that carried over the top of the SecDef's. "And have been since I was asked to leave the marines. That is probably in one of the files you hopefully read before the meeting. If you had called me 'boy,' it would still have been offensive and demeaning." He put up a hand to stop anything anyone might have said and continued. "If I had died with Kit—a situation that it seems you would prefer to this one—none of us would be here. I'd be dead and approximately ten unknowns would have had access to whatever they were after. Possibly without anyone knowing they'd been in and out at all. The only mystery would be why a couple of Hauptman guards ran off together, because those people were prepared to take bodies back with them, and I don't think they expected the bodies would belong to their own men."

Vincent Ortega took no prisoners, it seemed. Adam trusted that his face stayed blank. Only someone who had known Don as long as Adam had would have detected the amused pleasure in his old comrade's face.

After a breathless moment, the SecDef settled back in his chair with a slight smile. "I spoke to your former commanding officer, Mr. Ortega. I am happy to see that he was right." He rubbed his face—and suddenly looked every bit as tired as Ortega. "But it would be useful if we knew who it was—homegrown or international terrorists. Spies. Thieves. *Something*."

Kidnappers, Adam added silently. There were, he knew, several potentially high-value targets who habitually worked at night in the labs. He didn't say it because he didn't indulge in speculation with people he didn't know. Instead, he texted it to Don.

Don nodded once and said, "We're running DNA tests on the blood at the scene—"

Don's voice kicked over to background noise as anxiety struck through Adam's mating bond. He waited—Don's succinct outline of Hauptman Security's investigation to date sliding past his ears—for something to happen. One minute passed. Two. Instead of texting him, she fiddled with their bond until he couldn't sense her distress at all.

There were only two reasons Mercy would work so diligently to keep him unaware that something was bothering her. This didn't have the feel of the ongoing issues she'd been having after the Soul Taker, that damned ancient artifact, had tried to remake her magic in its own image. Those tended to have more pain attached to them.

Bonarata had called again.

He picked up his phone and texted Ben, the pack's computer expert. Ben would notify the rest of the people working on the Bonarata problem. It was unlikely to come to anything—they might manage to get his location for the duration of the call. But Bonarata, they had learned, was a lot more mobile than they'd previously understood. He was supposed to be located in Italy. Ben's traces had proven that the old vampire had some way of traveling that allowed him to be in San Francisco one day and Barcelona the next without leaving a trail. That was why the Marrok—whom Adam and his pack no longer belonged to— allowed Adam access to Charles, the Marrok's son, who was working on how Bonarata managed to get to Mercy through number, phone, and carrier changes.

In the end, Adam thought, it was going to come down to a battle one-on-one. But if they could stop the harassing phone calls, they'd force Bonarata to find another, possibly less effective means of terrifying Mercy.

Something Adam could sink his teeth into.

"—thought that the least you could do is pay attention," thundered the SecDef.

Adam continued to watch his phone for another heartbeat. Though Ben's "on it" had come through on the heels of the text, Adam's wolf still wasn't happy. SecDef's attitude didn't help.

Adam thought he had it under control, but when he looked up and saw his image reflected back at himself in the computer screen, his eyes were bright yellow. SecDef flinched—which wasn't good. Scaring powerful people was not going to make anyone safer.

"I hear you," Adam said. He paused to get the growl out of his voice. "Sorry. I had an emergency that I needed to deal with." And then he lied. "It didn't keep me from listening." And followed it up with a truth. "Don has been keeping me briefed on this situation, so I am already up-to-date from our side of this— and it sounds like nothing is coming up on yours, sir. Your people are certain that no one got in?"

"Yes," they all said with differing degrees of emphasis. Evidently this was something they'd already established and he hadn't heard.

Well, people asked questions to make certain of things they already knew all the time.

"Good," Adam said. "Vincent?"

The former marine corporal met his eyes.

"Good job. Thank you."

The young man took a deep breath and his shoulders relaxed. He looked, Adam thought, about fifteen. Twenty-two was too damned young to be embroiled in this kind of bloody mess.

"Thank *you*, sir," Vincent said.

Adam gave him a smile and said, "I'm not an officer—never was." And withdrew from the virtual meeting before he could say something else that proved he hadn't been listening to the last ten minutes. Don could finish up; he did diplomacy better than Adam. When they were through, Don would call him and they would have a meeting about the meeting.

Adam called Ben.

"Fucking Canada," Ben said in a harried voice without greeting. "We think. He's using a sodding stealth phone again."

A stealth phone lied to the cell towers about who it was and what it was doing. It switched its own number by various fairly easy and quick methods depending on the make and model. The ones Bonarata had access to were better than anything Adam had heard of.

"Charles got a trace on him just before he hung up, though, and we're following him," Ben said with an edge of the moon madness in his voice. A hunt was a hunt.

"In what part of Canada?" Adam asked.

"Montreal," Ben said. "That is now a for certain. Come on, you—" And some very British and a few American curses boiled out of Adam's phone.

If Bonarata was in Montreal, he was not in Pasco, where Mercy was. Adam was reasonably certain that she'd be safe in Uncle Mike's, even from the Lord of Night. Safer, anyway, than when she was in Adam's company.

He'd done such a good job against Bonarata the last time.

He deliberately loosened his jaw. The past could not be changed. In the present, he carried a few more weapons on his person and in his SUV. Weapons were great equalizers; give him a big enough weapon and he could kill anything. He had also found a new sparring partner to step up his training.

Ben got creative with a few new expletive combinations that would doubtless find their way into the vocabulary of the pack, and ended them with "Lost him."

"Next time," Adam said.

"Or the one after that," Ben agreed with a sigh. "It would be handy if we could keep track of him."

Adam made a neutral sound. They weren't going to track him down and destroy him. Bonarata was going to bring himself to them in his own good time. Adam wished he were more certain of the results. In the meantime, knowledge was power.

Ben grunted. "I could put a trace on Mercy's phone if she's not going to let us know when he calls her."

"I know when he calls," Adam said. "Leave Mercy's phone alone."

Ben grunted, but not as if he was unhappy. "How is she?"

"Today?" Adam asked. "Same."

Neither said how worried he was about Mercy.

"Okay," Ben said. "Would you let me know if someone—Sherwood or Zee or anyone—figures out how to fix her?"

"I will," Adam told him, and they disconnected.

Adam stretched and played a few rounds of solitaire on his laptop.

Don phoned about ten minutes before Adam expected him to. This SecDef wasn't as long-winded as the last one had been, then. Some changes were for the better.

"I was waiting for you to eviscerate him at the start," Don said without greeting.

Adam grunted. "Looked to me like Vincent had things in hand. SecDef couldn't throw too much sewage on him without looking like a bully."

"Hasn't stopped some of them in the past," Don said.

"If he'd been one of those, I would have stepped in."

"Good," said Don. "I think SecDef might have come a cropper trying to squish him even if he'd really tried. Speaking of the good gentleman, did you really not know who we were talking to?"

"No," Adam said. There was no excuse for that, so he didn't bother making one.

Don laughed. "Well, you handled him spot-on. I thought the 'I don't talk but my eyes turn scary' might be a bit much, but

SecDef seemed to think that meant we were competent. So thanks for that."

And the secret for making people think you knew what you were doing was keeping your mouth shut about what had *really* happened. If Don wanted to believe Adam planned all of that, it was okay by Adam.

"What did you think of Ortega?" asked Don casually.

Orson hadn't told Adam that Ortega was trans when he'd hired him last year. But though Adam might have let the changes in the Pentagon slip by him, he'd never have okayed a hire without a thorough check.

"That was a good pickup," Adam said. "You said one of your old friends recommended him?"

Don gave a sudden little laugh. "That boy doesn't have an ounce of quit in him, does he?" There was a little pause. "He doesn't bother you? Really?"

"I change into a wolf at the full moon," Adam said dryly. "Who am I to worry about someone making decisions about who and what they are?" Don grunted, but Adam knew him inside out. He heard the relief.

"Yep," Don said. "Ortega was fast-tracked for good things until people on top decided his kind of people weren't good for the armed forces. He's a crack shot and quick-witted." He paused deliberately before saying, "And he is careful and willing to keep information to himself when necessary."

"Were we keeping something from the SecDef?" Adam asked.

"We were indeed. It wasn't a bullet that killed Kit, though they shot him in the head as soon as he went down. It was your kind of stuff. Ortega thinks it didn't work on him because his grandmother was a bruja and he wears a protection of some kind that she gave to him."

"Bruja" did not necessarily mean the kind of witch that Elizaveta had been.

Elizaveta.

Adam hurt whenever he thought of her. She had been a comrade in arms and reminded him so strongly of his own grandmother, also a Russian immigrant, that she felt like family. He'd called her for advice now and then. She'd been the head of a large and powerful family. She understood his job. But she'd also been a much bigger monster than he'd understood, and when he'd figured it out, he'd killed her.

Because of Elizaveta, he needed to find out what kind of a bruja Ortega's grandmother was or had been. That might be a clue. Or a reason to distrust Ortega.

He really didn't want to deal with witches again. But he would if he had to.

He spoke with Don for a while more, coordinating next steps. Once Adam understood that magic had been involved, his traveling to New Mexico was a given.

When he got off the phone, Adam continued making arrangements to go to New Mexico. He bought an airline ticket. He texted his office to tell them he wouldn't be in for a few days, possibly more. When he'd done that, he punched in Darryl's number. Darryl, whom Adam was about to drop into the middle of a screaming mess.

He made himself stop smiling before he hit the last number. People could hear when you were smiling.

His second answered on the third ring.

"I've been waiting for your call," Darryl said with just a hair too much aggression.

Adam considered that tone, and also the words Darryl had used, before he said anything. There was no way that Darryl could have anticipated the reason he'd called him. He must feel that there was something else.

"Because?" Adam asked.

Darryl gave an almost angry huff. "Moon hunt."

Three days ago. Adam's wolf surged with satisfaction at the joy of that hunt. Speed had made his blood sing as they ran through the snow. The hunting sense connected all the pack so tightly, he felt as if he and they were one and the same. Their breath, their fangs, their strength all belonged to him—as his did to them. The power of the killing strike and the taste of blood.

Hastily Adam shoved the wolf back. He needed to pay attention here. What had bothered Darryl?

The beginning of the hunt had not been smooth. It was uncommon for beginnings to be without incident, and the pack was running hot all the time. When the wolf was tasting the moon, knowing a hunt was in the wind, it was hard to keep control. There had been a few pockets of violence, but they'd all been resolved without anyone dying, so Adam hadn't considered that anything needed saying.

"No," Adam said evenly. "I'm not calling about the moon hunt. I don't need to. You handled it."

A rumble of a growl echoed out of the phone. "I let *Post* do my job."

Currently, Adam had a surplus of very dominant werewolves to manage. They were desperately needed, given the pressure the pack was under to defend their territory from all comers, but it wasn't making life easy for any of them. Especially since Sherwood Post was considerably older and more dominant than Adam himself was.

Adam could feel his wolf bristle in defiant refusal at the thought of Post being more dominant. There was something that happened to a wolf once it had been in charge for a while. Very few Alphas were able to resume being answerable to anyone. Adam's wolf's determination gave him a lot of sympathy for Darryl, who was also supposed to be in charge of Post.

Darryl should be Alpha of his own pack. Adam and the Marrok had been in talks about finding the best fit for Darryl— something that would work for his career as well as for his wolf—when Mercy had made their pack responsible for maintaining the only place on earth where humans were safe from the things that go bump in the night. At that point, all of their options had changed.

If they were going to keep their promises and their bargains with the fae, Darryl was necessary. Post was necessary. Warren was necessary.

Now it was up to Adam to keep the three (four, if he counted himself, and he probably should) dominant werewolves functioning as a team.

He'd been privileged to serve for a few months under a staff sergeant who was gifted at team building. He'd put together a highly efficient crack team and managed to make them happy to serve under their idiot captain who should have been shot—and eventually was, amazingly enough by the enemy.

At the time, Adam hadn't realized those lessons would be just about the most valuable things he learned from being in the army.

Which was why he intended to let them sort some things out

on their own while he was gone. He knew his wolves. They understood what their pack had taken on and why it was important, necessary, not to fail. And if they were going to *not fail*, they would need every wolf. Without Adam, they would have to find a way to work together. He wished he could be a fly on the wall to witness it instead of running around New Mexico trying to figure out what happened on one hand and playing politics on the other.

"What was the job, the one you should have done, that you let Post do?" asked Adam.

"You were there," growled Darryl.

"I can't read minds," Adam growled right back. "I want to know what you think. Post did a lot of things. Answer the question."

"He broke up the fight between Mary Jo and George," Darryl said.

"What were you doing instead?" Adam asked, though of course he knew. That wasn't the point.

There was a pause while Darryl decided if he was going to let Adam lead. The length of the pause told Adam that it was a close-run thing.

"Guarding Zack," Darryl said, but went on more quickly, as if he were arguing with Adam, "I could have stopped Mary Jo and George before it got violent. They would have obeyed me."

That was true. Sherwood had been forced to tear into them hard enough that both still had open wounds until they had shifted back to human, well after the hunt was over.

"Werewolves are dangerous," Adam said. "Being a werewolf is dangerous."

"My job is to protect our pack, even from each other," Darryl said.

"Yes," agreed Adam. "You protected Zack. Our heart."

Darryl growled. "No one was going to hurt Zack."

"Even with the moon's call riding them?" They both knew the answer to that. No, Zack hadn't been safe from harm before Darryl had made him safe.

"Zack is a werewolf," Darryl tried.

Adam let that hang in the air. Zack had come to them broken. Adam didn't know what had happened to him, just that he'd bounced around from pack to pack for the better part of a decade until the Marrok had sent him to them. Their pack's lone submissive wolf was healthier than he'd been when he'd joined them, but he wasn't up to handling scuffles breaking out with him in the middle of them.

Darryl finally grunted acknowledgment.

"Zack needs to know we have his back," Adam said. "Sherwood broke up that fight—and you kept Zack safe." He let that sit a moment and added, "Protecting Zack was the most important job. That means you or me—not Post."

"But," Darryl said, "if I had stopped Mary Jo and George, they would not be hurt—and Zack would have been safe, too."

"There was another fight brewing right behind Zack," Adam said. "Honey and Luke. If you hadn't been right where you were, Luke couldn't have used you to put distance between him and Honey."

Darryl grunted.

"I know you saw that," Adam said.

At the beginning of the hunt, with the moon madness easing into their bones, it didn't matter how close their human halves were. Before they started the hunt, sometimes all the werewolf wanted was blood.

"I did," said Darryl, though he still sounded ruffled. Then he muttered—as much as anyone with a chest like Darryl's *could* mutter—"I didn't know if you saw it."

There was the key. Darryl knew he'd done the right thing. He needed to know that Adam understood that, too.

"I saw you and Sherwood working together to keep the bloodshed down," Adam told him. "You trusted Sherwood to do his job. He trusted you to do yours. I trusted both of you to keep Zack safe. We are pack."

"Sherwood is strong," Darryl said. "Dominant."

"So are you," Adam returned. "I can't tell you how this will play out between the two of you."

"And Warren."

Evidently Darryl was through pretending that Warren wasn't dominant enough to have been Adam's second, if dominance alone had been the decider. Good. That meant Darryl would have to figure things out there, too.

Adam thought Warren had been correct to take the third position in the pack when he'd joined—though he and Adam knew Warren was more dominant than Darryl. Their pack was, as Mercy put it, about half a century behind contemporary social norms. She'd usually add, "That means that you are about a century ahead of most packs."

Adam had had to force the pack into accepting Warren. They wouldn't have allowed a gay werewolf to step into a position that meant he might have to take over as Alpha—not then. But now their pack found themselves standing alone in the worst game of king of the mountain Adam had ever participated in. After the last six months, there wasn't a wolf in the pack who wouldn't follow Warren straight into hell and back again.

Some change was for the better.

"And Warren," Adam agreed.

There was a pause, and Adam let Darryl think for a moment.

"*You* could have stopped that fight. All the fights."

Adam was pretty sure Sherwood Post could have done it, too. But Darryl didn't need to understand that yet.

"Yes," agreed Adam. "I could have used the pack bonds and put everyone on the ground." He decided to let Darryl in on a secret. "And even back in their human bodies if I'd had to. All of you."

"What?" Darryl asked, sounding appalled.

It was supposed to be the kind of thing the Marrok could do to you. Not an ordinary Alpha. In fact, Adam had never done it to more than one wolf at a time. But Adam's wolf was certain.

"Yes. I could have. But it would have hurt them a lot worse than Post hurt Mary Jo and George. It would have told them I didn't trust them to control their wolves. It might have made them lose trust in themselves, in their ability to keep their wolves under control, when sometimes the only thing that allows them to do that is the belief that they can."

Silence hung in the air for a moment.

"I've been in a pack like that," Darryl said. Adam felt the muscles in his back release at the sudden lack of tension in Darryl's voice. "With an Alpha so busy making sure no one lost their cool that not one of them could function without him."

"Except you," Adam said, because that had been something the Marrok had told Adam when he'd sent Darryl to join Adam's pack.

"Except me," Darryl agreed, and Adam could hear that the

events of the moon hunt had been dealt with to Darryl's satisfaction. "So why *did* you call me?"

Darryl had government clearances that were higher than Adam's—working in a think tank made that a necessity. That meant Adam could lay the whole problem out for him.

"Sabotage?" Darryl said thoughtfully when Adam was finished.

"Or spies. Or someone on the inside playing games. Kidnapping, even." He paused. "Vincent said they had been ready to carry off bodies. He thought that meant they intended to kill both of my people and take their bodies. Maybe they were intending to carry off a live person as well."

"To what end?"

Adam shrugged, though Darryl wasn't going to see him. "I don't know. I don't know what all they do in those labs—I'm not sure SecDef does, either. But one of my people got killed, so I'm going down. I need you to take charge of the pack for a few days—maybe a couple of weeks—while I go and bless some hearts and take some names."

"Everyone knows that's your security company down there," said Darryl. "If I wanted to get you to leave the pack to its own devices, this is how I would do it."

That thought had not escaped Adam. He had it every time he had to go to DC, too, for the same exact reason. "Yes."

"Why aren't you calling Sherwood to hold the pack?" Darryl asked, his voice carefully neutral. "Since he quit hiding his light under a barrel, it's pretty obvious that he is tougher than I am."

Than I am, too, thought Adam, but that wouldn't be useful to say aloud. He wasn't sure his wolf would let him do that, anyway.

"Who cooks the pack Sunday morning breakfast?" Adam asked softly.

Darryl didn't answer.

"You love this pack. Warren loves having a pack to belong to, but there are some of our wolves that he'd be just as glad to kick to the curb. Sherwood is just finding his balance. He lost a lot, and sort of regaining his memory"—the whole pack now knew about that—"has been a mixed bag."

"He's got pretty good balance from where I'm sitting," muttered Darryl.

"So do you," Adam said. "And my wolves look to you to take care of them. They trust you. Being a second, being an Alpha, is a two-way street. The pack has a place in those decisions."

"Okay," Darryl said. "I hear you." He cleared his throat, evidently done with that subject, too. "I felt a flash of something through the pack bonds tonight. Mercy get another call?"

"Yes," Adam said.

"She tried to hide it from you again." Darryl sounded grimly amused. "If she hadn't, I'd have felt more than a flash."

Darryl was getting sensitive to the pack bonds—another sign that he was ready to take on his own pack. That was understood between them. But Darryl wasn't going to desert this pack until the heat was off them, even if it took years. Which was a good thing, because Adam was very much afraid that he couldn't let him go until that time. His wolf wouldn't let him weaken the pack like that.

"Mercy doesn't want me to worry when there is nothing I can do. We're tracing the calls when we can. Knowledge is power and all that. But we're in a waiting game."

"Sucks," Darryl said, agreeing with the sourness of Adam's

tone. And with those words Adam felt the bond between him and his second settle back into place. And for the first time since the moon hunt, it felt right. Darryl had been correct; Adam should have called him sooner.

"Yep," Adam said. "Defense always does."

Darryl made a sympathetic noise. Then, gravely, he said, "We'll take care of her while you're gone."

He wasn't talking about Bonarata. Neither of them thought Bonarata was done playing with them yet. He was talking about the way Mercy wasn't recovering from the Soul Taker.

"I know," Adam told him.

Darryl let him leave it at that, knowing that there wasn't anything either of them could really do for Mercy except hope she'd get better.

They were deep in a discussion about a planned pack activity that was now going to have to go forward without Adam when a small red light flashed on his desk. The front door had been opened. It was too soon for Mercy to be coming home. Jesse was out there alone.

"Done," Adam said, and cut the call.

His office was soundproofed so that even a werewolf could not overhear what went on inside it. That meant he couldn't hear what was going on in the house, either. He'd taken some pains to make sure that didn't become a liability. He stood up to go see why the door had been opened.

A soft buzz filled the room.

Jesse was the only one home, and she'd just hit the silent alarm.

The wolf roared so loud he had to fight to breathe—but it didn't slow him down. At all.

He jerked open the door—registering the crack of wood as

unimportant—and had to check himself so he didn't bowl right over the top of Jesse, who was standing in front of his door with her finger on the button.

The analytic part of his mind—which was just watching the action—noted that she didn't smell afraid. Not very afraid, anyway. And that might just be of him. He was aware that he could be alarming.

He picked her up and set her in the office. The only reason he didn't close the door was because she'd gotten her foot in the way. Which she'd managed because there was something wrong with the hinges. Only then did he figure out she was speaking.

"—*safe*," she said. "I'm safe. It's not an emergency. I'm safe." Mercy had taught her that—that Adam sometimes needed reassurances repeated when the wolf was in ascendance.

He took a deep breath and shoved the wolf down. Only when he was sure it was subdued did he step back and let her wiggle past him out of the office. It was probably too soon for relief, but he felt it anyway.

"Sorry, Dad," she said. "I didn't mean to scare you."

She was very nearly an adult, his Jesse. He could see her mother's features and his eyes in her face. But when she started college, she'd let her hair go back to its natural dark blond. And every time he looked at her after that, he'd also seen his own mother. But sometime between when he'd shut himself in the room and now, she'd dyed it again.

She looked more herself with bright purple hair.

"What's wrong?" he asked, fighting the adrenaline still pumping through him.

She pursed her lips. "I'm not sure, exactly. There's a guy on our front porch. He knocked on the door, stared at me when I opened it, muttered something"—she looked uneasy—"something really weird, and sat down."

Adam frowned and took a deep breath, but she must not have left the door open long, because he couldn't pick out any strange scents.

"He looks pretty harmless," she said. "Not a threat. I interrupted you because it's cold outside and I am a little worried about him dying on our doorstep." She paused. "I probably should have just knocked, right?"

"You can interrupt me any way you want," he told her. "You come first."

She rolled her eyes. "I know. But I don't have to be stupid about it."

The exasperation in her voice made him grin—which she returned. Jesse wasn't stupid, though. If she had hit the alarm, it was because something had struck her as an emergency.

"He's in bad condition," Adam said, not making it a question. "Or do you think he's dangerous?"

She had said he looked harmless.

"He's in bad condition and it's cold out there," she said. Then, more slowly, "Yes. I think he could be dangerous." More hastily, probably in reaction to his expression, she continued dryly, "If he wasn't freezing to death on our porch. There's something about him—like the wolves, Dad. Dangerous but not wicked."

His daughter was pretty sharp about people. If she didn't think this stranger was a threat, he probably wasn't. He didn't ask her to stay back when he went to the front door and opened it.

The figure huddled on his stairs looked miserable and cold, visibly shivering in the icy northern wind. His jacket was a good one—it should keep a man warm in colder weather than this. He smelled sweaty, like someone who was breaking a fever, though he didn't smell sick. He smelled of fur and forest and a little like Mercy.

For a moment Adam wondered that Jesse hadn't known who this was. But the man curled over on himself, his face drawn tight and hollowed, didn't look like Gary Laughingdog. Jesse wasn't a werewolf to identify people by scent.

"Gary?"

Mercy's brother didn't react to his name.

"Gary?" Adam said again, taking two quick steps until he was right next to him.

The man didn't even twitch.

"Gary?" Adam softened his voice and put a hand on Gary's shoulder.

That's when it all went south.

Gary snapped up, the leg nearest Adam planting itself behind Adam's foot. He got a wrestler's hold around Adam's leg, hands clasped just in front of Adam's knee, with Gary's shoulder laced over the top—turning Adam's leg into a lever. Gary drove his head into Adam's ribs to keep Adam from leaning forward and regaining his balance.

It was a good takedown, one that Adam used himself. It wouldn't have worked if Gary had been a normal human. But he, like Mercy, was just a bit faster than Adam—and werewolves were supernaturally quick.

The natural progression of the move would have allowed Gary to knock Adam off his feet and away. If Adam had been thinking, if he'd kept his head, he would have allowed the move to do what it was supposed to do. Gary wasn't his enemy—and this wasn't a move designed to cripple or kill. It was designed to let Gary get away.

But Adam was surprised, the head in his ribs had not hit gently, and it was three days since the full moon. His instincts—powered up by the moon's call and the unexpected pain—took over. As he told his pack over and over, you fight how you train. And he had trained for decades, for more than half a century, how *not* to allow an opponent to get what he wanted out of a fight.

He took advantage of his superior strength and the frost on the porch to slide his raised leg and Gary around just enough that he regained his balance. Gary had ended up on the top of the steps. When Adam didn't fall as Mercy's brother had intended, Gary threw his weight backward and sent both of them tumbling down the stairs.

On the ground, Gary pushed away with impressive speed and force. Maybe if the moon had been fainter in the sky; maybe if Gary's frantic scramble away from Adam hadn't meant that he was moving toward Jesse, who was standing in the doorway; maybe if Adam hadn't hit the corner post of the porch railing with his shoulder and if the burn of magic healing the crack in his scapula wasn't more painful than the original injury . . . maybe if all of that or some of that had been different, Adam could have stopped the fight right then.

But the moon was still large in the sky, and the adrenaline of hearing the alarm in his office when he knew Jesse was alone in the house sang in his blood. And Gary smelled—and acted—like prey. Adam could no more have stopped the wolf, his wolf, from going after his brother-in-law than he could have stopped the sun from shining.

Once the wolf took him, Adam retained only bits and pieces

of the fight. Usually it didn't work that way. Usually Adam could break down his werewolf's actions with clinically sharp memory.

The next clear thought Adam had was when he sat on top of Mercy's brother, who was face down in the snow. They were in the backyard.

Gary was pinned but showed no sign of trying to throw Adam off. He was absolutely still. Limp.

I've killed Mercy's brother.

For an instant he couldn't move, couldn't breathe, couldn't think. And then Gary's whole body shivered and Adam realized he—Gary, not Adam—was breathing in little gasping pants, like a terrified rabbit.

"Dad, don't hurt him," Jesse said urgently.

She was, he thought with gratitude for her common sense, all the way across the yard. He didn't look at her—you never look away from your prey. Your opponent, he corrected himself.

Except it is okay to look away if you have them immobilized— and Mercy couldn't break this hold, so he assumed Gary couldn't, either. He glanced over at his daughter.

Jesse was standing in the back doorway. "That's Mercy's brother. He's not an enemy."

She'd heard him call the man by name. Or maybe she'd recognized him once they'd started fighting. In any case, he hadn't been about to kill Mercy's brother. Probably. If the wolf had wanted Gary dead, Gary would be dead.

"He's okay," Adam growled to Jesse, and saw her whole body relax in relief. She started forward—but Adam didn't trust himself that much. "Stay back."

She nodded and stayed where she was, allowing him to turn

his attention to his prisoner. His *brother-in-law*, he reminded himself.

"Gary," he said, and he tried to keep the roughness out of his voice with indifferent success. "Gary, what's wrong with you?"

Instead of answering, the wiry man under Adam tried to get free. But Adam had wrestled in high school, and he had Gary in a highly illegal but effective hold.

"That dog won't hunt," Adam told him. "Settle down." And then, because the smell of fear was still tugging at Adam's control, he said, "Easy now. You're safe, you're safe here."

If it had been Mercy he was holding down, Adam figured that would have set her into a fit of sarcastic laughter. Gary was trapped, face down, under a werewolf—in human form—on six inches of freshly fallen snow, not something that screamed "safe." Adam glanced over his shoulder and saw, by the disturbed snow, that they *had* gone right over the top of the house. Adam didn't remember going over the roof. It had been years, decades, since he'd let the wolf out far enough that he didn't remember what the wolf did.

His chest gave a familiar zing of pain, and he hastily took a deep breath to expand his rib cage. Happily, the bone moved just a little as the lupine power that kept his body and face young, when his youngest brother was an old man, healed the broken rib.

"I promise, you are safe," Adam said. And this time he could hear the truth ringing in his words.

Gary's body gave one convulsive jerk, went totally limp again, then began shaking like a man kept out in the cold too long. Possibly because he was face down in the snow. The shaking stopped.

Adam released him cautiously, finally getting off him altogether.

When Mercy's brother didn't move, Adam put a hand to his shoulder and rolled him over.

He was unconscious.

"Is he dead?" asked Jesse tightly.

"No," Adam said. "Go find a blanket. Let's get him inside and warm him up."

Abruptly, Gary clenched into a fetal position. Adam had to check an instinctive urge to land on him again. But Gary didn't move after that. Adam thought Gary's ability to curl that tightly probably meant that his spine was okay, but before Adam picked him up, he did a quick exploration anyway.

He hefted Gary carefully, but apparently there was nothing painful enough to make him struggle. Also a good sign. Adam's wolf hadn't wanted to hurt Gary any more than Adam did.

Jesse brought the big comforter from her bed out onto the porch, but didn't approach farther than that. "I have the blanket."

"Not out here," Adam said, starting toward the house. "Let's get him inside."

Mercy's brother was a little taller than Adam, but he didn't feel much heavier than Mercy did, maybe twenty pounds more. The steps were icy—he'd shoveled them a few hours ago, but the snow had been falling ever since—so Adam was careful to keep his weight centered.

"I can't believe I didn't recognize him," Jesse said, holding the door wide so Adam could maneuver through without slamming Gary against the frame. "What's wrong with him? Why did he attack you?"

"I don't know."

In the distance, a coyote sang. The coincidence made Adam pause.

Jesse's eyes widened. "Do you think . . . ?"

"Let's get him warmed up and maybe he can tell us," Adam said.

Jesse threw the comforter on one of the big recliners in the living room. Adam set him in it and bundled him in the fluffy thing like a baby. He would have taken off Gary's boots if he'd been awake. But Adam didn't want to have his head down around the semiconscious Gary's feet—the man kicked like a mule, and he'd already demonstrated that he was prone to panic.

Jesse frowned. "He's soaking wet. I'll go downstairs and get him some dry clothes."

They kept clothing on hand, both in the basement and packed in the vehicles. Mostly a mix of unisex sweats and T-shirts. She should be able to find something that would fit.

"I'll call Mercy," Adam said.

INTERLUDE

COYOTE

COYOTE WATCHED IN SATISFACTION AS HIS DAUGH-
ter's mate carried the limp body inside the house. He'd been worried, for a moment, that he might have to stop the fight.

It had not previously been his habit to save his children. He
wasn't sure when that urge had first come upon him—but it also
wasn't his habit to examine his own motivations too closely.

3

MERCY

"WHY DID I MARRY ADAM?" I ASKED, A LITTLE INCREDU-
lously.

"Yes," said Mary Jo.

"Because I love him."

Mary Jo shook her head and waved a hand, casually (and
maybe a little drunkenly still) dismissing the thing that lay at the
heart of a couple of years of bitter resentment on her part.

"I *get* that. But you were already mates and had been taking
all sorts of crap from the pack. We are werewolves, not coyotes—
you were an interloper trying to take our Alpha from us. And we
were pretty convinced you were a weakness that was going to
bring us down."

She paused, her mouth finding a frown. "A coyote. And not a
supercoyote, or one brimming with Native American magics. A
coyote who is even easier to kill than your human form. Which is
as easy to kill as a normal human."

Yep. That was who I was.

She narrowed her eyes at me. "Why *aren't* you dead?"

I raised my eyebrows at her. "Is that a question or a wish?"

She waved a hand at me again. "No. No. I'm done with that. I don't want you dead anymore." She shook her head. "As long as we never have to clean up dead water fae glop again. The clothes I wore still smell like rotting fish and I've washed them three times."

I was beginning to enjoy this sloshed version of Mary Jo—though the effect of whatever Uncle Mike had provided for her seemed to be coming and going.

"I suppose I'm not dead for the same reason you aren't dead," I told her.

She raised her eyebrows in mute question.

"Because no one has managed to kill me yet." I'd meant to be funny. But a chill drifted over my skin and I remembered lying in the dirt while Bonarata walked away from Adam and me. I changed the subject. "But you asked me why I married Adam. I married him because I wanted to."

"Okay," she said. "I know that. But you'd spent most of your life trying to get away from us, from werewolves and our business. Why did you marry Adam—no. Before that. Why did you agree to be his mate in the first place? The cost to you, to your way of life, was so high—and you knew that it would be."

That. He hadn't asked. But he hadn't needed to, really. I'd been lost and struggling and Adam had thrown me a lifeline that had saved me. But it had also hurt, and completed the process of burning to ashes the quiet, safe life I'd built for myself. I didn't know if I owed Mary Jo that answer. I didn't talk about that time, even to Adam.

"It wasn't his good looks," my mouth said dryly before I'd made up my mind to speak.

My mate was movie-star beautiful. The kind of looks that, if he chose to emphasize them, would have stopped people in the street. I thought they were part of what made him so dangerous—a distraction for his enemies.

There was a brief silence.

"Do you know," she said, sounding almost surprised, "I believe you."

She shook her head and murmured, "This is the wrong way to go about this." She slurred the last "this" and looked surprised. Frowning, she took a gulp of the cider, then squared her shoulders. "Renny asked me to marry him."

Renny was a deputy with the Franklin County Sheriff's Office. He was so in love with Mary Jo it made me feel like songs should start spontaneously playing anytime they were together.

"Okay," I said carefully. Because she hadn't sounded happy about it.

Her hands tensed and her eyes lightened with her wolf again.

"He is human," she said. "If this were a few years ago, that would be okay. But we're under siege now. We have to keep our territory safe for everyone. That means our whole pack—and anyone we love—is a target. The bad guys already went after Renny once, and there are more and bigger bad guys all the time."

As if in answer, my phone rang. I flinched. But I picked it up and looked at the caller ID.

"Ben," said Mary Jo, who must have seen my phone's face as I moved it. "You should answer."

"I'll call him back," I said, hitting the red button so my phone shut up.

My phone chimed with an incoming message from Ben. I glanced at it.

Fuck you, woman. We know who called you. Who do you think you're trying to fool? Don't be a silly twat.

I sighed, then turned my attention to the problem at hand.

"Mary Jo," I said. "Tell me about Renny."

"He's going to die if he keeps hanging around with me—and now he thinks we should get married," she said, a growl in her voice. She must have heard it, too, because she took a calming breath, and when she continued, she sounded steadier. "I never minded not having children—I didn't want them in the first place. But Renny should have, I don't know, twenty kids. He volunteers for Big Brothers and for the Special Olympics. He teaches tae kwon do for kids at the Martin Luther King Center."

I was not surprised.

"You told him no," I said.

She nodded, looked away from me, then after a moment wiped her eyes. When she looked back at me, those wet eyes were also yellow.

"I love him," she said. "Who wouldn't? *Of course* I told him no. It was the right thing to do. It was. And now I can't sleep or eat."

That was bad. Werewolves need to eat. I gave a quick thought to her behavior since I'd come into the room and rapidly replaced "ticked off at a dunk in the outhouse and a little drunk" with "sleepless sad werewolf who had too much to drink without eating properly," and I shoved her bowl of stew at her.

"Eat that right now," I said in the voice of authority that I no longer always had to borrow from Adam.

She gave me a startled, uncomprehending look—as if I'd responded in Cornish or Mandarin or something. I gave the bowl another push.

"Eat."

I waited until she'd taken a couple of bites, then asked her, "How long since you turned down Renny?"

"A couple of days," she said, and from the way she said it, I thought she could probably have given me the hours and minutes.

She settled down to eat in earnest. I ate mine, too. It was good stew, and after I've been terrorized, I'm usually hungry.

Two days. She knew better than to let her wolf starve for two days, especially when the full moon was so recent. She was lucky she hadn't gone after one of her own team or the boy who'd fallen into the outhouse.

She needed more calories than she'd find in a single bowl of stew, no matter how filling. "Stay there," I told her. "I'm going out for more food."

I got up and opened the door to find Uncle Mike standing there like the Addams Family butler, with another, larger bowl of stew and a sliced loaf of bread with butter on the side.

I did not squeak in surprise.

Uncle Mike smiled, amused. "Any good tavern keeper knows when his guests are hungry." Which was his version of "*You rang?*"

I took the tray from him and wondered how much else he could tell about his guests. I swallowed my discomfort. "I appreciate the food," I said, which was not quite a thank-you.

He glanced at the table and said, "Drink the rest of that glass, Mercy."

"Yessir," I said dryly.

Unbothered by my sarcasm, he nodded. I backed into the room, shutting the door between us and the green man. I put the food on the table, took Mary Jo's empty bowl, and set it on the tray and the tray on the floor because there was no room for it on the table.

"Renny asked you to marry him, and you broke up with him instead," I said.

I picked up the glass and drank some more of Uncle Mike's magic-spiked cider. More of my headache slid away, allowing some of the tension in my shoulders to release, too.

"I told him we were done." Mary Jo looked miserable even as she dug into the larger bowl.

There were other humans in our pack, mates of werewolves. But they predated our ascent—or descent, depending upon your view—into our current job of being the protectors of the Tri-Cities. Mary Jo had been absolutely right that anyone associated with our pack had a target painted on their back. We'd been able to safeguard our vulnerable members, but none of the humans currently in our pack were adrenaline junkies like Renny. His job required the willingness to run toward danger when everyone with a lick of common sense would run away. He wasn't going to stand back and let the werewolves keep him safe.

My phone rang and, distracted by Mary Jo, I picked it up.

"This is Mercy," I said.

A soft dark laugh rang in my ear.

Mary Jo jerked up her head and stared at my phone.

"Hello," I said in what I hoped was a disinterested tone. He didn't usually call twice in one day. I found that I was terrorized out. Oddly, sitting across from Mary Jo steadied me, too. "Is there something I can do for you?"

A shivery tension filled the air. When silence answered me, I ended the call.

"He really defeated Adam?" Mary Jo asked in a smaller-than-usual voice.

My mate had cut his teeth in Vietnam and was one of the toughest werewolf fighters I had ever seen—and I'd grown up in the Marrok's pack with the bunch of crazy werewolves he'd deemed too dangerous to inflict on any other Alpha. Adam was a born warrior.

"Yes," I said. I tried not to picture my mate's broken body on the ground, curled around an artifact that was trying to turn him into its slave. It had been so close.

Mary Jo looked at my phone.

"He found your number," Mary Jo said heavily.

I shrugged. Worrying too much about it wasn't useful, but shoving it to the side extracted its own toll. I wasn't going to talk about Bonarata anymore.

"Let me guess," I said. "You didn't ask me to come here and tell you that you did the right thing in refusing Renny. You wanted me to argue with you, because I'm not any better armed against the bad guys than someone like Renny is."

"Probably," Mary Jo admitted.

"I can't do that," I said. "He is not equipped to deal with folks like—" I tapped the screen of my phone. I didn't use Bonarata's name any more than necessary.

She flinched but stiffened her spine and raised her chin.

"You didn't come here to ask me why I accepted Adam as my mate," I said. "I'm the wrong side of the equation. You came here to find out how Adam had the courage to take me as *his* mate."

"Yes," she said. "That."

"I don't know," I answered her honestly. "*I take great comfort knowing that Adam is very hard to kill.* Bonarata left us that night thinking Adam would die—and he was wrong. I don't know how Adam deals with the fact that I would not have survived the wounds he took that night."

"You are hard to kill, too," said Mary Jo. "You shouldn't be, but you are."

I wasn't going to argue about that. It didn't seem useful. Instead, I said softly, "Renny has a dangerous job. How are you going to feel if he gets shot trying to interfere in a domestic dispute or a standard traffic stop? Just because you don't accept his marriage proposal, that doesn't make him safe. It doesn't mean that he won't die in a car wreck on the way home tonight."

The wolf in her eyes lit right up, and my phone rang.

"How are you going to feel then?" I asked.

I answered my phone. This time I didn't check the caller ID because I didn't want to. I wasn't going to give Bonarata that power. Not with Mary Jo—*my pack*—here with me.

"Mercy," said my husband. "You need to come home. Your brother is here." There was a noise—I couldn't quite make it out. And then Adam grunted and disconnected.

Mary Jo grabbed her wallet. "I'll take care of the bill," she said. "My invite. Go."

"You need to wait before you drive," I told her.

She smiled. "I promise. Go."

I DID NOT SPEED ON THE WAY HOME. I WAS VERY, VERY careful about when and how I broke the law, and right now a speeding ticket would cost me more time than the few minutes I would save speeding. When a light turned red in my face, I stopped.

I'd called Adam back before I left, but he didn't pick up. The noises I'd heard before he'd disconnected had sounded like combat. But I couldn't be sure. Who would he have been fighting?

I tapped my foot as I waited for the light to turn green.

Why had Gary come to my house? Gary and I weren't close.

I had first met him this spring—I hadn't known I had a brother, half brother really, before that. Though maybe I should have. There are a lot of tales about Coyote marrying beautiful women, and many of the stories mention his children. Gary was older than me, probably by at least a century.

I had the feeling he'd been alone a very long time.

He hadn't been particularly friendly when we'd first met. He was rough around the edges. But I thought he was a good person, and he could be unexpectedly kind. He reminded me, in that way, of Kyle, Warren's boyfriend.

We weren't friends, Gary and I. I thought about that for a moment, because there was some kind of connection. We were fellow prisoners, maybe, both of us serving out the sentence of being our father's children. But Gary had kept in touch with me—and I'd found myself talking to him more than I'd expected. My life had been in a constant state of upheaval for a long time, and Gary knew more than I did about what I was.

The last time we talked, Gary had been training horses for a quarter horse breeder in Montana. Jobs like that tended to be mobile and seasonal, so he could simply be visiting because his job had ended. His being in the Tri-Cities was unnecessarily dangerous because he was still wanted in Washington for escaping from Coyote Ridge Corrections Center.

Adam hadn't sounded like it was a casual visit.

My phone—face up on the passenger seat—dinged and showed a message from Jesse.

We are okay. Come home. Don't speed. Dad says quite reading this and pay attention to your driving.

My phone dinged again as Jesse corrected herself. *quit

The light turned green while I was looking at my phone, and the car behind me honked. As I stepped on the gas, I wondered if the reason Adam hadn't answered his phone was because he was dealing with the police. Maybe they'd figured out Gary was connected to the pack, to me, even. That didn't make sense. Even Gary hadn't known we were related until I tracked him down.

Maybe the police had followed him to my house?

The crime he'd been in jail for hadn't been violent. No one should be dedicated to searching for him as long as he refrained from thumbing his nose at the justice system too hard—by, say, running around a mere forty-odd miles from the prison he'd escaped.

Proximity was why he'd relocated to Montana, where, in his words, "even if they send out bulletins or whatever they use now, one Native looks like any other Native—as long as the cop who is looking isn't Native, too." And he added, "Besides, no one in Montana cares about what happens in Washington anyway."

But in the Tri-Cities, if someone recognized him, Gary's presence in our house could expose us to criminal charges.

I took a deep breath and forced myself to relax. We had a couple of werewolves who worked at Coyote Ridge. They told me that Gary's breakout was legendary, that it had been elevated to urban myth. Prisoners escaped from time to time, but they always left a trail. Gary had left his locked room and disappeared without a trace. No one, I'd been assured, was seriously looking for him anymore.

But the noises I'd heard on the phone sounded a lot like combat.

There were no police cars at the house when I got there. I pretended I wasn't relieved as I pulled into the driveway between Adam's and Jesse's cars. There was a battered old Ford truck with Montana plates parked somewhat askew, presumably Gary's ride.

It had been snowing off and on all week. There were winters when we never got accumulated snow, but the snow around the house was currently a bit over ankle height. There was enough to make decent snow angels or—as demonstrated all over the porch and front yard—to leave impressions of what had clearly been a violent fight.

I inhaled deeply and did not smell blood. My nose said the only people who had been out here fighting were my brother and my mate.

I jogged up the stairs and opened the front door to a living room filled with upended furniture. Unusually for a fight involving werewolves, nothing was broken. I gave the fainting couch a frown. Sadly, even upside down, it seemed to be fine. Before I had time to wonder where everyone was, Adam called out from the basement.

"Down here, Mercy." He didn't sound particularly stressed, but I didn't like the solemn note in his voice.

Downstairs I found Jesse and Tad, our neighborhood halfblood fae, seated near the cage we used to lock up dangerous wolves. Adam was standing beside the cage, looking at me with worried eyes.

Behind the silver bars of the cage, a man was curled in a fetal position, his back to the room. He reeked of sweat and fear. His hair had been French braided at one time, but the braid was disheveled, with hair sticking out every which way, as if he'd slept on it more than one night. Or maybe just engaged in a battle with a werewolf. He did not, I noticed with relief, smell like fresh blood. He wore jeans and a ripped and wet winter coat he hadn't taken off. Huddled up like that, my brother looked smaller than I remembered.

Adam gave me a quick hug, which I returned before dropping to my knees next to the cage.

"Gary?" I said. He didn't respond to my voice at all.

"I don't know what's wrong," Adam told me, his hand warm on my shoulder. "He wouldn't talk to us. It felt like he *couldn't* talk." He glanced at Jesse, who nodded.

Sometime since this morning, when I'd last seen her, Jesse had dyed her hair bright purple. I thought she'd given up on outrageous colors when she started college a couple of months ago. When Gary was sorted out, I'd ask her why she'd gone back to dying her hair.

"Who had the fight in the front yard?" I asked, just in case there had been a scent I hadn't detected.

"Gary and I did," Adam said. "I don't think he's hurt—beyond bruises. Nothing seems broken."

He sounded defensive.

"The fight wasn't Dad's fault," Jesse said.

"I could have stopped it," he told her.

"What happened?" I asked. "From the top, please?"

"He knocked," Jesse said. "Dad was in his office and I answered the door. He didn't look right at me—not at my face. Mumbled something and took a seat on the porch. I didn't realize he was your brother, Mercy. He didn't look like who I remembered. I thought he was a lone wolf. He's not the first of those who has shown up here. I got Dad because I thought he was going to freeze to death on our porch."

"Werewolves don't freeze to death," observed Tad, who'd been silent up to this point. He sounded a little upset.

"He was shivering and sort of hunched." She nodded toward Gary, but there was a bite in her voice directed at Tad. "He looked like he was going to freeze to death. I'm not equipped to tell werewolves from not-werewolves." She gave Tad a look and said, "But I'm also not *stupid*."

"You opened the door," Tad said. "Your father wouldn't have heard him tear your throat out."

"When I got out here"—Adam said, evidently deciding that argument had gone on long enough, though I thought Tad had a point; maybe Adam had already had it out with Jesse—"he was sitting at the top of the steps."

He wasn't happy about the danger Jesse had been in, either; I knew Adam. But unlike Tad, he knew better than to rebuke Jesse as if she were a child. I foresaw more cameras around the house so Adam could better monitor things when he was in his office.

"He didn't respond when I talked to him," Adam continued. "He didn't appear to hear me at all. I put a hand on his shoulder and he reacted as if I were an enemy. That's when we fought."

I looked up at him, and he flushed a little. "Too close to the full moon. He's lucky I didn't kill him."

"Dad just pinned him," Jesse jumped in, as if I'd already gotten mad at Adam.

I figured if Gary was still alive, it was because Adam hadn't wanted to kill him—wolf in charge or not. Gary had a knack for making people want to kill him. That's how he'd ended up in jail in the first place.

"I was putting my trash in the bins outside and I saw the two of them come over the roof," said Tad.

Despite my concern for my brother, I could feel my eyebrows rise and I looked up at Adam. "Over the roof? I thought you just pinned him."

He rubbed his face with the hand that wasn't holding on to me and gave me a sheepish look. "I don't remember that part. You know what a fight is like. And the moon is just past full."

"He pinned him five or six times," Jesse said. "But Gary kept escaping. He just wiggled out until Dad really landed on him."

Adam winced at the last few words, maybe because of the enthusiasm Jesse used.

"He sort of gave up then," she told me. "Or we thought he did. Dad checked him out and carried him into the house."

"Unconscious?" I asked.

"No," Adam said.

"Catatonic," said Jesse.

"I'm sure you don't have the medical qualifications to assess that," Tad said dryly.

"Unresponsive," Adam said, stepping into the argument.

And it had been an argument, hadn't it? I wondered, briefly, if it had something to do with Jesse's eggplant hair.

But I was more concerned with my brother.

"If he was catatonic," I asked, "why is he in the cage?"

"Dad called you," Jesse said, "and right in the middle of that he jumped up like a jackrabbit. We'd wrapped him in a blanket. He sat up and the blanket sort of trapped him. He panicked."

"I came in about the same time," Tad said, "so it could also have been my arrival." He looked at me. "Smelling like I do, yeah?"

Fae, he meant.

"We're not sure," Jesse added. "Because neither Dad nor I heard when Tad came in, and Tad didn't see Gary jump up."

I glanced at Adam, because not hearing Tad's entrance was weird. Particularly if Adam had been revved up from a fight with the wolf near the surface.

He shrugged. "The wolf part of me stopped noticing Tad's movements a while ago. Not enemy. Not pack. Not dangerous to us."

I nodded.

"I heard Tad come in," Adam clarified, "but I didn't pay attention to him. I was more concerned about stopping Gary from jumping out the big plate-glass window. I caught him, but he's as quick as you are. If I hadn't been moving and close, I wouldn't have."

"He's scared, Mercy," said Jesse. "Really scared."

"It took Adam and me both to get him down here without hurting him," Tad told me. "Though once we got him inside the cage, he just collapsed."

Tad had been slouched back in the chair since I'd gotten there, but I'd been distracted by my brother. I finally took note of the deceptive casualness in Tad's pose that was designed to hide that he was ready for action.

I'd known Tad since he was nine. He'd worked with me in my

garage until he'd found a better-paying position as an undercover bodyguard. That meant he was going to school with Jesse, because being the daughter of the Tri-Cities' own Alpha set her up for nastiness no one would have dared to take against a real werewolf. He'd moved into my old house across the back fence from us a few weeks ago for added security for our home.

Tad wasn't a werewolf. He didn't look like a badass. He looked like a nerd, complete with stick-out ears and a big, goofy smile. But looks were deceptive. He was the half-human son of a powerful and grumpy fae. He could take care of business.

I wondered why he thought he should be worried about my brother, who was looking pretty helpless just now in a cage designed to keep werewolves trapped.

"I called Honey," Adam told me. "She should be here shortly."

I glanced up at him in surprise.

He smiled faintly. "I'm not oblivious."

"Peter's only been dead a year," I said. Peter's ghost still followed Honey around, a faithful attendant to his living mate.

"Honey and your brother have been talking," he told me. "Texting, mostly."

I frowned at him. "Honey didn't say anything to me."

"Honey didn't say anything to me, either," he said. "I have ways."

"Our wolf pack gossips like nobody's business," observed Jesse.

I decided I'd gotten as much information out of them as I was going to. Time to deal with my brother.

I tried his name again.

"Gary?"

He didn't respond to my voice, which wasn't a surprise. I'd

been down here for a while now, and he'd had plenty of time to react to me. I took a deep breath, but the overwhelming smell of sweat and fear made it difficult to get anything more subtle.

"You think it could be magic?" I asked.

"I don't know," Adam said.

"Maybe," Tad said slowly. "But it's nothing I'm familiar with—and I can't read anything through that cage."

I gave Tad a surprised glance. Silver shouldn't have any effect on fae gifts.

"Sherwood's been playing with it," Adam said with faint disapproval.

Sherwood, our no-longer-amnestic werewolf, had some unusual magic at his beck and call. He could remember who he was now, but he still had a lot of holes in his memory—and his magic. It made for some interesting times.

If Sherwood had a go at it . . . I decided—without much basis for my judgment—that he wouldn't have done anything that would hurt anyone. I reached through the bars to touch Gary. I wasn't a werewolf, so the silver didn't bother me. But my arm wasn't quite long enough from this side of the cage. I crawled to the side nearer to Gary and tried again. This time I managed to get my fingertips on his shoulder.

He jerked as if startled, even though we'd been making a lot of noise. After a bare instant he rolled over and up, until he was crouched over his heels. He grabbed the hand I'd had on his shoulder before he'd moved and brought it to his face, inhaling deeply.

He made a garbled sound that tried and failed to be a word. He followed that with a dozen other noises that also might have been words. I didn't think they were, though. There was something about them that felt wrong—the opposite of communication.

Gary looked up and his gaze swept over mine as if he couldn't see me. Then he closed his eyes, nodded once, and banged his hand against the bars of the cage. After the second bang he released my hand and waited. He was obviously making an effort to be still.

The cage locked with a key, but it also had a fingerprint lock that was much more convenient—as long as Adam was in the room. I gestured, and Adam opened the cage. There was a high-pitched beep and the lock clicked. I pulled open the door.

Gary kept his eyes closed and, nostrils flared, crawled out of the cage and to me. Not stopping until his arms were wrapped around my middle and his face was buried under my jaw, knocking me on my butt on the floor in the process. He sat there, rigid, for a long moment, then his whole body went limp and he began sobbing. Adam sat on the edge of the couch and put a hand on my brother's head as if he were one of the pack who needed comforting.

Quietly, Tad said, "I am increasingly uncomfortable with the knowledge that he drove from Montana in that state."

He wasn't wrong.

Gary was damp—wrestling in the snow could do that. This close, the scent of his terror and sweat was unpleasant. We'd have to get him a shower followed by clean, dry clothes. But that was something for later, because I was picking up a new odor stronger than any of the other scents Gary was carrying.

Sherwood had done something to that cage, all right. He'd created some sort of barrier that had locked away the magic swirling around my brother so well, I hadn't sensed it until the door opened. I thought of the time we'd locked Ben in the cage when the smoke dragon had controlled him, and wondered if Sherwood's modification would have helped Ben by cutting off the smoke dragon's magic.

We are all preparing to fight the previous war, I thought. Maybe the cage's new properties would come in handy the next time an ancient fae predator decided to make puppets out of our wolves.

"He reeks of magic," I told them. "It's a bit odd—it reminds me of fae magic, but it isn't anything I've been around before."

I had one hand on the back of Gary's head and the other on his shoulder. Even through the padding of the ripped jacket, his body was rock-tight. He did not react when I spoke.

"I can't sense it," Tad said—which was unusual, I thought, though I wasn't sure. Tad's power, since he was a half-blood fae, was weirder than mine, as well as an order of magnitude or two more powerful. I could smell magic, but Tad could work it. "Do you want me to call Dad?"

Zee had been . . . strange . . . since he'd destroyed the Soul Taker, an ancient and sentient artifact. Tad and I had decided that the resolution of Zee's long hunt had brought some part of his older, more dangerous self back into the forefront. I sometimes felt as though the older beings I knew had their personalities in geological layers. We'd cracked the ground to release the Dark Smith once more into the world. Now Zee didn't always fit neatly into the shape of the old mechanic who had been Tad's father.

I was glad Tad saw it, too. Otherwise, I'd have to put Zee's sudden strangeness down to whatever the Soul Taker had done to me.

"Zee was fine at work today," I said, rubbing my temple with a finger. "What do you think?"

Tad touched the side of Gary's face with his fingers, then withdrew them and shook his head. "I can't sense anything at all. We should talk to either my dad or Uncle Mike."

"Call Zee," Adam said.

I looked at him.

He gave me a faint smile. "You'll break his heart if you go to someone else with this."

Tad let out a breath. "That's true. But it doesn't make it a good idea."

I met Adam's eyes.

"Have Tad call Zee, Mercy," my mate said. "The Dark Smith of Drontheim destroyed a fascinating power for your sake. He won't hurt you."

"We made a bargain," I said. "It wasn't for my sake."

"I forgot," Adam lied—which he only did deliberately. He was making a statement, and he stared me down.

My brother's sobs had slowed to uneven breathing. I petted his head and nodded at Tad. "Call him, please. Jesse, could you get some water? And maybe some food."

HONEY CAME BEFORE ZEE ARRIVED.

She wore a red sweater over leggings and managed to make it look like she was ready to attend a board meeting. But she crouched beside Gary and me without reacting to the way he smelled. She leaned close but didn't try to touch Gary. For his part, he didn't seem to notice her. In fact, he seemed to be actively trying not to notice anyone or anything.

I hadn't been able to tempt him with food or water. He'd quit sobbing, but he kept his head down and he hadn't loosened his hold on me.

The various witnesses to Gary's arrival repeated their parts of the story. It had already acquired bits and pieces that were told in the same words. Honey had a good game face, but I was pretty sure she was as worried as I was.

"He hasn't said anything since Dad brought him in the house," Jesse told Honey.

"That's not quite true," Adam said. "He tried to say something when he figured out Mercy was here. I didn't understand the language he used."

"Not words," I said with emphasis, because the memory of the sound that had left my brother's lips still freaked me out. "It wasn't words. It felt like the opposite of speaking."

They all stared at me.

Honey frowned at me. Somewhat cautiously she asked, "Is that some more of what the Soul Taker left you with, Mercy?"

I hadn't thought so. Most of what I had noticed had been the sometimes overwhelming sensitivity to magic and unwanted insights into people. But once she asked, it seemed more probable than not. I shrugged uncomfortably.

"Huh." Honey frowned again. "He smells like magic to you?"

"Yes," I said.

"My dad is coming," Tad said. "If he can't sort it out, he should be able to point us in the right direction."

She nodded. "Okay. Let's get some food and water into him."

"Good luck with that," I said.

ADAM HAD BEEN RIGHT TO CALL HONEY.

Gary was easier with her than he had been with me, once he'd figured out who she was. And when he was unwilling to move, she just picked him up and moved him. He didn't fight her the way he had Adam. Eventually she got him up the stairs and into the kitchen.

He sat, his back to the bay of windows, with the table between him and the rest of the room. He was hollow-eyed and twitchy, but he ate whatever food we set before him—though only with one hand. With the other, he kept a fierce hold on Honey's hand, as if to remind himself she was still there. Periodically he'd glance around the room, but hunger kept most of his attention on his food.

I couldn't figure out why he was that hungry. He didn't look like he'd been missing meals. When I shifted back and forth between human and coyote, I got hungry like that. Working magic was draining. I wondered if he'd been shifting a lot—or if he was using magic to try to resist whatever made him smell of foreign magic.

Jesse had put together a couple of steak sandwiches from leftovers while Honey got him into the kitchen. When he fell onto them with ravenous hunger, she and Tad set out to build an omelet of epic proportions full of whatever odd ingredients were in the fridge. In the midst of their chopping, the front door opened in a fierce whirl of wind and weather—evidently the fat snow had given way to wind and sleet while we were downstairs.

My brother in safe hands, I headed to the front door to find Zee, coatless and soaked to the skin, standing in the doorway with iridescent silver eyes. For a moment he looked like a stranger—as if the forces driving the storm drew out his magic. Even though I knew he still wore his everyday glamour, I saw the malevolent and powerful fae that his magic disguised. The familiar if rain-drenched T-shirt clinging to his skin appeared to me as though it was a finely worked chain mail shirt.

I blinked and he turned to push the door closed. When he turned back, he swiped his wet white hair out of his face with an impatient hand, and when I saw his eyes again, they were a more familiar color and intensity. Everything about him had toned down now that the storm was firmly sealed outside.

"Where's your brother?"

He looked, now, as he had in the garage, wiry and tough— dried out by age to sinew and bone, a grumpy old mechanic feared only by people who didn't change their oil regularly.

Wordlessly I waved him in the right direction. He carried authority in his wake with the same ease that my husband did. Familiar and safe.

But in the back of my head, I knew that was not really true. Or not always true.

INTERLUDE

Earlier That Day

JESSE

JESSE LOOKED UP FROM HER TEXTBOOK WITH AN IRRI-
tated frown when someone knocked on her door. Her irritation
was not appeased when she saw Tad standing in the doorway.
Being caught belly down on her unmade bed in her oldest set of
sweats made her feel uncomfortably exposed.

"What?" she growled.

He pulled out his hand and showed her a rectangle of silver-
embossed card stock he held between his fingers, fluttering it to
draw her attention.

She sat up indignantly and grabbed her backpack, unzipping
the front pocket. It was empty. Her best friend had stolen the invitation and given it to Tad. Another time she'd have understood
how concerned Izzy must have been to call in Tad when their
on-again, off-again romance was currently on pause.

"Tell your girlfriend she's a traitor," Jesse growled.

"Don't go," he told her.

"It's a wedding invitation," she said dryly, "not a summons to a duel. Really, Izzy is making too much of it. Gabriel and I were friends before we dated."

"It's an attack," he said.

Gabriel had no reason to want to hurt her. He was the one who broke up with her. Even if he'd felt wronged, he wouldn't have tried to hurt her. Gabriel wasn't like that.

She stood up and made her bed, because the rumpled sheets were making her feel vulnerable. Tad waited patiently while she righted her bedding, then set the stuffed elephant in its proper place on top of her pillow.

Her emotions tucked away as effectively as her unicorn sheets, she turned back to him.

"If I don't go," she told him, "it will look like I'm still pining for him. It's not an attack. Gabriel isn't vindictive."

"No," Tad agreed. "He isn't. But he and I were friends, too. And I didn't get an invitation to his wedding." He paused. "And neither did Mercy."

She didn't know what to say to that. She couldn't tell him he was right. Or that she'd rather rub her heart with sandpaper than go watch the man she'd loved marry someone he'd started dating as soon as he'd left the Tri-Cities to attend the UW in Seattle.

She walked to her closet and rummaged through her box of hair dyes. She grabbed a bottle at random and walked past him.

"I'm going to dye my hair," she said airily. "I'll see you in the morning."

"Don't go," he said.

And because going to Gabriel's wedding was the very last thing in the world she wanted to do, she said, her back to him, "You aren't the boss of me, Tad Adelbertsmiter."

Then she retreated to the bathroom and dyed her hair purple.

4

MERCY

"I DON'T MIND SNOW AND I DON'T MIND RAIN," ZEE growled as he stumped into the kitchen. "But this place likes to spit water that turns to ice."

Tad, chopping vegetables, didn't look up when his father entered. Zee glanced at him but quickly looked away.

Jesse exchanged a worried look with me. I had thought matters between father and son had improved. Apparently not.

When Tad started dating Jesse's best friend, Izzy, Zee had taken an interest in her. Not in a creepy stalker way, but in a scarier "if you hurt my son, I will destroy you" way.

Tad was angry—and I think a little worried. Zee had a habit of dealing permanently with people who hurt his son. I thought Zee could probably tell the difference between an overstepping Gray Lord of the fae and a young human negotiating the confusing new adult version of romance. But Tad, like his father, was protective.

Fortunately, our kitchen was sized like one of those old-timey farm kitchens: fit for a family to gather in. There was more than enough room for the seven of us without forcing Tad and Zee into interacting with each other. For that matter, it was big enough to give Gary some space, too.

Honey looked up from tending to my brother as we approached the table, giving Zee a sharp appraisal. Honey was old, and old wolves tended to be more wary around the fae. At her increase in tension, my brother stiffened and set the last half sandwich back down on his plate. He saw us—I mean he knew there were people in the kitchen—but he plainly didn't see anyone he recognized.

Zee stopped well short of the table, frowned for a bit, then stretched his right hand in front of him, fingers spread, palm out toward my brother. Like mine on most workdays, his hands were stained with burnt oil. Scars covered his knuckles, and he was missing half a nail on his thumb. His ring finger was crooked where it had broken and healed badly—I couldn't remember if his fae form, his real form, had a broken finger or not. His hand looked old.

And powerful.

Zee closed his eyes and inhaled audibly. He mumbled in something that might have been German, except it didn't hold any words I was familiar with. I'm not fluent in German, but as in English, the little common words tend to sprinkle through normal speech. He opened his eyes, put his hand down, and turned to me with a scowl.

"What?" I asked.

"This"—he waved in my brother's direction—"is not something you should be able to feel. Tad told me that he couldn't sense it."

His scowl deepened, the wrinkles on his face growing to crags. He took two steps toward me and touched my forehead with his crooked finger.

"Is it worse?" asked Adam. He was sitting on the island, trying to give Gary as much room as possible. Gary was more agitated when Adam got too near.

"With Mercy, everything that can be worse is. Always." Zee's voice was a grumble, and I couldn't help but snort a laugh.

He dropped his hand from my face and told me, "I do not like how you have been left wandering through the world with your senses wide open like this. Vulnerable." He pursed his lips. "I keep hoping what that artifact did to you will correct itself."

"Yeah," I said. "Me, too." But talking about it wasn't going to change things. "Am I right about Gary? Is it fae magic doing this to him?"

He shook his head. "No. But I understand why you would think so. My own power, metal based as it is, has as much in common with the Jötnar as it does with other fae." He used the German pronunciation: *Yoot*-nahr, rolling the final "r." "But the Jötnar are mages of great power and greater stealthiness. And you shouldn't be able to feel this spell at all."

"The who?" asked Tad.

"Giants," said Honey and I.

"Loki," said Jesse at the same time, her knowledge of Norse mythology owing more to Marvel movies than study. She wrinkled her nose at us. "Loki wasn't a giant."

"The Norse giants and the Celtic ones were different," I told her. "Two words got conjoined when moving them from one language to another."

Zee snorted, but when I looked at him, he made a rolling gesture with his hand.

I raised an eyebrow, but this wasn't the time to get lost in translation. "Some of the Jötnar in the stories were larger than human size, but mostly they were antagonists of the Aesir—the Norse gods. They came from different places."

"The nine realms." Jesse gave a little nod.

"Those movies have a lot to answer for," Zee said, flashing Jesse a wry smile. He'd always had a soft spot for her. "More truth than they know and more ridiculousness, too. And the pronunciation. *Bifrost. Odin.*" He mimicked the way they were pronounced in the movie, hitting the long "i" in "Bifrost" and the "d" in "Odin." Which was how I'd always pronounced them— apparently incorrectly. "But yes. Sadly for us, the Jötnar were and are powerful mages, not the Pictish giants who became mountains when they lay down to rest."

"Did they?" asked Jesse. "Really? *Mountains?*"

Zee just gave her a Cheshire cat sort of smile, lingering and mysterious.

"Can you fix Gary?" asked Adam, pulling the room back to the point.

Zee's face twisted, but not in its usual sour expression. This expression was *wrong*. His lids lowered and his eyes darkened to flat deep gray, sending a chill up my spine. I'd been seeing a lot of this part of Zee, the older, more dangerous version of him. Or maybe that was just me and the Soul Taker's gift. Maybe he'd always been this dimensional and I'd just never noticed. But, I reminded myself again, Tad was worried about him, too.

I shivered even though the kitchen was warm. But no one was watching me.

"It depends." Oblivious to my doubts, Zee studied my brother, who, after his brief pause at Zee's entrance, was eating the last half sandwich as if he was afraid someone was about to yank his plate out from under him.

"It's not that he's blind," I told him. "And he can hear things. It's like he doesn't understand—"

My brother's head jerked up and he inhaled sharply, emitting a growl as his lips pulled away from his teeth. Honey moved her free hand to his forearm, a reassuring move that not incidentally gave her leverage on his right arm that would allow her to keep him from doing anything dumb. She was right. He didn't know Zee. If all that he could interpret was smell—and if he could scent like I could—then this could go badly.

"—what he sees or hears," I continued. "But it's not everything. He drove all the way from Montana, and his truck doesn't have any fresh damage. He sees objects like stairs and doors, but he can't see people as people. Or hear words as words."

"Almost like glamour in reverse," observed Tad to the room. The frying pan he held hissed as Jesse poured the egg mixture in.

His analogy was close, I thought. Glamour very seldom covered up scent entirely. It wasn't that the fae didn't have, some of them, a keen sense of smell—it was that most of them didn't use it. Humans were like that, too. Oh, normal people couldn't scent as well as I did, but they could have used their noses a lot better than they chose to. It was why blind people's other senses seemed to gain unexpected strength—they actually started paying attention to them.

"I'll need to touch him," said Zee.

But he took no more than two steps closer, and my brother rose to his feet, using the arm that Honey should have had control of to put her behind him, the table upending with a lot of drama—though it was sturdy. It would probably survive. Gary's plate and glass were toast.

Honey looked at that hand that held hers with an expression of astonishment.

Me, too. I didn't have any more strength than I would have if I'd been wholly human. *I* wouldn't have been able to shove Honey around like that. I knew it, I'd tried a time or two—mostly in training fights. Werewolves are *strong.*

I understood that walkers, people like me who were descended from avatars—Coyote, Hawk, Raven, and others—all had different abilities depending upon which avatar we were descended from. And also how close the generational relationship was. I hadn't thought any of us were stronger than the average human, though. Evidently, I was wrong.

Unworried by my brother's stance, Tad grabbed the table and righted it. He didn't put it back where it had been, though. He hauled it out of the way. Jesse grabbed a broom and dustpan. She was a little more circumspect—staying back from Gary and Honey. But she cleared the mess from the floor. If anyone started a fight, at least they wouldn't end up rolling in glass.

"I can't see into this magic without touching him," Zee said to me. "I can hold him still, with your permission, as he is not in a state to give it."

If Zee needed permission, it meant he felt that however he needed to hold my brother, it would not be something he'd normally do to an ally. Magic, of some sort, I was sure. Physically restraining Gary, if that was a real option—I gave my brother an assessing look, as I was still unnerved by the ease at which he'd moved Honey—would not have required permission.

"No," said Honey.

"No," I agreed with her.

"I can hold him," Adam offered.

"Wait," I said.

I considered the interactions I'd had with Gary over the past hour. His vision and hearing were screwed up. I looked at the grip he had on Honey and thought if his sense of touch was really okay, he wouldn't have had to hold on to her so hard. But he seemed to be getting good information through his nose. That's how he'd known me, and that's how he'd known Honey.

If scent was all that we had to communicate with, we'd have to use that. What kinds of things could *I* figure out from scent?

Werewolves all carry a whiff of pack. It grows to something more easily detected when we're acting in concert with each other—a hunt, a battle, even a baseball game. I pushed power through the pack bonds, but it wasn't enough to trigger any kind of scent flare.

Before I asked him, Adam did it for me. He lit up our bonds—and only the ones of the people in our house, so we wouldn't end up with the whole pack converging here. I'd noticed that he could do a lot of things I had never known were possible. I'd have put it down to me not being a werewolf, but I knew that he surprised some of the older wolves, too. I'd heard Zack, one of the three oldest wolves in our pack, call Adam "the Maestro" because of his command of pack magic.

As the bonds flared to life—Honey's to Adam, Adam's to me, Adam's to Jesse (that last one was a different kind of pack bond, but still a claiming, father to daughter)—I could see Gary feel it and heard his sigh of relief. I stared at him. Gary's secrets were coming to light today. Because he hadn't scented our bonds, he'd *felt* them.

It was wrong. I was taking advantage of him when he was defenseless. I—*we* had no right to this knowledge. But none of us had any choice, not even Gary.

Only Tad and Zee were outside of the pack bonds.

My brother closed his eyes and inhaled, breathing deeply now that he scented the bonds. He kept his eyes closed and tapped his free hand on Honey's, then nodded at Adam, at Jesse, and finally at me.

But we needed him to accept Zee's touch—and Zee wasn't pack.

I turned to Zee. "I need to give you my scent, so he knows that you"—I almost said "are mine" but thought it might be unacceptable, because the ties between Zee and me were mostly unspoken and worked best that way for us both—"are here at my invitation."

Zee frowned at me. "How are you going to do that?"

He didn't sound offended. But I didn't know exactly how to answer. Lovers smell like each other, but a casual touch wasn't going to transfer my scent to him. Maybe if I put a shirt I'd worn on him—

"Zee's hands smell like a mechanic's," Adam suggested. "Just like yours do. Might be enough to have Zee run the inside of his wrist along the side of your neck."

Adam took his own wrist and ran it under the line of my jaw to show what he meant. He sniffed his wrist, then shrugged with a hint of humor.

He always carried my scent.

"I can do that," Zee agreed. "With your permission, Mercy?"

I tipped my head to allow him access, and his wrist slid across the soft skin of my neck with a slight rasp of warmth that was cooler than Adam's wrist had been.

Adam raised an inquiring eyebrow, and Zee lifted his wrist in invitation. Adam sniffed.

"Almost," he said. "Try one more time."

It took three times—a number that gave Zee obvious satisfaction. The number three had magical significance to the fae.

I stood between Zee and my brother and put my own wrist to Gary's nose. After a second, I backed away and Zee put his wrist near my brother's face and held it there.

Gary tipped his head, put his nose closer to Zee, and nodded.

Zee put Gary's free hand under his own and carried both up to the side of Gary's neck, just over his pulse point. Gary bent his head and hissed, the muscles of his body tightening, and he broke out in a light sweat. But he didn't fight.

After a few seconds, Zee jerked his hand away and walked back to the other side of the kitchen to give Gary space, shaking out the hand he'd used on my brother as he did so.

I was surprised I hadn't felt a surge in the magic in the room, given how much reaction both men had shown. Maybe my senses were just overloaded. I tried not to feel hopeful that maybe whatever the Soul Taker had done to me was fading. Or could get overwhelmed and fizzle out. I'd take either option.

"*Pest*," Zee said. "I am sorry, Mercy. This is not something I can break without damaging him."

And my concerns about myself disappeared, telling me how much confidence I'd had that Zee could take care of it.

"The Jötnar work their own kind of magic," he said. "This is

subtle and powerful—the work of one of the old ones, I think."
He frowned. "There is one who could tell you more and he feels
obligated to you, but I am not sure it is a good idea to involve
yourself with him."

I knew who he meant. I'd just seen Ymir at Uncle Mike's.

A couple of years ago, under the influence of someone else's
malicious magic, Ymir had shown his true form and nearly destroyed Uncle Mike's pub. Mary Jo had been killed—or almost
killed, depending upon who you talked to. It hadn't been the Jötunn who had damaged her, but he'd been part of the problem.
I'd broken the spell and—though fae do not say thank you—it
had been implied.

The Jötnar weren't properly fae. Or maybe they were; I knew
that the lines between fae and not-fae were blurry. In any case,
the Jötunn at Uncle Mike's called himself an ice elf—and elves
were a type of fae.

There were a lot of classifications of fae that had been made
up to satisfy government forms—Zee called himself a gremlin,
which is a term that he predates to a ridiculous degree. "Ice elf"
was no more a real classification for the being who'd run amok
than the abominable snowman would have been. But when a
frost giant told you to call him an elf, you did it.

"The ice elf?" I asked.

"Snow elf," Adam corrected me absently, staring at Zee.
"Ymir calls himself a snow elf."

"Oops," I said without meaning it. Either way, they were ridiculous terms, conjuring up something that should be helping
Santa Claus deliver presents instead of destroying the world in the
fated Ragnarok.

"Ymir," Adam said, talking to Zee, "has power over wolves."

That was true, assuming our Ymir was the one in the stories.

"*Ja*," agreed Zee. "That is one reason not to invite him to your home."

"Omelet's done," announced Jesse. "Tad, can you move the table back so I can feed my step–half uncle?"

Once Gary was eating again, I said, "I've been wondering about this since I heard Uncle Mike call him Ymir. Ymir is supposed to be dead, right? Odin and a couple other Norse deities killed him and used his body parts to form the earth, right?"

"Origin story," huffed Zee dismissively.

"So he's not dead?" I asked. "This is the real Ymir we're talking about?"

"I don't know whether or not the landmasses were formed from Ymir's body," Zee said. "I wasn't alive yet. But I have my doubts. I suppose that your mate is the first human because he uses that name? He is the husband of Eve and Lilith, who came before?"

I narrowed my eyes at him. "Don't try to be funny. It doesn't suit you. It's not my fault that I've spent the last few years meeting people—*beings*—who I'm just finding out are real and living here. Baba Yaga. Guayota." I narrowed my eyes even more because I was really grumpy at this one. "Wayland Smith."

Zee grunted.

"If Wayland Smith is repairing Volkswagens in Kennewick, Washington, then it is not out of the realm of possibility that Ymir died to form the land we stand upon," Adam said, his tone just this side of amused—enough to take the temperature down without leaving Zee insulted. When he wasn't angry, my mate was pretty good at managing situations.

Zee threw up his hands. "All right. Yes. I see how you might think that. Most origin stories are ridiculous, which does not make them untrue—or at least does not make the allegory of the story untrue."

"Well, then," I said. "Ymir is supposed to be dead."

"Ymir is . . ." Zee let his tone drag out as he translated his thoughts. "Ymir is an honored name among the Jötnar. There is only one who wears that name at any time. They must hold the power of Winter"—I heard the capital letter there—"and call wolves, but it is more than that. They must be a worthy Power and able to defend their use of that name. There are none among the Jötnar who have objected to this snow elf—who now lives here, in this time—taking that name. Or none who lived." He frowned. "Ymir becomes a worse idea the longer we talk about him. Instead, we could call in Uncle Mike, who is better with this kind of spellcrafting than I am. Or your Sherwood Post."

"You don't think they can help," I said. I could read this Zee.

He shook his head. "No. But they are safer options."

Adam looked at my brother, who was dividing his attention between us and his food, tension never really leaving his body. "Would you invite the Jötunn to our house for us?"

Zee assessed my mate, and for just an instant I could see that unfamiliar *something* look out of his eyes. He glanced at me and as quickly as that, he was my friend again.

Phone in hand, Zee peered out the window with a grimace. Then he opened the back door and walked into the storm. The strength of the wind meant that there was no chance we could overhear him. I don't know why he needed to keep his conversation from us, but I trusted Zee to know what was best.

Tad brought the pan, cutting board, and assorted cutlery

they'd used for Gary's omelet and set it in the sink. He glanced out the window at his father, then over at Adam.

"You should probably go before Ymir gets here," he advised. "Ymir is . . ."

"Dangerous?" asked Adam dryly.

"Yes," Tad agreed. "But that's not what I meant. 'Malicious' is too strong of a word." He hesitated. "Bored. Ymir is bored. I think that all of the werewolves around are going to be too much for his self-control. It would be best if you all were gone."

He looked at me. "I don't think Ymir can do dogs. Which means you should be safe, Mercy."

"Not a dog," I told him.

"Dog is as far from a wolf as a wolf is from a coyote," he answered.

"And a werewolf is from a wolf," I argued back.

"Ymir can call werewolves," Honey said, but her voice was very quiet, and I don't think anyone else heard her because Adam spoke at the same time.

"So I should leave you, Jesse, Mercy, and Gary to meet with Ymir while I run away?" Adam's voice was too mild.

Tad flushed but persisted. "Dad will be here, too. No one is touching Mercy if Dad is here."

Something came and went on Adam's face. A flicker that my instincts told me was important. But Adam covered up whatever it was.

"Ymir is not my enemy," Adam said. "And he doesn't want to be my enemy."

"Adam." Honey's voice was careful. "He is not wrong about Ymir. Ymir can call werewolves." She paused, then said, "I've been in his power."

Adam's body stiffened and he took a step toward her.

"Centuries ago," she said, her voice calm even for her. "He needed backup, but perhaps more than that, he needed us to impress his enemies. He came to our pack house and called us. The whole Kraków pack numbered around sixty, but there were only seventeen of us at our Alpha's house when Ymir called. None of us, not even Kazuch, our Alpha, hesitated when Ymir asked us to come." She made a humming sound, as if considering what to say.

"It felt so *wonderful* to serve him," she said. "All of my doubts, all of my desires and wants, just vanished, subsumed in his presence. You've seen those dogs who focus on their owner with all their being, right? Just vibrating with the need to follow the next command. I know exactly how that feels."

Honey's voice and demeanor were matter-of-fact. But Gary's eating slowed and his head canted toward Honey. Behind her, her dead mate's shade wrapped his arms around her, his face twisted in sorrow. I hadn't noticed him when she first came in.

"When he was finished with us, Ymir took us back to our pack house and left us—all seven of us. Ten of us died in his service, including our Alpha and our first. We just . . . the pack dissolved. Today is the first day that I feel angry about what Ymir did to us. Kazuch was a good man, a good Alpha, and I didn't mourn him. None of the wolves Ymir took mourned him."

She looked at Adam and said seriously, "We should leave before Ymir gets here."

Adam might have agreed then, but Zee came into the kitchen, closed the door behind him, and said, "Ymir is coming. You who are wolves should go. I will keep Mercy and her brother safe. That will be easier if I do not have to contend with you."

———

TWENTY MINUTES LATER ADAM AND ZEE WERE STILL arguing about it in short savage sentences that sounded as if a physical clash were only moments away. The testosterone in the air made the kitchen feel a lot smaller. It was a big kitchen, but if the two of them actually started engaging with fang and axe (with Zee in this mood, nothing else was going to do), a football stadium would have felt too small.

Tad stood next to the stove, just a little in front of Jesse, who looked a lot less worried than she had when they'd started in on each other. I'd caught Tad nudging her attention toward my face. I couldn't help but grin when Zee resorted to German—a wonderful language to swear at someone in—and Adam answered in Russian. I understand a lot of German, but Russian is beyond me. Adam's speech was not as consonant heavy, but the rich vowels made it sound like Adam was purring epithets in preparation for biting Zee's head off.

If I'd been Jesse, I'd have been worried, too. But I could feel Adam's pleasure—relief, even—at being able to just let fly at an opponent who was capable of meeting him full force. He'd been eating a lot of frustration for the past year, and Zee wasn't someone who was going to misunderstand an argument for a war.

But time was passing.

I slid off the counter I'd retreated to when it had seemed the verbal combat needed more room.

"Okay, Adam," I said. "If you keep this up, you're going to still be arguing when Ymir gets here."

Adam's white teeth flashed in a grin, and he dropped the aggression. "Too true."

He wasn't stupid; he'd heard what Honey had said. Zee had ruffled his fur, though. The fight hadn't been playacting, exactly. But it hadn't been serious, either.

Zee scowled at me and then at Adam. "You," he said in an aggrieved tone, "have as much sense as earwax."

"Thank you," Adam said serenely. "Okay, Honey, we need to head to Tad's."

Zee looked at his son. "It would be helpful if you go with the wolves. It would give them some protection if they do encounter Ymir. And I would prefer that he does not notice you unless he makes it necessary."

Father and son stared at each other for a moment. I couldn't read either of their faces.

"Come on, Jesse," Tad said, turning away from Zee. "We'll take the werewolves to my house and have cookies."

"You made cookies?" Jesse asked him.

"Nope," he said. "Izzy's mother did."

"Yum."

ADAM TOOK HIS DUCKLINGS—AND HONEY—OFF TO Tad's house to eat cookies.

It had taken some finesse to pry my brother off Honey. He was more on edge without her, his grip on my wrist near bruising. Zee had dragged the kitchen table away again so Gary and I weren't trapped behind it.

My timing had been a little too close for comfort. Adam and the others barely had time to get beyond the fence in the backyard when I heard a car coming down our road about a quarter of a mile out.

There was something weird about it.

I frowned as it purred to a halt in the driveway, and Zee looked at me expectantly.

"That's a rotary engine," I said. "Renesis. I haven't heard one of those in years."

"He drives a 2004 Mazda RX-8," said Zee in satisfied tones. "I keep it running for him myself." He looked at me. "I don't want him going to the garage. Too many werewolves hang out there. And although he hasn't eaten a person in years, I don't want him to start with you."

The first time I'd met Ymir, he'd struck me as hesitant and polite, once he'd quit trying to kill everyone.

"I appreciate that," I said.

A car door shut quietly and then nothing. As minutes passed, Zee turned to give the wall between him and the front door a frowning look.

"Wait while I check this out," he said to me.

But then we both heard the sound of booted feet on the wooden steps and the doorbell rang.

"Come as guest and as guest depart," said Zee, staying where he was.

Ymir opened the front door. "Accepted," he said before the sound of his feet told me he was inside. I heard the door close gently. "Threshold to threshold."

In the house, he was soft-footed—if I hadn't been listening for him, I wouldn't have heard him walk from the doorway to the kitchen. That meant he had intended for us to hear him on the porch. He stopped as soon as he could see us, a slight man a few inches shorter than me—and I'm average height for a woman. He was wearing glasses, and he blinked at us as if they weren't quite strong enough.

Then he ruined the whole look by exposing his white, slightly crooked teeth at Zee. The expression muted itself into a smile when he turned it to me.

"I am pleased to see you once more, Mercy Coyotesdaughter. Zee has explained to me that your brother is suffering from a spell cast by one of my kind."

I nodded. "Yes."

"I will examine him and remove it if I can. If I cannot, I will tell you what I know about it. Is this acceptable?"

"Payment?" Zee asked before I could say anything.

"Payment has already been made," Ymir said mildly.

Because I'd broken the spell on him at Uncle Mike's, I thought, assuming that the Jötunn obeyed the same laws as the fae. It felt like the right sort of balance for what we were asking of him tonight.

Zee glanced at me, then gave a brisk nod, accepting my judgment.

"Here's my brother," I said, raising my hand and, because he was gripping it tightly, Gary's.

Ymir approached us; with his hands clasped behind his back and his face thoughtful, he examined my brother. Bored, Tad had said. Ymir didn't look bored now.

Gary figured out that there was something going on. He inhaled strongly and squeezed my hand. I squeezed it back. He held up three fingers with his free hand, gestured at himself and made it four. I squeezed his hand four times, one for each of us in the room.

Ymir dropped to a knee in front of Gary and tipped his head like one of the werewolves catching an interesting scent. My brother's whole body stiffened and a growl rumbled in his throat.

I squeezed his hand again, but he didn't relax. I didn't blame him. I found the Jötunn unnerving, too.

Ymir's vivid blue eyes had brightened to near-white in a way that reminded me of the Marrok's son Samuel, and he smelled of ozone and chill air—like an incipient ice storm. But there was something else, too, a quality of wildness my other senses observed, something that made me believe this being was able to call wolves.

Ymir stood up after a while and paced slowly around the kitchen, the picture of a man in deep thought. He raised his face as if to speak, and Adam boiled through the back door, coatless and shoeless.

Rage hot in his yellow wolf eyes, Adam stopped, weight balanced over his feet in a stance that spoke of his readiness to fight.

"Release her," he growled. "She is not yours."

It wasn't me he was talking about. I looked at Ymir.

A cold smile grew over the frost giant's face. "She is payment for what I do here. It has been agreed. Mercy is your mate, empowered to make bargains on your behalf."

It wasn't the time to do anything stupid like ask what the two of them were talking about. But I hadn't spent a decade fixing cars with Zee without learning to pay attention to my words. I thought back over what had been said.

But Zee got there first.

"Mercy made no bargain," he said. "Accepting your word that a payment has been made is not agreement. And I have no hold on the wolves that you can use my approval to take one of them. No bond to Mercy that I can make bargains in her stead. If you chose to accept some past action or inaction of mine for your aid with Mercy's brother, that is not our fault."

Ymir stiffened and made a gesture at the air, and I felt a fizz of unfamiliar magic. It seemed to tell him something.

"I am not a mortal child," Zee said, menace easing into his voice, "to be fooled by the likes of you. Nor do I lie. Your bargain is with me. That you chose to believe it was with Mercy is not her fault. And if you had been honest in your bargaining, it would not have mattered who you were making the agreement with."

Ymir looked at me, face so expressionless it sent ice down my spine. "I should have expected one of your kind to be duplicitous. Loki was always so—and I am told that he and Coyote are of a piece."

"Winter roads are treacherous," I said slowly. I wished that I'd gotten a chance to talk to Larry the goblin king instead of hearing his message from Uncle Mike. I might have been able to get more clarification. I'd tell Larry that he needed to give better warnings next time I saw him. "What did he do, Adam?"

"He's got Mary Jo," Adam said grimly.

"I found her spying upon me," Ymir said. He looked at Zee, and his upper lip curled derisively. "*Before* I accepted guesting rule. Bargain or no bargain, she stays mine," he said, his voice mocking, his attention on Adam now, "unless you can take her from me, remembering that I am a guest in your house."

When no one said anything, Ymir looked pleased. "Mary Jo. Is that her name? Pedestrian and Christian both. I will change it."

He snapped his fingers and I heard the crash of the big plate-glass window in the living room. A frigid blast of air swept through the kitchen, then a silvery wolf with black markings on her face that would have looked more at home on a cheetah or on the face of an ancient Egyptian queen stalked into the room.

Pieces of glass and drops of blood fell onto the tile floor in an irregular pattern.

Mary Jo's eyes were fixed on Ymir, who looked smaller next to her even though Mary Jo's wolf form was as compact as she was as a human. The frost giant laid his hand on the top of her head and turned gloating eyes to Adam.

My brother leaned his shoulder against me and let go of my hand. I couldn't tell if that was to free me for action—or to free himself.

"Mary Jo," Adam said, and I felt him light the pack bonds, as he had earlier for Gary, but this time he drew on one particular bond with a little more emphasis.

I was not so good with the pack bonds that I understood what Adam asked for, but I didn't need to be. The flavor of Sherwood Post in our pack bonds had changed over the past few months until he felt almost more like Joel, who wasn't a werewolf at all, than he did any of the rest of the pack. Through Adam, I felt Sherwood hesitate, and then he gave Adam what he'd asked for.

Our pack's ties strengthened and became something more, something that lived and breathed *magic*. When it was stable—a time both infinite and less than the tick of a clock—Adam made another ask, this time to Joel. The response he got was more immediate than Sherwood's had been but less sure, a hot vital spark that Adam's more subtle skill blended with the powers Adam already held. Then my mate asked me. Like Joel, I had no idea what he was asking for, less than Joel really, but I opened the barriers between us and offered him whatever he needed to gather from me.

Ymir's eyes widened and he sniffed the air. Zee's eyebrows rose and he allowed the hand that had been moving ever so slowly behind his back to return to his side. My usual carry was a gun in a holster in the small of my back, and even absorbed by whatever Adam was doing, I still wondered what weapon Zee carried there.

"Mary Jo," said Adam deliberately, and he shoved all of that—the pack magic entwined with Sherwood's primordial wild power, with the fire that was our tibicena Joel's weird addition to our pack, and with something that felt like Coyote smelled—and sent it blazing along the single strangled path that led to Mary Jo.

The hold Ymir had put on one of ours melted away in the fire of our Alpha's displeasure, as if it had been nothing.

Adam was good with the pack bonds. I knew that. I also knew that what he'd just done was more than mere ability. Someone had been working with him. I wondered if it was Sherwood or someone else.

Mary Jo flung herself away from the frost giant in a desperate leap and lost consciousness midair. Her limp body hit my legs with bruising force. She knocked me away from Gary, who shot his hand out, and I grabbed it even as I reached down to see if the wolf at my feet was still breathing. I counted on Zee and Adam to keep the three of us safe.

That had been a lot of power Adam had used. My own ears still rang with the echo of it. But Adam, who stepped between us and Ymir, didn't show any effect other than the light sweat that dampened the back of his shirt.

Ymir's white eyes locked with Adam's.

"What a surprise you are," Ymir purred, stepping forward.

Zee swung a staff he hadn't been holding when I'd last looked at him between the frost giant and Adam. The weapon buzzed through the air and then stopped, more or less waist height, in a horizontal barrier between Adam and Ymir.

It took me half a second to realize that the staff he held was my walking stick with the spear blade ascendant. Zee had produced the walking stick once before, so I wasn't astonished he'd managed it. I just wondered why he'd used the walking stick instead of the various weapons he had to call upon that belonged to him—or the one he was carrying on his back.

"You stand *guest*," whispered Zee. "You accepted hospitality while you assaulted the mind of one of those who belong to the house. You would have stolen her will and taken her from those who love her and who are loved. And now you would attack its master. While you are a *guest*."

That last word hissed out and a lick of silvery light flashed to limn the edges of the spear blade Lugh had forged. Ymir stepped back with a hiss. Adam backed up, too, and I didn't think it was voluntary.

"Think well what happens to those who violate guesting laws," Zee said, his voice once more belonging to an old grumpy mechanic and not a god of the forge.

Ymir stepped back several more paces, shaking his shoulders in a way that reminded me of a lion shaking his mane. Adam stayed where he was. No one looked like they were going to kill anyone else in the next few seconds, so I took a moment to actually assess what my free hand was telling me about Mary Jo.

"Breathing," I told Adam. Then realized that he'd know that through the bonds—and so should I have, if I hadn't been so panicked.

"She approached me," Ymir said, but not like he was talking to any of us here. "Wolves are mine to call. I called and she came." There was a short pause, and he said, "There are not so many wolves as there once were. It has been long and long since I had a wolf to call."

"She approached you as a guardian of this house," said Zee. "A house that you intended to enter as a guest."

Ymir closed his eyes, took a deep breath. As he let it out, his body relaxed, and when he opened his eyes, they were a deep, clear blue-gray.

"My apologies," he said with utter sincerity. "Adam Hauptman, Alpha of the Columbia Basin Pack, I have moved against you in this, your house. Instincts are powerful in my kind, and she is strong and beautiful. I could not resist the temptation of her."

As an apology, it was lacking.

"She belongs to me," said Adam, his voice deeper than usual with restrained rage. "She is *not* yours to call."

There was a flash of anger in Ymir's eyes. But he blinked and it was gone.

The frost giant nodded solemnly. "It is to my shame that I have done this. For this cause shall I complete what you have asked of me in recompense for my transgression."

All of my senses told me that he spoke the truth, and there was the ring of it in the air. But I knew, *I knew*, that he lied. Which did I believe? The instincts I'd honed over a lifetime of being Coyote's daughter? Or the insight I'd had shoved down my throat by the Soul Taker, an animated gateway for a dark god?

To make matters even more special, now that the temperature had come down in the room, the incident was trying very hard to bring on one of my inconvenient panic attacks. Like Mary Jo, I'd had my will stolen away once, too.

"Can you help my brother?" I asked—and almost didn't recognize my own voice. I had expected to sound shaky because of the increasing shortness of my breathing. But I sounded like Adam had—enraged.

"I cannot disarm the binding spell," Ymir said with apology. I didn't believe that any more than I believed his other apologies. "This is because it is magic that belongs to my name-brother Hrímnir. Unlike me, he is the original bearer of that name, and his abilities outstrip my own."

I was a little surprised that there wasn't more bitterness or something when he admitted another was more powerful than he was. But there was nothing like that in his voice or manner.

"Do you know how Gary can be freed?" I asked.

I'd had to force the words out through a throat that wanted to close. I deliberately tried to ignore Mary Jo at my feet because looking at her was making me worse. I understood what it felt like when someone stole your will. Maybe we couldn't trust Ymir's information, but I intended to make him talk as long as I could.

"My brother is the only one who can free yours," Ymir told me, then he gave a slight grimace. "I am bound not to tell you where or how he can be found."

"I'd expect it is somewhere near where Gary was living," said Adam.

I'm sure he meant his tone to be dry, but the rasp of his wolf was in it. He knew I was fighting off a panic attack, and he was doing his best not to add to it. I could feel the support he sent through our mating bond. Not calmness—we'd learned from experience that he could not be calm when I was freaking out. But strength and the knowledge I wasn't alone.

When a panic attack hit me when he and I were alone, sometimes his physical touch helped. But if he touched me right now, I'd lose the battle I was fighting to seem normal in front of the stranger in our house.

Gary released his hold on my wrist—I was thankful because that hold was making me feel trapped—and dropped to the floor next to Mary Jo. He felt her limp body with careful hands, then focused his attention on our *guest*.

"Is there anything more that you can tell us that would be useful?" Zee asked.

Ymir shook his head.

"Then go," Zee said. "And cause no more trouble for your hosts."

"Remember my name, old friend," Ymir said pleasantly. He looked at Adam. "I'll tell my brother to expect you."

Ymir bowed his head—but even in my distracted state, I could see that something raw and violent flared in his eyes as he glanced at Zee and away.

As soon as the front door closed behind the Jötunn, I gave Adam a frantic look.

"I've got this," he said.

I bolted for the stairs as Zee rumbled something. Before he finished, I was at our bedroom door.

I heard Adam say, "Leave her be," as I shut the door behind me and sprinted to the bathroom just in time to lose Uncle Mike's excellent stew. Nausea only hit me sometimes in a panic attack, but this one was a doozy. I stayed in the bathroom for a while.

Sounds traveled up. I heard Warren's voice. Then Mary Jo's. She sounded agitated, but she wasn't dead, so that was a win. Jesse came upstairs, walked past her room, and paused in front of our door.

She tapped lightly on the door. "Headed to bed, Mercy. Hope you feel better soon."

"I'm good," I croaked.

"Okay," she said wryly. "As long as you're good."

"Yes," I told her. And then more truthfully, "I'll be good in the morning."

She tapped the door twice and then I heard her bedroom door shut, leaving me to the unhappy task of making my breathing even out.

INTERLUDE

Six Weeks Earlier

ADAM

THE HOUSE LOOKED EMPTY, BUT ADAM KNEW BETTER. His wolf knew there was someone dangerous inside.

He knocked on the door.

When it opened, Zee scowled at him. "What do you want?"

It didn't sound friendly, but Zee was only friendly around Mercy.

"We need to speak," Adam told him. "I'd prefer not to do it where we could be overheard."

The old fae opened the door and stepped back in invitation.

"Kitchen," Zee said, leading the way, though Adam had been here before and didn't need guidance.

He took the seat Zee indicated and waited in silence while Zee brewed a fresh pot of coffee. Adam had dealt with old creatures before. He knew it didn't do to try to hurry them.

Eventually Zee set a cup of black sludge in front of Adam and sat down opposite him with his own cup. Adam drank the rich bitter stuff without grimacing. He was an Alpha werewolf; he knew a challenge when he saw one.

Zee's face softened in brief amusement, and he sipped from his own cup.

"Two things," Adam said.

Zee nodded.

"Mercy isn't as bad off now that you've destroyed the Soul Taker," he said. "But—"

"She stares into space for up to three minutes at a time," Zee said. "And she doesn't notice she's doing it."

"Twice today," said Adam.

"Three times at the garage."

"She has a constant headache, but she won't tell you that," Adam told Zee.

"She doesn't like to admit there is something wrong," Zee groused. "Stupid child. She doesn't think we know?"

Adam gave him a grim smile.

"I do not know how to help her," Zee said. "I have tried. I can do a little with body hurts, but this . . . this is damage to her soul and to her magic. I have asked for help—but Baba Yaga is unreliable. And . . ."

"And?"

"And she is a healer of rare ability; she can bring back the dead as long as they aren't very dead. But I don't know if she can fix what's wrong with Mercy."

"I called Bran," Adam said. "But he told me that if Sherwood can't fix her, he has no chance."

"And Sherwood?" asked Zee.

Adam shook his head. Then to this being who loved Mercy, too, he asked the question that had been haunting him. "If she can't be fixed?"

"It is early days yet," Zee said.

"If she can't be fixed?" Adam asked again, his throat dry. "What then?"

Silence spoke louder than Adam had been hoping for. Silence was not optimistic. But if he'd wanted optimism, he wouldn't have come here. The fae cannot lie.

"You said two things," Zee said eventually, his voice brisk.

"Bonarata is going to come for her," Adam said.

"Yes," agreed the fae.

"I don't have to ask if you'll help her," Adam said.

Zee nodded at him, and said, "Nor I you."

Adam leaned forward. "I was not strong enough, not skilled enough, to defeat him."

Zee nodded—that was no secret.

"Would you teach me?"

5

ADAM

ADAM WATCHED MERCY SCRAMBLE UP THE STAIRS, listened to her ragged breathing until she shut their bedroom door. His wolf wanted to go after her, and so did he. But he had a job to do—and Mercy didn't enjoy an audience. Not until she had matters under better control.

She wasn't in danger. She *wasn't* in danger. No matter how their bond felt, she wasn't in danger. His wolf was reluctant to believe that, no matter how many times Adam rebuked him.

"I thought she was done with those," growled a voice that set the beast, the one not his wolf, into high alert.

That had the benefit of making his wolf quiet. The two monsters who lived under his skin did not come out at the same time.

Adam turned cautiously to face Siebold Adelbertsmiter. The walking stick was gone to wherever it went, but Zee didn't look one bit less dangerous without it. Adam suspected Zee had used the walking stick to make Ymir and Adam back down so that he didn't have to do something more lethal.

Adam wasn't intimidated by Zee—which might or might not be foolish—but he was wary around him when Mercy wasn't in the room. Despite the tone he'd used, the tightness around Zee's mouth made Adam think he was hurt rather than angry.

"It's been a while," Adam said carefully. He didn't say it had been since last October, when the vampire who had his own ties to Adam's mate had commanded her to stop panicking. None of that was anything Mercy would want Zee to know.

Adam knew that Mercy was afraid that one of her beloved monsters would kill one of her others. It was why Adam hadn't killed Stefan already—that, and the knowledge that having the vampire on call helped keep Mercy safe, sometimes when Adam couldn't. There was also the distinct possibility that Stefan's death would not free Mercy but kill her, too. He didn't know why Zee hadn't killed the vampire, but assumed the old fae's decision tree had followed the same path as his own.

"A while?" Zee asked suspiciously.

Adam nodded. "She thought she was done with them, too." That felt true enough to appease Zee without betraying anything that Mercy hadn't told him. Mercy didn't like people to worry about her, so she didn't tell them things. Like the way she hadn't told him about Bonarata's call—even after Ben had warned her that they all knew.

The back door opened, and Tad, Honey, and Jesse spilled in, followed by Warren. Adam had known his draw on the pack bonds would result in a mass invasion by the pack, but he'd expected it to take longer. Warren must have been in the neighborhood.

Honey glanced at him, and he tipped his head to Mary Jo and

her unexpected guardian, who were still on the floor where Mercy had left them. Mary Jo was stable, so Adam had kept his attention on the biggest threat in the room, but having pack here to take care of Mary Jo was good.

Warren gave Zee a hard look, but Adam caught his eye and directed him to Mary Jo and Gary as well. Mary Jo would need all the pack support she could get for a while.

"What happened?" Jesse demanded.

"I will go," Zee said, pointedly not looking at his son. "I will talk to the people I know who might have information on this brother of Ymir's."

"That would be useful," Adam said.

Zee made a sour noise and left through the front door.

"Dad?" Jesse asked again.

The whole pack would have felt his power draw to free Mary Jo. "Wait just a second. If I don't let the pack know they can stand down, we'll have everyone here."

After he sent a text to the pack, he took the opportunity to text Darryl, Auriele, and Sherwood separately. Those three he needed.

That done, he evaluated his audience—while he'd been texting, Mary Jo had recovered enough to listen. Good. He gave them all a brief synopsis on how Gary got here and why they'd called Ymir in. Then he took them through a play-by-play from the moment he realized that Ymir had caught Mary Jo.

"He can't do that again?" asked Jesse, wide-eyed.

"I don't know," Adam said honestly. "But Sherwood might. He, Darryl, and Auriele are on their way over. That's one of the things we'll discuss."

He could feel Mercy's distress as a burn in his chest. But she wouldn't thank him for abandoning his duty. He moved on to the next thing.

"Jesse, it's late and you have school tomorrow." He was adjusting to thinking of Jesse as an adult who could make her own decisions. The decisions she made had so far been good ones, and that had made it easier.

She was his daughter; she would know he wasn't sending her up to bed like a ten-year-old—he hoped. He was sending her upstairs with a mission.

"Yeah," she said, giving him a rueful smile. "I should hit the hay. How about I check on Mercy on the way?"

And that made his wolf settle a bit.

"I would appreciate that," he told her, and watched her absorb the praise implicit in his words. Maybe he should praise her a little more often if it meant that much to her.

She gave Tad a playful shove with both hands. Whatever tension had been between the two of them earlier, it was evidently settled. "You have school, too. Get out of here."

"Test, even," agreed Tad, and he gave a nod to Adam. Then he went out the door and Jesse went up the stairs, leaving Adam to deal with the werewolves.

"I'm going home," Mary Jo said. She started to get up but wobbled back to the floor, snarling at Warren when he reached over to help steady her. Adam judged the wobbles to be as much from her still-finishing shift from wolf to human as from what Ymir had done. She wasn't usually disabled by the shift, but Ymir had ripped her from her human shape to the wolf in the space of seconds. It would be a few days before her shifts felt normal again.

But she would recover—Adam could tell by the way her attitude resembled the bonhomie of a shedding rattlesnake.

Gary, Adam's other problem, remained silent—much better than the strange noises he made when he tried to talk. Adam's wolf winced from those sounds the same way he did when exposed to something too loud or sharp. Gary's body language was alert but not combat ready. Adam didn't think that he'd break for it and try to run again.

Gary had put his body between Mary Jo and the frost giant to protect her. As far as Adam knew, Gary had met Mary Jo briefly, but hadn't spent any time with her that would make him treat her any different from any person on the street. And Gary didn't seem to be able to recognize anyone. But Mary Jo had been in distress, she'd smelled like pack—and Gary had thrown himself into danger without hesitation.

Before he'd seen it himself, Adam wouldn't have put money on Gary being protective of anyone. Mercy said that her half brother was a better person than he pretended to be, but Mercy always thought the best of people. It wasn't really that she was a good judge of character, but mostly that people tried to live up to her view of them. Adam had taken her opinion of Gary with a grain of salt.

Now Adam could see who Gary was when all of his defenses were removed.

Seated beside Gary, Honey had her calm face on, telling Adam that she was really disturbed. Gary was leaning against her lightly, like a blind man keeping his sense of place rather than for reassurance.

The other bookend of the four, Warren, looked both relaxed and awkward with his too-long legs taking up a lot of room on the tile. Like Honey, his face was calm despite the rage that Adam felt through the bonds. Warren was keeping it buried deep enough that Adam didn't think anyone else would find it. Adam hoped he was doing as well with his own fury.

Ymir had taken one of theirs.

"I'm going home," Mary Jo said again, as if someone was arguing with her.

You aren't wrong about that fight you're about to get into, Adam thought with amusement. *No one here is going to let you go off by yourself. We're all just hoping someone else will stick their neck out first.*

He wasn't surprised when Warren took the lead.

"How about you give a call to Renny, darlin'. Or I could. If we knew you weren't alone, we wouldn't fuss at you."

"I broke up with him," Mary Jo snapped, answering the mystery of why she'd felt off to Adam for the last few days. "The whole point of that was to get Renny free of my life."

Raw hurt rolled out with her voice, and hearing it, she flushed, closing her eyes. When she spoke again, her tone was filled with calm dignity. "That was the point. I'm going home."

Honey tried next. "You need to be with people."

Mary Jo gave the room a cool look. "I am a grown woman. A werewolf. A monster. If I'm not safe, no one is."

She stood up—this time with a lot more success—and brushed her arms off, as if that meant she could brush off the rest of the conversation with it.

"Mary Jo."

Three of them jumped when Adam spoke, and Gary stiffened a moment later, tilting his head in Adam's direction. Adam hadn't intended to put so much power in those words, but the moon was still strong and Mary Jo wasn't the only one who was going through some things tonight.

"Yes, Adam?" Mary Jo said, with an edge in her voice.

He could give her orders. But living with Mercy had taught him that sometimes going around things was so much easier than bulling through them.

"I am sending Gary home with Honey tonight," Adam said.

Honey raised her head to look at him, but she didn't seem displeased.

"We don't know what's wrong with him. I need you to go with Honey," he said. He held up a hand when Mary Jo looked at Warren and started to say something. "I can't spare Warren tonight. I know you are hurting, but I can't leave Honey alone with Gary when he's damaged and I have no real idea what he can do."

Mary Jo was a fireman. Fire*person*? He sometimes lost track of what terms were polite this decade. She fought fires and saved people, anyway. She was fierce. As driven to duty as he himself was. They would never have gotten her to go with Honey for Mary Jo's own good. But to keep Honey safe?

And it had the benefit of being true. He *would* feel better—with the memories of how easily Gary had moved Honey and of the speed and strength with which he'd fought Adam fresh in his mind—if he didn't send Honey home alone with Gary.

"Okay," she said grudgingly.

Warren helped Honey escort Gary out to her car while Mary Jo ran downstairs to get clothes to wear from the pack stores. Adam went out to the garage and found the plywood they'd used the last time the big window in the living room had been broken. When he got back into the house, only Warren remained. The two of them secured the plywood, sealing the winter outside once more.

Then, with Warren left on guard duty, Adam was *finally* free to go to his mate.

THE ROOM WAS DARK AND QUIET EXCEPT FOR MER-cy's ragged breathing. She'd found a corner and wrapped herself in a blanket that didn't do enough to warm her, judging by the way she was shivering.

Adam left the lights off and sat on the floor beside her, his back to the wall. He left a little space between them. If she wanted touch, he was there.

"Fat lot of use I am," she said, struggling to get the words out around the vibrations of her jaw. "If we had had to fight him, all I would have been able to do is collapse in a corner."

He didn't tell her that if Zee and he hadn't been able to take care of Ymir, she didn't stand a chance. He didn't say it because no matter how much that looked true, Mercy had proven it wasn't. She could face off with volcano gods and come out of it with nothing more than a scar on her cheek.

He considered his words.

"Nah," he said.

He'd tried to make it playful, a contrast to what she was feeling. But his monsters, roused by his mate's condition, lent their darkness, so the casual word came out rich with . . . something not playful.

He waited and tried again, and this time he sounded more normal. "You pushed this off until the enemy was gone. You'd have held out until you did what you had to do."

She shook her head fiercely. And for a moment he hoped she'd argue with him—arguing was sometimes useful in her battle with her panic attacks. But when she spoke, it was to direct the conversation away from herself.

"Ymir is a problem," she said raggedly, "if he can take our wolves."

She was absolutely right.

"Sherwood is on his way over," Adam told her. "I don't know if he'll have suggestions, but he's our best bet."

Mercy tried to say something, but it didn't come out. Adam fought back the urge to look at her, because she preferred not to be stared at. This was a bad attack. He'd expected her to be mostly done with it by the time he'd been able to come up.

If he'd only gotten to Tim sooner—

He wound that thought up tight and shoved it down where it belonged before one of his beasts got even more stirred up. The important thing was not yesterday—the important thing was tomorrow.

Mercy thumped the back of her head against the wall. "Six weeks." She growled. "Six weeks without a panic attack. Anxiety attack. Stupid attack. Whatever. Not since Stefan—"

Her voice broke off and she quit breathing.

Every muscle in Adam's body locked up with the need to help her. There was nothing he could do—not unless he was willing to use the pack bonds to force her recovery. In a life-or-death circumstance, he might do something like that. But she wasn't going to die today.

And he wouldn't take advantage of her vulnerability like that.

After a few seconds, she caught a breath. Then another. She scooted over an inch and leaned against him, resting her forehead on his arm.

"Mary Jo?" she asked, her voice hoarse.

"She's pretty scared," he admitted. "She's going home with Honey and Gary. The women don't seem to fret Gary as much as the men do."

Mercy gave a hiccup of laughter. "No surprise there."

But Adam didn't think it was like that. He'd gotten the impression that Gary didn't care about the sex of the people he took to his bed—or flirted with. But women felt safer. Or maybe it was just Honey and Mary Jo.

Mary Jo. That reminded him he had a few questions.

"Warren was trying to get permission from Mary Jo to call Renny and get him over there, too. Something happened between them?"

"He proposed to her, so she broke up with him," she told him.

"That makes sense," he told her, because it didn't.

She huffed a laugh. "He's human, and being her boyfriend has already gotten him hurt."

Oh, that. Yes. Adam understood that in a visceral way.

"She really loves him, then," Adam said.

Mercy nodded. "She really does." Her voice was sad.

He was quiet for a while, wondering, as he often did, whether joining his pack had put Mercy in more danger or less. He used to think he knew the answer, because his pack had been quiet before he'd decided to court Mercy. But lately he'd found himself wondering if all the stuff they'd been hit with the last few years hadn't been going to happen anyway. Maybe if Mercy's life and his had not merged, none of them would have survived this long—they were stronger together.

"I didn't even know what to tell her," Mercy said. "Except that she should talk to you."

He couldn't help but give her a wry laugh. "Thanks for that."

"He's human," Mercy said. "He works in a dangerous job— and the Tri-Cities are not getting any *more* safe for police work. He could pull the wrong car over tomorrow—or trip coming down stairs."

Neither of them mentioned Changing Renny. His chances of survival weren't high, and being a werewolf came with its own set of worries. The average life expectancy of a werewolf who survived the initial Change was now around eight years. The drop was due to the increased pressure on the Marrok to take care of troublemakers before they drew the attention of the human authorities. Being out to the humans had been unavoidable, given modern technology, but it hadn't made their lives easier.

"Honey might be the best person for her to talk to," Adam said. "She's seen more than I have."

"What do you think she'll tell Mary Jo?" Mercy asked. Her body was softening against him, and the tremors were subsiding.

"To do what will leave her with the fewest regrets," Adam said. "But to have a clear eye on just what that means. And you are forgetting one part of this."

She looked up at him and he ran a gentle finger along the scar on her cheek, the one that looked a little like war paint. As much as he regretted the wound, he loved that scar. It was a reminder to him, and to the pack, that his mate could hold her own.

"What am I forgetting?" she asked.

He couldn't tell if she was okay with his touch yet or not, so he let his hand fall away.

"Renny," he said. "If that man lets Mary Jo walk away again, he doesn't deserve her."

That got him a watery smile, and she hummed a few bars of a song. Her pitch was usually spot-on, but tonight wasn't "usually," so it took him a moment to recognize the Beatles' "Revolution."

"Yeah," he said. "A determined person can change the world."

She leaned away from him to drag up the edge of the blanket and used it to wipe her face.

"Good thing snot washes out," she said, looking at the wet spot her face had left on the fabric.

"Can I hug you yet?" Adam asked, his voice sounding wistful even to himself.

In answer, she crawled into his lap, snotty blanket and all. What was a little snot compared to the overwhelming relief of her? He wrapped his arms around her, being careful how much of his strength he used.

She tucked her face under his jaw, wiggling until she was where she wanted to be. His body was honed to maximize his ability to protect her and his pack; he knew it didn't have much more give than a cement bench. Her body wasn't exactly squishable, either, for that matter. But she always seemed to find a way to fit against him.

With her safe in his arms, his beasts—the wolf and the other monster—gave him some peace. Sometimes he wished that his world could be only this: he and Mercy curled together in the dark.

But he knew he wouldn't last long like that. Peace was, for him, a momentary thing that rapidly turned into boredom. Mercy rubbed her cheek on his neck and he couldn't help but smile. She was worse than he was. Always up and doing something was his Mercy.

He waited while her breathing slowed. For the first few minutes of sleep, her breath stuttered like a baby's after a crying jag.

He heard the quiet sounds as Sherwood arrived, followed shortly by Darryl and Auriele. He ignored them for the moment. When he was sure Mercy was asleep, he rose to his feet, the wolf's strength making his awkward position on the floor trivial. He wasn't often grateful to be a werewolf.

Mercy was heavier than his first wife had been. Christy had worked out, but not the way Mercy did. Especially lately. Asleep, her face appeared gaunter than it had a year ago. He wondered, not for the first time, if he was driving them all too hard. There was a fine line between peak performance and broken.

Adam didn't want to break his mate. He wanted to give her everything he knew, every bit of training to help her survive, and hope it would be enough.

The best way to save a drowning man, his father had liked to say, was to teach him to swim before he fell in the river—so he could keep himself safe instead of depending upon you. His dad had been big on independence. He would have adored Mercy.

Adam set her on their bed and stripped off her clothes. She wasn't usually a heavy sleeper, but a bad panic attack damn near put her into a coma. She also slept cold.

He rustled up one of his T-shirts, soft from wear, and put it on her. He was pretty sure that she had woken up sometime in the process, but she didn't give him any help. He covered her up and kissed the soft spot between her jawbone and the back of her ear. She made a grumpy noise and rolled over to bury her head in her pillow, leaving her knees folded and her rump sticking up.

She looked like Jesse had when she was a toddler and they'd let her get too tired. After a moment, Mercy rolled onto her side, patted his half of the bed. Finding it empty, she tipped her face until one eye peered at him.

"You need to do Alpha stuff?" she asked, her voice foggy with exhaustion.

"Yes."

"Got a call from the Prince of Darkness on the way to the pub," she said.

"I know."

She blinked at him, her other eye opening for a moment as she tried to read his expression.

He wasn't sure what she saw, but it seemed to make her happy. "Okay. Didn't want to lie to you. Tempted, though."

"I get that," he said. "Me, too, sometimes."

Both of her eyes narrowed on him, more alert than they had been. "Anything I need to know?"

"Not tonight," he told her. "We can talk in the morning."

"Anyone die?"

"No one you know," he assured her. "New Mexico business."

She nodded and closed her eyes. "Gonna sleep now."

"You do that. I'll be up when I'm done with my Alpha stuff."

"Okay," she said, and her body went limp.

These were the things that he was privileged to see, vulnerabilities his tough-like-Timex mate kept well hidden. She had to be strong. It was a good thing she was.

His grandfather's voice rang in his head: *A man protects his woman, Adam.*

He and his whole pack had been uprooted from New Mexico to protect her. Bran's little coyote might have thought she'd been abandoned at sixteen by the pack that had raised her, but the Marrok hadn't given up responsibility for her. When she'd moved somewhere without a pack to serve the Marrok's purposes, Bran had given Adam his transfer orders.

Adam had resented that at first. Then he'd been bewildered by it. For nearly a decade he'd lived next door and a few acres away from her, and nothing had happened. *For years* nothing had happened.

Until it did.

When he first noticed his attraction to Mercy, Adam had mapped their relationship out. He had craved her kindness, her humor, and her body. He'd thought that her toughness and independence were an obstacle he had to overcome to get her to accept him. He had looked after his first wife. He would take care of his mate.

Hah.

On his way out of the bedroom, Adam stopped and looked back. Mercy had burrowed under the covers again until only a lump showed that their bed was occupied.

Thank God Mercy was tough.

He closed the door behind him and took one step down the dark hallway. Then he returned to his bedroom door and placed the flat of his hand against it. Then he leaned his forehead against the varnished wood and closed his eyes, expanding their mate bond.

She was sleeping, dreaming of something only a little worrying. It had to do with Medea—he'd gotten the feel of the cat's purr. He slid his attention to the pack bonds, listening, for lack of a better word, to the general health and well-being of the pack.

He could feel Mary Jo's emotional disturbance—and Honey's, too. More of Honey's distress than he'd have thought based on what she'd been like before they'd left. But Honey was good at concealing things.

Pack bonds only went so far. Adam couldn't invade their privacy deeper to find out how much of their distress was due to Ymir's attack, and how much was other things. Renny. Gary. Some boundaries shouldn't be crossed.

He stayed there, basking in the power of his pack for a minute. Then he opened himself up to the new thing—the awareness that had begun after Mercy had faced down a troll on the suspension bridge and claimed the Tri-Cities as pack territory. That had been magic; they had all felt it when something happened. At that moment, he'd gained a link to the land his pack claimed for their own. He hadn't figured out just what it was good for yet—he'd never gotten a warning of trouble from it.

A while ago, he'd dismissed it as one of those weird things magic sometimes did. He'd found it neither threat nor help, so he'd mostly ignored it. Until October.

Mercy wasn't the only one the Soul Taker had affected. Since he'd fought that damned artifact, this bond had grown deeper in a worrying way. It was too easy to lose himself in the exploration of every roadway, every blade of grass, the ancient sheets of basalt that lurked beneath the earth. *His* territory.

"Is she okay, Adam?" Warren said, his voice calling Adam back to himself.

He blinked. If he'd been in wolf form, he'd have shaken the numbness off. In human-seeming, he just rubbed his face with both hands.

"Mercy?" Warren stood at the top of the stairs and looked worriedly at the door between them and Mercy.

"She's okay," Adam said. "Or at least she'll be okay after some sleep. I was just recharging."

As he followed Warren down the stairs to where his people

were waiting, he realized that was true. He did feel better. Re-freshed. And he hadn't drawn that from the pack, had he. Had he?

MERCY CROSSED HER ANKLES AND RESTED HER FEET on the dash because she knew Adam hated that. He wasn't worried about the car, but he'd seen photos of what happened to people in car accidents. He was a very good driver, but there was a "wintry mix" dripping down and he wasn't the only person on the road.

Mercy wouldn't walk away from a car accident the way he would.

One of the first things he'd noticed about Mercy was that she understood people. She really knew how to get under their skin. Under *his* skin.

Her feet on the dash told him that she was really annoyed with him. He wasn't sure why. He dealt with it for a few miles, giving her a chance to tell him. Just outside of Eltopia, the car behind them fishtailed violently and pulled off onto the shoulder.

Mercy wiggled her feet.

"What did I do?" he asked in what he hoped was a reasonable voice.

She gave him a look that said his tone had been less inquiry and more demand. But she took pity on him because, when push came to shove, his Mercy was the more reasonable of the two of them.

"You need to be in New Mexico," she said. "Darryl isn't military, and neither is Auriele. He doesn't know how to thread the needle between threat and cooperation that allows your company to work with the various military arms of the government."

"Darryl will be fine," Adam told her. "He's smart." Brilliant, in fact, which was why he had a bunch of letters behind his name and a big check for working with a think tank. "Auriele can charm the birds out of the sky."

That last drew an incredulous look from Mercy that made him wave an acknowledging hand.

"Nothing you have seen her do," he said, a little sadly.

Auriele had adjusted to Mercy as his mate. Mostly, she'd even quit blaming Mercy for hurting Adam's first wife with her very existence. Christy was good at making her friends forget that Christy had left Adam a long time before Mercy had looked at him with anything besides exasperation. But Auriele didn't go out of her way to be friendly with the woman she'd always see as Christy's replacement.

"Can they handle the business in New Mexico as well as you would?" Mercy asked.

There was a problem with living with someone who could hear even the whitest of lies. He chose not to answer—which was an answer in itself.

"You left the pack with Warren and Sherwood," she continued. "The first time they disagree, they will pull the pack apart."

Ah. He knew what she was so angry about.

"If they do," he said, his voice rough with some emotion he couldn't quite label, except that it made his wolf stir under his skin. "If the pack can't manage a few days without me to babysit, if Darryl and Auriele between them can't run down the problems in New Mexico—that is on me. My choice."

"Because of me," she said, her face turned away from him. He didn't need to see her expression to know he'd nailed it.

"Mercy," he said, quelling the growl that wanted to exit his throat.

"I would have been fine on my own," she said sharply. "Or you could have sent Warren or Sherwood with me. Or Warren *and* Sherwood. That would have helped Darryl run the pack without our three most powerful wolves killing each other in your absence. You could take care of New Mexico."

The SUV slid a little, sending the traction lights into a quiet frenzy.

"Would you please take your feet off the dash?" Adam asked.

She looked at him, heaved a sigh, and pulled them down.

"Thank you," he said fervently, feeling his back loosen just a bit.

"Sorry," she mumbled at the window. "But you didn't need to do this. You *shouldn't* have done this."

"I did, though," he told her. "I absolutely needed to."

He waited until she looked at him—though he kept most of his attention on the road, which was getting a little dicey. Once they got into the mountains, it would be colder and the icy mix should turn to honest snow. Snow was a lot safer than wet slush.

"You didn't," she insisted. If something happened to the pack, to the people in New Mexico, Mercy thought it would be her fault.

He held up a finger. "I left the pack in the hands of two very competent wolves. Warren is very, *very* good at negotiating rough water. Sherwood is focused on our pack's safety. And"—he was a little smug about this—"I made Honey the third vote in any disagreement between Warren and Sherwood."

Mercy drew in a breath. "They agreed to that?"

He nodded. "They aren't dumb, either. They know that they

needed a path to compromise, and both of them respect Honey's judgment."

He waited, but she didn't have anything to say about that. He put up a second finger. "Neither you nor I know what's really going on down in New Mexico. I don't know what skill set would be more valuable, mine or Darryl's. But I have a cell phone, and Darryl is not prideful in that way. If he needs advice, he'll ask for it. And no one, no matter how many stars or bars they have on, is going to disrespect Darryl."

Darryl was good at being scary.

"Especially not with Auriele around," he added. Mercy made a huffy sound that tried not to be agreement.

"We are headed into the mountains of Montana," Mercy said. "The chances of cell reception are not great. Darryl might not be able to get through to you."

He shrugged. "I have good people in New Mexico. They just need a werewolf or two to manage things. Auriele and Darryl know how to manage."

She grunted.

"Third, and most important, Mercy." He held up three fingers, then touched them to his lips. "I could live if I lose the pack. I could live if my business folds. If a bunch of people I don't know die in New Mexico when I might have been able to save them, I could live with that, too. None of those things would make me happy—but I have a lot worse things on my conscience."

She was staring at him.

"I could not live with losing you," he told her, his throat tight. "There are times when I have had to let you go out into danger without me. More times when I haven't known about threats to your life until they were long past. But this time . . . this time I have the privilege of being backup while you head out to see if we can rescue your brother."

She didn't say anything to that. A few minutes later the weather turned more serious and took his attention. She liked to think things through sometimes, his Mercy. But she put a hand on his leg and he wished for the Chevy truck he'd driven in high school because it had had a bench seat.

Eventually she said, "It was easier when I was mad at you. I can't shake the feeling that this is stupid. Running to Montana to try to talk a frost giant out of cursing my brother? If that's really what happened. I'm not inclined to trust any word that came out of Ymir's mouth."

He'd always known his Mercy wasn't stupid. "I agree with you. But Zee said it was Jötnar magic at work, too. If we hadn't talked to Ymir at all, I would have suggested going to the place where Gary was damaged as a logical next step."

She didn't say anything, but when he glanced at her, she had her bottom lip between her teeth.

"Ymir just gave us a name to check out," he said gently. "We'll figure out what happened to Gary." He wanted to say that they'd fix it. But he was looking at living proof that things weren't always that easy.

He hadn't been able to find a fix for what the Soul Taker had done to her—or even enough of a fix to take to Mercy as a possibility. He wouldn't lie to her, so he didn't promise they could help her brother, either.

"Okay," she said after a few miles. "But it was easier to be mad at you instead of scared for my brother. Could you do something to make me mad, please?"

"I need inspiration," he apologized. "Maybe if you could say something stupid or offer to risk your life for people I don't care about?"

She laughed, as he meant her to. It didn't last long, but she didn't resume chewing on her lip.

They stopped in Coeur d'Alene to get food and fuel up. The temperature had dropped nearly fifteen degrees from when they'd left home. The cold didn't bother him, but Mercy stamped her feet to get warm while the diesel tank in his SUV filled.

"Would you go inside and get me a lot of black coffee?" he asked.

She gave him a sharp look that said *I know what you're doing* but walked briskly into the busy convenience store.

While his tank filled, he overheard two truckers. The fill stations for the semis were a ways off, but the pair were shouting over the sounds of the big engines.

"Big storm brewing in the Montana mountains, Jenny," a small man with a big bass voice rumbled.

"I heard," said the other trucker, who was so bundled up that Adam hadn't realized she was a woman until she spoke. "I'm stopping in Sandpoint. I have friends there with space to park the truck."

Adam pulled out his cell and texted Mercy a request for backup food. Just in case. Because the address Honey had given him for the last place she knew that Gary was working was outside of Libby, Montana. According to the map app on the SUV, they would be driving through Sandpoint, Idaho, to get there.

The storm worsened the whole way from Coeur d'Alene up the panhandle of Idaho to Bonners Ferry, where he stopped to put chains on. The roads were bad enough to spawn multiple winter advisories, and traffic disappeared entirely except for an occasional snowplow and a few cars off to the side of the road as they climbed the mountains above Bonners Ferry. Mercy fell silent again, and not because she was mad at him. Her hand on his leg grew tense until she let go of him.

He glanced away from the snowdrifts that fought to pull him off the mountain pass and into the valley below. Mercy was squinting into the blizzard, leaning forward in her seat as if that would allow her to see farther. Her arms were wrapped tightly around her midriff, and he wished she'd put her hand back on his leg. He missed her touch.

"If you had a car manufactured in this century, we could have taken that and you could be driving," he told her, his eyes on the road again.

"My van could have handled the roads, but she would have traveled slower," she told him. "Her center of gravity is too high for speed in this kind of terrain."

"Speed being a relative thing for a Vanagon," he observed.

"There is that," she agreed, and he could feel the grin he didn't take his eyes off the road to see. "And you're a better driver for this kind of road than I am."

Her reply shouldn't have surprised him. He wasn't sure it was true—Mercy was a good driver and knew it. But her opinion made him want to puff his chest out like a teenager. Ridiculous.

"I love your dimple," she said. "Like a promise of the soft middle in a crusty roll."

He laughed at that as he changed the angle of his tires to account for the drag of a deep bit of snow that the wind had gathered in a protected curve of the road. "I'll show you a crusty roll."

"No nudging when you are driving on snowpack," she warned him.

"I am the Alpha," he informed her with mock smugness. "I can nudge anytime I want to."

The SUV chose that moment to fishtail, and it took a bit of finesse to get it traveling in the direction of the road.

"Anytime within reason," he admitted. "Though there is something to be said about flirting during these life-or-death moments."

She laughed—but it turned into a squeak when he came around a sharp turn to find a car stuck, wheels spinning, in the middle of his lane. He dodged it and pulled over, hoping he didn't catch a soft edge and have his rig roll down the mountain. Mercy hopped out before the wheels were fully stopped. By the time he made it to the stuck car, she was already talking to the driver.

"You aren't going to get a two-wheel-drive anything up the rest of this hill," Mercy was saying. "Do you have chains?"

He didn't. Mercy gathered the three kids and two car seats and organized them in the SUV while Adam and their father pushed the car out of the traffic lane. On a dry road, Adam could have pushed the car at a brisk jog. But no matter how strong you were, the coefficient of friction mattered. He could only push until his boots lost traction.

Satisfied that the car was as far off the road as they could manage without pushing it down the side of the mountain, Adam chivvied the driver into the shotgun seat of the SUV. Mercy had shoved their luggage to the side and put herself in the far back, behind the kids. No seat belt back there, but it couldn't be helped.

It took them half an hour to deliver the small family to their intended destination—a house a couple of miles up a country road behind the cluster of gas stations where Highway 2 broke east and 95 kept going north. In better weather, it would have been a five-minute drive. By the time they parked in front of his house, their adult passenger had recognized Adam.

Being rescued by a werewolf should have terrified him, but instead their new friend Wayne was thrilled. Adam found himself smiling for selfies and posing with each of the children as he simultaneously turned down heartfelt offers of lodging and food. It took some effort to extract himself without offending anyone.

Mercy—who had managed to stay in the SUV—regarded him as he left Wayne's mother's house with a little more speed than was prudent under the driving conditions.

"Say it," he growled.

She unbuckled so she could turn in her seat and kiss his cheek, then she belted herself back in. "You're cute when you're embarrassed."

The delay, the driving conditions, and the short winter days meant that it was already dark when they hit Libby, Montana. He fueled up and Mercy managed to get "Montana directions" for where they were heading.

"The ranch Honey told us he was babysitting is on the same side road as someplace called Looking Glass Hot Springs," she said, putting a large cup of steaming coffee in the cup holder beside him. "There will be two signs. The second one is right next to the road we need to take. If we don't feel a cattle guard as we leave the highway, we need to stop because we've missed the turn and there's a drop-off on either side of the road that tends to get filled with snow and look like it's level ground. Gary's ranch will be at the end of the road, about a mile after we pass the resort." She took a sip of her own drink, grimaced, and set it aside.

"Gas station hot chocolate is dangerous," he murmured, taking a swig of coffee. It wasn't the worst he'd had, and it was hot.

"That's fair. Sounds like the place we're looking for is a dude ranch open in the summer months. They hired some stranger, meaning someone not native to Libby, to watch the place and keep the water pipes from freezing—which they did last year. That would be my brother. He was all alone up there. The owners take their horses to California for the winter months, but sometimes they leave a pair for the resort to use for winter weddings, which apparently are a big moneymaker."

He smiled. "Worried about the horses?"

"Got to keep the watering troughs filled and ice-free so they don't colic, and plenty of food so they keep warm," Mercy said. "Perils of growing up in Montana with a bunch of people who still think of horses as their primary source of transportation."

"Charles?" Adam asked.

"Could be." She sighed. "He scared a whole bunch of information into me that comes out at odd moments."

"December weddings in Montana seem pretty optimistic," Adam said. He did not have fond memories of Montana winters—and this storm wasn't going to help that.

"There's supposed to be one this weekend," Mercy said. "Some famous billionaire marrying a regular working-class girl." She paused, gave him an amused look, and whispered, "It's a secret."

"So how did you find out about it?" Adam asked. "Was it in the local newspaper?"

She laughed. "I thought you grew up in a small town. The clerk who gave me directions told me about it. The guy behind me in line used his cell phone to show me photos of the groom. No one knows who the bride is except the local baker who made the cake—because the father of the bride paid for it. Not that they are going to use it now."

People talked to Mercy. He thought it was because she listened. She was interested in their stories.

"The baker was sad about the cake," she told him. "It wasn't huge, but pretty. Paid for, of course. You don't make a wedding cake without making them pay for it up front." A little mournfully, she said, "It's a lot of work to build a wedding cake, and now it will probably just get cut up and used for sampling."

"Shame," he said. "Didn't we get our cake because someone ordered one and didn't pay for it?"

She flashed a smile at him and leaned her head briefly against his shoulder. "So we did."

Outside of Libby, the already ferocious wind picked up. Adam had to pay attention, conscious of fatigue trying to fog his reactions. This kind of driving was harder on his brain than his body. He finished off his coffee. He was pretty sure that caffeine worked differently on him than it had before he'd become a werewolf, but it still helped to keep him sharp.

Mercy opened her window and dumped her cup of sludge. He'd probably be washing hot chocolate off the side of his SUV when they got home. She stopped the window as it started to roll back up, and he felt something flash in the bond they shared.

"There's magic in this storm," Mercy said.

As bad as the road was, he still glanced at her, getting a quick snapshot. She was holding on to the grab handle above the door with a white-knuckled grip—as if without that hold, she might fly out the window. Her eyes, normally a dark chocolate, were bright yellow, as if she were a werewolf, too. He'd seen that happen before—more often since the incident with the Soul Taker. For a werewolf it was a sign that their wolf was trying to take over. He wasn't sure what it meant in Mercy.

"Magic?" he asked.

"Can't you feel it?" Her voice was dreamy, and she tipped her chin to allow the cold wind to blast over the skin of her face more effectively. Their bond was lit up with a fizzy static he couldn't read anything through.

He hit the button on his side of the SUV that would close her window.

"Mercy?" he asked. "Are you okay?"

INTERLUDE

Last Night

HRÍMNIR

THE PAIN OF THE THEFT WAS NOT LESSENED BECAUSE he was old. Experience meant he trusted less often and with more sureness.

He had believed.

When the phone rang, he'd been sitting in his chair before the dead fire for a full day, held suspended by sorrow and despair. By his trust, he had ruined everything. He let the telephone ring itself into silence.

When the phone rang again, the being known in this time and place as John Hunter refused to answer it. There was no information the phone would provide him that would make the situation better. The effort of centuries, in the face of fate, was brought to nothing because of him. Because he had trusted the wrong one.

The second silence lasted for long enough he believed they would not call again. He heard the memory of the music of the lyre transforming this mundane little cottage into something

149

more, a magic that had less to do with the power of the artifact than it had to do with the roughened hands on the strings.

When the phone rang a third time, he picked it up.

He did not speak. Not once. But he didn't need to. His name-brother knew what had happened in astonishing detail. He had suggestions—and he had a warning.

If this had been yesterday, John Hunter would have wondered how Ymir knew so much when Gary would have been in no condition to tell him anything. But it was not yesterday, and the frost giant was not Loki or Freya to pick information out from what was not said.

Hrímnir listened.

"They are coming, brother mine. Do not underestimate them."

He set down the phone as Ymir's words slid through him like poison.

His dog, who had been faithfully sitting at his feet, whined uneasily. But the dog had always been smart. Smarter than his master.

John Hunter died in the molten heat of Hrímnir's fury—because anger was better than sorrow. Than pain. It felt good to give in to his rage.

"You want to go?" Hrímnir said, knowing his voice was nasty. He opened the door and let the growing wind and snow blow into the cabin with its false sense of home. With its vanishing warmth.

The dog cowered from his wrath—and the storm filling Hrímnir's veins and bones insulated him from shame. Of everyone in this tale, the dog was the most innocent.

"Go, then," he thundered. "It won't save them."

The dog ran from him into the forest outside as Hrímnir called winter's wrath to the world.

6

MERCY

WIND-BORNE MAGIC FILLED MY LUNGS AND COVERED my skin. As if it were oxygen, it filled my muscles and lit me from the inside out. I couldn't see, couldn't feel, couldn't breathe, suspended in a whiteout of icy power.

Adam's voice centered me and I clutched at it, even as the magic fought to drag me free, drag me into the wind.

Something changed, a channel narrowed and closed. Abruptly, I was back inside my body, curled into the warmed seat of Adam's SUV. The window I'd opened was closed. I let the empty cup fall onto the floor.

"Mercy," Adam demanded. "What happened?"

"At a guess," I croaked, all but crawling across the center console until my forehead found the heat of his shoulder, "Ymir may have told us the truth. It feels to me as if there might be an immortal frost giant helping this storm along. It tastes like the same magic that has my brother. And finally, I am now officially not angry that you abandoned the pack and your business to come with me."

Winter roads are treacherous.

"That bad?" he asked.

"I have never felt anything like that," I answered, opening the bond between us as wide as I ever had, just so I could surround myself with him. So that I wasn't alone with the memory of that magic that had come very close to remaking me.

My husband's warm hand came off the steering wheel and wrapped around the side of my face. The scary magic was still out there. But Adam was my lodestone. With a touch he made me feel centered. Not safe. There was nothing safe in a world that contained Bonarata. But he gifted me with his confidence, his support, and his belief that I could handle things.

All of that without saying a word.

It was a brief moment of relief, though. He had to put his hand back on the steering wheel. I was raised in the Montana mountains and lived in the capital of freezing rain, and these were the worst roads I'd ever been on. When the truckers quit driving, it was seriously bad.

"You closed the window, right?" I asked.

He nodded.

I peered out of the car to the forests, where the snow had buried everything except for the evergreens under a white blanket. The storm had not lessened just because the magic wasn't trying to rip through me anymore.

"I don't understand why rolling up the windows blocked—is presumably still blocking—the magic," I said.

"Sherwood," Adam told me. "He took a silver Sharpie and

drew all over the doorjambs and inner frames on all the doors. Runes, I think. I am not sure what they do."

"When?" I asked, startled because I hadn't heard anything about that.

"Last night," he said. "While you were sleeping."

"Why don't you know what they do?" That seemed a bit out of character for my Adam. He was a real believer in "knowledge is power."

He sent a faint grin my way, though he didn't take his eyes off the road. "I am not sure Sherwood knew what they were supposed to do. He wasn't about to admit it, though, so I let it go."

Sherwood's fragmented memories made his magic somewhat odd. And dangerous. Ben told me a few days ago that Warren and Kyle were still finding alarm clock pieces in random places in their house. The clock had exploded in Sherwood's house a couple of weeks ago. Sherwood did not know why the pieces ended up at Warren's house. Darryl postulated that there might be some analogue of quantum physics in magic—I couldn't tell if he was joking or not. Darryl's multiple PhDs could make it difficult to follow his humor.

"This storm has engulfed all of Montana, parts of Idaho, Washington, and over the border in Canada," Adam said thoughtfully, distracting me from worrying about the dangers of riding around in a car Sherwood had done something to and back to the dangers of driving in a blizzard. "Montana is what? A hundred thousand square miles?"

"About a hundred and fifty thousand square miles," I said. Montana history had been a requisite class when I'd been in high school, and some things stuck.

"We were supposed to have bad weather," Adam said. "This is a storm that has been growing for a few days, but when we left this morning, it wasn't supposed to be the storm of the century."

"I know."

"On a scale of one to ten," he said, "how much power do you think a creature has to have to drag a once-in-a-century storm down on a couple of hundred thousand square miles?"

"The kind of creature that most of Northern Europe thought could bring about the end of the world," I said, remembering the power of the magic that had tried to consume me. "Ragnarok."

I should have been more afraid, but knowing that there was a being, presumably Ymir's brother frost giant, out here calling the storm—that made me think saving my brother was a possibility.

Adam drove for a bit. Then he said, in a voice that was more thoughtful than worried, "I guess we better not tick off Ymir's brother, then. Look, there's the first sign."

It was painted on the side of a dilapidated barn with a roof that would be lucky to survive this storm. Unlike the barn, the sign looked like someone was keeping it in good shape. LOOKING GLASS HOT SPRINGS, it read, ESTABLISHED 1894. EXIT TWO MILES AHEAD.

Two point two miles later there was a much, much smaller sign poking bravely out of the snowbank that read just HOT SPRINGS with an arrow directing us to take a left turn.

Adam slowed to a stop on the highway. He was probably safe doing that. There had been no one on the road since Libby, even though I'd been assured the snowplows were out doing their thing. Somewhere that wasn't here.

Impossible to tell if the road was in front of the sign or on the far side. There really wasn't much of a way to tell where the highway was, either, except that it was a suspiciously wide space without trees or brush. Adam had been driving right down the middle of that space for a while.

I stared at the blowing snow outside for a second, and then popped my door open and jumped out. I paused involuntarily, waiting for the magic to hit me again.

"Mercy—" Adam stopped speaking, his eyes fixed on me.

Though the wind still tasted of magic, it made no effort to crawl through me. Too bad I didn't know if that first time had been some sort of attack, or if my weird and unreliable immunity to magic had decided to kick in. Or, possibly, the thing the Soul Taker had done to me was relenting for a bit.

"I'll find the road," I told him, grabbing my coat out of the backseat and putting it on. I didn't have to tell him to watch for traffic, because he wasn't stupid. It was pitch-black outside. Even with the snow falling sideways, we should have some warning of other idiots out driving so long as they had their headlights on.

For lack of any other guide, I trotted through knee-high snow toward the sign. I'd planned on slowing when I got near it, but I misjudged and found myself tripping in the suddenly deeper snow when the ground disappeared under my feet. Shoulder-deep in a drift, I scrambled awkwardly back up the drop.

I made it to higher ground, but everything I wore was covered in a layer of snow. I should have put on the gloves currently sitting, warm and dry, on the floor behind my seat. I pulled my hands into the sleeves of my jacket.

The snow was deeper here than it had been on the road. I guessed the snowplows had helped the highway a bit. Even on the raised flat ground I was wading knee-deep. With a general knowledge of how rural roads and cattle guards interacted in this part of Montana, I shuffled along the edge of the drop until my shins banged into something hard and metal and possessing many different angles. I would have interesting bruises in a few hours.

I turned ninety degrees, putting my back to the sign, the buried thingy that I was pretty sure was one end of the cattle guard my gas station informant had warned me about on my right. I found a hump with the side of my foot that I decided was the first bar of the cattle guard. I wasn't going to dig down with my bare hands to make sure. If I was correct, I was on the road.

I used the straight line of the hump to guide me across the flat, snow-covered ground that looked very much like the flat, snow-covered ground that had just dumped me in a hidden ditch. My knee found another upright something that ended below the snow level and I stopped.

I turned back to survey the roughly thirty-foot-long line my tracks made in the snow, a line that should cross the road we needed to take, while Adam waited in the middle of the highway. There still hadn't been a car on the highway in either direction because even truckers and native Montanans didn't travel in this kind of storm in the dark. You had to be pretty stupid to do that.

I moved to the midpoint in my line and waved Adam over. When the SUV stopped in front of me, bumper skimming the snow, I walked to the driver's-side door instead of the passenger side.

Adam rolled the window down.

"We can't follow a road we can't see up the mountains without falling off the side of a cliff or into a creek," I informed him, waving vaguely behind me at the path we needed to take, where, about a quarter of a mile away, the rugged foothills of the Cabinet Mountains rose. Between the blizzard and the night, they were almost invisible. "I think we need to go back to Libby and try this in the morning."

My stomach hurt at the thought. My brother was caught in a trap, and I didn't know when he was going to start thinking about a way to chew his foot off to get free. He was old, but I knew he wasn't immortal.

Adam rolled the window back up, then got out of the SUV. He frowned ahead, then brushed the melting snow off the seat of my pants. He lifted me into his seat, which startled me by moving to adjust for the change in drivers without anyone pushing a button. I'd been hijacking Adam's SUV enough that it recognized me. I needed to get my own daily driver.

"Take this." Adam handed me his coat.

"What are you doing?"

Adam glanced up at the sky. There wasn't anything to see, not in the middle of this storm. But Adam, his eyes already full of his wolf, knew where the moon was.

"We don't know what we will be heading into," I said. "My brother was on his own. The hot springs are supposed to be open now, but I don't know if anyone actually lives there—and no one has been over this road in the time it took for more than a couple of feet of snow to fall. It makes more sense to turn around and come back in the morning." The snow would still be here in the morning. "Maybe the spring."

My brother would not last until spring. I wasn't sure he would last a week.

Adam pulled his shirt off with less care than he'd used on his coat, and I could hear stitches give way. His knuckles were a little more defined when he gave me the shirt.

"Camping gear in the back of the SUV," Adam's wolf said. He

breathed the frigid air with joy. "If we need it. I can find the road. Just follow me."

In snow this deep, my coyote self would not sink to the ground. I could have run on top of the snow—but I couldn't have been sure of the road. Adam's wolf was nearly ten times heavier than a coyote and his paws were armed with large retractable claws that would dig down beneath the snow.

"We could drive back to Libby and bribe a snowplow," I persisted.

"Spoilsport." The wolf laughed, though Adam was still mostly human-shaped. "Don't want to be trapped with me in a snowstorm?"

I rolled my eyes in a fashion his daughter had taught me. "Fine. When they shovel our frozen corpses out next spring, they can put 'They thought it would be fun' on our gravestone." But inside, I was grateful. I needed to find Ymir's brother and get him to release the spell on *my* brother—and the thought of retreat when we might be close to our goal felt like I was failing Gary.

Adam pulled off his boots without untying them. Rather than giving me his snowy boots, he tossed them over my shoulder into the back. His jeans ripped when he tried to unzip them with transforming hands now more suited to rending the flesh of his enemies than manipulating delicate things.

"I liked those jeans," I told him sadly. "They hug your butt just right."

He laughed again—though I knew that he had to be in a lot of pain already. "You can see my butt anytime you want, my love."

I heaved a sigh as I took the wet shreds. "It's not the same when you know I'm looking," I told him, and tossed the mass over my shoulder, presumably on top of his boots. Maybe on top of my gloves, too.

I wasn't as good at ignoring the cold as the wolves, though I did a lot better than they did in hot weather. I turned the vents toward me and activated the seat heater, but I left the door open as Adam changed. Closing the door on him felt too much like abandoning him to the storm.

Even if he had forgotten the magic that had tried to take me, I hadn't. Adam was an Alpha werewolf, but he couldn't feel magic like I could, even before the Soul Taker had had its way. Not that I could do much about any magic that came at us—but at least I could warn him if I felt it change.

The actual temperature wasn't all that cold for a Montana winter. Seventeen degrees, the SUV said.

When the mountains got really cold, the skies were bright and clear because the air could hold no moisture at all. If it had been colder, every piece of fabric on me wouldn't have been wet. I was wearing a coat, but my fall into the deep stuff had forced snow up the back of my coat.

I held my icy hands to the warm air blasting from the vents for relief from the wind that howled through the open door. Even with the nearness of the last full moon, it took a while for Adam to change to his wolf. He staggered to four feet and swung his head in my direction, pinning his ears in disapproval.

Shut the door.

They weren't really words. A werewolf's mouth and throat aren't shaped right for speaking. But I picked out his meaning anyway, and the bond carried his unhappiness that I'd sat shivering and wet when I could have shut the door and been toasty warm . . . though still wet.

"When you are done," I told him.

He growled, but most of his attention was on the final, most painful parts of the change now. He'd blocked most of it, but I could feel the edge—like the bite of a dentist's drill when the numbing agent wasn't quite good enough.

It took another five minutes. Being away from the pack really had slowed his change down—or else he was saving his power in case we ran into trouble. He could have drawn from me, if he'd needed to, but he didn't. He shook himself off at last, his fur—silver and black—blending into the storm. The Marrok's older son, Samuel, was a white wolf. He'd have been invisible.

Adam gave the open door a pointed look.

I shut the door. Unlike a werewolf, I didn't have supernatural healing abilities, so I put on the seat belt. When I drove the SUV over or into the side of a cliff, the seat belt might be useful.

Adam jumped the length of two cars to clear the cattle guard, which wasn't any more pleasant to cross for a wolf than a cow. When he landed, he slid off an invisible bank. Presumably that meant that the road curved just past the cattle guard. I stopped before I got to him.

Rolling down the window, I said, "It's not too late to drive back to Libby."

He leaped out of the snow, shook himself off, and gave me a laughing look that displayed his many sharp white teeth. Tail sweeping the air, he crouched, shoulders nearly on the ground, and then danced off in a clear invitation to play.

"Alabama boy," I told him. "This is *winter*. You don't know what you're messing with."

He did, of course. He'd been born and raised in the South, but he'd spent some time in the Marrok's pack. It had been before I was born, but it would take more than a few decades to make someone forget what real winter was like.

I could feel his laughter in our bond as I rolled the window back up and he turned to face the mountains. He threw his head back and howled, his challenge echoing through the night. When nothing answered him, he set off again, zigzagging across the road in a pattern designed to take him from one edge to the other while the SUV and I crawled along behind him.

When we left the flat ground and the road climbed in the narrow valley between two steep hills, the deep snowpack lessened, replaced by drifts I could mostly avoid. I got stuck once, but shifting into four-low got me out of it. I left the SUV downshifted; we weren't going fast anyway.

I couldn't see the road under my tires, but with less snow, the SUV bumped in ruts and over rocks. I was able to use the feel of the car to tell me where the road was. That was the good change. The bad change was that the wind increased and I could barely see Adam—his silver-and-black coat blended a little too well with the winter night, even though I'd turned on the SUV's big spotlights and he was only a couple of car lengths ahead of me.

I could tell we were still winding our way through the bottom of the ravine, but any smaller visual cues were obscured by the night and the blowing snow. It felt as though we'd been traveling for hours and traversed a hundred miles. According to the SUV, we'd been driving for twenty minutes since crossing the cattle guard and had covered around three miles. I wished I'd thought to ask my helpful informant how far up this road my brother's ranch was.

There was a very real possibility that we'd drive right past it and end up somewhere lost in the Cabinet Mountains Wilderness.

Adam had a sat phone, I reminded myself. If we got that lost, we could call for help. We weren't too far from Aspen Creek, I could call—

I hit the brakes and the horn at the same time.

Adam stopped and turned to me. Driven by the need to keep him safe, I threw open the door of the SUV. I was on the road beside him when I realized I should have had Adam jump in the Sherwood-protected SUV and shut the doors instead of hopping out like an idiot. But it was too late to retreat now.

I couldn't see it. Couldn't see *him*. But I could feel him, a dense mass hidden in the heart of the storm and the darkness. And the magic.

The wind stopped as if someone flipped a switch. Not the whole storm—I could hear that continuing around us. But in the ravine in which we stood, it simply stopped. All of the snow that had been whirling about fell abruptly, leaving the air crystal clear.

The sudden-fallen snow covered me, and it covered Adam in an inches-thick blanket. The amount of snow felt as though it was too much, even with as bad as the storm was. The consistency was wrong, too—it didn't feel like snow. It was too heavy, too stiff. And I couldn't feel any magic at all, anywhere, as if the weird snow insulated that part of my senses.

I could have laughed in the relief of it. Except that we were not alone and my feel for magic was the only way I had to understand what we might be facing.

Everything was still, the only sound the raging storm that surrounded our little pocket of calm. I stared in front of us where something huge—half again as big as the SUV—blocked the road. Like us, it was covered in the snow. Staring at it was like looking at a piece of furniture covered with a sheet—all the important details were missing. But it moved, so whatever it was, it was alive. Breathing.

Snow tickled my nose, I sneezed, and the snow blanket fell off me in unnaturally large pieces, like a clay-mold reverse of my body. When it hit the ground, it turned to powder, as if it had been normal snow all along.

Adam shook himself clear as well. I threaded my fingers into the ruff at the base of his neck. Both of us kept our attention on the mound of white.

Finally, the shape gave an avian, rattling shiver. Instead of breaking free of the thick white covering, it absorbed the snow and grew. It rose up and unfurled huge wings, oversized even for the bulk of the creature. The wings were odd, composed of giant, snowy feathers that melted and re-formed in a way that made my eyes hurt. Fully extended, the wings stretched—improbably—from one side of the ravine to the other.

Illusion, I thought, but I wasn't sure.

Like the feathers, the edges of the wings were hard to focus on, changing subtly moment to moment in a way that wings were not meant to.

The body the wings attached to had four legs that were covered in thick feathers of frost and snow. The front legs ended in scaled raptor's feet complete with foot-long silvery claws that, unlike the feathers, looked as solid as Adam's. The feathers of the back legs covered the limbs all the way to the ground, hiding the details—but I didn't think the back legs ended in bird's feet.

The creature's head completed the mythological winter raptor effect, looking vaguely like that of a giant horned owl, but one that wore the colors of winter instead of autumn. Above the great dark beak were cold eyes the deep secret blue of a winter's night. It was a being that invited a metaphorical description.

I could not see pupils in those eyes. My night vision is coyote-good, sharp-focused but sometimes uncertain about colors. The thing's eyes were as dark as the night—I don't know why I was so sure they were blue.

The creature stepped forward and changed as it walked, the wings folding down and smoothing into a hefty winter coat built of layers of furs like the old mountain men had worn. The being took on man-shape, tall and broad with a full white beard and hoary hair that looked like a wild pony's mane, thick and wind-tangled. He was maybe six inches taller than Sherwood, whose human self was the largest in our pack. The frost giant wasn't quite outside the realm of human possibility—but he was definitely on the edge of probability.

His eyes were still the eyes of the gryphon.

"Gryphons are Greek," I said. When I am cold and scared, when I am faced with primordial and terrifying forces, when my life is on the line, sometimes the history degree makes itself felt. Because fear also tends to make me rash, my voice was accusing. "Or Persian. Or Egyptian. *And* they have eagle's or hawk's heads."

He stopped moving forward and looked at me.

I lifted my chin as I remembered Adam's admonition that the best path forward would be not to tick off Ymir's brother. I stopped before I actually told him that he had done it wrong, which were the next words that wanted to come out of my mouth.

"I am no hound of Zeus," he said, his voice softer than I expected, but there was something odd about the quality of it, piercing. "No creature of Mithra or Osiris."

I thought I could have heard him in the middle of a roaring crowd—or battlefield. What he didn't sound was angry, which was good. I drew a breath to figure out how to respectfully request he free my brother.

Then the Jötunn said, in that same voice, though now it seemed to rattle in my bones, "I am the wind and the storm. Hear my name and tremble, all you mortal children of weak and puling gods. I am *Hrímnir.*"

He sounded as though he expected me to bow to him, or tremble in fear. I was afraid, but his expectation that it was his due was annoying. The trembling I was doing had more to do with being wet and cold, or so I told myself staunchly. *The wind and the storm.* Hah. He was lucky I had a liberal arts degree so I knew what "puling" meant.

Adam bumped me hard because he knew me inside and out. *Don't be funny,* he was telling me. *Don't be a smart-ass. Remember this is the guy who pulled up a storm that is blanketing three states.*

The knowledge of how far out of our league this one was, was not useful, because when I'm really scared, really *really* scared, the other thing I get is angry.

Remember your brother, Adam's second bump said.

Adam was very smart, even when I was putting words into his mouth.

It was the thought of my brother's plight that allowed me to swallow what I wanted to say and change it into something that was more in keeping with good manners and common sense.

"We've felt your magic in the wind," I said, "but we knew of you before that, Hrímnir." My tongue didn't want to make the rolling "r." I ended up putting too much emphasis on it, so his name came out sounding more sarcastic than I meant it to. I went on before he had a chance to notice. "My brother came to our house unable to understand what he sees or hears. Unable to make himself understood. Ymir tells us that it's your magic that holds him. I am here to ask you to free him of your magic."

He stared at me with cold, predatory eyes—and I *knew* better than to meet the eyes of a predator unless I wanted a fight. There was something about his gaze that made it impossible to look away, the way I should have. I couldn't sense any magic, but it was very, very hard to breathe. I was pretty sure there was a lot of magic around that only my lungs were aware of. Maybe he was hiding it. Maybe there was so much magic that I'd overloaded my ability to detect it.

At least I wasn't drowning in insight. I had a feeling, call it self-preservation, that Hrímnir wasn't someone whose soul I wanted to read accidentally. Or otherwise.

"I know why you are here and what you want," the frost giant said. "My brother told me to expect you." His eyes went from me to Adam. "Are you his? Wolves are his to call."

A low growl rumbled out of Adam before he could stop it. And that's when I figured out that the Jötunn wasn't asking if I belonged to Adam. Hrímnir thought we might belong to Ymir. I wondered if that would be a good thing or a bad thing as far as getting the frost giant to fix my brother.

"Werewolves belong to themselves," I said firmly.

Hrímnir made a scoffing noise.

"Ymir took one of our pack," I told him. "Adam took her back." I waited a beat. "Ymir apologized."

The frost giant gave me a look of utter disbelief.

"He didn't mean it," I acknowledged. "But we did get her back."

"He *said* you weren't his."

Yep, I thought, even his brother knows Ymir can lie.

"We aren't."

He stared at me again, but this time I took care to keep my eyes on his beard. He gestured to the wintry world around us and a gust of wind cut briefly through the stillness.

"I thought you would take the hint that you were not welcome. He—" He broke off abruptly, and his breath fogged in the chill. The ambient temperature dropped—my childhood senses, attuned to winter, told me it was down by twenty degrees or more. There is a feel to the air when the world achieves below-zero temperatures.

"If you take the spell off my brother," I told him, "we will be happy to leave."

It was the wrong thing, and I knew it as soon as I said it. He didn't have to wait for us to leave. He could kill us here and now, and neither my brother nor Adam and I would be any bother at all. I didn't need Adam's warning bump to tell me I'd screwed up.

Hrímnir turned away, the skins flaring around him like a cape. I was pretty sure those were wolfskins, very large ones. The relief of being out from under the frost giant's regard, of being able to breathe again, made me a little light-headed. He paced in an angry, agitated circle, and when he was looking at me again, he shook his head.

"No," he said. "No. You should leave."

I was pretty sure he hadn't been considering letting my brother go. We were lucky in his choice—but it didn't feel that way. I *had* to persuade Hrímnir to release my brother.

I needed a way in. Something we had in common. What did I

have in common with an ancient frost giant except my brother? And I'd just proven that was less than useful just now.

Reading fairy tales had become something of a passion with me because I dealt so much with people who had inspired them. More than once I'd found a kernel of truth that helped me. The fae love to bargain, I thought. I was pretty confident that the Jötnar weren't fae, no matter what they had told the government. But a bargain was almost legal tender among the creatures of power I'd met, not just the fae.

"Is there anything we can do for you that would change your mind?" I asked carefully.

Hrímnir started to reply—a negative by his body language. Then he hesitated, closed his mouth, and frowned at me. "What is it you think you can do for me?"

Not a freaking clue.

"I am Mercedes Hauptman, daughter of Coyote and mate to Adam Hauptman, who is the Alpha of the Columbia Basin Pack." I didn't try to match his proclamation-of-greatness tone, but a little hubris was necessary. "This is my mate, Adam Hauptman, who took our wolf back from your brother when he would have claimed her for himself."

"Daughter of Coyote?"

I had thought that might get his attention.

"As my brother is son." I wasn't sure it was smart to bring my brother back into the conversation, but it also seemed counterproductive to leave him out. He was the reason I was here—I dug my fingers into Adam's fur—the reason *we* were here.

Hrímnir rocked back on his heels a moment, then said in a completely different voice that had lost the German or Germanic accent entirely, "Gary is your brother?"

"Half brother." It didn't seem smart to say anything that he might read as a lie.

"Is Gary Coyote's son?"

His voice was still not a frost giant's voice.

I thought of my brother, living up here all alone. He wasn't the type to enjoy being alone. I thought of the way I had been able to taste the frost giant's magic in the storm. Would my brother have chased that down? Had they been friends? Acquaintances? But an acquaintance would not have engendered the complicated emotions I sensed in this . . . well, not a man. Being.

"Yes," I said.

Slowly the frost giant nodded. "That explains . . ." Then he shook his head and drew in a breath. When he spoke again it was in that soft voice designed to make gods tremble, accent firmly back in place. "He stole from me."

Adam ghosted in front of me, standing between me and the frost giant.

"Are you certain?" I asked, risking his temper.

He looked at me. "Can you lie? Can your brother?"

The answer was yes, of course. I didn't want to tell him that.

"I am not fae," I told him as a compromise, quickly following it with a question of my own. "What was stolen from you?"

But Hrímnir had turned away from me again and was pacing in his circle. Talking to himself.

"He was my friend. Our friend. He couldn't have taken it. Taken him. He lied. They *wouldn't*. He is our friend," he muttered, then followed it with a louder and more heated statement. "He lied. He is a liar. He took it and lied."

He seemed to be stuck there.

I loved being faced with a being of godlike powers who might

be in the middle of a psychotic break, complete with vague pronouns. I didn't know if I should interrupt or hope he forgot about
us entirely.

His voice dropped again. "He hurt us. Hurt me. Did they do
it together?" He stopped and looked up at the sky, where the stars
were hiding behind the clouds.

"What was taken?" I asked.

He turned to me, face lighting with rage. "My harp. He took
my harp."

"I don't know if he took it," I told him. "He can't tell me because of your magic. But he came to my home, a day's journey by
car. He did not bring a harp with him."

I'd looked in his truck to see if Gary had brought any clothes—
which he hadn't. I was pretty sure I'd have noticed anything as
big as a harp.

"He got away," Hrímnir growled. "But he didn't take it with
him. It's here. I can feel it, but I can't get to it because he has
taken refuge."

"Someone took your harp," I said, parsing through his words.
I couldn't tell if he was certain it had been my brother who took
it or not. Maybe that's what the argument he'd had with himself
had been about. Maybe not. "You know where it is?"

His eyes narrowed on me suspiciously. "I do."

"And it is not with my brother."

"He took it," he snapped with such force that I wouldn't have
been too surprised to see bits of teeth fly out of his mouth. He
turned his head away in a motion that brought lashing tails to
mind. "He didn't take it. He wouldn't. Not from us. He didn't
know what it meant."

I'd grown up with very old and sometimes irrational creatures who could kill me if I pushed them too far. I knew what was possible and what was not. I needed to redirect Hrímnir to more useful thoughts.

"You know where the harp is," I said. It wasn't a question because he'd said as much. "But you can't get to it."

"They won't keep it," he said slyly. "They will all die. None of them will keep it."

"Of course not," I agreed. "Where is it?"

"In the holy place of fire," he said.

I blinked at him while I assimilated that. The snow was still deep enough it was hard to see where the road was, the road that my helpful informant at the gas station had told me led to two properties. The dude ranch my brother worked on, and Looking Glass Hot Springs. One of those fit the phrase "holy place of fire" better than the other.

"You believe the harp is at the hot springs," I said. "The resort. And you are going to let this storm rage until everyone there is dead. There are people at the hot springs now?"

"It was taken there. They took it there. *He* took him there."

Truth shivered through his words. Which was very helpful because I couldn't tell if what he said was true—which is what it felt like. Or if it was that he believed what he said—which was a different thing entirely. And it didn't matter, because what he said didn't make sense to me at all.

"Why can't you just go get it?" I asked.

"They fled before me to a place they knew I could not follow," he told me with sudden coherence. "But they will die there." He paused and said, with the force of a prophecy, "*He* will die there."

Sadness came and went so fast I wasn't sure I had seen it at all. "I may not be able to go there, this is true. But it is also true that they cannot leave unless I let them."

"If they escape—"

"They die," he said with a fierce smile, and I thought of the gryphon—or whatever the beast had been.

I rubbed my forehead as if pressure could make the Soul Taker's damage go away. Wind I did not feel lifted the skins on his back and made them flutter.

"Why can't you just go to the hot springs and retrieve the harp?" I said, holding up a hand as his anger began to rise. "I am ignorant about holy places of fire and also mostly ignorant about Jötnar. Maybe if I knew more, I could help."

He considered me.

"This is a place where the heat of the heart of the world rises in the water," he said. "Rich in magic and healing." He closed his eyes and turned his hands palms up—and the air became thick with a magic as pure as the snow. Evidently, from the rush of effervescent power on my skin, my senses were noticing magic again.

He closed his hands and I could breathe, though magic still rippled around us.

"This fire I may sup upon," he said simply. "But the land has been held sacred and the element opposes my own. Generations upon generations have made the springs a refuge. If I get too close to the fire of the holy place, I burn."

Hot springs were not uncommon in the Rocky Mountains, of which the Cabinets were a small chunk. Many of them were secrets—there was one in the Marrok's territory that I was pretty sure only Charles and I knew about. But at the turn of the previous century, building hotels and health spas around largish and safe-ish hot springs had been popular. Most of those naturally occurring hot springs had been considered sacred by the original inhabitants of the land. A place that held the touch of God, by whatever name people addressed him by. Holy.

Holiness was one of those things that I knew when I felt it—but I couldn't have described it coherently if my life depended upon it. I was unclear if holiness was something that was independent of belief or not. I wasn't even absolutely certain what it was—a force, a warding, or something else entirely. I did know that it could affect magic strongly, and sometimes unpredictably.

"Someone stole your harp from you and ran to the hot springs, where you couldn't follow them. The harp and presumably the person or people who stole it from you are at the resort. They can't leave, and you can't go in to get it."

"Yes."

"You have made it so they cannot leave. They will die. Your harp will stay there, and you will *never* recover it."

Hrímnir roared, a sound that carried with it the force of the winter wind. Cold bit at my face and burned everywhere I had skin exposed.

"Unless . . ." I said, letting my voice trail off.

He turned his head to me, and I felt his attention as a wave of cold. I didn't shiver, but it took an effort.

"What if we go in and get it for you?" I suggested.

INTERLUDE

ZANE

"DID YOU HEAR THAT?" EZRA SAID. "THEY'VE CANCELED the flight to Missoula—winter storm."

A cold chill went up Zane's spine. They had to make it to the wedding.

"You might not make it to your own wedding, buddy." Leon's big grin split his face. "Don't look like that. Have you even met Tammy? She's not going to hold the biggest storm in a hundred years against you. You should wait until the weather dies down and go to Hawaii—which is where all December weddings should be held."

Ezra shook his head. "Nah, this is where generational wealth does its work. Go to it, Zane." He waved a hand at him, as if inviting him to work real magic.

"I don't have a wand," Zane told him, imitating the Harry Potter gesture Ezra had given him.

"Nah," Ezra said with a grin. "You have real magic. Get your phone out and work your spell."

With a reluctant smile, Zane pulled out his phone, quickly discovering their flight to Missoula wasn't the only one canceled. He couldn't get a flight into Kalispell, Helena, Butte, or Bozeman. Billings *was* a possibility. When he checked it, Billings was more than five hundred miles from Libby—the nearest town to Looking Glass Hot Springs.

Wealth or not, it was Ezra with his military connections who found a pilot willing to fly into Spokane as long as they didn't close the airport.

Two hours later they were climbing into a twenty-year-old Cessna 172, having shed most of their luggage.

The pilot gave the three of them an odd look—saying something in Spanish to Ezra, who laughed.

Zane knew they seemed an odd lot. Ezra was a forty-something retired MP and looked it, the son of migrant parents who had grown up working hard and continued to do so. Leon was twenty-seven, and he'd grown up harder than Ezra—whose family was still tight.

Leon was an inner-city kid and wore gang tattoos on his shoulders, though that part didn't show—much. He'd gotten himself out on scholarships, had a newly minted medical degree, and was working on his internship—the reason that they hadn't gone to Montana days ago. Medical interns were at the mercy of their programs. Finally, there was Zane himself, who was an advertisement for a life of privilege.

The avenger and the caretaker and the scion. Part of the carefully balanced magical equation that was his destiny. Two years ago, he'd known neither of them—now they were his best friends.

They shouldn't have been friends at all. But, his inner selves told him, fate was a funny thing. He knew they'd continue to be friends throughout his lifetime. They always did.

Leon caught his elbow. "You okay, Zane?"

"Fine," he said, planting himself firmly in the here and now. "Let's get going."

7

MERCY

THE STORM RESUMED ITS FURY AS SOON AS THE gryphon flew away.

"What do you think?" I asked Adam.

It had been too bad he'd been stuck in wolf form, unable to help negotiate. He was better with words than I was. I hoped I could deliver on my part of the bargain.

"Maybe I should have tried to contact Coyote instead of coming here." As soon as I said it, I realized that might have been smarter. Instead, I'd dragged Adam out into this storm on a wing and a prayer—and the word of a lying frost giant who lusted after our pack. "Coyote might have been able to free Gary without this journey to winter hell."

Or not. Coyote was unreliable help at best—and I knew exactly what Gary would say about asking our father for anything. Gary knew Coyote better than I did.

The wolf gave me a sly smile, and warmth blossomed through our bond. Apparently, my husband preferred the path we'd taken. I hoped we could deliver on my promise. Finding a stolen harp and returning it didn't sound too difficult, given that we knew it was at the resort. I hoped it wouldn't take very long.

The wind hit my wet jeans, and my toes burned from the cold. My boots were too short, although I wasn't sure they made boots tall enough for this kind of snow. Snow had snuck in from the top, and my socks had wicked the moisture all the way to the soles of my feet. Adam bumped me toward the SUV.

I shut myself in the blessed warmth of the car, leaving Adam outside to continue his role as guide. My wet jeans clung to my knees, fighting me when I put my foot on the accelerator. Once we left the area Hrímnir had cleared, the snow got deeper. There were a couple of times that even in four-low, I had to back up and hit the drifts at higher speed before the SUV could break through.

We'd traveled another two miles in about twenty minutes when the road made a few sharp turns and ended abruptly in front of a huge log building fronted by a massive porch. A giant rustic sign hung from the rafters in two parts. The top sign read MOUNTAIN HOME GUEST RANCH. A larger sign hung below it, connected by two thick chains. It read WELCOME FRIENDS.

I turned off the engine and got out of the car. The wind whistled around the buildings, and there were a few shingles on the otherwise pristine white surface. The covered porch had a few feet of wooden planks visible, where the wind had scoured the snow. The rest of it was buried deep. Beyond the ranch house, set at a little distance, was a huge red barn.

"We missed the turnoff for the resort," I told Adam, who huffed an acknowledgment.

"Since we're here, I might as well see about those horses that could be tucked up somewhere in the barns." The horses had been bothering me since the conversation I'd had with the people at the gas station.

It was legitimately an accident that I'd missed the turnoff. But I'd have felt driven to find my way up here tonight anyway. I was here on Gary's business, and part of that was taking care of his responsibilities.

There were other buildings visible—cabins and garages—but I didn't care about those. The barn, painted bright red, was maybe a hundred yards behind the main building. I picked it as the most likely place to confine a couple of horses out of the weather. In the summer, the barn was probably a convenient distance from the main building. In knee-high snow with drifts up to my hips, it was a trek.

Even with Adam breaking trail in front of me, I was dripping sweat from effort by the time I made it to the barn, though my toes were still freezing. My coyote could have made this trip a lot easier—and I'd do it that way tomorrow. Because I could hear and smell the horses in the building.

From the SUV, the barn had looked as traditional as the house. But up close, it was a thoroughly modern building with a pair of twelve-feet-wide roll-up doors the same shade of red as the barn itself. There was a control panel next to each door. I pressed the one nearest me and nothing happened.

Of course the electricity was out. Doubtless there were generators around somewhere, but I wasn't going to be able to locate them easily.

Around the corner from the big doors was a person-sized door. The snow was a lot less deep here. I couldn't decide if someone had been here recently or if the wind had blown most of the area in front of the door clear.

It was unlocked. The minute I opened the door, I was greeted with a chorus of whinnies, the mysteriously satisfying smell of horses, and the rich scent of alfalfa.

Adam preceded me into the cavernous building. It wasn't as dark as I expected, mostly because there were translucent panels in the roof that let in what light was available. At night, with a blizzard outside, there wasn't much of that. A normal human would probably not have been able to see anything.

Traditional stalls lined both sides of the barn, maybe ten on a side, and all of those were empty. The center was obviously meant to be an open arena, maybe a hundred feet by a hundred and twenty feet. Temporary fencing had been set up to create a large pen in the arena that held two sleepy great horses. Belgians, maybe? Though these were some lighter color, and I had the impression from somewhere that Belgians were usually darker—bay or black. They weren't big enough to be Clydesdales, and Belgians were the only other breed of draft horse that I could name. To one side of the pen was a sleigh.

The big horses watched us curiously but not anxiously. Their water trough was filled to the brim with crystal clear water. The barn felt warmer than it was outside by virtue of being out of the wind. But it still wasn't above freezing in here. Their drinking water should have ice, if only on the edges.

There was a stack of forty or fifty hay bales just out of reach of the horses. While Adam took a sniff around the barn for hidden threats, I broke off a couple of six-inch-thick flakes from an open bale and tossed them over the fence.

Leisurely, the big animals moved to the hay and began eating.

They appreciated the nighttime snack, but there was no urgency to their feeding like I'd have expected in horses left on their own for as long as Gary had been gone. There was no manure in the pen.

When I was growing up, my foster father had kept a couple of horses, and one of my chores had been mucking stalls. This pen had been cleaned recently, probably within the last few hours. I reached through the fence and touched the trough. The aluminum was warm. After a second, my fingers tingled with a hint of magic. I'd expected the magic, but I hadn't expected it to feel like my brother. I couldn't do magic like that. It wasn't a kind of magic I would have expected from Gary, either. Useful magic was more a fae thing. Or a frost giant thing, maybe.

When I next had the chance, I was going to pin my brother to a chair and make him talk. Hopefully, the next time I saw him he would be *able* to talk. To that end, I needed to finish up here and head for the Looking Glass resort or hotel or whatever it was.

The water might have been Gary's work; however, my brother hadn't cleaned the pen or fed the horses today. Under the stronger, more usual barn scents, I could detect something that smelled of winter, magic, and wolfskins.

"The frost giant is taking care of the horses," I said out loud.

Adam, finished with his inspection, huffed his agreement, turning my presumption into a certainty. In his wolf form, Adam could catch scents better than I could as a human.

"After he damaged my brother, Hrímnir took over his duties." Why had he done that? To protect innocents? Maybe he just loved horses. "If it weren't for what he's done to my brother—and his whole disregard of the kind of damage he's doing, and the people who are going to die because of his storm—I think I might like him."

I pulled out my phone to check with Honey on how my brother was—maybe she could figure out a way to let him know the horses were okay. But there was no reception. We were pretty far from civilization, so it wasn't surprising. When we got to the hot springs, if I still didn't have a signal, I could use Adam's sat phone to make the call.

"Do you think we should spend the night here?" I asked Adam. "I could shift and we could stay in the barn, or I could break into the main building. There are chimneys—there should be firewood somewhere."

Adam shook his body as though shedding water, and trotted to the door we'd used coming into the barn, impatience in his body language.

"Okay," I said, relieved. Staying here would have been smarter. I let us out and then shut the horses in their safe space. "The sooner we find that harp, the sooner we'll be done."

I was pretty sure the harp was an artifact of some sort, a magical item. It could be something of great power or mostly sentimental. But I didn't think the frost giant was a sentimental creature, and the last great artifact we'd encountered hadn't been a picnic for anyone. I rubbed my temples, wishing I didn't have to listen to the magic in the storm.

"Vulnerable," Zee had said.

We found the road to the resort about a mile back down the road. The storm had pulled down the sign and flipped it backward—which is why we missed the road the first time. Well, that and the snow that had gathered about two feet deep over the roadway so it looked no different than the terrain around it.

I stopped before I turned off the main road, rolling down the window. Adam trotted over to me.

"Hrímnir said magic is weird at the resort. Maybe you should take on human shape before we get there."

Adam considered this, then shook his head.

I felt something pass through our bond. But though sometimes we could talk through that path, it was intermittent. Just like my part-time immunity to magic. But I caught a bit of his confidence. He thought that wouldn't be a problem, but if he had to get stuck in one form among possible enemies, he'd rather be the wolf.

Fair enough.

The SUV roared as I scaled the steep road through the trees behind the wolf. I'd learned to drive in this kind of country, and it still took every nerve I had to keep going. I couldn't see the road in front of me most of the time—not because of the storm or the darkness but because of the way the road humped up and down, leaving my headlights illuminating the sky or the trees. And if I slowed down at all, I'd be in a world of trouble. Only my speed allowed the SUV to keep climbing instead of sliding down the mountain backward.

It was probably less than a quarter of a mile before we breached the top, but it felt like a thousand years. When the chassis was level, I stopped to catch my breath. There had to be another way into the resort.

In front of me, all I could see was snow flying sideways, illuminated by my headlights. I couldn't see trees or any sign of which way the road went. Before I could worry too much, Adam appeared, trotting toward me.

I rolled down my window. "When we go home, *you* are driving back down that excuse for a road."

He gave me a look.

"Okay," I admitted. "That was really fun." I held up my hands to show him how much they were shaking. "But you still get to drive on the way home."

He gave me a laughing look and turned to lead the way forward. There were no trees or cliffs to indicate where the road might be. The road was flat, and the ground to either side seemed to be flat, too. We traveled slower because even Adam was having trouble finding the road.

I knew what flat, treeless ground in the mountains meant. Chances were that under the snow on either side of the road was swamp or lake. Probably we wouldn't sink through—it was really cold, and frozen water was as good as asphalt for driving on. But considering we were heading for a place with hot springs, I'd just as soon not risk it.

The sound of the roadway changed as we crossed a bridge. My eyes didn't see it, but I could feel the flow of water beneath me. It tasted like magic. My foot came off the gas pedal, but I didn't notice until the SUV slowed to a stop as the power beneath the vehicle dragged at me. Called me.

A sharp sound by my left ear interrupted the water's song. I turned to see Adam's face right on the other side of the window. The sound had been his claws scoring the side of the door.

I blinked at him, then put my foot down on the accelerator. When the SUV pulled forward, a sharp pain slid through my chest, a pain that stopped as soon as we were off the bridge. The frost giant had been right that there was a Power here. The grip of the water, whatever the cause, had felt impersonal—like an avalanche. It was simply a barrier, designed to catch creatures like me.

I concentrated on Adam after that. We'd entered some kind of fog bank; between that and the driving snow, the first inkling I had that we'd reached our goal was when I realized that the lump of snow on my right was in the shape of a truck. Beyond it, now that I was looking for it, was a huge building, almost lost in the storm and the fog.

Following the wolf, I piloted the SUV into a space between two snowed-in cars and parked, steaming water about five feet in front of my bumper. I opened the door and slid to the ground. Adam leapt inside the open door to begin his change.

Through the snow beneath my feet, I felt it, a queer sort of warmth that was magic and not magic. Something nearly sentient, a guardian.

"Refuge," I said out loud. Then chose a different word. "Sanctuary."

Power swept through my chest as if in agreement or warning before sliding away and taking with it the taste of warmth, leaving behind a cold night and the smell of sulfur from the hot springs.

I went to the back of the SUV to open the rear hatch and grab our gear—and stopped.

On the other side of the parking lot there was a lake, or at least a very large pond—it was hard to be sure in such poor visibility. It was bitterly cold but the water at the edge of the parking lot was not frozen. A vast wall of mist rose up, like a great white dragon obscuring the view of the shoreline nearest the resort as well as the edge of that giant old building.

I waded through the parking lot snowdrifts and almost bumped into a sign that told me I stood on the shore of Looking Glass Lake. It also advised me not to swim in the lake, as the hot springs could be dangerous.

In my experience, hot springs were usually just that. Small pockets of water bubbling up from the ground steaming hot. Sometimes there were lots of pockets of water. Here, apparently, those pockets were underneath the lake.

The resort—which is what the locals had called it at the gas station in Libby—had been built on the edge of the lake. The building was half-obscured by darkness, storm, and mist, but it didn't look like a resort to me. It had the spare, efficient lines of something erected with an eye to efficiency—probably at least a century ago.

And it was haunted.

I tried to pretend that the wisps drifting between me and the building were just an effect of the hot springs, but I could hear their quiet, ghostly voices. A lot of people had died here at one time or another. I eyed the rectangular building and thought sanatorium or hospital—and the label fit.

A random swirl of wind allowed the bare bones of a wrap-around porch to emerge briefly from the mist and shadows, hinting at a past or possibly future attempt to soften the stark lines as the narrow white boards it was sided in did not. The roof of the porch was completely gone, but from the winter-dormant wood that draped over the structure, some kind of climbing plant grew over the frame in the summer.

Maybe if it had been daylight or if the numerous lights around the parking lot and building were lit, it would have looked more welcoming. As it was, three floors of blank windows stared out at me in a way that did not feel friendly. I could not imagine seeing this place and thinking, "This is where I want my wedding to be held."

Hrímnir had called this a holy place and a refuge. I'd been

given the word "sanctuary" by whatever being claimed this location. Sanctuary, in the medieval meaning of the word, had been both holy and a refuge. Historically, a person who had been given sanctuary could not be arrested as long as they stayed upon the holy ground. In real life, of course, this had been more true in some times and in some places than in others. But the tradition still lingered in modern times, culturally if not legally.

It didn't look like a safe place. Unease finally got the better of me and I retraced my path through the snow to the SUV, putting it at my back so I could watch the lake.

I wondered what the clear warning I'd been given that this was a sanctuary would mean for our quest. Recovering stolen property shouldn't be a problem. Hopefully, we wouldn't need to hurt anyone. I tried not to wonder what Hrímnir would do after he got his harp back. Somehow, I couldn't see him just letting the thief go—even if we did have a bargain. The frost giant wasn't fae; maybe he wasn't bound the way a fae would see themselves bound. What would I do if I brought the harp back to Hrímnir and he didn't take the spell off Gary? Maybe if I proved Gary hadn't done it?

He was my brother. I wanted to think he would never have been so stupid as to steal an artifact from a frost giant, but I couldn't manage that.

I rubbed my face with cold hands. If I wasn't going to use my gloves, I should have just left them at home. I remembered that I'd intended to grab our luggage, but I couldn't make myself turn my back on the hot springs. Something out there was watching us. I squinted, but I couldn't see anything.

I put my hip against the quarter panel of the SUV for the connection to Adam—it felt like it was taking him forever to change.

In the dark, with the SUV's tinted windows, I couldn't see him, but the subtle rocking of the vehicle told me he was in there.

I pulled out my phone, but was unsurprised to see that I still had no reception. I couldn't look this place up on the Internet. Or contact Honey or Mary Jo to check on Gary. We weren't cut off, I reminded myself. We could use Adam's sat phone.

Cold seeped up from the damp legs of my jeans and into my bones.

Eventually the door behind me opened and shut. Safely back in his human body, Adam nudged my shoulder with his own.

"Let's get you out of the cold," he said.

He grabbed his duffel and my backpack and took the lead on the way to the main entrance. I was braver with him, so I could take my attention off the lake and look at his backside instead. The jeans he wore weren't as good as the ones he'd destroyed, but the view was still nice. I trekked behind him, in the path through the drifts that he made, humming an old carol softly to myself.

He laughed. "Not a king or a saint," he said. "No heat lingers in the very sod where I tread."

"But the winter bites less coldly," I said. "You make a pretty good windbreak." And keeping my eyes on him meant I didn't have to notice the ghosts. Hopefully, they wouldn't notice me, either.

As we got to the entrance, I saw that there were Christmas lights strung all over the bare trusses that used to bear the roof of the wraparound porch that clearly, now that I had a closer view, was an original feature. They'd have looked pretty all lit up, but unlit, they only contributed to the bleakness of the place.

I'd thought the door might be locked for the night, but Adam had no trouble opening it. Sleigh bells on the door's Christmas wreath gaily announced our arrival as a wave of warmth engulfed us. We stepped out of the storm and straight into the first half of the twentieth century. Here, inside, and unexpected given the grimness of the exterior of the building, was the expensive elegance I'd have expected from a resort where billionaires get married.

"Huh," I said. "I guess you really can't judge a book by its cover."

The reception area was small for a building this size, but that made it look more expensive rather than less, a kind of "good things come in small packages" experience. There was room for an elegant couch and a couple of chairs. Two original oil paintings hung on the wall. I would have bet money that they were worth a small fortune. I couldn't name the artists, but they had the look of art that should be displayed in a museum and not a lodge in the Cabinet Mountains.

Rather than a reception desk, there was an open window into a small office. The counter was figured oak, presumably original to the building from the wear and tear carefully preserved in the varnished surface.

The whole reception area and the parts of the office I could see were immersed in Art Deco design, down to the vase filled with five or six peacock feathers and the burled walnut paneling on the walls. Even the Christmas wreath on the door was done with the sort of spare elegance of the late flapper era.

Adam said, "I feel like I'm a passenger on the *Titanic*."

"Or walking onto a movie set," I agreed, not bothering to correct him. The *Titanic* sank in 1912, a decade or two earlier than the Art Deco period.

I surveyed him and then looked down at my own travel-stained wet clothes.

"Both of us are terribly underdressed, dear sir." I borrowed my posh English accent from the one our English werewolf used. I knew I'd gotten it right when Adam grinned at me.

The only touch that was out of place was the pair of plastic battery-operated lanterns illuminating the room. One of them sat on the beautiful counter and the other on the floor beside the couch.

Adam leaned over the counter and grunted. He dropped our baggage and hopped over the barrier and into the office without so much as disturbing the little paper tent that announced that the office was closed for the night.

"Yep," he said from the other room. "They still use keys. Assuming that the rooms with three keys available are not in use—and the ones that have three keys bound together with a zip tie are rooms that aren't ready—that means the entire third floor and most of the second are out of commission or occupied. Are you okay with ground floor?"

"Sure," I said.

If Adam hadn't been with me, I'd likely have bedded down on a couch, though hopefully there was one somewhere that would be more comfortable than the one in this lobby. But he was right. In a storm like this, no one would begrudge us helping ourselves. We could pay for our room in the morning, assuming there was an employee to pay. Adam took a key and then found a piece of paper and a pen, doubtless to record our absconding with the key and use of the room.

There was a light switch just to the right of the counter. I flipped it, but nothing happened. "I wonder why it's so warm in here if the electricity is off."

"There is a generator," a woman's voice said from the narrow opening between the reception room and the dark hallway beyond.

I was startled. I'd had no inkling there was anyone around. She must have been standing there in the dark when we'd come in. I would have heard someone moving.

She continued in a friendly, informative manner that was very much at odds with her having been lurking in a hallway, watching us. "It's confined to essential services—the kitchen and the walk-in freezer, as well as the water pump for the well and to keep the hot spring water circulating in the pipes and radiators. The building can run—without lights, of course—on minimal electricity."

I wouldn't have thought Adam could see her, either, but something galvanized him. Maybe he was more upset about her lurking than I was. He dropped the pen and abandoned his half-written note. Key in hand, he vaulted the counter again, landing lightly between me and the dark opening that led to the hallway beyond, as if to put himself between me and an enemy.

"Good to know," I answered.

"I sounded like a tour guide, didn't I?" The floorboards showed their age by squeaking a bit as the woman walked in, though she wasn't very big. Slender, with big dark eyes and light brown curly hair cut short to highlight her fine features, she looked like she was in her midtwenties.

Despite the lateness of the night, she was fully dressed in a green silk shirt and herringbone-patterned trousers. She had pearl drops in her ears and a single pearl on a gold chain around her neck. Maybe there had been a party or reception earlier in the evening?

"You must be with the groom's family," she said. Her smile lit her face. "I'm sorry no one warned you about the weather. What are you driving, that you made it up those roads? And in the dark?"

Adam, uncharacteristically, did not respond to her friendliness. He'd come across the barrier as though he was prepared for a fight. But it wasn't until he spoke that I understood why.

"Vampire," he said.

Her smile died as though it had never been.

I honestly hadn't noticed the scent until Adam spoke. The sulfur of the hot springs was pretty strong—and I was dog-tired. Once Adam drew my attention to it, though, it was obvious.

Vampire. Bonarata. Chills spread up my spine, and my stomach hurt. Was this whole thing a trap?

I'd grown up in the Marrok's pack, and Bran Cornick was capable of engineering the situation that had forced us here, away from our people and our home. Vulnerable. Anything that Bran could think up was well within the capability of Bonarata.

But there was a danger in giving Bonarata more power than he had, wasn't there? I looked at my husband's hostile back and thought that his mind had gone to the same Bonarata-inhabited place that mine had. I put a light hand on his shoulder.

"Vampire," the woman agreed coolly.

As she spoke, a man strode in behind the woman, as if he'd been lurking in the hall. The floorboard didn't creak under his weight, even though he was a big man, a little over six feet tall and built wide. His skin was pale, and I thought in brighter light I'd see freckles to go with the light skin and the hair that looked to be red, though the yellowish lanterns played havoc with my ability to judge color.

It struck me that his clothing, like the woman's, was a little formal for the middle of the night. He wore a snow-white dress shirt, set off by the black braces that held up his sharply pressed trousers.

He stepped between Adam and the vampire, the same way Adam had put himself between me and her. The big man looked from Adam to me, his face unhappy. When he spoke, the Irish in his voice was riding high—both in temper and sharp lilt. "Who the hell are you?"

Adam had been rude, maybe. But the stranger's attitude was gauged to raise the tension in the room by a bit—especially since he directed his ire at me. There was going to be violence in a few seconds if someone didn't try to calm the waters.

But I was *tired*.

"Who the hell are *you*?" I snapped in return.

His blue eyes shot to my face with every evidence of surprise, which cut short his anger. The female vampire's voice was frosty as she said to me, "Who wants to know?"

I opened my mouth to respond to both of them, when I realized that Adam wasn't acting as if an aggressive man had just tried to start a fight. My mate hadn't taken his eyes off the female vampire. He didn't even look at the Irishman. Adam never ignored a threat.

For a second I worried that the vampire might have caught him in her gaze, but Adam knew better than to let himself be trapped so easily.

I replayed the last few moments in my head and almost groaned. We didn't have a second vampire. We had a ghost.

"You can hear me," the dead man said, his voice dropping to a purr. He paced forward, ignoring Adam and the woman, all of his attention on me—as if he were a lion and I was a gazelle who'd just thrown herself in his path.

Even now when I had proof positive, he didn't *feel* like a ghost.

The clothes that he wore should have clued me in right away because they weren't modern. They'd just blended so well with the theme of the reception room, period correct down to the handmade shoes, that I hadn't taken note of them.

I'd always been able to see ghosts. I knew about them. Knew the difference between the repeaters—the poor remnants caught in emotionally fraught moments that they repeat endlessly—and the sentient ones. I could tell the difference between a ghost that was a fading record of the person they had been and one whose soul was trapped beyond death. A few times I'd seen ghosts that were so real-looking they could almost pass as living. This man was different.

Or maybe, I thought, a chill climbing down my spine, I was.

I hadn't seen one of the *real*-seeming ones since the Soul Taker had ripped my mind open—except for Aubrey. Aubrey had been lifelike, too; but he'd been as influenced by the Soul Taker in his own way as I was. This ghost was a lot more like Aubrey had been than he was like any other ghost I'd seen. Maybe this was what one of those real ghosts looked like to my new awareness.

I was scared down to my bones, but not of the ghost.

"Mercy?" Adam asked without turning his head from the vampire, whom he perceived as the greatest threat in the room.

The vampire . . . *she* was looking at me with interest bordering on hunger.

And that was another weird thing. Ghosts, like cats and certain other sensitive creatures, avoid vampires to the extent that I can sometimes tell there is a vampire in the room because there are no spirits at all.

"You can hear him," she whispered. "See him."

Adam took a step back until I rested against his body. He gave the sort of grunt that told me he understood that there might be a second threat. One he couldn't see. I patted him to let him know that a ghost wasn't a threat. Or at least I didn't think a ghost could be a threat to me.

I didn't answer the vampire.

"She can, can't she?" The Irish lilt was lighter when the ghost wasn't angry. The dead man rocked back with a broad grin. "Hello, doll," he said to me. "Aren't you an interesting find, then?"

He was wearing a shoulder holster with a big pistol. A 1911, I thought, though I couldn't pick out the make other than it was different from the 1911 model Adam carried as his backup. The ghost hadn't been wearing a gun when he'd come through the doors, but ghosts could be changeable like that.

The vampire glanced toward the Irishman, looking a little high and to the right of him. She couldn't see him. She took a deep breath—vampires didn't have to breathe except to talk, but most of them are pretty good at maintaining the illusion.

She looked at Adam, tried to meet his eyes, I think. But Adam moved his head, tipping it so she was in his peripheral vision, making it harder for her to capture him—if that was her intention. My mate seldom made unforced errors.

Finally, she turned to me.

She pursed her lips. "I think it is time for introductions. I am Elyna Gray."

"O'Malley," said the ghost with a frown.

Her lips quirked up. "O'Malley."

She couldn't see him, but she could hear him. I thought about the last few minutes and changed that to she could hear him some of the time.

"But I go by Gray," she continued. "I live—my home is in Chicago. I'm here because my good friend's daughter is supposed to be getting married this weekend. Travel is complicated for people like me—vampires—so I came early, just in case."

"Jack O'Malley," said the ghost, extending his hand to me with a challenge in his eyes. "Also from Chicago."

"Mercy Hauptman," I said.

I stepped around Adam so I could take Jack's hand. It felt real, solid and warm—and a breath later it felt like nothing, though I could still see it. Disconcerted, I let my hand drop back down to my side, rubbing my fingers together to let the feel of his flesh dissipate.

"Jack O'Malley, Elyna"—I dispensed with the last name issue by dropping hers entirely—"my husband, Adam Hauptman."

"Hauptman?" Elyna said with a faint frown. "I didn't see your names on the guest list."

"We're not attending the wedding," I told her.

Adam made no effort to join in the conversation except for a faint nod of acknowledgment when I'd introduced him. Because I could deal with both of them, vampire and ghost, while Adam could see only her, he would play backup. Adam didn't say that was what he was doing—but I knew my husband.

Jack bent to his wife. I didn't see his lips move, but Elyna nodded. "He says you feel like Gary Johnson, the caretaker of the ranch up the canyon."

Johnson? I thought. *Really, Gary. You couldn't have come up with something better?*

"My brother," I said.

"Is there a reason you're here rather than at the ranch with him?" she asked.

"Yes," I told her. "He's not there. The rig he drives is gone, and I'm worried about him. We were hoping there might be people here who know more about what's going on."

Honest answer. It wasn't my fault she—they—would get a few false impressions from that.

Something skittered behind me, and I glanced over my shoulder. It was only a big house spider running across the tiled floor.

I returned my attention to Elyna—but that spider had been in a frantic hurry.

"Gary was supposed to bring down the sleigh today for a dress rehearsal, but he didn't make it," Elyna was saying in a determined effort to pretend Adam wasn't still treating her like the enemy. "Jack was pretty sure it was the weather. The landlines are out—"

I should have been listening. Spiders, the ones I was familiar with, didn't hunt down their prey like a coyote did. They waited for prey to come to them. That spider wasn't hunting anything. It hadn't been a predatory run; it had been a get-out-of-Dodge run.

I turned to see what the spider had been running from. I half expected to see nothing, having hesitated long enough for anything of the insect variety to have disappeared from sight. Maybe it was something as simple as a hotel cat or, in this lobby, a falcon, though I trusted it wouldn't be a Maltese.

But it was there, all right—the thing the small spider had run from. It was a bigger spider, a much, *much* bigger spider. I felt the quietness that overtook the others as, alerted by my sudden tension, they, too, saw the spider.

The last time I'd seen her, this spider had been on the tree at Uncle Mike's.

A thimble wasn't a big thing, but a spider with a body the size of a thimble was a very big spider. She wasn't as large as some tarantulas I'd seen—there's a kind of tarantula in South America that's so big its legs could hang over a dinner plate. But tarantulas weren't metallic silver, either.

In a strange way, like the ghost, she fit with the decor of the room. The metallic silver and the spider shape was exactly the sort of combination that looked so Art Deco in design that I wouldn't have been surprised to see it echoed in the vase that held the peacock feathers.

"That's not a normal spider," Elyna said.

The spider made a leisurely, if intent, trek along the same path the other—the *harmless* spider—had taken. She appeared to take no notice of us. But I knew that wasn't true. I had to look at my arms to make sure that there was no silvery spider silk sliding across my skin.

Adam shifted his weight, and I put a hand on his arm to keep him where he was. I didn't think trying to squish the spider or throwing her out into the storm was going to be a good move. It took maybe twenty long seconds for her to find the crack between flooring and wall where the first spider had sought refuge. It didn't look as though there was going to be room for her to follow it.

"Does this have anything to do with the Soul Taker?" Adam asked. "The spider-fae?"

My feet itched with the memory of the bits and pieces of the fae spider-thing that had served the Soul Taker and its absent god.

I shook my head. "No."

The silver spider didn't feel like something fae. She felt like something that belonged here in a way the fae did not.

When I spoke, the spider turned around to face us, face *me*.

"What the *fuck* is that?" asked Jack O'Malley, sounding freaked-out. "What's she doing to me?"

I had to fight to make myself look away from the spider so I could see the ghost.

The whites of Jack's eyes were showing as he shook his head, staring down at his arms. His hands were simply gone—and as I watched, the pale forearms, corded with muscle, grew less solid.

Feeding, the spider told me.

INTERLUDE

GARY LAUGHINGDOG
(JOHNSON)

GARY SAT UP ABRUPTLY, KNOCKING A PIECE OF PAPER onto the ground. He was in a strange bedroom, on an unfamiliar bed. His head ached and he could hear a murmured conversation from a room on the other side of the closed bedroom door.

It sounded like Honey—and someone vaguely familiar. They were being quiet. He caught the words "sheriff" and "stupid."

He got slowly to his feet. He understood what he was hearing. He had *recognized* Honey's voice. He even identified the other voice. It belonged to the firefighter in Mercy's pack. Mary Lou. Mary Jane. Something like that.

He was *free*.

He started for the door, and paper scrunched under his bare foot. He bent to pick it up.

You did pretty good. But I decided to have Mercy finish this up instead of you. She's at the hot springs now. Communi-

cation of any kind is not possible. Don't try to return to Montana. There's a BIG STORM just now. You might know something about why that is.

Instead of a signature, someone had drawn a little coyote. Gary crumpled the paper into a ball and threw it at the wall.

8

~~~

MERCY

I WASN'T SURE I HAD *ACTUALLY* HEARD THE SPIDER'S voice—a warm, amused feminine voice that quivered a little around the edges, as if the speaker were elderly. I could have just imagined it—though it wasn't the type of voice I'd expect such a creature to have.

Just now it didn't matter. Real or imagined, the "feeding" part was accurate. I could see it as soon as I *looked*.

"Jack?" Elyna sounded worried. "What's wrong?"

"Mercy?" Adam asked.

"The spider," I said absently, trying to understand what I was *seeing*. "It's not really a spider—not only a spider. I think it's feeding on Jack."

Elyna pulled off her shoe, but when she tried to approach the spider, she ran into some sort of a barricade. When she threw the shoe instead, it hit the spider with a crack, like a baseball hitting the side of a barn, then rolled to the side. The spider appeared unharmed.

And amused. I didn't want to know how I knew that.

I raised a hand. "Hold off. I don't think you can do anything to her that way. I might—" I lost track of what I was saying.

Jack was a ghost—and a disturbingly strong one at that. He wasn't a friend, or even an acquaintance. Maybe if the spider consumed him, it wouldn't be a bad thing compared to the damage a strong ghost could cause.

But my instincts told me it was wrong, and I was in the habit of listening to my instincts.

Afterward . . . afterward I wondered why I knew what I had to do in order to understand what the spider was doing. And why I thought that I had to understand it before I could stop it. But that was later.

I'd spent the better part of the last two months trying to shut down the way the Soul Taker had ripped open my senses. Yes, I sensed things in a way I never had before. But that raw knowledge, that *seeing* into people without them or me having any say over what I saw—that intrusive, overwhelming ability had disappeared when Zee destroyed the Soul Taker.

Mostly. The quick glimpses into people—like the way I'd seen forests in Uncle Mike's gaze—were nothing compared to the overwhelming comprehension the Soul Taker had given me before it was destroyed.

At that moment, I knew, *knew* that the only way to save Jack was to see the world as the Soul Taker had forced me to see it.

Opening that extraordinary, abominable sight felt like peeling bandages off and opening wounds that were raw and oozing. Festering. I exposed the changed part of my mind that the Soul Taker had made and forced it back into the light.

I was very careful not to look at Elyna, and I tried to only observe the stuff Jack was made of—energy and magic and soul. I told myself I didn't notice the events of his life and what kind of person he had been when he was alive.

I tried not to see the bonds of spirit and soul that entwined him with the vampire. When I failed at that, I tried not to get lost in the sudden understanding of how her vampiric nature allowed him to hover so near to being alive, not a vampire but held by the necromancy that kept vampires walking when they should be corpses.

There was no time for that, and it was knowledge I should not have.

Dangerous knowledge, agreed the spider, sounding intrigued.

What I was doing was reckless, dangerous. My mind wasn't built to hold this much, to understand this much. If it lasted too long, I didn't know if I would die or turn into someone—something—not me.

"Mercy." Adam's voice was a growl, and it centered me.

I focused on the strands between Jack and the spider, but those didn't tell me enough. I had to examine the way the spider was feeding, and my choice was to see too much of Jack—who he was and how he was made—or to see too much of the spider. Reading the spider with my mind open like this struck me as a good way to get lost.

Jack was covered in fine silver threads that encircled him and wove around him like a lovingly knit sweater. The spider silk concentrated around the ends of his arms, and the bright magic made me want to close my eyes against the power of it. Instead, I stepped closer to Jack and reached out to touch the threads.

My head ached with the amount of information pouring into me, from my eyes and my fingers and my skin. Most of the information didn't matter; I needed to know how the spider was feeding from him so I could see how she could be made to stop.

I couldn't prevent her snacking on him by manipulating the web, but there was a chance I could do something else. It was the only option I could find. Knowledge acquired; it was time to stop *seeing*.

That proved easier said than done. I fought to reseal the Soul Taker's rips in my mind, but it was harder to close those paths than it had been to tear them open. I flailed, drowning in the river of enlightenment.

My mouth tasted of copper and salt—and then I was safe, my feet on the ground and my mind my own. I stared into my mate's golden eyes and all that I saw was him, the taste of blood on my tongue.

I thought for a moment that I'd bitten my tongue or something and the pain had brought me back. The blood in my mouth tasted like pain. Then I saw that Adam's mouth was bloody, too, and there was a fresh wound healing on his forearm.

He'd bitten himself and pressed his mouth to mine. Blood strengthens bonds, and he'd used his to give me the power to save myself from the Soul Taker's cursed gift. Adam was the most loving person I'd ever met, though sometimes his love language was painful to everyone involved. I'd learned that I had to be brave to love him.

Worth it.

He stepped back, and turned me to face the fading ghost. I hadn't been lost in the flood of understanding for long, I thought. The spider had only consumed a few more inches of his extremities. But when I looked into Jack's face, I saw that his awareness, his sharp fear, was fading, too—his bright blue eyes were dulling.

"Jack," I said urgently. He looked at me, but I couldn't tell if he really saw me. This wouldn't work if he didn't help.

"*Jack O'Malley*," I said, stealing all the dominance I could from Adam. My voice carried an Alpha's authority and my own power over the dead.

The demand hit the ghost and he swayed, lifting one of his arms in a futile effort to touch me. There was so little of him left.

I had understood what I needed to do just a second ago. But while I wasn't paying attention, that knowledge had drifted away like a half-remembered dream. I couldn't tell Jack how to save himself because I couldn't remember.

Memory. Ghosts are like a memory, I thought, and in that moment, I understood exactly why that was. Then the understanding left me, but I didn't need to know why.

When we see a ghost, pay attention to it, it becomes more attached to our world, my brother had once told me. His next words, if I remembered them correctly, had been, *So don't do that.*

"I see you," I told Jack, focusing on him, trying to capture his eyes as if I were a vampire instead of a . . . whatever I was.

"Rory," Elyna said urgently. "His name is Jack Rory O'Malley."

Names are important—the fae won't reveal their true names, and change them as often as they can. Names have power. Names *remember.*

How was it that Peter Pan saved Tinker Bell? It wasn't the

children clapping their hands—although they had. *Peter Pan* was a story. Fiction. A lie. But stories are powerful lies because they are true in a way that real life isn't.

"I *see* you, Jack Rory O'Malley," I said.

Peter Pan had saved Tinker Bell with belief.

"Jack Rory O'Malley." This time I said Jack's name with authority, knowing with absolute certainty that Jack stood before me now. In that moment, I believed that he was real.

The spider couldn't feed upon him if he was real.

I wasn't expecting the crack of sound, like a blown fuse, or the sudden flash as all the lightbulbs in the big chandelier over my head, all the lightbulbs in the reception room, the little connected office, and at least some of the ones in the hall lit up.

For just a moment, the moment it took for the lights to remember that there was no electricity to power them—for that instant, when the little reception room was lit up as bright as day, Jack O'Malley was visible to everyone, whole and complete, and as real and solid as flesh and blood and life. I could hear the thump of his heart.

Adam stiffened.

Elyna cried, "*Jack?*"

She reached for him, but before she could touch him, the lights went out and her hands passed through him.

"Jack?" This time Elyna's voice was nearly a whisper.

There was a soft sound that did not originate from anyone in the room. It might have been a laugh. It might have been "Good girl." I looked, but I didn't see the spider.

"Is he gone?" Adam had his command face on, and that told me he didn't know what to think, either. At some point he'd cleaned off his lips. The wound on his arm had healed, though his skin was still stained with blood. "Is Jack gone?" he clarified, directing the question at me.

"No."

Jack was trying to comfort Elyna, though he could not touch her and she could not hear him. But I wasn't worried about him just now.

"Did you see where the spider went?" I asked.

Adam helped me look. The room wasn't big, but then neither was the spider, by comparison. We started at opposite ends and searched thoroughly. I noticed that Adam had quit treating Elyna as an enemy. I thought it was probably due to her obvious distress over Jack. My husband was a romantic at heart. He was still keeping an eye on her, still alert, but not wary.

"If it's here, we're not going to find it," Adam said, moving the couch back to its original position.

I crouched so I could look under the end table. There was a wad of bubble gum, but no silver spiders. I flopped down on my butt.

"Oh, it's still here," I said direly.

Beside me, the chair creaked as Elyna sat on it with the grace of someone who'd grown up in an era when women only wore dresses, knees and ankles together. She rubbed her hands before putting them on her thighs to still them.

She was uncomfortably close. I turned to face her and shoved myself back a couple of feet in the process.

"Mercy," the vampire said. Then she looked away from me and blinked rapidly. Tears, I thought. But it could have been some other emotion.

"I don't have any photos," she said in a small voice, still turning her face away from me as if there was something fascinating about the wreath on the door. "The ones I'd had . . . before . . . were gone. I haven't seen my husband's face since . . . for nearly a century." She looked at me then, and I couldn't read the expression on her face at all. "Since the day I killed him, in fact."

There was nothing I could say to that.

"I am a monster, after all," she said. "We are all of us monsters in this room, I think." She pointed at Adam. "Werewolf," she said. She pointed at herself. "Vampire." She made a whirling "somewhere" gesture and said, "Ghost." She pointed at me and waited.

"*Not* a werewolf, vampire, or ghost." I didn't owe her my identity, and too often others' ignorance of who and what I was had saved the day. Instead, I gave her a part of the truth, the part she already had. "Psychopomp sometimes."

She looked blank. That was okay. It was a weird word.

"I have a knack with ghosts," I clarified.

"Okay," Elyna said after a moment that she used to tell me she knew I wasn't giving her the whole truth. "Okay. That spider—"

"*That* was not a spider," said Jack with emphasis.

I'd been looking everywhere but at him. I'd spent the last ten minutes searching for a spider I knew we weren't going to find and trying to figure out what to do about Jack. More specifically, what to do about whatever I'd done to him. I worried about it. He didn't feel the same as he had before the spider—or whatever she was—had tried eating him. He felt more solid, grounded.

There was a path dead souls were supposed to follow when they left the realm of the living. I always knew where that path was; I could feel it in the same way I knew where the sun would rise each morning. I didn't like any of the words I'd been given for it. "Heaven" felt too small, "the light" too vague.

Jack wasn't going *there*, whatever I called it, not without more help than I could provide. He felt—permanent.

I, on the other hand, felt as though I had been manipulated into doing that to him. I didn't know why it was important for Jack to be trapped here, neither alive nor quite dead anymore, but I was pretty sure I was following the spider's script.

"Not a spider." Elyna corrected herself because she'd heard Jack, not because she'd read my mind.

Jack had been able to make her hear him before this. Sometimes. I was afraid it would take him a lot less effort now.

"Not a spider," I agreed. "Or not one of the usual ones."

"You seemed to know something about it," she said.

Adam looked at me, too. I shrugged and decided I didn't want to have a conversation while I was sitting on the floor. I got up and noticed there was a wet Mercy-butt spot on the polished surface. I was tired of running around in wet clothes.

"I've only seen that spider once before," I told them. "Yesterday." I glanced at the clock on the wall in the office and watched the second hand tick past midnight. "Day before yesterday now."

Adam's eyes narrowed. "You didn't say anything about a spider."

"It was at Uncle Mike's," I said. "Uncle Mike had a Christmas tree"—outside of a fae-dominated bar I could call a spade a spade and a Christmas tree a Christmas tree—"that had spiders spinning tinsel-like strands. Lots of little golden spiders, and the one silver one. I didn't tell you about it because it was at Uncle Mike's."

"Lots of strange creatures at Uncle Mike's," agreed Adam. "You are sure it doesn't have anything to do with the Soul Taker?"

I shrugged again. Instead of telling Adam that my newly acquired weird senses didn't think the spider tasted like the Soul Taker or its god, as I might have if we'd been alone, I said, with equal truth, "Uncle Mike hustled me away from the tree. If he thought the spider had something to do with the Soul Taker, he'd have said."

"And he'd have known," Adam agreed.

"Uncle Mike?" asked Elyna.

"The fae who runs our local fae bar. He's someone who knows things," I told her. Then to Adam I said, "The spider did seem to take an interest in me. Maybe it was because of our recent supernatural spider encounters? Or maybe she was bored and thought I was interesting."

"So did she follow you here?" Elyna asked. "Or did she hitch a ride? Where did you drive here from?"

"I don't know," I said. Surely I'd have felt it, if she had been in the SUV with us. But I couldn't be certain. I didn't know which was worse: that I hadn't been aware of her presence in the confined space, or that she could somehow transport herself to where I was.

Adam answered the other part of the vampire's question. "The Tri-Cities in Washington State."

Elyna nodded. "Is she going to attack Jack again?"

I shook my head. "I have no idea. I don't know what she is. Absolutely no idea."

"What *did* you do to me?" asked Jack.

I looked at him reluctantly. Even when I hadn't been looking at him, he'd felt real. Now I could see things I hadn't noticed before. His blue eyes had a dark gray ring around the pupil. He smelled of something familiar. After a moment, I identified it as ink. There were faint black smudges on his fingers. Ballpoint pens had come into common usage in World War II, I remembered. Before that, it had been all fountain pens.

"Were you a journalist?" I asked.

He frowned at me. "Architect."

"Architect," Elyna answered, too.

"What did you do to me?" he asked again.

"What does it feel like I did?" I asked.

He opened his mouth, shut it again. Finally, he said, "I don't know." He walked to the window between the reception room and the office and knocked a pen onto the floor. "That was a lot easier."

"I can't see you, Jack," Elyna said. "But I can hear you more clearly."

She hadn't heard everything he said, though.

"Will it last?" Jack looked as though the answer mattered to him very much. I could see why it would.

"I don't know," I told him honestly. "Usually I try not to make the ghosts I see stronger than they already are."

He grinned at me, a charming, boyish expression—but he was still wearing that gun. As soon as I noticed it, I could smell the gun oil.

"I can understand that," he said. "Encouraging ghosts doesn't make for restful sleep." Then he sobered. "If they knew what you can do, they'd never leave you alone."

"No," I said. "If they—*if you*—knew what I can do, you'd all stay far away from me."

I usually tried not to think about the night in Prague when I'd destroyed all the ghosts, using the power of that destruction for my own purposes. It still made me sick.

He looked at me a moment. "Wow. Okay. I'll keep it in mind, then."

Abruptly, there were only three of us in the room.

"He left," I told the other two, then yawned, one of those jaw-cracking, inescapable yawns. "Is there any chance I could get to sleep sometime before the sun rises?"

Adam held up his purloined key. "Ms. Gray, we should head to bed."

"Good night, then, Mr. and Mrs. Haupt—" She stopped mid-word. Frowned. "Hauptman. Tri-Cities, Washington. Werewolf. You're them. Adam and Mercedes Hauptman."

"Yes," Adam agreed.

She whistled softly. "You are the Hauptmans the Lord of Night has taken such interest in."

"Bonarata," I said, and watched her flinch just a little. I wondered if she thought he'd appear if I said his name three times.

Maybe he would.

"What did you do to enrage him?" she asked me. "Your husband and pack he wants dead—he offers substantial rewards to the vampire who manages to kill any of them. But you, Ms. Hauptman, you he wants alive. Any vampire who harms you will regret the day they were made. He has made it clear he wants you for himself."

"Do you intend to try for Bonarata's reward?" I asked without answering her question. It was a long story, and I didn't feel like sharing it. It was also the second time I'd said his name out loud.

She smiled. "To the extent of not harming *you*, yes." She looked at Adam and shook her head. "I highly doubt Bonarata knows I exist, and I'd love to keep it that way."

The third time his name had been spoken here tonight, and he hadn't shown up or called. Maybe that was because my cell phone wasn't working.

Elyna paused. "In point of fact, I owe you quite a lot. Jack is—" Her voice cracked. "Jack is necessary to me."

She gave a short nod, as if to herself, then she spoke briskly. "You are looking for your brother. I will help you in any way I can. If you fear that he is lost in the woods, I can help look. The winter holds no fear for me. Vampires can freeze"—her face tightened just a bit, but her voice continued on pleasantly—"but we are rather like goldfish and will thaw without many issues. I am strong and I see very well in the dark. I can also find heat signatures"—her lips quirked up—"rather like a mosquito."

"Thank you," I said warily.

"You saved my husband," she told me. "Without him . . ." She chose not to finish that sentence.

"Would you be willing to talk to us about the other people trapped at the resort with us?" Adam asked.

"The lodge," she said. "It's not really up to resort standards yet, is it? The entryway and some of the rooms, yes, but not the whole building. Everyone calls it the lodge—especially the people who work here."

The people at the gas station had called it a resort. But I had to agree that "lodge" fit the building better.

"But you don't expect someone here is involved with your brother's disappearance, do you?" Elyna went on. "Most of us are just here for the wedding."

I looked at Adam. For all we knew, Elyna was the one who'd taken the harp.

"Elyna Gray," Adam said, "from Chicago."

She looked surprised and a little wary. "Yes?"

Maybe no one else would have been able to tell, but I could see Adam relax.

"I've heard stories about you, Ms. Gray," Adam said. "You killed the Mistress who made you—and she was an old and powerful vampire. Then instead of taking over the seethe, you chose to move to Chicago and live as a lone vampire. When the Master of Chicago objected, you killed him, too. The new Master treats you with care and leaves you alone."

She let out a burst of ugly laughter, and for a second there was nothing human about her face. She recovered quickly. "That makes me sound like a total badass, doesn't it?"

"Yes," I said honestly.

Her mouth twisted bitterly. "I killed my Mistress and left the seethe because I lacked the power to hold it. They would have killed me in a day. I fled to Chicago. It had been my home, and it is a big city. The Master who ruled there kept a small seethe, and I thought I could stay hidden from him. I was wrong. I didn't kill him, at least I didn't kill him by myself. But he died *because* of me. The new Master is grateful for the old one's death. And it is a gratitude that has no fear of me—he knows just how powerful I am *not* in the world of the *nosferatu*. I live by his grace as long as I cause no trouble."

Adam looked at me. His face told me that he thought it would be handy to have the vampire as backup. He thought we could trust her. Maybe he knew more about her than what he'd said. But Gary was my brother; this was my call.

I considered her. "Have you stolen or rightfully recovered an object from anyone in the past week?"

She blinked at me. "I begin to think that your quest is more interesting than I expected. No, Ms. Hauptman, I have not taken anything from anyone in the past week. Not as a gift. Not as an unwilling gift. I have stolen nothing this week, nor have I recovered property belonging to me—or anyone else. Is that good enough?" She gave me a sudden grin. "If you have a mystery, I want in. Our wedding preparations, never intended to be elaborate because there were fewer than thirty guests invited, have been halted because of the storm. The power is out, so I can only use my laptop sparingly, and when I do, there is no Internet. This evening's events aside, I have found myself as bored as I've ever been in my somewhat-longer-than-usual life."

Adam asked, "Is there somewhere we could talk where we won't be overheard?"

"By someone who might have very good hearing," I said. Because if we were dealing with a stolen fae artifact, there was a good chance that the thief might have better than average hearing. Supernatural hearing.

Elyna's grin turned triumphant. "Yes. I know of just the place."

ELYNA BROUGHT US THROUGH THE HEART OF THE lodge and out the far door. We forged through less-deep snow on a covered walkway, woefully inadequate for the current weather, that led to a cluster of small, picturesque buildings at the edge of the steaming lake. There were more of the strings of Christmas lights that decorated the entrance of the resort, as well as faux-Victorian streetlamps, none of which were lit.

Elegant signs, gold on black, noted the use of each smallish building—changing rooms, showers, storage. Snow covered the sides and tops of the buildings, and I glanced back at the lodge's roof. Hard to judge from my angle, but it looked to me like the snowpack there was nearing a foot despite the steep slope of the roof.

Snow had weight. I wondered if someone was planning on getting up there to clear it or if the building would collapse before the storm was over.

Adam saw me looking—and raised an eyebrow when he examined the roof, too. "Lot of snow up there," he said. "Someone should clear it before it collapses."

"The lodge is nearly as old as I am," said Elyna unconcernedly. "We've both survived a lot of winters."

At the end of the path was a taller-than-me stone wall with a heavy rustic door that looked so forbidding that I was a little surprised when it opened easily.

Beyond the door, cobblestone pavement stretched from the wall to the side of the lake, half of it covered by a roof, the other open to the sky. Along the edge of the lake were five soaking tubs, and to either side of them were soaking pools built into the side of the lake with what looked like native stone. Steam rose from the lake, the tubs, and the cobblestones as the heat of the lake met the frost giant's storm.

Against the back wall under the roof were a series of hooks that held fluffy white robes. Elyna walked past those and flipped a switch—and soft moody music accompanied the trickling sound of water. If we talked quietly, even sharp ears wouldn't be able to hear us.

"I thought the power was out," I said.

"Everything out here is part of the system that pumps the water into the pools and the resort to heat both," Elyna said. "That pump is integral to keeping the place habitable, so it's part of the infrastructure supported by the generators."

She laughed at my expression. "Jack is . . . *was* an architect. He is fascinated by this place. He can't ask questions, so I have to."

Still under the roof, if only barely, was a propane fireplace surrounded by benches. Elyna lit the fireplace, brushed the accumulated snow off a bench, and sat down. Adam and I were wearing coats and boots—Elyna was still in her light shirt and trousers. Cold bothered vampires even less than it bothered werewolves.

Adam brushed the snow off the bench next to her, sat down, and lifted his arm for me to sit beside him, because even the fireplace and the heated floor could not fend off the bitter wind.

We'd dropped off our luggage in the room Adam had chosen, but I hadn't taken time to change. In the warmth of the lodge, I'd forgotten my clothes were damp. I remembered as soon as we stepped out into the snow. I appreciated the windbreak.

"It's supposed to be haunted, you know," said Elyna in a thoughtful voice, her eyes past my shoulder.

I didn't look behind me. I knew what the old building looked like—and I knew it was haunted.

"Jack doesn't talk about such things," she said. "I don't know . . . how much of him is still left. It occurs to me that I am talking to someone who might know."

She pinned me with her eyes. It wasn't a vampiric power—it was raw need.

I closed my eyes against her question, then opened them. She had the right to ask.

"Ethically, I'm in uncharted territory," I said, and Adam's arm tightened over my shoulders. His coat was well insulated, so it was just pressure, not warmth. It still felt good.

"I have guesses," I told her, "but they are only guesses. I don't know if I helped either of you tonight. Furthermore, I'm not sure telling you what I think is going to—" Make you happier. Add to your peace. Make anything better. "—be useful."

"I *saw* him tonight," she said. "I've lived with him—with him as a ghost—for nearly a decade."

I cleared my throat. "He's been dead longer than a decade."

Her mouth tightened unhappily. "Closer to a century. But I didn't find him again until about a decade ago." She paused. "When I returned home."

I nodded.

"I can hear him sometimes, sometimes not," she continued. "He has opinions and he's saved me. More than once. But we don't converse. He seldom touches me, and I can't touch him at all. I read him books."

She stopped speaking, and tears welled up in her eyes, spilling down her cheeks.

"I've read all the books about ghosts," she said.

"Most of them are garbage," I told her. "But I don't know which ones."

She gave me an unhappy smile. "I understand you aren't certain of what you know. But I need to know this is really Jack." She looked around.

"He's not here," I told her.

She wiped her eyes. "I murdered my husband, Ms. Hauptman. And I need to know that he's forgiven me. That he is capable of forgiving me."

"Oh," I said. "That. I have seen ghosts my whole life. I used to think I knew about them. Now I think I don't know *any* of the important things."

All around us, the formless wisps of white that might have

once been ghosts blended in with the fog off the lake and the blowing snow. There were dozens, if not hundreds, of them. They didn't approach us, though. Something, the vampire's presence maybe, kept them at bay. I tried not to notice them, dropping my eyes to my boots. We were sheltered from the wind and snow, but my toes were cold again.

"One thing I've been *almost* sure of is that a person's soul is not meant to linger here after the body is gone," I said. "It's bad for the dead person—and it is harmful for the living."

Elyna had quit breathing and leaned forward, the firelight reflecting in her eyes.

"Most ghosts are just a lingering impression," I told her. "It still can act like the original, but it is not the person who died, any more than a photograph or a video is. And that's right and proper. I've seen what happens when the soul is trapped in its ghost, and I worked really hard to stop the—" *Vampire*, I almost said, but I thought that might lead to a digression. Frost had been a monster even among monsters. "—the creature doing that. It was an abomination." I didn't know how to explain the *wrongness* I'd felt about what Frost had done. One of his victims had been a friend of mine.

"Jack—" I fumbled as I tried to express something I sensed, something I didn't entirely trust, in a way that would do the least harm. "His soul is trapped."

Elyna's face closed down, though that had been the answer she'd hoped for before I started talking. "I see."

"Here's where it gets unclear," I said.

"Woo-woo," murmured Adam with more humor than the situation called for.

"Well, yes," I snapped. "I am going by instinct. Jack doesn't feel like an abomination. He doesn't feel *wrong* in the same way that other ghosts with souls have felt to me." For whatever that meant. "But his soul is still stuck, and I'm very much afraid I made that permanent tonight."

She sucked in a breath and looked away. "Ah. So, he's really here?"

"Yes."

"And it is bad for him." She stared at the row of white robes on the back wall. "Is this something I have done to him? Called him back with my need and trapped him here?"

I shrugged uncomfortably. "I don't have those answers."

When I'd been trying to help Jack with the spider, I'd understood why that was—how something about the necromancy that kept Elyna up and moving affected what Jack was.

"Spilt milk," said Adam briskly. "He is here. You can't change it. Make the best of it and move forward."

The icy wind blew through my jacket and I shivered, tucking myself closer to Adam. The fire was pretty, but it was too small and too far away to provide any warmth.

Elyna wiped her eyes and kept her face covered for a moment before she brought her hands down to her lap and straightened her back. "Thank you," she said.

"Be careful what you ask for," I offered.

"No," she said. "Information is good. Speaking of which, you wanted to know about the people trapped here in the storm."

"That's right," Adam said, accepting her change of subject.

"And you want to know about something someone stole? Something that you think might have some bearing on why Gary Johnson isn't up at the ranch where he should be."

I was keeping my chin tucked in my coat so I couldn't see Adam's face, but I heard the smile in his voice. "That's right, too."

"Maybe," she said, "if you tell me more about your mystery, I will be more use to you."

Fair enough.

"My brother has been cursed," I told her. "Because of the nature of the curse, he can't communicate. He showed up at our house yesterday. We came here looking for a way to help him. But before we can do that, we need to find an artifact—you know what those are?"

Not everyone did. There were a lot more fae in the Tri-Cities than there were most places in the US. Artifacts were mostly a fae thing.

"An artifact?" she said. "Like a fae artifact?"

"Yep," I said, my voice wavering with the chattering of my teeth. "Well, not fae, I don't think. But an object bound with magic." I thought of the deal we'd made. "If we don't find it, the being who is causing this storm isn't going to let anyone leave here alive."

Silence—except for the howl of the wind—hung in the air.

"There is no reason for you to freeze while we talk," Elyna said. "Let's go soak in the hot water."

I glanced at Adam. He'd been treating Elyna like an ally since he'd matched her to a vampire whose story he had heard. I didn't know if that would make him willing to share a hot tub with her. It sounded like a good idea to me. Except for the "stripping naked in subzero temperatures in a snowstorm" part.

Elyna didn't wait for us to agree. She stood up and removed her clothing.

When Adam stood up, I knew we'd be doing it, too. I was a

shapeshifter—nakedness didn't bother me. All of my reluctance was temperature-based.

Adam frowned at me. "Are your clothes still wet, Mercy?"

There was a bite in his voice that I ignored.

"What happens after we are all toasty and have to get up and run for cover?" I asked, fumbling with the zipper of my coat.

"You can run pretty fast," Adam said. "I noticed that when I was courting you."

His words were teasing, but his mouth was tight as he brushed aside my hands, which were being pretty fumbly. Sitting out here talking had made me colder than I had realized. My jeans wanted to cling—and Adam ripped them down both outside seams.

"Hey," I protested, stepping out of the pile of rags that used to be my pants. "You werewolves might destroy clothes on a daily basis because they get in your way, but I've had those jeans for years. They have good pockets."

I expected him to make some quip like the ones I'd made when he'd ripped his own jeans.

Instead, he said, "You need to warm up, and they were in the way of that." He picked me up and pulled my boots off. One sock came off with the boot, but the other one stayed on.

His voice was biting when he said, "Before God, Mercy. Were you going to wait until your toes fell off?"

I took a good look at my bare foot. "That's not—"

I was still wearing my T-shirt, bra, underwear, and one sock when he strode to one of the steaming tubs and dropped me in. When my cold extremities hit the hot water, I made a sound I wasn't proud of and instinctively tried to hop out. He put his hands on my shoulders and kept me there. Only when I quit struggling did he start to take off his own clothes so he could climb in, too.

"—not frostbite." I completed my sentence once my brain was functioning past the pain. "Which is good, because you aren't supposed to stick frostbitten toes in boiling water."

My toes ached all the way up to my knees, and I bounced my legs, trying to defer the familiar pain of flesh warming up to normal temperature, while I struggled to remove the last of my wet clothing with fingers that burned from the sudden warm-up. The utter agony of the process told me that Adam's diagnosis of frostbite hadn't been that far off.

He was right to be angry. I'd been stupid. I knew better than to stay wet in this kind of cold. I wasn't a werewolf or vampire, and I couldn't judge my endurance by theirs.

He should have been angry *at me*—but he wasn't. He was angry at himself. I'd scared Adam. He counted on me to take care of myself, to draw boundaries with him and the pack so neither of them put me in a situation I couldn't handle.

The hot tub Adam had chosen could have fit maybe eight people comfortably, more if they were good friends. It had enough space that we three predators could share it for a time. Elyna had climbed into the far side sometime when I wasn't paying attention. Adam climbed in next to me.

"You," he said, "warm up a bit while I tell our new friend what we're doing here."

I sank lower in the water, closed my eyes, and drifted for a moment. The ache of my feet and hands subsided as Adam's voice rumbled beside me.

Elyna's voice got a little shrill now and then. She knew what frost giants were, but not that they weren't figments of Norse mythology. It is always an uncomfortable adjustment when the rules of the world get rewritten over the course of a conversation. But Elyna's problems weren't mine.

When he finished speaking, we all soaked for a little more and listened to the hissing as the storm met the waters of the lake.

"There's a piano here," Elyna said, "and one of the staff members has a guitar she's learning to play. But I haven't heard any harp music. Do you know what it looks like?"

"He said we'd know it when we saw it," I offered. "Silver with blue gemstone inlay. Not crystallized stone, but turquoise shaped to fit. A pair of wolves on the ends of the arms—or yoke."

I had a sudden thought and sat up a little straighter before ducking back down to keep my shoulders in the water. "He called it a harp. But now that I think about his description, it sounds more like a lyre"—I made a yoke shape with my hands and then a straight horizontal line across the imaginary top—"than a harp." I swooped my hands in the graceful fall a harp makes as the strings vary from the deep-toned long strings to the shorter, higher-pitched ones.

"A woman's face at the base," Adam added, "with gemstone eyes."

"I'll ask Jack," she said. "He's not . . . reliable about things like that. But it would be stupid not to put in a request."

"Tell us about the people trapped here with us," Adam said.

ABOUT TWENTY MINUTES LATER, WRAPPED IN THE BIG fluffy robes and carrying our wet and frozen clothes, including the rags left of my jeans, Adam and I made our way back to our room.

Adam had chosen one on the corner of the first floor. It had windows on the north and the west walls, and shared only one wall with another room—and that room was empty. The windows were original to the lodge, which meant that the room was a little breezy, though the hot spring–fed radiator had no trouble keeping it plenty warm.

Adam had brought a flashlight, but with two sets of windows, the room was light enough for us to see. A human would have had trouble, though, between the storm and the night.

After the elegance of the reception room and hallways, the room felt distinctly utilitarian. With spare, beautifully made furniture, its tribute to Art Deco style leaned harder on the Great Depression side of 1929 than the flapper era that had preceded it.

A thick, dark green quilt folded on the foot of the bed contrasted with the white chenille bedspread, setting the color scheme in the room. The end tables and the headboard were genuine antiques, while the mattress and the chest of drawers were new. I was not an antiques expert, but anyone with a nose as good as mine could tell the difference between antique and modern. Age carries a much more complex scent.

I dropped my clothes on the floor, stripped off the robe, and dropped it, too. Then rethought that. I kicked the robe off the wet clothes. It took me two kicks. I would have crawled right into bed if Adam hadn't caught me and dragged me into the bathroom, which was lit by his flashlight on the floor.

"You'll thank me tomorrow when you, I, and the bed don't all stink like sulfur," he assured me, grinning when I growled at him.

"Why aren't you tired?" I snipped at him as he shoved—I mean, urged—me into the large shower stall.

"I am," he said, turning the hot water on both of us. "What I don't have is a killer headache from saving ghosts from mytho-logical spiders."

I shot him a look. "I haven't complained."

He gave me a smile. "That's how I know it's bad. Turn around."

When I turned, the water beat down on my back. It was very hot—only a few degrees cooler than the hot springs had been. It felt wonderful, and warmed up the parts of me that had refrozen in our dash from the hot tub to our room.

I rested my throbbing head on Adam's shoulder, and he pressed his fingers against the back of my neck, working the knots out.

"I am, at this moment, really, really glad you abandoned all of your duties to come with me," I announced. "Just so you could—Eep!" I couldn't stop the yelp as he hit a knot just under my shoulder blade. "Right there."

The stiffness left my whole body, and I sagged against him in relief. He laughed—a low, soft sound that made me want to purr. Eventually he said, "Can you stand on your own for a minute?"

I did, and he soaped himself up with such brisk efficiency that I found it sacrilegious and told him so. He smiled when I reached out and touched his chest and let my hand drift down his belly.

"Careful," he cautioned. But he didn't mean it.

Both of us were too tired for that to lead anywhere. But the feel of his skin under my fingers soothed the restless worry of all the problems I didn't know how to solve: My brother. Me.

My fingers were less sensitive than usual, wrinkled from all the water exposure. I examined them and said, "That was a bucket list item I never thought I'd satisfy."

"Which item was that?" Adam asked as he grabbed a small hotel bottle of something and opened it.

A strong mint scent battled with the sulfur of the hot springs and won. He dumped some on his hands, rubbed them together, and then he rubbed them on me. The small bar of soap was sufficient for his skin, but apparently not for mine.

"I think that's conditioner," I told him as my skin grew slick but not soapy.

The flashlight yielded plenty of illumination to take a shower with. But it was angled wrong for reading labels.

He grunted. "What bucket list item, Mercy?" His voice was a low growl, but I figured it was because of where my hands were, and not because he was unhappy about my bucket list or impatient with me.

I lost it, pulling my hands away to avoid damaging anything important as I found myself laughing helplessly. "What a day—and a night. Jeez, Adam."

"Bucket list?" He sounded serious, but I could tell he wanted to laugh, too. He put my hands back where they had been.

"Sitting naked with you and a vampire in a hot tub. Of course, I thought it would be Stefan—or, because our lives have been very strange lately, maybe even Bonarata. But Elyna was an acceptable substitute."

He released my hair from its braids, working it free with gentle fingers. "Kinky of you. If that bottle is conditioner, this one must be shampoo, right?"

INTERLUDE

Last November

A Desert Somewhere in the American West

THERE WAS A WHOLE LOT OF NOTHING FOR MILES IN all directions. No, that was a little bit of an exaggeration, Tracy LaBella thought, getting out of her bright green Maserati SUV and stepping into sand that immediately tried to swallow her five-inch stiletto heels. Tried.

The ground wallowed in hillocks as small as her SUV and as large as a mountain, providing homes for small creatures in its meager plant life. Tough creatures survived—thrived, even—in this barren landscape. Tracy respected tough.

The dwelling—calling it a hut would have been insulting to . . . one or the other of them—blended in with the landscape so well that someone less observant might have driven right by it. As she got closer, she noticed the fit of the untreated, age-grayed wood was surprisingly tight in this hot, dry climate. The temperatures here sucked the moisture out of most wood, shrinking it in the first years so that gaps should have formed. There should have been repairs for that, and there weren't. This building had been here a long time. The wind and sand had scored the surface, but it was largely unchanged from the day it had been built. Assuming, of course, it had been built.

Her own home, her first and oldest home, had been hatched.

The porch in front, covered to provide shelter from the sun, was larger than the whole of the building. She stepped onto it to knock at the door.

A rough piece of wood moved and an eye appeared briefly before the wood returned to its place. Nothing happened.

Tracy knocked again. "Grandmother, grandmother, grandmother."

"That rot doesn't work with me," an amused voice answered her. "I'm not fae. And to that end—I don't speak with liars."

Tracy contemplated that. Heaved a sigh. "Really?"

Silence answered her.

She shrugged. "Very well."

Dropping her magic and her illusions, Baba Yaga dusted off her heavy skirt and snapped the steel of her teeth together a couple of times because she enjoyed the sound.

The door opened, and a wizened old woman with Native American coloring and features came out, a tray with two cups of hot tea in chipped mugs in her hands. One mug read *Proud Parent of a Valedictorian at Morris Middle School*. The other one read *#1 Witch*. The old woman crossed the porch and walked around the side where a small table and a pair of cheap metal chairs awaited.

They seated themselves, and the old woman handed Baba

Yaga the cup that read *#1 Witch* and took the other for herself with a contented sigh.

"What brings you here?" the old woman asked.

"A mutual friend who now owes me a favor."

The old woman smiled, and the wrinkles in her face deepened. "Oh, that scoundrel," she murmured. "Better that you don't collect favors from him. They don't turn out quite the way you expect."

"He says that you've been bored. He said, 'Perhaps she might consider decorating a fae tavern for the season. The green man who runs it has agreed—and something interesting might drop in her web.'"

"Well, now," said the old woman.

9

~

MERCY

I AWOKE TO A FINGER DRIFTING OVER MY CHEEK. AC-
cording to my inner clock, it was early morning—still dark this
time of year. I smiled at the gentle touch and pressed my face
into it.

But both of Adam's arms were wrapped securely around my
waist, holding me against his chest.

The hand on my cheek was icy.

Adam's hands, like his body, were usually a few degrees
warmer than a human's would have been.

I opened my eyes and there was a stranger's face not an inch
from mine. If he hadn't been dead, I'd have been breathing his air,
he was that close. Panic held me frozen as he lowered his face and
pressed his chill, *hungry* lips to mine.

I don't know how a hungry ghost is made. There are stories,
but they are told by the survivors, people trying to explain the
inexplicable.

Gary once told me a tale he had heard from an old man at a pub in Yorkshire. A ship had capsized and the crew escaped on a boat. They drifted, lost at sea, for a very long time. After the food and water were gone, they ate each other—the last one starving to death.

Eventually, the boat washed ashore at a small fishing village. The ghosts of the sailors had nearly consumed the whole town before some bright person burned the boat and buried the ashes in holy ground. Hungry ghosts are dangerous.

Other ghosts could and would feed from the living. Once, when I'd been rendered defenseless, I'd had a ghost feed on me without consent. But hungry ghosts are different. They kill their victims.

Some kill in a single feeding, but others drain their prey for weeks or months before they die. Having fed once from a particular person, a hungry ghost can follow that person across oceans and continents. They don't stop until their chosen quarry is dead.

Fortunately, they are rare. I'd only encountered a few of them, and they usually left me alone. I wasn't food for them; my natural shields kept them out.

This one frightened me because he'd caught me asleep. That was all. I didn't get scared by ghosts just because they touched me.

All I needed to do was move or push it away. But somehow, I couldn't. It wasn't panic holding me still—it was the ghost. But that was impossible. I was *immune* to them.

His lips grew warm as gooseflesh rose on my skin. He wasn't stealing body heat, but the theft of spiritual energy chilled me to the bone as it warmed him.

I thought of what I'd done to myself last night to save Jack. I'd ripped off the hard-won bandages protecting me from what the

Soul Taker had done. But I hadn't needed to do that, had I? It had seemed necessary at the time, but when I had a chance to look back on it, what I had done for Jack I could have done without all the drama.

Vulnerable, Zee had called me in my kitchen. I'd chosen to believe Adam's pack-magic kiss had fixed what I'd done, brought me back to where I'd been before I'd been stupid.

Demonstratively not, if I couldn't send this ghost packing.

Frustrated in my efforts to move, I thought maybe I could wake Adam up. He was a light sleeper. If I could so much as tense a muscle or change my breathing, he'd wake up.

But I *couldn't* move. Maybe I could reach Adam through our bond—I stopped that thought before it went any further. I wasn't absolutely certain that wouldn't give the ghost a way to attack Adam through me. And if I couldn't defend myself, when ghosts were my bailiwick, I didn't know what Adam could do against it.

If I didn't figure out something pretty freaking quick, I was going to die.

What did you expect to happen, with you displayed like a lantern in the night, a picnic for any passerby? asked an impatient voice. She was a dozen words in before I realized I wasn't actually hearing her with my ears.

One of Coyote's get makes a rare meal for a spirit eater, she chided. *That poor starveling likely traveled miles to feast upon you.*

I couldn't see her. I couldn't blink or shift the direction of my gaze away from the dead man's predatory eyes. But I recognized that voice.

Change, child, the spider told me in the tones of a disappointed teacher dealing with a willfully dim pupil. *They can't feed upon animals.*

I had changed into a coyote before I could crawl. It was as basic to me as breathing. I couldn't hold my breath or twitch a finger, but when I tried to shift, the familiar zip of magic shot through me.

The ghost jerked away from me with a hoarse cry that sounded more like a flutter of dry bones than any sound a human might make. I squirmed out of Adam's hold and hit the floor, putting more distance between me and the ghost, which was flailing soundlessly on the floor as if the brief contact with my coyote self had been damaging. The dead usually had no physical presence, but a brass lamp on a table about ten feet from where the ghost held his solo struggle fell to the ground with a loud clatter.

Adam didn't move.

That meant he was held as I had been. Helpless.

The thing writhing on the ground didn't look dangerous anymore, but I put myself between Adam and the ghost anyway.

Now that he wasn't touching me, I could get a good look at him. He was all bones and rags, a gray and off-white mass on the Persian carpet, smaller than he'd felt when he'd been feeding, barely recognizable as human.

The damage he'd suffered trying to feed from a coyote lessened after maybe thirty seconds. For a moment he lay motionless, then he rolled to hands and knees and looked at me.

I felt a buzz of my magic and I saw him, not the ghost but the man he'd been before he'd become this monster.

I'd expected him to be Native because the land we were on had been occupied by Indigenous people, by my people, for a long time before the white settlers had come. But now, even in the dark room, I could tell that his hair had been several shades lighter than mine was. His features were Anglo, with a narrow chin and a prominent nose that had been broken at some point. His body was so thin that although he was clothed in the flesh he'd worn in life, I could see both the radius and ulna bones between his wrist and elbow.

The Cabinet Mountain Range was a dangerous and difficult area to try to survive in. There was a reason that it had still been largely uninhabited when it was made a protected wilderness in the middle of the twentieth century. Starvation was only one of the weapons the great mountains had used to kill interlopers.

I blinked, and the man the ghost had been vanished, with only the monster left behind. And then it, too, disappeared, because ghosts don't need to move like real people.

I knew what that thing wanted. I was moving before the ghost reappeared on top of Adam. One hand gripped my mate's bare shoulder, and the other caressed his cheek as the ghost kissed Adam's lips.

I vaulted onto the bed and opened my jaws to grab the back of the ghost's neck and wrest him away—my instincts working before my brain reminded me that he was probably not something that tooth and claw could affect. My teeth sank into *some-thing* that was not flesh. But because ghosts are *not* limited to moving like normal creatures, something caught me under my ribs. My teeth couldn't hold on as the blow propelled me across the room until I hit the chest of drawers with enough force to rock it back on the wall with a crack.

I rolled to my feet and bolted back to Adam.

The second time the ghost threw me, I hit the wall next to the bathroom.

I am curious why you are running around unprotected, like an invitation to any spirit-predator you happen by, the spider said.

I ignored her. Magic spiders talking in my head were something for future me to worry about. Right *now*, I had to save Adam. But her words broke the mindless frenzy that would have had me throwing myself at the ghost now feeding from Adam in earnest.

My previous actions hadn't worked. I had to try something different.

Panting, more from terror than exertion, I stared at the thing killing my husband in front of my nose—and a flash of silver caught my eye as the spider descended down a line of tinsel-thick spider silk to land on the back of the ghost's neck, just where I'd been attempting to seize it.

In return for answers, I will give you a gift, the spider told me.

I couldn't tell what she did, but the ghost fell away from Adam, curled up into a fetal ball, then melted into a pile of stinking, unidentifiable goo.

Adam exploded out of the bed. He stood naked, breathing hard, his wary attention on the bed. I couldn't tell if he was staring at what was left of the ghost or at the silver spider picking her way out of the wet mass and into the folds of the bedclothes.

Pretty man, said the spider with approval as she hid herself in the white chenille. As soon as I could no longer see her, her presence was gone from my head.

I shifted back into my human shape and hurled myself at Adam. I had almost had to watch while he was eaten by a ghost.

"Oh God," I whispered in his ear as his arms closed around me with fiercely tempered strength. "Oh God, Oh God, thank you, God." It was prayer. Unfinished, but I trusted it was still heard, as honest gratitude should be. "I thought he was going to kill you. Are you okay, Adam?"

His arms hurt the forming bruises on my back and made it a little hard to breathe. I was grateful for the pain. It meant we were both alive. And it gave me an excuse for the tears staining my cheeks.

I had almost lost him, because one of my few magics had failed me when I most needed it. Because I'd been stupid.

"I'm okay." His voice shook a little, not with fear—he didn't smell like fear. It was adrenaline fueled by frustrated rage. Pressed against him, I felt his stillness when he noticed my tears. Softer, he said, "I am okay, Mercy."

I kissed him then. The kind of kiss required when your mate tries to die on you. Desperate didn't cover it.

"What was that thing?" he asked eventually, after my heart admitted he was safe, so I wasn't clinging quite so tightly. "I take it you *are* sure it's not going to get back up and try again?"

"No," I told him. "It's gone."

He set me on my feet and went to check the body anyway.

A ghost's body, I supposed. It was certainly organic from the smell. I'd never encountered a ghost who left behind physical remains. Maybe a hungry ghost was more like a zombie.

I watched as Adam prodded it with an umbrella that had been hanging near the door for guests' convenience in warmer weather. The unhealthy grayish mass seemed to have the consistency of Jell-O. It wiggled a bit before the end of the umbrella pierced its surface. It didn't move on its own, but he did succeed in making it smell worse.

The spider had told me the hungry ghost had been attracted

by my presence—called by the damage the Soul Taker had done, like a shark summoned by blood in the water. I had to figure out how to fix myself.

Once Adam had made certain the thing wasn't going to rise again, we coped with our fears in our various ways. I told him about hungry ghosts in a babble of information that helped me calm the freak down. I would have told him about the spider, but he decided he needed to explain why I should have escaped and left him to deal with it as soon as I'd realized my ghost-mojo was broken.

That went well for him, with me still on edge from the utter terror of understanding I could do nothing while a ghost ate my husband, a ghost I should have been able to drive away except that a stupid ancient artifact decided to play around in my head.

Adam and I didn't fight very often. He didn't enjoy being mad at me, so mostly I tried to resist the temptation. I couldn't say why it was such a turn-on or why it made me feel safe when he was angry. Perversity, probably—it was my besetting sin, after all. Sometimes you just had to accept who you were and move on.

Eventually I made him laugh by calling him a word I'd learned from the pack's foul-mouthed British import. By that time, both of us were done fighting.

"I haven't heard that one before," he said. "Are you sure Ben didn't make it up?"

"*Urban Dictionary* says not," I assured him, and he laughed again.

"What does it mean?" he asked.

I bit his neck lightly and said, "Allow me to demonstrate."

"You don't have to nudge me twice," he growled. And when I bit his neck again, he added, "But you can if you want to."

By mutual unstated agreement we avoided the bed with its reeking mass of goo and made love on the floor.

Sex with Adam is never boring and seldom follows the same path. This time it had the give-and-take of a good conversation. I was never quite sure where the discussion was going, but we visited some interesting places. Sometimes our path covered emotional territory, sometimes we got a bit heated. In the end, we had a genuine exchange of views, to our mutual satisfaction.

Not even the sting of my elbow where it had hit something at some point in the proceedings put a dent in the joy that was my body. He'd started out on the bottom to keep my elbows safe.

"The floor's hard," he'd said. "Any bruises I get will heal up quick."

That had lasted for a bit, but my elbow and both knees attested that sometimes passion and good sense have only a passing acquaintance. We'd ended up back where we started, though I was pretty sure I was way more comfortable than he was. Adam's hard body only made a good bed if I was relaxed enough to achieve near bonelessness, which I was.

"I've got to get up," I told Adam's chest reluctantly. "Now that you aren't quite so distracting . . . that smell."

His quiet laugh bounced me up and down. "Rank," he agreed.

The remnants of the ghost reeked like a skunk ten days dead on hot pavement—considerably worse than it had originally smelled. If we left it in here much longer, the room would be uninhabitable.

I got up and examined the problem. Coagulating on the bedding was a gelatinous mound roughly the mass of a large watermelon, with what looked like a few bone fragments in it. A grayish stain that might have had green overtones in better light spread around the remains where the bedding had absorbed liquid.

"I don't think that a washing machine is going to clean that bedspread," I said. "The obvious answer is to chuck the whole mess outside where it can freeze."

But when I tried to open them, the windows proved to be old, fragile, and frozen shut.

"How did you stop it?" Adam asked.

"It wasn't me," I told him. "It was that silver spider."

He'd been heading over to help me with the window, but stopped at my words.

"I thought the spider was an enemy," Adam said cautiously. "Why did it save us?"

That's right. We'd gotten into a fight before I could tell him what I knew about the spider.

"I'm not sure," I said. "She told me to change to coyote when it had me. Apparently, it is an obligate human predator. Foiled, it went for you. When I couldn't stop it, the spider informed me that I was to repay her efforts with information and then dropped down on the hungry ghost and turned it into goo."

"You bargained with her?" asked Adam, and not in the tones of someone admiring their spouse's intelligence.

"The spider isn't fae," I said. "She didn't wait for my consent, just made an assumptive close like a pushy salesperson."

I shoved again at the window—which remained stubbornly in place.

"Are you going to keep staring at my butt or help me with this window?" I had no idea where he was looking, but I was done arguing with him for the day. Distracting him from the (hopefully harmless) bargain I'd made seemed like a good idea. "I can't get enough force at the right angle, and if I keep going, I'm going to break it. Which seems stupid given there's a blizzard going on outside."

He patted my bare butt with an appreciative hand and a huff of a laugh. "Let me get the bedding bundled up and ready to go. That way we don't have to leave the window open so long."

Thanks to a waterproof cover, the mattress had escaped being destroyed, but the bedspread and the pretty quilt were toast. In a few quick moves he had everything in a neat bundle, the goo on the inside and the waterproof cover clean-side out. He set that on the floor and had the window open in a couple of wiggles and a crack that worried me.

"It's just the ice," he told me. "Nothing broke, but I have to hold this up. Can you—"

I grabbed the bundle of bedding and dropped it into the snow outside.

"What about the umbrella?" I asked.

"Chuck it."

I did.

With the remains of the dead thing outside and the window closed again, the room smelled a lot better. It would be a while before it was pleasant again, though. The radiator rattled in an effort to bring the temperature back up.

"I didn't think ghosts left a rotting corpse behind," Adam said.

"Me, either," I told him. "First time for me. I was able to bite it—sort of—when it was feeding off you."

As soon as I said it, I felt my gorge rise, though there was no lingering taste in my mouth. But. Ugh. "Excuse me while I brush my teeth."

I returned from the bathroom and contemplated the bare mattress.

"It's still dark out," I said. "But it feels like morning. Are we getting up?"

"It's seven thirty or thereabouts," Adam agreed. "Six thirty our time. We might as well get dressed."

We'd had about five hours of sleep. I could function on five hours, but I wasn't going to be happy about it. Adam was a machine. If he needed to, he could go days without sleep. That didn't have much to do with being a werewolf—werewolves need sleep like anyone else. It had to do with being Adam.

I dressed in my only clean clothes. I hadn't packed with the idea of getting snowed in. With the power out, I thought it was unlikely that the lodge would have a functioning laundry. I picked up yesterday's wet clothes, rinsed them off, and hung them up to dry on the towel racks, the shower rod, and a couple of chair backs. There was no saving my jeans, so I tossed the remnants into the inadequate garbage can in the bathroom.

Adam had put on his clothes and taken a seat on the mattress. He watched me with a thoughtful expression. Drat. I'd given him time to think. I smoothed out my socks so they would dry without wrinkles—something I cared nothing about.

"We should check in with the pack," I said, and hearing my own words I was suddenly concerned with doing just that. "Let them know we made it here and see how my brother is."

"We can't call out," Adam said. "My sat phone isn't finding reception."

I stared at him. "I thought those things picked up signal in Antarctica."

"I suspect that something is interfering," he said. "The storm—"

"Or the frost giant," I said. "We're stuck in the dark until we make it out of here."

"Yes." My mate looked thoughtfully at me. "And that was a good distraction—or would be if I didn't know you better."

I frowned at him, and his eyes warmed. "All right, Mercy, what don't you want to tell me?"

I bounced on the bed next to him and put my head on his shoulder. "You're going to make me talk." I sighed.

"Yes," he said.

I heaved another sigh. "That ghost shouldn't have given me any trouble. It shouldn't have been able to trap me. I shouldn't have needed someone else to destroy it."

Adam kissed the top of my head and let the silence continue, because he was good at interrogations.

"I don't think it belonged here at the lodge," I told him. "The spider said the hungry ghost sensed me and traveled here to enjoy a meal. Apparently, something the Soul Taker did made me a good snack for hungry ghosts and probably other things that feed that way." I paused. "I'm pretty sure that I didn't help matters when I fixed Jack."

Adam's muscles were tense against me. "Whatever the Soul Taker did to you, it's not getting better," he said. It wasn't a question.

I shrugged. "Comes and goes, mostly."

"How often do you have a headache?"

Busted. I shrugged. "Nothing too bad."

"Mercy."

"I think I need to go look for help," I said.

"Good," he said. "Where?"

"That's the eighty-four-thousand-dollar question," I said. "And that's the reason I haven't looked for help before this."

"Sixty-four," he corrected.

"Inflation," I offered. More seriously, I said, "There's Sherwood."

Adam shook his head. "I asked him. He says he can tell there's something wrong with your magic, but it's deeper than that. He is afraid that if he tries to mess with it, he'll only make it worse for you."

I lifted my head so I could see his face. "You've been going behind my back?"

"You weren't doing anything about it," he said without shame or remorse. "We've all been worried."

When I attempted a fierce stare, he said dryly, "You'd have done the same thing for me."

"Fair enough," I had to admit, resettling myself until I was lying next to him, my head on his thigh. My head did hurt, and the warmth of his body was soothing. "I assume you've talked to Zee?"

"He's been looking since October," Adam said. "He told me he has something he is pursuing, but he has that sour expression when he talks about it. I don't think we should count on Zee pulling your fat out of the fire."

"Well," I said after a minute, "there's my brother. But any help he can give is stuck in the world of 'There's a Hole in My Bucket' territory. We need to fix him before he can help. And to fix him we have to find the harp that looks like a lyre."

Neither of us mentioned my father. But both of us thought about it. Coyote's methods of fixing something were terrifying.

"I think I smell food cooking," I said. "And, dear Liza, the sooner we get out and meet these people, the sooner we can find the artifact and get my brother free."

Adam took a deep breath and said, "I suppose we go look for some straw, then, dear Henry." He hummed a few bars of the song as we headed out.

THE RECEPTION DESK WAS STILL UNMANNED, AND Adam's half-written note was undisturbed. Adam popped into the office to finish writing the note and added an addendum about the bedding and umbrella we'd destroyed. He didn't say what had happened to them.

When he was finished, we followed the scent of breakfast down the long hall to the opposite side of the hotel. We walked by a wall of smoked glass that protected a speakeasy-style room with a dozen small tables and two large ones. A sign proclaimed that The Gunner's Moll was closed for the season.

According to Elyna, Looking Glass Hot Springs closed down on Labor Day weekend and reopened on Memorial Day. The restaurant was a separate business that was open for the regular season. The resort opened in December every year on a limited basis for weddings.

During December, the hotel staff cooked breakfast and made sack lunches for guests. The guests were encouraged to take themselves off to one of the local communities for dinner—or hire a caterer or chef who could use the kitchen facilities. The groom's family had planned on bringing their own cook, but like most of the party, he had been scheduled to arrive yesterday.

We passed the door leading outside to the hot tub area and

took a left through a short corridor and into a dining hall still
(according to the signage) awaiting renovations.

The plank pine floor had seen better days, and there were water stains on the dropped ceiling tiles. Five out of the eight fluo-
rescent light fixtures worked—and those were better suited to my
garage than a hostelry of any kind. But the music piped into the
room—presumably generator powered, because the kitchen
was—came from a decent sound system. Elyna had told us the
lodge had fuel enough to keep the generators going for a couple
of weeks. I hoped that we could resolve the cause of the storm
before the fuel supply was put to the test.

The room might be ugly, but it was big. The three sizable
round tables looked a little lost. Efforts had been made to brighten
them up with white lace tablecloths and small bouquets of fresh
flowers—Elyna had mentioned a greenhouse. The flowers and
lace were completely outmatched by the general seedy air of the
room.

Last night, Elyna had divided the people here into groups: the
bride's party, the groom's party, random refugees from the storm,
and the lodge staff. Around the tables, the lodge guests had organized themselves in much the same way, probably for different
reasons.

*"There are thirteen people here now, not including you, me,
or Jack," Elyna had told us.*

Seventeen people. Four of us were definitely not hiding the
frost giant's artifact, which left thirteen. Thirteen didn't feel like
an unreasonable number of suspects. I'd suggested that maybe my
brother, acting alone, had hidden the harp somewhere, and that
was still a possibility. But it wasn't likely.

Artifacts are difficult to hide. The warm water in the horse barn told me that my brother had tricks I didn't know, but hiding an artifact was another level. Artifacts hummed with magic. Werewolves might not be able to hunt them down, but anyone with an ounce of fae blood could.

"We could just ask if they've stolen a lyre," I'd suggested to Elyna and Adam last night, sticking my feet out of the tub to cool off, because the water was a little too warm to keep every part of me in it all of the time. "And make them give it back."

"You'll run into trouble with that," Elyna said.

"She isn't serious," Adam told her. "We need the lyre back, not broken or thrown into the lake as a sacrifice or tribute."

He'd accepted that we were looking for a lyre rather than a harp. I wondered why an ancient, presumably knowledgeable being hadn't known what to call his own artifact. I wondered if it would turn out to be significant. Still, a silver stringed musical instrument with a face carved on it should be easy to identify whether it was a harp or a lyre.

"We're getting off track," said Elyna. "Let me tell you about the people trapped here with us." She eyed me. "Maybe it would be best to keep your questions for the end."

Adam waved a hand in invitation.

"The largest group," she said, "even if you don't count Jack and me, is the bride's party. We arrived before the storm got so bad. The bride, Tammy Vanderstaat, is in her midtwenties. She has a master's in social work and is employed by a nonprofit."

Standing in the dining hall now, it was easy to pick out the bride's party. They occupied the table farthest from where Adam and I stood. The bride definitely drew my eye first—and I wasn't sure why. She wasn't beautiful, but her face was full of character, lit from within. She had more muscle than I was used to seeing on someone who wasn't a shapeshifter. Maybe she was into martial arts or gymnastics or something.

"The other members of the bride's party are her father, Peter, and four of his crew—all Chicago police officers who moonlight in remodeling." Elyna had stopped there, then said, "I've known all of them for nearly a decade. They've never been to Montana before. We arrived here the day before the artifact was stolen, but I judge it highly unlikely that any of them are involved."

"Artifacts can make people do very strange things." I answered her from a wealth of unwanted experience.

Elyna's eyelids lowered, and there was a growl I had not heard before in her voice. Not quite a threat, but nearly there. "They are mine, these men. I will protect them."

That was why they had traveled to the lodge before the rest of the wedding party, missing the storm. Elyna had to come early because travel was complicated for vampires. Feeding along the way would be dangerous. Feeding at an isolated place in Montana in the winter would be very dangerous. Vampires need to feed often. Most of the ones powerful enough to live on their own find it more convenient to have a pool of humans who are regular donors: sheep.

"Understood," Adam said easily. He knew vampires as well as I did. "We are here to get the artifact back, not to hurt anyone."

Even without Tammy among them, I could have picked out the table of police officers. Not because I was so good at picking out policemen or vampire donors. And not even because it was the largest group seated in the dining room. It was because I could spot a pack at a hundred yards.

All of the laughing faces were turned toward their Alpha. The father of the bride, Peter Vanderstaat, I assumed, because he looked like Tammy. And also because when Elyna had spoken of him, she had done so with affectionate respect—and she hadn't named the other men. It might have been because she didn't care about them, but I thought it was to protect them from us. They were hers. But she hadn't felt the same need to protect Peter. Or his daughter. She considered them her equals.

The second table held only two people, a man and a woman. Both of them bore a clear resemblance to each other in features and coloring, though her build was slight while his was heavier. He was dark haired and dark eyed. Her face was turned away, so I couldn't see her eyes, but her hair was dark and, even braided, reached down past her hips.

"Then there are the refugees," Elyna said. "They came here yesterday—no. It is after midnight. That means they came here the day before yesterday."

The day my brother arrived at our house.

"I haven't met them. I am a writer with odd hours." It was said so airily I couldn't tell if she really was a writer or if she used it as an excuse for not appearing in daylight. "They are hikers who go to bed early and, presumably, rise early, too. Victoria and Able Morgan, Peter told me, brother and sister. Midtwenties— about Tammy's age."

"What were they doing out here?" I asked, levering myself up on the edge of the tub for a while because, even after nearly freezing my feet earlier, I was now too hot.

"They were hiking." She smiled at me. Neither she nor Adam had had to get in and out of the hot tub. I used my toe to splash some water in her direction.

She said, "I know, that's what I thought, too."

So her smile hadn't been because I wasn't as tough as she and Adam were, but because my face had shown what I thought about human people hiking for fun in the Cabinets in the middle of the winter. When I was growing up, not too far from here, my foster father had been part of a group of volunteers that went out to find people who had gone hiking in the winter. Once in a while they found them when they were still alive.

"Still think, actually," she said. "I might be a city girl, but I know stupid ideas when I hear them. Peter tells me they are experienced winter hikers who have done winter hikes in Alaska, Northern California, and even, once, the Swiss Alps. This is the first time they've been here. The sudden cold snap that preceded the storm caught them unawares, and when they saw the lights— we had lights then—they decided it was smarter to take shelter for a few days and resume their hike when the weather subsides. Peter says they keep to themselves. Jack says he can't get into their room."

"Is that unusual?" Adam asked her.

Elyna shrugged. "He sounded like it was."

"Curiouser and curiouser," I said, sliding back into the tub until the water hit the bottom of my chin and wishing my head didn't hurt. "What about the groom's people?"

"Zane's not here," Elyna said. "He was supposed to be on a plane landing in Missoula. But that wasn't looking good last I heard."

"Zane is the groom?" Adam asked.

Elyna nodded. "I haven't met him, but Peter likes him—and after decades in the CPD, Peter's instincts are pretty good. The only members of Zane's party here are his parents." She grimaced. "His parents—"

"*The billionaires?*" *I said sympathetically.*

She looked at me, eyebrows raised.

"*The gas station attendant in Libby said it was a billionaire's wedding.*"

She laughed. "I don't know about billionaire, but rich, yes. The family owns Heddar's."

"*The grocery store chain?*" *Adam asked.*

She nodded again. "And has controlling interest in two other chain stores I know about. Andrew and Dylis Heddar. Andrew's grandfather started the grocery chain. Andrew's father turned it into a national business concern, and Andrew, the biggest shark of all, has taken it international. They are not happy that their only child has chosen to marry a social worker from Chicago. Not happy at all. At least, Andrew isn't pleased, and his wife . . . Peter says that she feels however her husband tells her to feel. She was an heiress of some sort, I think. Her family money was what allowed Andrew to expand."

"*Are they trying to stop it?*" *I asked.*

Elyna shrugged. "Peter says there's nothing they can do. Zane has his own money, inherited from his grandfather. He runs the company's charitable arm—that's how he and Tammy met. But he doesn't need to work."

At the table nearest to Adam and me, an elegantly clothed woman, presumably Dylis Heddar, pushed around her food—an egg white omelet—without enthusiasm. The man sitting next to her, his arm possessively on the back of her chair, conversed with a teenage girl who had a serving tray on her hip. The girl was Native, like me—nothing unusual in that, given where the lodge was located.

I found my eyes returning to Dylis Heddar. Elyna had dismissed Zane's mother as a society woman who happened to be married to a dangerous man. The vampire had sounded both pitying and dismissive. But my instincts warned me to keep my eyes on Dylis—the nonentity wife rather than her business-shark husband—as if she were the more dangerous of the two.

Dylis was racehorse thin, with sharp cheekbones and skin as white as the snow outside. Her hair was white, too. Long and fine, it was caught up in a simple twist at the nape of her neck. She wore makeup, but it was subtle stuff. Her husband, Andrew, looked like he should be on a horse out on the range. He was tall and had a mobile face, given to sudden changes of expression. I was close enough to see that his eyes were clear blue.

One of the abilities I'd been born with was that I could usually tell what kind of magic a person held.

Mr. and Mrs. Heddar carried fae blood. He wasn't even half-blood, though without the assist of the Soul Taker's tinkering—which seemed to be in abeyance just now—I didn't entirely trust that assessment. Dylis . . . Dylis felt different. She was fae, full-blooded, even. But there was something wrong with her magic.

The teenage server tried to take a step away from Heddar. He caught her wrist. It was just for an instant, long enough for her to stop trying to leave. When she quit, Heddar released her. Beside me, Adam tensed.

The girl moved her tray so that it was between her and the older man. She had a tight smile on her face, while her whole body told anyone with eyes she was very, very uncomfortable. I couldn't hear what was being said over the music. Which was, I suppose, the point of having music. I recognized the girl from Elyna's description as one of the three staff members; I assumed that the other two were in the kitchen.

Of her, Elyna had said:

"Emily's responsible for cleaning rooms and whatever they need her for. She usually stays at the lodge for her workweek when there is a room available, going home to Libby on her days off. She works here summers and during school breaks and has since she was fourteen or fifteen. She's seventeen now, will graduate from high school this year, and has been accepted to college at Montana State with scholarships. Pre-med."

There was a sound out in the lake, and Elyna paused to stare into the mist before going back to her description. "Peter says she's another quiet one. People like him, though, and he got her talking."

Andrew Heddar knew he was making the girl uncomfortable and was enjoying it. I would have disliked him even without Elyna's distaste.

"I know who I hope has the artifact," I told Adam.

"He needs to leave the children alone," Adam said. "Pick on someone his own size."

I'd spoken very quietly, but Adam's voice was louder than necessary, deliberately pitched to carry over the music. Everyone became aware of us at the same time.

This one's for you, brother mine, I thought, taking a deep breath. *Showtime.*

"Who the hell are you?" asked Heddar, all the affable charm gone.

We were the center of everyone's attention.

Except for Emily. As soon as Heddar was distracted, she made for the kitchens as fast as she could without actually running. I couldn't tell if she was taking her moment to escape unwanted attention—or if she was going to get help. Maybe both.

At the far table, Peter rose to his feet in a measured movement that spoke to his training. He kept everyone else in his pack—his group, since they weren't werewolves—seated with a short gesture of his left hand. He didn't move quickly, but he pushed the chair out of his way in case he had to move. Standing, he wasn't tall, but that didn't matter. He owned the ground he stood upon in a way that reminded me of Adam.

I was pretty sure Elyna's police officer friend was carrying a weapon from the way his right hand strayed a little farther back along his side than was natural. But his real power was in his shrewd, cool eyes and his trained calm. I had no doubt that he was, outside of my husband, the most dominant person in the room.

The hiker pair, Victoria and Able, moved at the same time as Peter stood. Their movement was more subtle. If I hadn't been on high alert, I might not have noticed how the woman, Victoria, turned so she had a better view of Peter, or maybe Peter's table—though I knew which way I'd vote on that. While she did that, her brother turned more fully toward Adam and me.

At the table nearest us, Dylis Heddar surged to her feet, accompanied by the crash of her chair.

"I know you," she declared, her glassy eyes fixed on my husband. "I know who you are." Her voice was soft, but it cracked on the beginnings of the words and sometimes in between. She sounded like a drug addict, pushing through lethargy with something that seemed like panic—or a very bad actor in a mid-century horror movie that probably featured a guy in a rubber monster costume. Her eyes were an even lighter shade of blue than her husband's, but equally unusual.

Heddar's expression sharpened. I could see he was still offended by Adam's words but was rapidly rethinking his initial reaction. His peripheral vision must have been terrific, because he didn't look over when he grabbed his wife's arm with an unkind hand.

"Enough, Dylis." To Adam he said, "I asked you. Who are you?"

Heddar had tried to assume control of the room and failed. I was pretty sure that at least some of his irritation with his wife was because she was holding the room's attention without appearing to seek it. And his second attempt wasn't doing any better than his first.

Dylis jerked her arm in an unsuccessful attempt to free herself. Like her voice, her movement was off, a little convulsive and awkward, the most effort put into the motion at the least efficient time.

"No," she said breathlessly, still struggling. "No. He's here to get it. The thing I hear in the walls. He's here to save us all."

"Dylis," Heddar said sharply, his voice louder than the situation called for. "Stop."

None of the other people in the room looked surprised at her outburst. At Peter's table, Tammy Vanderstaat started to get up, her face concerned with a hint of anger ascending, eyes locked on Andrew Heddar's hand. Her father said something in a low voice and she sat back down, but she wasn't happy about it.

"The music," Dylis said.

A *clue!* I thought in my best Inspector Clouseau imitation, caught up in the half-histrionic spell of the woman.

Dylis caught Adam's gaze, and when she did, her body quit moving, stilling from her center of gravity out to her extremities. Briefly, the pupils of her eyes were hourglass shaped, like a goat's, before they resumed a normal human appearance, even if they retained their startling sky-blue color.

Dylis Heddar's power swirled around her, overwhelming her husband's faint aura of magic as easily as her presence eclipsed his.

"The music in the walls," Dylis whispered, as if we might have missed the clue the first time she'd said it.

Silence fell.

Able, the male half of the pair of hikers, broke the spell. "Hauptman?" He stood up, eyes widening in some strong emotion. "Who are you hunting here?"

I took a step closer to Adam—and it was as though the room was bathed in magic. It was hard to breathe, hard to hear—like Uncle Mike's had been the day before yesterday—as if all of the protections in my mind went down at once.

I closed my eyes and grabbed Adam's arm, using him, using our link, to center myself. I could feel the power of the Heddars' magic. His not so negligible as I'd thought, hers far more vast and old—but still wrong in a way that I could not define.

I could feel the power of Elyna's presence. Not just emanating from the room where she now rested, but in the ties she shared with all the people gathered around the farthest table—the bride's table. She had been right; they were hers. She'd lent them power—as vampires do. They'd be a little harder to kill, a little faster, and age more slowly.

In the middle, between the Heddars' fae magic and the bride's table's necromancy, were a pair of goblins—I presumed those were the two hikers.

In the kitchen . . . in the kitchen was—

Then Adam stepped into me, powering up the bonds between us, and I was back to normal.

There were, I thought, a lot of magical folk trapped in a lodge in the middle of a blizzard. What were the odds? There was more going on here than a stolen artifact. What had my brother gotten himself into?

"I am Hauptman," Adam said. "Have you done something that means you need to be hunted?"

I'd forgotten that one of the goblins had challenged Adam. The spell of Soul Taker woo-woo must have only lasted a second or two. I would have been less surprised to find it had been hours.

Able raised his chin. "Not by the likes of you."

"What's going on out here?" asked a congenial voice in an accent even a little more Irish than the one Elyna's dead husband had used. A man stepped out into the room, drying his hands with a dishcloth. He was tall and handsome yet somehow effacing, like the perfect British butler. The effect was only a little ruined by the Irish accent.

But the magic . . .

It rolled over the room like a warm wave that calmed and soothed as it drowned its victims. Able sat down, his face relaxing—though I noticed that his companion's face didn't seem to be reassured. Dylis sat down, too, and her husband released his punishing grip. Peter stayed on his feet, but he looked less like a policeman ready for anything and more like a mildly interested observer at a high school basketball game.

The green man said, "Ah, new flotsam from the storm. Welcome and more to all who seek shelter."

INTERLUDE

In the Tri-Cities

SHERWOOD

THE ROADS WERE BAD. BUT SHERWOOD WAS A GOOD driver. He was also too smart to be driving in these conditions. When Honey had called to ask him to come over and check Gary because something had happened last night, Sherwood had debated just changing to wolf and running there.

But he needed to be human-shaped to deal with the situation with Gary. Without one of his prosthetic devices, he'd be forced to hop around. Just the thought of being that vulnerable made his wolf stir.

So he drove.

The lights began to flash on the railroad crossing just ahead. He eased off the gas and tapped his brakes lightly. The car in front of him twisted a bit but stopped in plenty of time. Sherwood did, too.

The impact, when the vehicle behind him failed to even try to stop, was loud—louder when Sherwood's car hit the one in front and his airbag inflated, smacking him in the face. He felt the bone in the bridge of his nose go. Something slammed into his legs—and he heard a crack. He ripped the airbag out of his field of vision.

Down the tracks there was a train coming, and the car in front of him had just been forced through the crossing gate and onto the tracks.

Sherwood's door opened in a protesting squeal of metal and he had to grab the base of the steering column and lift to free his legs. More metal popped and bent.

Behind him a woman shrieked, "It's not my fault. It's not my fault. I didn't see you."

He ignored her. If she could scream that loudly, she was going to be okay for a minute. Unlike the still figure in the car ahead of him.

Sherwood scrambled out of his car and ran. He didn't have time to do this pretty—not with the train making the ground rumble. From the sound he had about fifteen seconds to get this done. The trapped vehicle was pressed up against the base of the crossbar on the right side, so instead of pushing he was going to have to pull it around.

It and his car, too. Because they were crushed together.

There wasn't enough traction. And no time for magic. Magic performed under these kinds of circumstances meant blowing things up—not saving people.

Sherwood didn't hesitate. He reached down and grabbed the foot on his very expensive prosthetic and ripped it off. The remaining broken metal post dug into the ice like a pickaxe.

He dragged the cars sideways, stumbling with the awkwardness of having one leg slipping like crazy and the other six inches shorter. He ended up pulling the car half over him as he rolled onto his back.

When the train came through, no one died.

The car door next to his face swung open and the edge caught Sherwood's broken nose. Behind him, the woman, who was still screaming, was now screaming, "What are you? Don't kill me. It wasn't my fault."

The man he'd saved was almost worse with his horrified apologies. Sherwood rolled and stood, balancing on his good foot. He waved a hand at both of them, a sign to back off. Then he hopped back to his car. It took him a minute to find his phone—the accident had thrown it into the backseat.

He was in pain—there was more wrong with him than the broken nose. Though everything was healing just fine, the healing hurt, too. He'd destroyed his very expensive prosthetic two weeks after the doctor had finally figured out why it was rubbing so badly and fixed it. It was less than a week since the full moon, and he could feel the change in the season as the winter solstice neared. He was vulnerable in front of strangers—and that woman *would not* quit making noise.

Last of all, there was something about this snowstorm that set all of his senses on edge. It felt *malicious*.

He needed help or he was going to kill someone.

He stared at his phone. Who did he trust when he was vulnerable? Who could keep people safe if Sherwood lost his battle for control?

He hit a button and put the phone to his ear.

10

~~~

MERCY

"FLOTSAM?" I HEARD MYSELF SAY TO THE FAE WHO'D emerged from the kitchens. I thought I sounded normal, but Adam's hand moved to rest on the small of my back. "I thought you needed an ocean for us to be flotsam."

Our host was a green man. I didn't need the Soul Taker–born curse to feel his magic. It tasted like Uncle Mike's power.

"Liam is the night manager," Elyna had said, picking at the ice trying to form on one edge of the hot tub. "He was manning the desk when it became obvious that the roads were becoming too dangerous for travel. He called upper management and told them to keep the staff at home, that he and Emily—with the help of Hugo, a retiree who usually works a couple of days a week as the custodian and gardener—could handle it." She paused. "Hugo can't talk above a whisper—throat cancer or something—but he's a sweetheart. He tends the greenhouse and brings each of the guests flowers every evening."

As I stared at the smiling Irish fae who had been working as a night manager at a very small in-the-middle-of-renovations lodge in the wilds of Montana, I thought, *sixteen people*. Seventeen with Jack. All of us trapped on sacred ground by a snowstorm controlled by a frost giant. Seventeen people, and there was a werewolf, a vampire and her necromancy-augmented people, a ghost, and not one, not two, not three, but *five* fae—goblins count as fae. Also me. The only actual normal humans here might be Emily and Hugo the gardener.

We weren't flotsam, because flotsam was accidental and random. We had been brought together deliberately. I wondered who had done that and why.

I wondered if I was going to be able to save my brother.

"Perhaps you are right," said Liam, the desk clerk and night manager, whose power flowed around me like the mist rising from the hot lake had last night. "Not flotsam."

The green man who was not Uncle Mike made a show of considering his words. He said, "Let us say, then, far travelers who have arrived at our doors, blown in by the north wind. Winter lost." He spread his hands. "Welcome, guests, to Looking Glass Lodge." He smiled. "Resort. I meant 'resort.'"

Emily had followed the green man out of the kitchen. She gave an exasperated hiss. "Dramatic much? Don't mind Liam. He grew up in Ireland." She said it the same way my mother said "She was raised in a barn" to apologize for one of her more socially inept friends. "And all the signs say Looking Glass Hot Springs."

I used my senses to check Emily again. Nope, still human.

The green man, Liam, threw the dish towel he'd been holding at her and laughed when she snatched it out of the air.

"You go help Hugo with the dishes, you troublemaker," he

admonished. "There's not a thing wrong with Ireland—or my manner."

She grinned and vanished through the doorway again.

"Adam and Mercy Hauptman," said my husband, stepping forward with an outstretched hand. "We came in last night. I took a key and left a note at the front desk."

"Mr. Hauptman." Our host shook Adam's hand and then his eyes widened just a touch. I saw comprehension dawn and he quit meeting Adam's gaze by briefly looking at me, rather than by dropping his own gaze. A move that did not challenge Adam's rank—nor admit to a lesser status. People learned those kinds of manners when they hung out around werewolf Alphas. Or when their magic was geared to making their guests feel welcome and comfortable.

"Ah, *that* Hauptman," the fae said. "Forgive me for not making the connection. It is an honor to have such guests. I am, for my sins, Liam Fellows—please call me Liam. I have not been to the desk yet this morning, not expecting anyone could make it through the roads. I hope you find our hospitality up to your needs."

"Sir," Adam said. When Adam is wary, he gets military. I was pretty sure he couldn't feel what Liam Fellows was, but he knew that I had been surprised.

He also didn't accept the role of guest that our would-be host offered. Offered again. Guesting laws are very important to the fae. They'd provide some protections—but also restrict what we could do.

If we were Liam's guests, we could not, for instance, steal the lyre without consulting him about it ahead of time. If the lyre was a *fae* artifact—not all of them were, and the frost giant had not been clear—I wasn't sure any fae would be okay with us giving it back to someone who was not fae.

"Mrs. Hauptman." Liam held his hand out to me. I wasn't surprised that he air-kissed my knuckles. Uncle Mike did that kind of courtly greeting occasionally, too.

"Mercy, please," I said.

There was no way around it. If we were going to remain at the lodge, it would have to be as guests. We wouldn't be able to find the artifact if we were staying however many miles up the mountain at the ranch my brother worked for.

"With that storm outside we are"—not grateful, good grief, Zee would have my hide if I said something that stupid to a fae, especially a powerful fae I did not know—"happy to be your guests."

Liam's body relaxed. I was surprised that he let me see that— or that it mattered so much that we accepted his hospitality.

I'd asked Zee one time why Uncle Mike wasn't a Gray Lord. Zee had told me that within the walls of his pub, Uncle Mike's power was formidable, but outside of his center of power, he was too vulnerable to be a Gray Lord. We were in Liam's territory here. He would have no trouble chucking us out if he wanted to. I wondered why he didn't want to.

"Good, good," Liam said. "Let's hope this storm ends soon, but we should have sufficient fuel for the generators and food for our guests for the next few days." He smiled. "I am not ashamed to say that I am a good cook. So perhaps the food will make your stay with us worth the price of the storm."

Uncle Mike would have known if someone brought an artifact into his pub. Adam and I needed to talk to Liam Fellows at a time and place when there weren't all these other ears listening. The first step to that was to establish that though he knew who we were, we also knew who he was. Or at least *what* he was.

"You remind me of a friend," I told him. "He likes to feed people as well. Most of us call him Uncle Mike."

Beside me, Adam drew in a breath—so I'd been right. He hadn't known what Liam was.

Our host's smile became careful, and he assessed me more deeply. "Runs a pub up your way, doesn't he? Aye, I know him. You also remind me of someone, Mrs. Hauptman." He paused and said, deliberately, "Mercy."

"My brother, Gary, is a caretaker for the ranch up the mountain from here," I said.

"Ah, of course," he said, as if that had not been the person he'd been thinking of. "You do remind me of Gary."

Had he been talking about someone else? Who else could I remind him of? Coyote? A green man living in the wilderness might have met Coyote.

"Sure and your brother's a fine fellow," Liam, the green man, continued. "He was supposed to come down with the horses yesterday, but I expect the storm derailed his plans. With the phones being disobliging, there was no way to check. Do you intend to try to reach him today? I feel it's my job to discourage that. It's not the kind of storm to be careless with."

"We've already been there," my husband told Liam. "He's not at the ranch. The truck he usually drives was gone."

All true, if misleading. The deception wasn't directed at Liam, but for our audience, I thought.

I glanced around the room and was surprised to see that we were no longer the center of attention. Given our sudden appearance, I was pretty sure that their disinterest was probably something Liam was doing. I'd seen Uncle Mike redirect a crowd now and then in the same way.

Peter had retaken his seat. His fellow police officers and his daughter were cleaning the last bits of food off their plates. The hikers had their heads together and were speaking rapidly. I should have been able to hear what they were saying, but the perfectly judged volume of the music did its job. All I could catch was the occasional consonant.

At the Heddars' table, Dylis was back to picking at her food with even more disinterest than before we'd come in. I was starting to think that my initial impression that she was on something was correct. Addiction could be the source of the wrongness I felt in her magic. I wondered what medication she could possibly be on.

The only person who was still paying attention to us was her husband, Andrew. He was staring at Adam the way one Alpha looks at another, assessing the threat. He saw me observing him and abruptly pulled out his charm and smiled.

I smiled back. With teeth.

Liam noticed the exchange, glanced around the room, then took a step away from us toward the kitchen.

"Your brother is a man of rare sense," Liam told me. He was a fae and could not lie. Maybe "rare sense" meant something other than "good sense."

He must have seen my disbelief, because his smile widened and turned genuine for a moment. "He is. A storm—even this kind of storm—is not going to harm him."

"I'm glad you think so," I told him rather than agreeing.

"We *should* talk more about Gary," Liam said. "But you have caught me in the middle of making breakfast, so talk will have to wait. The house is serving eggs, bacon, and pancakes today. Or I can whip up something special if you wish?"

"No need to make anything special. Breakfast sounds lovely," I told him, carefully avoiding anything that would put us in his debt.

Liam smiled (again) in appreciation of my considered wording, and this time his expression was more than a little sly. I found myself wanting to like him, and had to remind myself that he wasn't Uncle Mike. He was our host and he'd abide by the guesting laws, but that didn't make him our friend.

"It is no trouble at all," he said. "Food will be out shortly. Pray take a seat wherever you like."

As if he had already made his calculations, Adam led us to the hikers' table without hesitation. I would have chosen the Heddars' so I could ask Dylis about the music she heard in the walls.

But the hikers' sudden appearance in this remote location had made them top candidates for most likely suspects, even before I'd known they were fae. I couldn't argue with Adam's decision. It was good I was happy, because the hikers were unhappy enough for all of us.

Able stiffened when Adam pulled out a chair opposite Victoria and motioned for me to sit. As usual, Adam had chosen our seats strategically. Our backs were to the kitchen, but we had good views of all the people at the other two tables.

It was an unnecessary strategy, though, because everyone at Peter's table rose when Adam and I sat down. As soon as the last of that group exited the room, the Heddars left, too. No one stopped to introduce themselves—just as they would not have had we been staying in a generic hotel under normal circumstances.

That probably meant that no one realized just how bad the storm outside was.

The pair at our table started to get up and leave with everyone else. But Adam waved them back into their seats.

He was an Alpha—it hadn't been a request. They sat back down, though I could tell that neither of them quite knew why.

"We met Elyna Gray last night," Adam told them. "You must be the hikers that she mentioned—Able and Victoria. Not part of the wedding party."

They didn't respond.

"Able and Victoria," Adam said. "Siblings and mountain climbers."

"Yes," Victoria said tightly.

"Goblin killer," her brother hissed at Adam. "We've done nothing. Leave us alone."

Adam hadn't killed any goblins that I knew about—which would be anytime in the last decade. I hadn't killed any goblins, either. I had led a team of pack members with the intention of confronting a fugitive goblin who had killed a human child. He'd ended up dead at the hands of the goblin king, but I'd been there, too. I would have killed that goblin if I'd had to.

I wondered what stories were going around that had Adam labeled as a goblin killer. Or maybe the question should be who was telling the stories.

Victoria's hand shot to her brother's knee, and he quit talking. Adam bumped me lightly with his shoulder. They were more worried about him. Adam thought I needed to be the one to talk to them.

Fair enough, I thought.

Elyna hadn't known anything about them other than that they apparently made good money GoPro-ing themselves climbing mountains, then posting their adventures to social media.

I needed to find out who had the artifact so I could return it. I didn't think arguing that Adam hadn't killed any goblins was going to help with my main goal, so I set it aside.

A rather long silence had stretched out between us as I decided how to approach this. We were alone in the room, and that opened up a few possibilities.

"Nasty weather out there," I said to Victoria, ignoring her brother. "Do you know what caused it?"

"A low-pressure system bringing in arctic air?" she answered. She had a death grip on her brother. "Are you some kind of meteorologist?"

I'd hoped for a more direct answer. Questions were neither truth nor lies.

"No," I said. "I'm a mechanic. But I *know* why this storm is going to keep going for a while."

The timing was right for them to have been involved with the theft. For the first time I wondered if my brother had really been the thief. I'd just accepted Hrímnir's assessment. It didn't make sense that he'd stolen the artifact, left it here, then run to me.

Goblins were excellent thieves, and this pair knew about mountains in winter. If I had to pick someone to go rob a frost giant, this pair would be a very good choice. They had enough magic to slip in and out of locked places, but not so much that they drew attention. They had opportunity, and possibly the means for the theft.

As for motive . . .

If I reached out and closed my hand, I'd hold Lugh's walking stick. There were a lot of fae who resented that, an artifact held by someone who wasn't fae, even if they couldn't do anything about it. The walking stick had decided, for whatever reason, that it belonged to me.

Hrímnir wasn't fae. I didn't know if his missing artifact had been created by the fae. But I did know that most of the fae looked upon all artifacts as theirs. Zee certainly did. And Underhill had not yet forgiven me for giving the Soul Taker—which had certainly not been fae—to Zee for destruction.

Motive enough. *If* the goblin siblings knew that Hrímnir had an artifact. And where he lived. And that he couldn't come here. The simplest explanation was still that my brother had stolen the artifact and left it with someone.

He was more likely to have done that with someone he knew better than any of the guests—someone like Liam, maybe. Liam wasn't here, though. For now, I had a couple of goblins to question.

"Someone is missing his lyre and wants it back," I said. "Until he gets it, none of us is going to leave here alive."

"I told you." Able's voice was urgent as he leaned toward his sister. "I *told* you there was magic in this storm."

True.

Victoria gave her brother a look and he subsided. No question who was in charge between the two of them.

"It would take a Power to do this," Victoria said. "Not just a Gray Lord—one of the elementals."

I didn't say anything. I didn't know what she meant by elemental.

"A lyre," Victoria said.

"An artifact," I told her. "It might be a harp. I'm a little unclear about that."

I couldn't tell if that was news to her or not. An artifact would make sense—not much else would move someone to expend the power that this storm cost.

After a moment's silence, Victoria said, "And it is your intention to return it? This lyre or harp? An artifact?"

"If it isn't returned, no one is leaving the lodge alive," I told them again.

"I don't believe you," Able spat angrily, staring at my husband. "You humans are all liars. Werewolves, too. If you find it, you'll take it to the Marrok, *werewolf*, won't you? Because he sent you after it, didn't he? An artifact—and oh so close to his territory."

"The Marrok has nothing to do with this," Adam answered. "If he wanted something, I'm not the wolf he would send for it."

"Charles," breathed both of the fae, stilling in their seats like a pair of rabbits who have just seen a coyote. It didn't make them look very human.

I wondered how Charles would feel about the terror he inspired in this pair. The Marrok's son scared me, too. And he *liked* me—I was mostly sure he liked me. But the fear he inspired was a useful thing. It kept people from getting hurt.

Just now, it also showed me what the goblins looked like when they were afraid.

They hadn't been frightened about the storm. Or about someone stealing an artifact from a being powerful enough to control the weather. I was pretty sure that if this pair had taken an artifact from a frost giant, they would have been more scared of the frost giant than they were of the mention of Charles.

Maybe the goblins hadn't stolen the lyre. Harp. Artifact.

"Charles doesn't hunt artifacts," I told them. "Nor does the Marrok."

The goblins both looked at me in utter disbelief. Or as if I were very stupid.

"Do you *know* what the Marrok has?" Victoria hissed as only a goblin could. She managed to shove a fair bit of contempt into her voice, too. "A treasury of dozens of artifacts—dozens of *named* artifacts. Who knows how many unnamed."

"How else would he amass such power if he doesn't hunt them?" asked Able. "Do you think they come to him when he calls?"

That could be a dig about my walking stick—or not. It didn't matter right now. I was considering whether or not Bran had a stash of artifacts. I could hear that the goblins believed what they were saying.

If Bran had a bunch of artifacts, I wouldn't know about it, would I?

Bran Cornick, the Marrok, was motivated by one thing: to keep the werewolves safe. There wasn't much he wouldn't do to accomplish that. If he'd found a use for fae artifacts, he would keep them. Even if he was only keeping them out of the hands of his enemies.

Oh hell. As soon as I'd had that last thought, I knew. *Of course* he was collecting artifacts. Zee was also collecting the weapons he had made—most of them artifacts of varying degrees of power. I wonder if Zee had started that because of the Marrok—to keep his most powerful creations out of the Marrok's hands.

"The Marrok might hunt artifacts," Adam conceded, as if he'd followed my thoughts. Or maybe he knew something I didn't—like that Bran had a massive collection of fae artifacts. "I have no useful knowledge about that. But he's not hunting them with us. We have a treaty with the fae."

One that did *not* say we were obliged to give them any artifacts we might find.

Victoria saw something over my shoulder, and whispered, "He's coming." She waited long enough for someone to walk from the kitchen to our table, and then smiled. After a second, the smile became genuine.

Liam brought two plates, overflowing with food, and set them on the table in front of Adam and me. We got glasses, which he filled with orange juice from a pitcher he'd also carried. He refilled the other glasses in front of our companions.

Victoria thanked him.

I had to work hard to keep from showing my shock. There was no way that she didn't know Liam was fae. Maybe she didn't realize that he was more powerful than she was? Or she was too young to know how dangerous thanking the fae was?

Liam accepted her thanks blandly, said a few hostly things, and took himself back to the kitchen. I wondered if he could hear what we were saying. I didn't think so, because I hadn't been able to eavesdrop over the music—and my hearing is very good.

"This elemental whose artifact was stolen is causing this storm?" Victoria asked. "It was stolen near here?"

I nodded.

"I thought you were here about your brother," said Able. "That's what you told Liam."

"I am," I said. "But it's turned into something more complex."

"Well," said Victoria, "I don't know why you're talking to us." She gave Adam a sour smile. "Neither of us has stolen an artifact."

That put the goblins in the clear. Fae couldn't lie. There were ways, I'd been told, very secret ways that goblins could lie. But her words struck me as the absolute truth—and I could tell truth from lie more accurately than any lie detector.

She pushed back her chair, stood up, and strode out of the room, Able trailing behind her.

"I thought we weren't going to tell people about the artifact and ask them if they stole it?" said Adam, but not as though he was upset.

"Time is short," I said. "My brother is—" I had no words for what had been done to him. I knew what it was like to be helpless. "My brother is in trouble. We can't even get in touch with Honey to check on him. Or the pack. Or what is going down in New Mexico. And this storm."

Even tucked deeply inside the lodge I could hear the winds blowing.

"I know storms like this, Adam. They kill people. People who are heating their homes with fireplaces and don't know their chimney is blocked until everyone dies of carbon monoxide. People who don't have enough money to heat their homes. Emergency workers."

"Other people, too," said Liam.

I hadn't heard him approach. Adam turned his chair around, but I stood up.

The green man looked at us and frowned thoughtfully. "I think we need to talk."

Adam leaned back and raised an eyebrow. "Here?"

Liam glanced over his shoulder to the kitchen, where I could hear the murmurs of voices. "My apartment, where we won't be disturbed."

That pretty much answered the question of whether he could hear what we'd been talking about from the kitchen, even over the music.

LIAM'S APARTMENT WAS ON THE THIRD FLOOR, WHERE the ongoing renovations were on full display. The flooring had been taken down to the original boards, and sections of the walls had great gaping areas where the lath and plaster had been removed to expose new electrical wiring.

There was a sort of creaking sound above us. Adam crooked his neck and looked at the ceiling. "Sounds like you need to get someone up there to get the snowpack off."

Liam stopped, looking up, too. I felt his power slide through the structure of the roof.

"Ice dam," he said. "I'd fix it, but this old building takes magic oddly sometimes. I don't want to bring the whole thing down on our heads. We'll have to get someone up there to clear it manually."

He looked at Adam, as if measuring him for duty. But then he said, as if to himself, "There is time for discussion first."

We wove through and over construction debris to the end of the hall and around the corner to another hall, where the destruction ended and material storage began. Four pallets of flooring held up five rolls of carpet. Another pallet of five-gallon buckets of paint. Large boxes, some of them unopened and others ripped open for inspection, disgorging masses of bubble-wrapped furniture or fixtures.

"Pardon the chaos," he said as he led us around a stack of drywall that reached past his shoulder. "Construction is not a neat or tidy business."

But once we were past the drywall, we emerged into about twenty feet of pristine hall that did not look as though it belonged in the lodge at all. Or not a lodge built in the last thousand years.

The floor under our feet was rough-hewed wood, eighteen to twenty inches wide, with narrow gaps modern construction would never have tolerated. The walls were fieldstone fitted far more tightly than the floor.

"Granite," I said, letting my fingers slide over the rough surface of the walls, though my eyes were on the door at the end of the hall.

Liam nodded. "That it is. Makes it feel like home."

The door.

There was an entrance to Underhill at the edge of our backyard. It wasn't fancy, made of thick and battered oak that looked as though it had stood there for a century and would probably stand there for another. It was a good door, solid, but not a beautiful thing.

Underhill herself had put it there when Aiden, a human child who'd been trapped in her world for uncountable years, had come to live with us. We'd moved him when our pack house had become too dangerous for innocent bystanders. We hadn't sent him away to keep him safe—but because he was needed to keep the world safe from one of our more interesting pack members.

Though Aiden wasn't currently living with us, the door was still there. Underhill, in her human-seeming, used it to visit us sometimes.

Liam's door was nothing like the door in our backyard.

His was a spectacular piece of art, though not at all in keeping with the sleek Art Deco of the renovated parts of the lodge's ground floor. Nor even the medieval castle construction of the hall the door stood in, though the rounded top and the heavy forged-iron hinges and knob were obviously a nod to the Middle Ages. Instead, the oak leaves—carved in bas-relief all over the door and frame—made me think of Art Deco's nature-loving fanciful predecessor, Art Nouveau.

It looked nothing at all like the entrance to Underhill in our backyard—but, like that one, Liam's door felt like a door between worlds.

"Nice door," Adam said.

"Yes," Liam answered with a sly smile. "I made it myself."

He opened the door, revealing a very modern apartment with a tile floor covered by thick area rugs. The kitchen was part of the living room and it was a chef's workshop. All business and no fripperies, but I was pretty sure that the big gas stove was a work of art in a different way than the door was.

"Welcome," Liam said, and there was a pop of magic as he stepped aside to allow us entry.

He hadn't unlocked the door, but that door didn't need a lock to keep people out any more than Underhill's door did. I was pretty sure if we'd pushed past him before he welcomed us, something fatal would have occurred. There was a tang to magic spells that were designed to kill, a sort of eagerness or anticipation. I could sense that here.

The windows looked out on the surroundings of the lodge, the storm raging outside. I hadn't expected that, somehow. It felt as if this room was both in the lodge and not in the lodge.

Magic doesn't have to make sense.

Adam and I sat side by side on a soft couch that the muscles in my body—still sore from the shivering cold of yesterday—found amazingly comfortable. Because Adam was here, I let myself sink down into the gentle support. My mate perched on the front edge of the couch. He didn't like soft seating that could slow him down if he needed to move.

"Here we cannot be overheard," said Liam. "This morning I arose thinking I knew why this storm decided to be so inconvenient. Imagine my surprise when you told our goblin twins that it is caused by someone trapping us here until you retrieve a musical instrument—though there seems to be some confusion about just what kind of instrument you are looking for. An artifact."

I noticed that his Irish accent was abruptly toned down, until it was only a faint lyrical note instead of a John Philip Sousa march.

Adam's eyes narrowed. "Uncle Mike would know if someone brought an artifact into his pub."

"Why did you think the storm was so bad?" I asked.

Liam sighed—and answered Adam. "Yes, of course he would." He dragged a chair across the room and placed it directly in front of Adam and me. Then he sat, legs crossed at his ankles, elbows on the arms of the chair with his hands steepled.

"We," he announced with a sigh, "are at an impasse. I cannot afford to trust you, and you cannot trust me."

"Why not?" Adam asked. "We are all trapped here until someone figures something out." He looked at me.

"I'm still hung up on why a green man wouldn't know if there was an artifact at his lodge," I said. I frowned. "And why were you surprised when we showed up for breakfast?" Had he expected the hungry ghost to take care of us? But that didn't make sense because if that were the reason, he should have known it hadn't. Uncle Mike would have known if something like that invaded his pub.

"Green man?" Liam said. "I haven't heard that term in a very long time. Is that what Uncle Mike is calling himself?"

I couldn't remember if Uncle Mike had ever named himself a green man.

"Other people have called him that," I said, because I knew that was true—then repeated the question he'd avoided. "Why didn't you know about us?" Or the attack on Jack. Anyone sensitive to magic should have felt *something*.

"What does Gary have to do with a stolen artifact?" Liam asked me, instead of answering.

If he didn't want to answer the question, he could just say so. And also, if he wasn't answering my questions, I wouldn't answer his, either. "We were attacked by a hungry ghost this morning," I said.

Beside me Adam stifled a laugh.

"You were what?" Liam stiffened, sitting forward in his chair, his hand reaching for something at his side.

"This isn't your lodge," I said with sudden certainty.

Almost as if it were an echo of my words, I felt something that rocketed up through the bottoms of my shoes and up through my spine. Not quite magic, but power of some sort. It felt a lot like an earthquake, like something was pulling a firm foundation out from under my feet.

Liam's nostrils flared and he growled, "*My* lodge. *My home.*"

His magic surged with his asserted ownership, and the trembling feeling subsided. Mostly. The hairs on the back of my neck still felt a little unhappy.

"If it is yours, why don't you know if there's an artifact here?" Adam asked softly. He'd thought Liam was talking to us. "Why didn't you notice the hungry ghost in our room?" His voice

dropped into the soft tones that were Adam at his most dangerous. "Or did you set that ghost on us?"

I shook my head. "He didn't. It didn't belong to this place."
Then I added, "He wasn't talking to us, he was enforcing his
claim on the lodge. How long have you been here, that it isn't
yours yet?"

Liam narrowed his eyes at me.

"You don't have to answer that," I said. I'd just wanted him to
know that I understood what I'd felt.

Liam tipped his head. "You aren't quite . . . whole." He shook
his head. "Not the right word. You are wounded and it leaves you
open in a way that is dangerous."

"Thank you for telling us something we already knew," Adam
said blandly. "Do you know what to do about it?"

He asked it so casually, I don't think Liam understood it was
an honest question.

"Not in the slightest," Liam said. "I've never seen anything
quite like it." He smiled a bit grimly. "Not in anyone who lived.
Would you share what kind of creature caused it?"

I could feel Adam's worry, though his face didn't change.

"Not a creature," I told him. "An artifact—not built by
the fae."

"Do you still have it?" Liam asked casually, a hunter's gleam
in his eye.

"Destroyed by a friend of ours," Adam said.

"A fae friend," I added at Liam's indrawn breath.

He regained his butler friendliness. "Pity. If you still had it, I
might have been able to figure out how it damaged you."

"My brother came to my house the day before yesterday,
cursed with an inability to understand or communicate with any-

one," I said, more to change the subject than because I had any plan in mind. But after I said it, I realized that withholding information wasn't going to make our task any easier.

Adam looked at me. I shrugged. "We're in the same boat right now. Maybe if we all talk, we might be able to come up with a solution. And, Adam, if he's like Uncle Mike, if Liam has the artifact, the only way we are going to get it from him is if he gives it to us of his own free will."

Adam hesitated but finally nodded.

Liam, for his part, didn't react to my naming him a suspect by so much as a twitch of his eye.

I told Liam the whole thing, from the moment my brother showed up until we were attacked by the hungry ghost. I didn't tell him about the silver spider. She seemed like something . . . *someone* dangerous to talk about. It was easy enough to do when I reduced our battle with the hungry ghost to "We won." Even easier when I left out Jack, too, because he was Elyna's and no business of anyone else's.

When I was finished, Liam closed his eyes. "Coincidences. I don't like coincidences. You tell me the storm is caused by Hrímnir, who wants his lyre back. And I believe you."

He uncrossed his ankles and moved a little, letting his body inhabit the seat rather than simply sit in it. His change in posture seemed to alter the nature of his chair. It became a throne, not the kind used in modern royal ceremonies, but the high seat earned by a chieftain.

I couldn't help thinking of a painting of a barbarian king, like something on the cover of a Conan the Barbarian novel. An incongruous thought, given Liam's outward tidiness, but it felt *true*.

In some other time and place, one that was bloody and messy, this man had been a ruler of a fae court.

I could almost see . . .

Liam's eyes widened. He leaned forward, saying something to Adam when my mate blocked his way. But I couldn't understand his words. All of my attention was focused on the vision I was experiencing of a different time and place.

—*blood on a wooden floor. So much blood. A man screaming.*

Liam's fingers brushed my forehead and the visions scrolling in my head drifted away, leaving me sweaty and shivering. Hot and cold at the same time. Adam's arm around my shoulder let me center myself.

"You need to find someone who can fix that," Liam told me.

"I intend to," I told him. The consequences of not fixing it were growing more obviously grave on a near-hourly basis.

Liam sat back again, once more a well-groomed, graceful man in a wingback chair.

I cleared my throat and tried to remember what we'd been talking about.

"Why do *you* think the storm has trapped us here?" I asked.

"To prevent a wedding," Liam said.

Interlude

New Mexico

Don Orson

THEY FOUND DON A VANTAGE PLACE IN THE HILLS that gave him a clear view of the compound below, well within his field of accuracy. He didn't have to worry about taking out civilians; there were none of them anywhere around here. He set up his tripod and gave a little groan—mostly theatric—as he lay down and got ready for his shot. If he was needed.

It had taken Adam's people less than a day to find the culprits. They'd checked out the place where their man had been killed, then wandered around the various buildings until Auriele Zao said, "I smell henbane."

Don had had no idea that one of their projects was entirely peopled by witches doing magic instead of chemists doing . . . what chemists did.

The pair of werewolves had called a meeting with the entire group of white witches to find out who had been stalking them.

Darryl Zao was a scary SOB, but in that meeting . . . Well, Adam said that being Alpha was as much about being a protector as being able to kill things. Don had been privileged to see that at work. Darryl had taken a room filled with terrorized, traumatized people and made them feel safe.

As they'd left the tearful, grateful bunch of witch nerds—Vincent's term, and it was sticking—Darryl had muttered, "Like putting a barbecue in the jungle and wondering why the predators keep coming around."

"Poor things," agreed his wife. "I'll have some suggestions for Adam about extra protections." She glanced at Don. "And you should have a word with someone. White witches are prey. You should have been told they were here, and accommodations should have been made for their safety."

Darryl made a few phone calls—apparently there wasn't a pack in Los Alamos, but there was a big one in Santa Fe.

"I thought Adam's pack didn't get to call for support from other packs," Don had observed to Auriele while her husband gave orders to the Alpha of the Santa Fe pack.

She'd grinned at him. "Don't remind them, and we won't, either."

Darryl hung up the phone and shook his head at her. "The pack Alpha is a good friend of mine. He doesn't like witches—and he tells me there's a compound about ten miles up into the hills outside of town. Auriele and I will do a quick recon to make sure these are our culprits, and we'll take them out."

Don didn't ask him about the legalities of the operation. Black witches were, all of them, killers of the innocent—and the human justice system was not built to handle them. If there were bodies, the wolf pack would handle it.

———————

BESIDE HIM, THE WEREWOLF LEFT TO GUARD HIM whined softly.

"I know," Don told her. "Don't shoot wolves or people with armbands."

Auriele's voice whispered in Don's earpiece. "Go."

He put his scope to his eye and waited.

11

~~~

MERCY

"WEDDING?" I SAID. "YOU MEAN TAMMY'S WEDDING?"

"The one scheduled to take place on the winter solstice," Adam said, which was something that I should have noticed.

Liam gave him a tight smile. "Exactly."

A marriage in which the very wealthy heir of the family fortune chose to marry a policeman's daughter sounded very romantic. It was probably the plot of a dozen different romance novels. But marriages had not always been about love.

A marriage was an ancient rite of passage. It was an exchange of vows—a contract, in the fae sense of the word—intended to represent the uniting of bloodlines for the future. As such, a marriage, the right kind of marriage, could be a powerful source of raw magic.

"What is so special about this wedding?" I asked slowly. "Magically speaking."

I expected the rite to be some sort of method for maintaining power—it might be wealth, of course. The Heddars were very wealthy. Or possibly it was some sort of influence. But my bet was that it was power. All of the fae lost a great deal of magical ability when Underhill closed herself to them, driving some of them to drastic measures.

Liam didn't speak right away. Finally, he got up from his seat and walked to the window, his back to us as he watched the snow fly outside. "Every hundred and forty-four years, the oldest child of the current generation of what is, in this age, the Heddar family must marry on the shortest day of the year on sacred ground."

I wondered if it was the Heddar family who received the power or if they were bound by some fae bargain. Liam didn't seem to be more powerful than Uncle Mike, so I doubted that it was him.

The green man turned to face us. "With such a binding is the beast known as Garmr kept captive."

That was so far from anything I expected that I just stared stupidly at him.

"Garmr?" asked Adam. "What is that?"

"Wait," I said. I had been reading every folktale story I could scrounge since the fae had become an unavoidable part of my life. There was a lot of important information sprinkled somewhat carelessly in fairy tales. But there were some sources that had been more carefully tended.

"Ragnarok," I said, pronouncing it like most Americans would. Then more properly with rolled "r's" and umlaut "o," the way Zee said it: "Ragnarök. You believe that this marriage holds fate at bay. By preventing Ragnarök."

"Indeed," agreed Liam.

"The end of the world." I wanted to scoff. I didn't believe in fate. Didn't *want* to believe in fate. But my instincts were standing up and paying attention, telling me that this explanation would account for our adventures thus far. This explanation was big and *fantastic* enough to include an ancient frost giant who could take the form of a gryphon. Big enough for a storm of epic proportions and a holy place in the wilderness full of supernatural people gathered under one roof.

What in the world had Gary been mixed up in?

To make sure I had this right, I said, "You believe that if we don't stop the storm so the marriage can take place, Garmr is going to be freed and the world will end."

Liam gave me a faint smile that held no amusement. "If the wedding participants cannot make it here because of the storm, if the marriage doesn't take place, Ragnarök will begin."

"You bring me on such interesting adventures, my love," said Adam. "What is Garmr?"

My mouth was dry so I had to swallow. I had thought we were here to save my brother, and prevent the dozen or so deaths that a storm like this would bring. The end of the world was a pretty exponential leap in consequence. Not that I *believed* in Ragnarok, I reminded myself.

"Garmr is the wolf—or dog, or something canid—who guards the gates of Hel—that's one 'l,' not two," I told Adam, because Liam had made no effort to answer. "According to legend, he breaks free from his chains"—I glanced over at Liam, who shrugged—"or some kind of binding, anyway. Once he is free, he bays or howls or cries out and announces the start of Ragnarok."

"The end of the world," Adam said. "Is that real?"

"This"—I gestured out at the storm and waved my hands to encompass the events since my brother showed up—"feels like someone believes this marriage is important to stop."

Liam said, his voice a near whisper, "I believe." He turned back to the storm. I couldn't tell if he was looking for something out there or if he didn't want us to see his face.

"When Zane Heddar bought this place ten years ago, I was called here to prepare it for this wedding."

He put his fist against his heart. The wind chose that moment to beat especially hard against the windows.

"Real enough, maybe, that someone enraged a frost giant to prevent the marriage," Adam said, linking our story to his. His words hung in the air for a moment.

Liam nodded. "That is my thought. If finding the artifact will stop this storm, I will help you in any way that I can—as long as it does not interfere with my primary objective, which is to see this wedding accomplished."

"Does that include information?" I asked.

"Of course."

"Andrew and Dylis Heddar are both fae," I said. "The fae are immortal. How does that work?"

"Ah." Liam took time to organize his thoughts. "Andrew is entirely mortal, though you are right that he carries fae blood. His great-great-grandmother was a fae woman. He has some magic, though I am unclear on exactly what he can and cannot do with it. Dylis . . ." He sighed. "The binding spell is a Great Spell. There have never been very many of them. Whoever or whatever created it, they used wild magic, and it resonates in the bones of the people tied by blood or vow to the family."

"She was attracted to the magic?" I hazarded. I remembered the glassy look in her eyes. "Addicted?"

"That's a good word for it," Liam said. "She feeds on it, and it feeds on her—as long as she is married to a member of the family."

"Are we talking about 'I am my own grandpa'?" said Adam somewhat obscurely. "Let me guess, she is also Andrew's great-grandmother."

"Great-great-grandmother. But she was also that husband's great-grandmother." Liam sighed. "She's been marrying her own descendants every few generations. Andrew figured it out after Zane's birth. I gather that is why Zane has no legitimate siblings. He's not only the oldest child in his generation, he is the only legitimate child in his generation."

Adam whistled in through his teeth.

"We think that the binding would also work with one of Andrew's illegitimate children—they are still descendants of the last sacred marriage—but we don't want to chance it."

"Who is 'we'?" Adam asked it before I could.

"Zane and I are," Liam said. "It's a secret—part of the protections bound in the spell is that only the people directly involved in the spell will remember it. To keep someone from trying to interfere. Zane was born knowing about it. I learned after I was called here—though I have officiated at several, if not all, of the previous weddings. His parents remember. This close to the wedding, though, everyone in the wedding party should be starting to understand what their roles will be." He smiled at us. "This close to the wedding, you'll remember about it until after the wedding." His smile turned wry. "And if the wedding doesn't happen, and the Great Spell is broken, I suppose you'll remember about it until you die."

I wondered if Coyote knew about this wedding. And then I wondered if he would try to keep the binding safe—or if he'd be more interested in seeing what happened if the binding did not continue. Had he sent my brother here to steal the lyre and bring about the end of the word?

I rubbed my forehead as if I could erase that thought, because it sounded all too possible.

"Could Zane still make it here?" Adam asked. "Mercy and I managed the trip last night."

"The last time I talked to Zane—yesterday afternoon, when my sat phone was working—he'd found out that his flight to Missoula was canceled. No flights are going in or out of Missoula or Kalispell because of the weather. He thought he might have a flight to Spokane on a private plane." He spread his hands. "He is resourceful."

"A Great Spell," I said, putting the same capital letters on the words that I'd heard in his voice. "Spells have requirements, right? A bride. A groom." The groom had bought the lodge a decade ago. "This place?"

"A holy place," Liam said. "Yes. There's a reason we find ourselves in the Montana wilderness in the middle of winter. Finding a holy place we could own so that we could control it when we needed to perform the marriage wasn't easy. There are very few holy places that are not controlled by religious orders."

"A holy place," I said. "Is that why the lodge isn't yours the way Uncle Mike's tavern is his? A holy place"—I tried to put words to something that I understood viscerally—"belongs to itself."

He looked at both of us and then shrugged, folding his arms across his chest. "Though I claim this lodge as my own, the lake has its own divine guardian. She is why this ground became sacred, or perhaps she *is* because this ground is sacred. I did not think, when I first arrived, that it would be a problem. The lodge isn't holy ground, or shouldn't be. Only the lake and the surrounds that the lake touches."

"The manitou is the spirit of the lake, of the hot springs," I said, using the word Charles had taught me for the spirits of place. "Her power is tied to the water." I remembered what the frost giant had said. "Or fire."

Liam's eyebrow rose. "Fire?"

I wasn't qualified to argue magic or magical things with someone like Liam. Instead, I kept going to make sure I understood the problem he had, because it might be important when we were looking for the harp.

"The lodge is on solid ground, so it should be separate." I paused, thinking about what I'd felt when we'd parked Adam's SUV. "But it's not just the lake that belongs to the manitou. It's the hot springs."

If the lodge had not belonged to the manitou of the lake in some way, the frost giant could have retrieved his artifact himself.

"There are underground springs," Liam said. "And the lodge is riddled with piped-in water from those springs. The lodge functions as my home—"

"Like Uncle Mike's pub?" I asked.

"Yes and no," he said. "That's the problem. My power is unaffected, but the lodge . . . has a mind of its own. A will that acts without me—or even the will of the spirit of the hot springs."

"Magic's unpredictable like that," I said.

Liam gave a short laugh. "That it is. How may I help you find the artifact?"

"Could you speak to this spirit?" Adam said. "Ask her if she knows about the artifact we're looking for?"

"I can and will," Liam answered. "But I don't know that it will do much good. She won't always speak to me. She isn't motivated by the need to prevent the end of days. I'm not sure it would matter to her at all. What is important to her, what is essential to her very nature, is that her springs are a sanctuary for healing and for people fleeing trouble."

I knew that. I'd been told.

"Too bad for us," I said. Adam and I weren't either of those. We were in pursuit.

Liam gave me a twist of his lips. "I think that's why she and I get along most of the time—our magics align. I take care of my guests—and so does she. You are a problem. You are *my* guests, but you didn't come here for sanctuary."

"Just to clarify," Adam said, because you always were careful about assuming things with the fae. "You cannot sense an artifact here?"

"I didn't say *that*," Liam temporized. "But I *am* certain that I cannot sense the one taken from Hrímnir. This is the only one I have felt arrive here in the last month." He bent down and felt along the floor beside his chair.

I wasn't surprised when he handed me the walking stick. It was icy cold when I touched it, but quickly warmed to its usual temperature. The carved gray wood felt right as I closed my fingers around it, as if the size not only fit my hands, but that my hands were whole and complete when they held the stick.

Disconcerted, I set it on my lap. It felt ruffled and protective. Had it been a dog, it would have been growling at Liam. I shouldn't be able to know that.

"What else *are* you certain of?" I asked.

"There are no magical items of any kind in the possession of the bride's party—outside of the vampire, if you are one of those who would consider her an object rather than a person," Liam said.

"What about the people?" I asked. "Someone who knows my brother well enough he'd trust them with an artifact."

Liam pursed his lips thoughtfully. "There's just the three of us who know Gary. Hugo has been here since the storm began. He usually goes home at night—he has a place a few miles down the road, I understand. But he said he'd stay here to help."

"Hugo—the gardener?" I asked.

Liam laughed. "Yes. He holds sway over our greenhouse. He and Gary do get on together." He paused. "But Hugo is forgetful, the dear man. He is forever leaving things—I found a hoe in the lobby yesterday, and a bucket of fertilizer out by the hot tubs." He frowned as if he didn't want to say this part. "He's a little simple, I think. I wouldn't entrust him with something I didn't want to have left in the hallway. And I wouldn't put him in that kind of danger—and I don't think that Gary would, either."

Liam looked at Adam, then nodded in agreement to something he read in my husband's face. "But I'll ask him. Please don't do it yourselves. I can manage without bullying him, and I can tell if he lies to me."

"What about the girl—Emily?" Adam asked, then added, "I wouldn't leave her alone somewhere Heddar could find her. He reminded me of a cat playing with a mouse downstairs at breakfast."

Liam looked unhappy. "Noted. I like to work the young ones in pairs when I can." He sighed. "At any rate, Emily. Well. I will ask her, too. But I just don't see it."

"If not your people, it has to be the guests," Adam said.

Liam relaxed a little. "Are you sure it was Gary who stole the artifact?"

"Hrímnir is," I said.

"No," Adam answered at the same time, but added, "Probably."

"Gary barely exchanged a word with any of the wedding guests," Liam observed. "I think that you are on the mark to be suspicious of the hikers. I don't know them; they aren't local. But that doesn't mean Gary didn't. Maybe they were working together."

"It's not them," I said at the same time Adam said, "I agree."

My mate turned to look at me.

"What?" I said. "It isn't them. They said they hadn't stolen an artifact, and they weren't lying."

Adam nodded. "They did say that. But if Gary stole it, he could have given it to them to keep safe. If he didn't—a goblin might not see liberating an artifact from Hrímnir as stealing."

"They weren't afraid," I said. "The thought of Charles made them freeze in terror—and they weren't worried about the creature who was capable of causing a storm like this. I think that if they had the artifact, they'd have been more afraid of Hrímnir."

"They weren't afraid of saying 'thank you' to someone like Liam," Adam observed.

"Goblins, eh," said Liam. "They aren't powerful—but there are a lot of them and they work together. More now, since Larry has taken the throne. He has turned his horde of misfits into an army. I don't know any fae except perhaps a Gray Lord who would take advantage of a 'thank you' given by a goblin in the past decade." He shook his head and smiled with genuine amusement. "And the little pests know it."

Larry really was the king of the goblins, then. Not just the ones in the Tri-Cities.

Adam wasn't distracted by thoughts of a goblin monarchy. "So a 'thank you' is—

"A way of thumbing their noses at the powerful fae," said Liam, a hint of amusement in his voice that faded as he continued. "But Charles is not a Gray Lord or a capricious Power. Charles is the hand of judgment. He is not spiteful or wicked. If Charles comes for a goblin, the goblin king would not stand in his way. He will tell his people that justice has been done. They have a reason to fear Charles—assuming they've done something to offend him."

Or planned to, I thought, remembering the way the goblins had sounded about Bran's presumed hoard of fae artifacts. Aspen Creek, the Marrok's pack's territory, was not too far from here. Maybe the goblins had been thinking about robbing someone who was not a frost giant.

"I cannot check their rooms," Liam said. "They came here as refugees. The spirit of Looking Glass protects them."

"I don't think it's them," I said stubbornly.

"Can you look in the other people's rooms?" Adam asked.

Liam nodded. "Maybe I will organize some work parties this afternoon. We need to clear out some of this snow. I doubt the Heddars will participate—but I can look in their rooms at dinner."

"This could be a very long storm," Adam said, getting to his feet and pulling me to mine.

Liam frowned and nodded. Then he walked to the door and opened it for us to exit. Something creaked over our heads.

"I'll clear the roof while the rest of them are shoveling snow," Adam offered as he led the way out the door.

I'd been reexamining what we knew. I had much better questions than I'd had last night, and I knew who I wanted to ask about them.

"Unless you need me to shovel snow," I said, "I think I'd better check on Gary's horses."

"Hrímnir is taking care of them," Adam said.

"But it's not his job, is it?" I said. "It's Gary's, and that means it's mine."

"If you're going up to the ranch, could you check and see if Gary has any eggs?" Liam asked, bringing up the rear. "He was using the kitchen in the main building because he preferred to cook on the gas stove. I have enough for a couple of days, but I'd be happier with another dozen."

"Eggs," said Adam with a frown.

"If I don't come home, check for me in Italy," I told him. He didn't look like he thought I was funny.

AS THE CROW FLIES, THE RANCH WAS ABOUT THREE miles from the lodge. On four feet it took me about forty minutes to make the trip. The snow had lightened up, probably because it was well below zero out. The winds cut through my coyote winter coat, so I stuck to the wooded areas where the trees blocked some of it.

I'd carried Adam's pack because mine wasn't big enough to stuff my winter coat in. The straps took a bit of jury-rigging— Adam's wolf is over two hundred pounds, and my coyote is around thirty-five. But when Adam was finished, it was secure and I could still wiggle out when I wanted to change.

The barn door was closed tight and it had a round door handle, so I had to become human to get in the barn. It was a good thing that years of knowing our foul-mouthed British wolf had expanded my vocabulary of power words. They lasted me until I was able to shut the door behind me.

The horses whinnied as soon as I opened the door. One of them put a hoof on the metal bar of the panel fence and made a loud noise. The other popped his lips together, like Donkey in *Shrek*. Or maybe it had been *Shrek 2*.

"I know, I know," I told them. "I'm dressing as quick as I can. Underwear. Bra. Socks. Oh, *good* socks. *Warm* socks. Jeans. Sweatshirt. Coat."

I indulged in a full-body shiver, then put on shoes. I'd brought my tennis shoes instead of my boots because even Adam's pack didn't have room for midcalf boots as well as my coat.

"No stepping on my toes, you two," I told the horses, flexing my toes in their meager protection. "You have big feet, and the tennis shoes aren't going to help much."

They had water, though they'd drunk the tank down by about four inches. It was still warm. That would be a handy bit of magic. I wondered again if Gary would teach me how to do it.

Not that keeping water unfrozen was likely to be all that useful. But it would be fun to have a magic spell I could work. Changing into a coyote was who I was. It didn't feel like magic, and it was most useful when everyone didn't know I could do it. But keeping water unfrozen . . . that might be a neat party trick.

They had eaten every wisp of the hay I'd given them last night.

The bale I'd pulled from didn't look like it had been touched since Adam and I had left.

"A third of a bale per horse per day," I muttered, hearing my foster father's voice in my ear.

But the bales I'd fed horses with when I was a teenager had been bigger, I thought. And the horses I'd been feeding had been a lot smaller.

I tossed the rest of the open bale over the panels for the horses to start on. Then I took the knife conveniently stuck in an unopen bale to cut the strings of another one. I stuck the knife into another unopened bale so it didn't get lost in the hay chaff. Habits were coming back to me.

I fed the horses half of the new bale. It looked like a lot of hay. Too much?

"I don't know that I'm going to make it back today," I told them. I dumped the rest of the second bale into their pile of food. They were hardly going to get too fat if I overfed them for a couple of days.

I had the trough filled and was using a manure fork to toss manure into a wheelbarrow when I heard a mechanical growling sound outside. Liam had said the lodge had a backhoe, but the engine I heard was way too small for that.

Snowmobile, I thought, as the engine shut off. I considered my actions—and decided to keep doing my job. I moved the wheelbarrow to the next pile of manure.

The barn door opened and shut.

I waited until I got the last round nugget before I looked up.

The man who watched me from just inside the door was clean-shaven. A few strands of pale hair peeked out from his stretch hat, which was pulled down over his ears. The hat was black with a small label I could read from where I stood: *Carhartt*. His jacket was red-and-white plaid wool felt. He looked like a rancher bundled up to take care of livestock.

His features were familiar, like an artist had taken a rough-hewn statue and refined craggy features into something more finished. More human. I thought of shapeshifters and gryphons. I thought of my old friend Zee and the even older fae I saw in his eyes more often than I used to—and the perception I had that they were two separate people.

"Hello, Hrímnir," I said. "I was hoping we could talk."

I had thought that maybe someone who took care of horses that weren't his responsibility might continue to take care of them. I'd expected the frost giant, though, the powerful, dangerous, but not-too-clever Hrímnir I'd met last night.

This man strolled over to the fence and put his arms on the rail second from the top, which was a convenient height for him. At least in his human guise. He even smelled like a human—though one who had been out in a winter storm.

"Have you found my lyre?" he asked, his accent pure American Pacific Northwest with a hint of drawl—a Montana rancher accent, to match his clothing.

"You said it was a harp," I told him, turning my attention back to my task.

"Oh? I had not noticed." There was a rustle of clothing; I thought he might have shrugged. Then tension sharpened the back of my neck as he drew in a sudden breath. "Harp. I said harp?"

"You did. When you told me my brother stole it from you."

"What year is this?" he asked.

I told him.

"Tomorrow is the winter solstice," he said.

It hadn't been a question, but I answered him anyway. "Yes."

"Tell me," he said, and there might have been a hint of urgency in his voice. "Is there a wedding taking place at Looking Glass tomorrow?"

"Yes." I moved to the next pile of manure and positioned the wheelbarrow so I could look at him. "Or maybe. If the groom can get there in time. There's this blizzard that looks like it's going to be messing everything up."

He turned his back to me and, after a pause, started pacing restlessly. I decided to let him walk it out while I finished cleaning the pen.

I hauled the wheelbarrow behind me, because the twelve-year-old me had found that I could balance it better that way. He quit pacing when I headed toward the gate, and opened it to let me through. I found a pile of manure where I could dump my wheelbarrow load. The pile didn't look like it was big enough to be more than a week's worth. Someone had been coming in with a tractor to clean it out.

"What have you found?" he asked.

I put the wheelbarrow back where I'd found it and used the time to think about what to say.

"Do you want to put a stop to the wedding?" I asked.

"No."

He could be lying. But I didn't think he was. "Why not stop the storm, then?" I asked.

Instead of talking, he found a pair of brushes and handed one to me. Then he hopped over the five-foot panel with an ease that was more than human. I used the gate—it required less effort, and I wasn't trying to show off. I didn't think that he was, either.

He started to work on one horse; I took the other. Kept in a clean, dry pen, neither horse was more than dusty, but grooming horses was soothing. I had been horse crazy when I was twelve and thirteen. When I was fourteen, my foster parents had died, one after the other; afterward, horses had not been as important.

"You know what the wedding accomplishes," he said. It wasn't really a question.

"Liam, the green man at the hot springs, told me," I said. "The wedding must take place tomorrow or the hound Garmr is released. If he is free, when he howls, Ragnarok begins."

"Do you believe that?" he asked me. "Does Coyote's descendant"—something happened to his voice, surprise maybe—"Coyote's *daughter* believe in fate?"

I gave that a little consideration. "Let's say that I'd rather be allowed to keep my belief that there is no such thing as fate than have my belief disproved when Garmr is released and the world is destroyed."

He might have laughed. My horse's back was taller than my head, so I couldn't see him to be sure.

The horse raised his head as I hit an itchy spot. I switched out the brush for my fingers so I could dig in a bit heavier. The big horse stuck his nose in the air and peeled his lips away from his teeth in pleasure as I rubbed his belly.

"The chances of this wedding happening look pretty bleak," I said. "Last we heard, the groom was going to try to fly into Spokane. The road between here and Spokane was bad when Adam and I drove it yesterday. I'd guess it's impassable by now."

He didn't say anything, and I said, pointedly, "There's this big winter storm."

"I made a vow," he said. "Upon my power, I swore that everyone at the lodge would remain trapped where they were until my harp is back in my hands." He paused. "Or until all of the people at the hot springs are dead. I *cannot* release the storm until one or the other of the conditions is met."

"That might take a while," I said. "The lodge has food stores and water."

"If the wedding does not happen," the frost giant said, "and the Great Spell is broken, the backlash will kill everyone at Looking Glass—excepting only the spirit of the lake. One way or another, this storm does not have long to live."

"That is added incentive," I said.

I supposed that if the end of the world was coming, it didn't matter that we were all going to die if Adam and I couldn't find the harp in time. It felt like it mattered, though.

"I, too, will be gone," he said, not sounding particularly upset about it. "I do not know if there is among the remaining Jötnar one who can claim my name and live. If not, then my magic will die with me."

"Why is that?" I asked.

"Because I created the Great Spell that binds the fate of the world," he said. "I know what a world ruled by my kind looks like. I did not—do not want it to happen here."

We worked awhile.

"I made it out," I said. "Out of Looking Glass Hot Springs, I mean." I wasn't sure that it was bright of me to point that out.

"I let you come here today," he said. "I could allow you, because you were not there when I made my vow."

"You knew I'd be here," I said.

"I hoped for it, yes." His voice deepened a little. "I felt that we two should talk." I heard the scruff, scruff of his brush. Then he said, "I thought if you came to take care of the horses, we might have a few things to say to each other."

"What does it matter that you called it a harp when it looks like a lyre?" I asked, moving from my horse's belly to his rump. He huffed a disappointed sigh but went back to eating. "And what does that have to do with the winter solstice—or the wedding?"

"The instrument is the key to the Great Spell," he said. "When the renewal is close, those bindings loosen. Then Garmr can choose the shape of the leash that holds him. A hundred and forty-four years ago, he chose a lyre. That I am now calling it a harp means that is the shape it is to become. A shadow of the future." I heard him pat his horse.

I stopped brushing. "Garmr chose the shape?"

"He had no say when I bound his voice," the frost giant said. "It is right that some part of the magic responds to his will."

I rubbed my forehead, and the gelding I'd been grooming gave me a look. It made a certain sort of sense that a being who cared for the needs of horses he'd put in jeopardy—by dealing with their caretaker—would concern himself with the needs of another kind of beast.

"You didn't realize that this is the year the spell needs to be renewed until just now. Or else you wouldn't have unleashed this storm."

"No," he said. He let out a heavy breath.

"Someone stole the artifact to stop the wedding and begin the end of the world," I said.

"It does seem likely," he said.

"Did they goad you into creating this storm?" I asked.

"Possibly," he allowed.

"How did they manage that?"

"I have spent the last few decades alone in the mountains here." He sounded a little apologetic. "The winters are long and the wilderness appeals to my power. Those of us who work with the weather are more changeable than other Jötnar. It is why this shape I wear now is as much mine as the gryphon or the Jötunn you have already met. Your mate is a werewolf; you know about two-natured things. When he wears his wolf, he also wears the nature of the predator."

"Yes," I said. "He's more violent and less wise."

"Yes. That is it. When I am in my other form, as a Jötunn, I am more likely to react and less likely to think." He paused. "It is easier to be that one. He does not feel the years go by." He gave a huff of self-directed unhappy amusement. "He doesn't feel the guilt of what I have done to my good dog, who has never done anything but what I asked of him."

"Garmr," I said.

He grunted a yes. "But there is danger in staying in that self. I do not see plots." His voice became a growl. "I did not, for instance, notice that your brother became my friend in order to steal from me."

"Someone is using you to prevent the Heddars' marriage," I said slowly. "I don't think that's my brother. If he has skin in that game, it's from the other side. He's probably not going to survive Ragnarok, either." I sucked in a breath. "Someone used him, too." I didn't need to guess at who that might be.

Dear Father. What made him stick his paw into this mess? Curiosity? Love of disaster?

He grunted. Based on living with Adam, I recognized it as a masculine reluctant-agreement grunt.

"My brother Ymir," Hrímnir said finally, "awaits Ragnarok with all the fervor of one who has never seen a battlefield, who has never seen gods lying dead in a sea of the blood of the innocent." He said it with such neutrality that I was pretty sure *he* had. "Ymir lusts after the glory of the old days of war. When death came at the bite of blades instead of rockets and bombs."

"I've met a few people like that," I said.

He sighed. "I think too small, our father always said. I react. Always react. Because I would prefer to be left alone and never to act at all."

"Is that just intuition?" I asked. "That Ymir is using you to free Garmr? Because I don't see my brother believing a thing Ymir says."

But he'd reacted to Ymir, hadn't he? Had that just been because Gary's senses had been scrambled? He'd attacked Adam earlier.

"Not intuition," he said. "I have no idea what Gary's motivation was or where his loyalty lies other than with himself."

The silence grew chill—and long enough that I wondered if I'd misread him. His horse raised his head from the hay and snorted, making my horse's jaws quit moving. Quiet fell, except for the breathing of the horses.

I'd thought we were working our way to becoming allies with a common goal. But maybe I'd underestimated the drawback of my being the sister of a man Hrímnir believed had betrayed him. Hurt him. I decided not to try to defend Gary. I didn't know if there was a defense for him.

"When Ymir called to tell me he was sending you," the frost giant said, "he told me you were coming to *demand* I release Gary. He said you were dangerous and dishonorable. That the world would be better off with you dead." He paused. "Ymir could have removed the magic I bound your brother with."

Ymir had lied. Of course he had.

"With that attitude, I'd rather not have him work magic on my brother," I said with absolute truth.

"Ymir thought it might be a good idea if no one left Looking Glass Hot Springs with the artifact. That I had the means to prevent that if I chose."

My horse started eating again, and Hrímnir's horse put his head down and followed suit.

"So why didn't you kill us?" I asked.

"I *do* know who your mate is," Hrímnir said. "Gary and I were friends . . . since sometime near the summer solstice. He liked talking about you. I know what purpose your territory serves to maintain the peace between the humans and our kind. *I* understand the humans have weapons that could vie with Jötnar magics for destructive power, should they choose to use them."

That whole bit sounded like a non sequitur, but I thought he was leading up to something. I kept my mouth shut and waited.

"I told him that I would not kill Adam, because of the role he and his pack played," Hrímnir said. "Ymir assured me that it was not a problem. That he, my brother, could take the pack and make them even stronger. The wolf is his to call."

"When he came to examine Gary"—I fought to keep a neutral voice, but it emerged sharpened—"he took control of one of our wolves without her consent . . . or ours. My husband took her back from him."

"So you said earlier." Hrímnir stepped around the horses so he could see my face. "Your husband is strong."

"Yes."

I was pretty sure that if Ymir tried to take the pack while Adam and I were here, Adam would notice. Even I, as a pack member, could still feel those bonds. The pack was okay, I reassured myself. They'd be okay until we got back.

I don't know what he saw in my face, but whatever it was, he apparently approved. He nodded once, then walked back, putting the horses between us once more.

"Are you going to find my harp?" he asked.

"Is there a reason we can't just line everyone up and ask who has the artifact?" I asked. I didn't mean to whine. "I can tell when someone is lying. Adam and I might not be able to force the Heddars or the vampire to cough it up—but Liam is anxious to let the marriage take place. The three of us—"

"They are all guests," the frost giant said, apparently unsurprised about the vampire. "Liam cannot allow you to take something by force regardless of his personal feelings on the matter. And if you scare whoever has it—they might destroy it."

I rubbed my temples to alleviate my headache. He was on the other side of the horse, but I felt the frost giant notice. I shouldn't have been able to know that.

I needed to get out of here soon. I did not want to be standing next to the frost giant when the damage I'd received from the Soul Taker decided to open my mind again.

"There's a pair of goblins," I said, to distract myself from my weakness. "They aren't with the wedding party—they were apparently planning on climbing in the Cabinet Mountains but were discouraged by the blizzard."

"Do you think they took the harp?" he asked me.

"Liam does, I think. Possibly Adam, too." Though Adam wouldn't say so unless he had proof.

"Do you think they took the harp?" he asked again, in exactly the same tone.

"No." I blew a bit of horsehair off my face.

"My brother took the harp," I said slowly, trying to work things out through the warning buzz in my head. "Then he dropped it off at the hot springs or hid it or somethinged it. But it makes the most sense if he left it with someone at the lodge. You wouldn't just dump an artifact somewhere and leave it by itself." I paused. "I wouldn't, anyway. There is no end to the trouble a loose artifact can cause."

"*Somethinged* it," said Hrímnir, as if he enjoyed the word. "And then came to tell me he'd done it."

I stopped grooming. Incredulously, I turned around.

"What in the name of little green apples did Gary do that for? I thought you caught him, or cornered him into telling you what he'd done. He just went up to you and said, 'Hey, you know that harp . . . lyre . . . thingy? Yeah, I'm the one who took it'?"

"You know," Hrímnir said ruminatively, "I should have waited for him to tell me why before I spelled him to shut him up. And to punish him." He stared at me. "Because you are just like he described you. And you risked running into me in order to make sure the horses had food and water."

"Maybe I came here to see if I could talk to you," I said. "Because you'd been up here to take care of the horses yesterday." I tapped my nose.

"Maybe," he said. "But that's how he described you, too. I would like to know what my brother did to make your brother befriend me, then steal my harp."

I scoffed. "There is nothing that your brother could do to make Gary take your harp." I was pretty sure about that.

"Ymir has money. More gold than Andrew Heddar."

"If my brother were motivated by money," I said dryly, "he wouldn't be babysitting a ranch in the winter and breaking colts in the summers."

Hrímnir grunted.

"Besides," I said, "there is no world in which Ymir and my brother managed a civil conversation for longer than it took one of them to open his mouth."

Hrímnir grunted again, this time in agreement, and went back to grooming. After a while, he stepped back, and then held out a hand for the brush I was using. "They're clean enough."

His hand touched mine when I gave him the brush. I think I expected to feel something—that his skin would be hot like the werewolves, or cold because he was a frost giant. I expected to feel the power of the storm. But it felt exactly like any other hand I'd ever touched.

"You still have no idea where the harp is?" he asked.

He sounded . . . odd. But not angry.

"No," I said. "But if we are all going to die tomorrow if Adam and I don't find it, I'd better get back."

I walked to the horse pen's gate, conscious that he wasn't following me. I unhooked the chain.

"What happened to rip open your mind?"

The question was said in virtually the same tone as his previous query had been; it took me a moment to process what he'd said. Open gate in my hand, I turned to look back at him.

Before I could figure out what to say, he narrowed his eyes. "Not your mind. Your magic and your soul."

That was more than I'd known about the damage. "I encountered an artifact called the Soul Taker," I told him. "I don't suppose there's any chance you could fix this." I tapped my head.

"I am not a healer." He tipped his head. "The Soul Taker. Time was that the priests who held the Soul Taker could see inside the souls of men."

I couldn't help but grimace. "And women."

"I met one once," he said. "He gouged his own eyes out."

Yep. I needed to get this fixed even if I had to ask Coyote. "Did that help?"

"I don't remember," Hrímnir said. "Where is the artifact?"

"Siebold Adelbertsmiter destroyed it," I told him.

He drew in a breath. "It's good that you destroyed it—or had Wayland Smith destroy it. As you said, stray artifacts do nothing but cause trouble."

"That's true," I agreed.

"Go back to the hot springs and find that harp, Mercy Hauptman," said Hrímnir, who was apparently done with the topic of me and my damage. "I cannot trespass there to help you, but I will give you such—" He stopped speaking for a moment as if searching for a word. I caught a flash of expression that I couldn't interpret. "—aid as I might. There isn't much time. You need to find out where the harp is and bring it to me. Then I can let the storm dissipate." He paused, then said softly, "I will do anything in my power to help you find it."

I nodded and left the pen. I shut the gate and stood for a minute. "If my brother took the artifact, it's because he thought he was doing the right thing."

Again, I couldn't read the expression on Hrímnir's face. Old creatures are good at hiding their emotions. "Possibly," he said. "Doing the right thing doesn't mean no one gets hurt."

"Did he know about the wedding?" I asked. "I mean, it would be stupid of him to leave the harp there if he wanted to stop the wedding."

"I didn't tell him," Hrímnir said. "I didn't remember. It's one of the ways I protected the Great Spell—no one remembers it until they need to. Only the couples who are the heart of the spell."

"You don't remember it?"

"I choose not to," he said. "Most of the time. It's another reason I do not use this self"—he waved his hands to indicate his own form—"much."

"What about Ymir?" I asked. "Why does he know about it? Why does he remember it?"

"Someone told him," Hrímnir said. "The spell that keeps it secret weakens as it nears its time for renewal. Ymir is powerful, and that power is ancient and deep. Now that he knows, he will remember until after the marriage. If there is another marriage."

"Who else could remember once they found out?" I asked.

He smiled grimly. "That may be the right question. A Power, maybe. Someone like your Wayland Smith. One of the old gods. Odin or Thor." He pronounced them like an American would have, not like Zee did.

I didn't ask him about that. There was someone else who might not forget. Liam had officiated at the last wedding—and when we'd first met, he'd told me I reminded him of someone.

"I rather think that you will remember," Hrímnir told me. "Mercy Coyotesdaughter."

I stared at him.

"Go now, Mercy," he said. "Go find my harp."

"I'll do my best," I said. I made it to the door, hefting up the empty pack before I remembered. I turned to see that he had not moved from where I'd left him. "I'm going up to the main building to look for some eggs to bring back to the hot springs."

"Electricity is off," he said. "Likely anything in the house is frozen."

I smiled at him. "I was just letting you know—I wasn't asking permission."

I shut the barn door behind me and cursed my tennis shoes all the way to the main building. He was right, it was very cold in the house—but the refrigerator was commercial quality and it had maintained its temperature. It was warmer in the fridge than in the house.

I found three dozen eggs, but there was only room for two dozen in my pack, once I had my coat jammed in it. Taking the second dozen eggs meant leaving my wet tennis shoes behind.

When I got back outside, the snowmobile was gone and the snow was once more falling heavily.

THE TRIP BACK TO THE HOT SPRINGS WAS A LOT MORE miserable than the way out to the ranch had been. On the way, the wind had been at my back; now I was forced to travel against it. The driving snow bit at my eyes and nose in a way that disoriented even my coyote self. If I hadn't had my mate bond telling me which way Adam was, I would have gotten turned around.

I lost track of time. I'd started out in a steady trot, but couldn't keep it up in the face of the storm. I hoped that Adam wasn't still up on the roof in this wind.

My eyes stung, and I was feeling pretty sorry for myself when I stepped onto the sacred land. The storm didn't lessen, exactly, but the despair that had piled onto my back decreased remarkably.

I traveled maybe another quarter of a mile through the trees and into a clearing. Even through the blasting snow, I could see the lodge. I paused then. For a moment I wasn't sure why. I couldn't smell anything but the storm, could barely see well enough to avoid running into a tree. But—

It coalesced from nothingness, blending in with the magic that saturated the land, then becoming denser with every breath I took until it stood in front of me, as real as the snow beneath my feet.

Garmr, I thought.

Looking at him, I understood the confusion about what exactly he was—dog or wolf, neither quite fit. He was nearly twice as tall as Adam's wolf and more massive. The size of a grizzly, at least. His muzzle was broad and flat, more like our Joel in either his presa Canario form or the volcano demon dog he could become than a wolf. But Garmr's heavy gray coat and his yellow eyes said *wolf.*

Other than his eyes, there was nothing obviously aggressive about his stance—and that he had taken form foursquare in my path. Hrímnir spoke to him, so he was intelligent. It was not an accident that he blocked my way.

I wondered if Garmr knew who I was and what I was trying to do. I wondered if he wanted to be bound for another hundred and forty-four years, or would rather break free to start a massive war that would destroy the world. He didn't look particularly violent.

I, too, had unwelcome ties that bound me in uncomfortable ways. If I considered what Stefan, my friend the vampire, could do to me if he chose, the panic closed up my throat so hard I could not breathe.

I jumped sideways a hair's breadth before he attacked, because I was not surprised that he'd want to stop me. That meant his jaws closed over the pack on my back instead of the nape of my neck. His jerk, a movement designed to snap my spine, still flung me powerfully to one side.

I had practiced this, though. I shifted to my human shape as my weight hit the straps and I twisted, then shifted back to coyote and twisted some more. Adam's pack, even modified, didn't fit as well as my own, and I was free of it sooner than I expected.

I ran. I am speedier than a real coyote. Quicker than most of the werewolves, too. I knew where I was going, and I sent a wild call out to Adam—though he'd have felt my fear when Garmr attacked.

The guardian of Hel was faster. His teeth closed over my haunch. I don't know that I had ever felt such pain. I couldn't hear or see through the searing agony of what those teeth did—but it hurt my head so badly I didn't feel any pain from my flesh.

I tore free more easily than should have been possible. And the leg he'd savaged still worked as well as it ever had. His teeth had passed right through my body—and done much more damage to my being than if he'd chewed on me physically.

I knew, *I knew*, I couldn't let him bite me again. Still running, but now adapting a zigzagging, random path like a drunken rabbit, I made myself more difficult to catch and gained some ground on him. Possibly he was just playing with me.

I shifted to human. Naked in the icy storm, I wouldn't be able to function for long. My toes burned and the wind cut into my flesh. I reached out into the air and closed my hand on the walking stick.

INTERLUDE

Bonners Ferry, Idaho

ZANE

HE LEFT EZRA AND LEON AT A HOTEL IN SANDPOINT when the radio announced the road was closed past Bonners Ferry. The two of them—the avenger and the caretaker—were necessary for the Great Spell, but they were also people he loved. And they were human. From the weather report—and his inability to contact Liam at the lodge—he assumed the worst. He didn't think any human could make it through this storm.

The Suburban he'd purchased in Spokane made it to Bonners Ferry only because of the chains he had on all four wheels. When he reached the barricade, he turned around and parked at the gas station a half mile back down the road. The lot was full of semi-trucks and stranded motorists.

He left the Suburban and headed into the storm.

12

ADAM

ADAM HAD TRIED TO TALK MERCY INTO EATING BE-
fore she headed out to the ranch. Liam was determined that his
snow shovelers should have lunch before he put them to work. But
once Mercy had decided that the horses needed tending to, waiting was not an option.

"When someone locks them up in a barn, they can't take care
of themselves," she told him. Then, with a frown, she asked, "Are
you sure you want to do that? I can just leave my coat behind."

He'd already destroyed the straps on his pack, so her words
came a little late.

"I can get another one," he told her.

"Yes, but I know how much that one cost."

Her coat didn't fit in her pack—which was much smaller to
accommodate her coyote. He was tired of watching Mercy shiver.
His pack was replaceable, and with a sharp knife and liberal ap-
plication of duct tape—which he always kept in his SUV—his

larger pack could be made to work. He was just grateful he'd thought to throw the packs they carried in their other forms into the SUV at the last minute.

"I can get another one," he repeated.

Keep it casual, Hauptman, he cautioned himself. If he smothered her, she would leave. If he smothered her and she did not leave, he would be making her weaker. Less safe. And that was unacceptable.

He measured the pack straps against her and cut off another three inches.

"Another hour wouldn't hurt them," he tried.

"You tend to your horses before you tend to yourself," she said, and he recognized both the cadence and the finality. Silently, he cursed Charles and anyone else who had taught Mercy about the care and feeding of horses.

He reminded himself that Mercy would be okay if she waited until she got back to eat. She'd eaten a big breakfast. She wasn't a werewolf; she didn't need the calories that the rest of the pack did.

His wolf wanted to insist on going with her. He'd already done that once, and it had gotten him here. But that had been different, and for a different cause. He didn't mistrust her ability to take care of herself—he had wanted, had *needed*, her to know that she came first. Before pack.

His Mercy was prickly about her independence, and it had taken a battering over the past couple of years. He didn't want to change her; he only wanted to keep her safe. Sometimes he had to admit he couldn't do both. He had to trust her to know her limits. She was good about asking for help when she needed it.

The ranch wasn't that far away, and the storm had subsided a little. Her coyote was probably even better equipped for traveling through this country in the winter than his wolf was. She was light enough to run on top of the snowpack, whereas he would have to break a trail.

He might still have insisted on coming if it hadn't been for the reconsideration he'd seen in Liam's face when Adam hadn't fussed about Mercy going out in the storm on her own. Mercy was safer if everyone saw that Adam respected her ability to protect herself. It made them understand she was dangerous—even though most of them wouldn't know why.

When Bonarata had demonstrated how easily he could have killed Adam, it had rubbed Adam's nose in the fact that, at the levels Mercy and he were now playing at, he could not count on his werewolf being powerful enough to keep her safe. But he'd been dumped on his own, under-armed, in a country where he didn't speak the language and had no good way of telling friend from foe. He'd been outclassed in Vietnam, too, and he'd survived. He'd done that by learning, by getting better at his job, and by figuring out how to do that job with inadequate tools.

So directly after Bonarata had finished educating Adam, Adam had gone to the scariest, most deadly warrior he knew and asked him for lessons. He was learning how to be more lethal, but he was also learning how to keep Mercy safe among the paranoid, powerful fae.

Zee told him that having your enemy overestimate you was as useful as having them underestimate you. Adam's casual acceptance of Mercy running out alone in the storm made Liam wonder what Mercy was capable of.

If letting Mercy go alone to the ranch without a fight made her safer from the assorted crazy and powerful beings here, he could do that. He'd still rather have had her eat first, but that was her choice.

"Stop growling," she said, stripping out of her clothes and

stuffing them into the pack with her coat. "It's cute but it won't get you anywhere."

Adam couldn't help his sheepish smile—and didn't bother fighting it because she wasn't looking at him anyway.

She held up a boot to size it against the space left in the backpack, shrugged, and stuffed her tennis shoes in. He didn't protest because she wasn't going to be wearing them out in the storm. But he took her socks out of her hands and put a pair of his woolen hiking socks in the bag instead.

She laughed and then went to work zipping up the pack. The light shone along her naked back and flank, highlighting the faint silvery scars where some Montana rancher had unloaded a shotgun at a coyote. At least there wouldn't be anyone out hunting coyotes in a storm like this.

He ran his hand over the scars—a reminder that his mate was a target, that he couldn't protect her from everything, but also that she was a survivor. She leaned into his touch, and he bent until he could wrap both of his arms around her waist and pull her into his body.

"Not going to get this pack zipped up this way," she said with a huff of laughter.

He tucked his head between her neck and shoulder, just below her ear, and breathed in. "You come back safely," he said. "I don't want to live in a world without you in it."

"Don't worry," she told him. "If I die, I'll be like Jack and come back to haunt you."

He bet she would, his stubborn love. Oddly, that reassured him enough that he could let her go—though not before he kissed her bare shoulder.

Standing, he said, "Get a move on. How can I miss you if you don't go?"

"Way to ruin a tender moment," she mock-complained, tightening the compression straps so the pack was dense instead of puffy and sloppy.

Then she shifted to coyote.

He put the pack on her, making sure the straps around her shoulders and belly were just right—too tight and she wouldn't be able to get out of it or shift safely back to human, too loose and it would hinder her travel. She could have put it on and then shifted, but she let him do that for her.

He understood her, and tried very hard to give her what she needed. She tried very hard to do the same for him.

He opened a window and she hopped out and was away. He stood, the winter blowing into the room, until he couldn't see her for the woods and the flying snow. Then, very quietly, he said, "Come back to me, love."

THE SCENE IN THE DINING ROOM WAS VERY MUCH AS it had been at breakfast. Adam contemplated the goblins, who were carefully not looking at him, and the Heddars—and sat down at the table with Elyna's people.

Peter was a little twitchy, but Adam had been getting a lot of practice at dealing with hyperdominant people. He had no trouble finding common ground at a table filled with those who dealt with humanity at their worst and best moments.

Peter and one of the other men had served in the marines. When Adam admitted to his ranger background, they exchanged the kind of ribbing the branches of military reserved for their allies. His security career was enough like police work that it gave him an entry with the rest of Peter's pack—as Mercy had dubbed them after breakfast.

By the time the teenager—Emily—came in with glasses, a pitcher of ice water, and sandwiches, they were exchanging absurd work stories. When it was his turn, he told them about how four of his men, responding to an alarm, chased the suspect down into a back office—and encountered a skunk. The skunk won handily.

Tammy came in late, picking up her food in the kitchen. She looked unhappy, and when she sat down, she said, "I tried calling Zane, but it looks like the phones are still down."

Adam's sat phone still wasn't working, but he didn't think it would be useful to tell them that.

The table looked grim.

"What happens if he doesn't make it?" asked Peter.

She glanced at Adam and said, "The end of my world."

That was so obvious that Adam decided to clear the air a bit. So he nodded at Tammy and said, "The end of the world."

The whole table looked at him with a fair bit of hostility.

What had Liam said? Something about how the wedding guests would come to an understanding about what the wedding was and their part in it. He wondered how that had happened. Had they just woken up knowing about the Great Spell and accepting it and everything that it implied?

"I'm here to help," Adam told them. "Or maybe to play some harp. Or is it a lyre?" He flapped his hands to imitate little wings on his shoulders.

"You're an angel?" asked Peter sardonically. "You don't look like one."

No one at the table had a reaction when he said either "harp" or "lyre." That confirmed that none of these people had the harp—and that Elyna hadn't told them why Adam and Mercy were here. Mercy had asked her not to, until they had a better handle on what was going on. But Tammy and her people for damn sure knew about the Great Spell now.

"You're right," Adam agreed. "I'm a werewolf. We did come here to help Mercy's brother. I'd prefer that we not participate in the end of the world."

Peter sat back. "Fair enough."

"How did you get caught up in a marriage that decides the fate of the world?" Adam asked the bride-to-be, deciding to take down the temperature a bit.

"For the money," Tammy said instantly. "Why not?"

She was a good liar. The blue eyes she'd inherited from her father helped that innocent look along. Police officers learned to be good at deception, too. Blandness spread around the table like butter on warm bread.

"I bet you gave your dad fits when you were a teenager," Adam said. "Werewolves can tell when someone is lying."

She cracked up. She had a good laugh—earthy and warm.

"I practiced that one for the reporters," she admitted. "It gives them something that will sell papers, and Zane knows it's not true. That's all that matters to me."

He judged that if he took the tension down one more notch, no one would notice he didn't tell them anything they didn't already know. He wasn't sure how the conflicting protections—the green man and the spirit of the lake—would sort themselves out with each other *and* with him and Mercy when they finally figured out where the artifact was. He decided keeping information close to his chest was still the best policy.

He asked the heart of the pack, "How did you meet?" and settled down to listen.

"It was the legs that caught his attention," Tammy said in a sultry voice, hopping her chair back a couple of times so she could display her jean-clad legs. The table erupted into laughter.

Shuffling footsteps headed their way from the kitchen at a rapid pace. Adam checked Peter's unconcerned face and didn't turn around to see who the stranger was.

"I was in my office when our director brought a couple of big-money donors to meet me," Tammy said, once the others had calmed down.

As the footsteps neared the table, a man's toneless whisper said, "Is this the leg story? You promised me the leg story."

"This is the leg story," said Tammy, her voice gentling. "Join us."

Adam turned to see an older man, his rolled-up shirtsleeves damp with dishwater, snagging a chair from the nearest table. He set his chair next to Tammy's and regarded her with earnest attention.

He'd never been a big man, Adam judged, but age had shrunk the newcomer until he looked almost frail—except for the calluses on his hands. And an inner fierceness that Adam's wolf noticed, though Adam didn't know why the wolf was so certain.

"You must be Hugo," Adam said, "who grew the flowers on the tables."

Hugo offered Adam a sweet smile. "I am Hugo," he said with odd emphasis, nodded, and repeated, "Hugo." He reached a hand across the table so he could exchange a handshake. "You are the famous werewolf Adam Hauptman." The whisper didn't change, and Adam remembered that Liam had told them that Hugo's voice had been damaged.

For all of his age, his grip was firm.

"I am Adam Hauptman," Adam replied, deciding to ignore the "famous werewolf." It had felt a little like a dig, though Hugo's smile was friendly and his expression was a little unfocused.

As soon as the introductions were done, Tammy continued her story. "Now, in that job, we went out and checked in with our local homeless population all the time. We knew them, and they knew and trusted us."

Hugo wasn't fae. Adam was sure of that. Nor was he a witch. Adam wasn't Mercy, who could pinpoint supernatural people by the scent of their magic, but he'd have been prepared to bet money that Hugo was *something*.

"—and because of that, I got a reputation. When anyone—park personnel, police, or even some of the homeless people—would find them, they would bring them to me—"

Adam listened to Tammy with half an ear. His wolf was *fascinated* by Hugo. Adam knew better than to discount the wolf's instincts.

Liam had said Hugo was simple. Neurodiverse, maybe, Adam thought. The old man's interpersonal communication was *off*. But there was a confidence in the way Hugo moved that belied any lack of intelligence.

Adam wished Mercy were here to tell him what she thought of Hugo. He was willing to bet—from his wolf's reaction—that there was something very special about the lodge's gardener.

"—'Any questions?'"

He could tell from the happy anticipation of the rest of the table that Tammy was nearing the climax of the story, so Adam brought his attention back to her.

"And Zane said, 'Just one. Why do you have three prosthetic legs on your desk?' And I said, before my good sense could intervene, 'Why? Are you a leg man?' He leaned over the desk and said, 'Absolutely. Would you come to dinner with me?'"

"And she said no," Peter said proudly.

"Dating donors is a good way to ruin your charity's funding," she said. "It took him three months to talk me into it. He sent his dating résumé, with letters of recommendation from all of his former girlfriends—and one boyfriend." She grinned.

Hugo asked her to repeat parts of her story—some he hadn't quite understood, and some he wanted more information about. Subtle humor didn't seem to be a concept he was very good with. The whole table chimed in, all of them, Adam thought with interest, protective of the gardener.

He was just getting ready to excuse himself when Liam came in to request help with the snow.

THERE HAD BEEN OTHER VOLUNTEERS TO HELP CLEAR the roof, but Liam had quashed them all. The roof was pitched properly steep to have survived nearly a hundred years of Montana winters, which was steep enough to be dangerous, especially since the old shingles had been replaced with metal a few years ago. If Adam fell off, even from that height, he was unlikely to do any permanent damage to himself. The same could not be said of any of the humans.

Liam showed Adam where the extendable ladder was stored in an outbuilding and helped him carry the unwieldy thing over the snowdrifts to the back of the lodge. Where the greenhouse extended from the side of the lodge, they found a nook that was somewhat protected from the wind gusts, and set the ladder up.

Even in the shelter of the greenhouse, Liam had to hold the ladder to keep the wind from dislodging it. Liam had borrowed some climbing gear from the goblins—who had not volunteered to help. The goblins, with their mountain-climbing experience, would have probably been better at this than Adam. But according to Liam, they had handed over the gear without a word and disappeared into their rooms.

"The goblins really don't like you," Liam said, giving Adam a speculative glance.

"Someone told them I kill their kind," Adam said, going over the equipment carefully. "It's not true, but I don't blame them for being wary."

Adam put the climbing harness on, making adjustments as necessary. Liam didn't say anything more, so Adam didn't, either. He put the rope over his shoulder and started up the ladder, trusting Liam to hold it steady.

The wind grew stronger the higher up Adam climbed, but he'd been expecting that. He had grabbed a pair of safety glasses from the SUV because the driving snow did a pretty good job of sand-blasting his eyes. But the second time he had to stop to clear them on the way to the roof, he put them in his pocket. His eyes would just have to deal.

Once at the top of the ladder, he examined the environment he'd be working in. He'd chosen to climb up the back of the building where the wind had blown the roof mostly clear. His initial plan had been to walk up this side of the roof and tie off to one of the chimneys that Liam had assured him were in superb shape and very sturdy.

From his current vantage point, though, he realized that plan needed some tweaking. He'd seen slides in playgrounds that looked less slick than this roof. Walking wasn't going to work.

He knew there was a grin on his face as he charged up the roof—hopefully where the joist two-by-fours supported the aluminum from underneath. He reached the nearest chimney and roped himself up without incident. He let out a sharp whistle, so Liam knew he was free to go run herd on the ground-bound snow shovel personnel.

Snow shoveling in a blizzard when the metal underneath his feet was slick and set steeper than forty degrees was much more entertaining than the ordinary sort. Especially when, finished with the less snow-packed south-facing side, he turned his attention to the front, where the ice dam had kept the snow in place. The first load he shoveled off the roof landed either on top of someone or on a path someone had just cleared, from the swearing that drifted up to him.

"Sorry," he called down, not really meaning it.

Adam had done his share of mountain climbing. The last time had been about twenty years ago, but he didn't have any trouble remembering how it worked. The goblins' equipment was a little lighter and more user-friendly than what he'd used, but that could have been as much due to price point as it was to a couple of decades of technological advancements.

Three stories in the air, the wind was more than brutal. After a few minutes of working on the north side, Adam put his safety glasses back on and pulled his balaclava over his face for good measure. He imagined Mercy making comments about bank robbers.

It wasn't a quick job. There was a lot of roof, a lot of snow, and a stubborn ridge of ice. He had to temper the force he used when he was separating the ice from the metal roof so his hardened steel shovel didn't go right through the aluminum.

After a bit the wind picked up and the temperature dropped, but by that time the work had warmed his muscles so he didn't much notice. Werewolves were built for winter, even in human shape. He found clearing the roof deeply satisfying. An old soldier learned to relish a task with clear objectives.

Eventually, even with the bite of the wind and the occasional face-plant when his boots slipped, he lost himself in the work. The snowball caught him by surprise when it hit the back of his neck.

He jerked around, but there was no one on the roof with him. The trajectory had been wrong to come from the ground—it would have had to come over the ridge of the roof. He looked at the nearest trees suspiciously, though it would take a werewolf to make a snowball fly that far. No one lurked in the trees.

When nothing more happened, he looked down to take the next scrape—and saw an arrow drawn in the pristine snow he'd been about to shovel. The arrow had not been there when the snowball hit him. He would have noticed.

He inhaled, but he didn't smell anyone. Though there was one person here he wouldn't smell, wasn't there?

"What's up, Jack?" Adam asked, his gaze following the direction of the arrow until he saw something big moving out there in the woods. It was maybe a quarter of a mile away as the crow flies.

He pulled his safety glasses off and tipped his head to protect his eyes from the wind.

Without knowing exactly how far away it was, he couldn't judge the size with accuracy—except that along the edges of the lake on the northeast side there were a series of picnic benches where, in better weather, guests could eat. One of those picnic tables was directly between Adam and the whatever it was—bear? It was the wrong shape for a bear, but closer to that than a moose. The picnic table, which was closer, was less than half the size of the creature. Grizzly, Adam thought. Or something with a grizzly size and shape.

Despite the distance, he breathed in, his wolf itching to identify the predator who had entered his territory, no matter how temporary that territory was. Adam agreed with the wolf, especially as the creature waited just along the path Mercy would be taking back from the ranch.

He stared at the distant creature for a few breaths. Thought about why Jack would be worried about a grizzly that far away from the lodge. Then he reached for Mercy through their bond.

It was his habit not to spy on his wife; he knew how she felt about it. Mostly he was content just to know that she was out there, somewhere. Instantly he could tell that she was close—and that was all he could pick up. She wasn't blocking him, and there was nothing wrong with their bond. Maybe, he thought, as his pulse picked up with the call to action, whatever was interfering with their bond was the same thing that interfered with his sat phone. Hrímnir's storm eliminating communication, maybe. Magic could be literal like that.

Mercy should be on her way back from the horses by now. He'd lost track of time, but he'd been up here awhile. And if she traveled cross-country, which would be faster than the road, he reckoned that her path would cross right where that beast was.

It—and it didn't move like any bear he'd ever seen—was waiting for Mercy.

Although this conviction came without facts to back it up, Adam had survived this long by not questioning his odd convictions. Instincts. And something had driven Jack to make sure Adam noticed the creature lying in wait.

Adam dropped the glasses, ignoring how they tumbled off the edge of the roof. He rid himself of his safety line by the simple expedient of breaking the carabiner that attached his harness to the rope. Free, he ran down the freshly cleared roof, picking up speed from the steep pitch.

Discipline kept the wolf from emerging as he leapt off the edge of the roof. Clearing the mess of the lodge's front gardens with a few feet to spare, he landed on his feet and rolled to protect his joints. They would heal if he damaged them, of course, but he needed them to get to Mercy.

He was conscious of Peter's shout as Adam started sprinting through the deep snow. Without the thirty-odd feet of elevation, he couldn't see the creature—and he'd never seen Mercy at all. But he knew where it was. He'd have to run around the edge of the lake.

He thought about traversing the lake. This side—he was on the far side of the lodge from the hot springs—was frozen solid, scored by drifts of snow. He might cut the distance by a third if he ran on the ice.

But werewolves can't swim. If he fell through, he would never make it in time to help Mercy. He vaulted over assorted raised flower beds and fences until he was running along something that might be a path that edged the lake, where there were no trees or shrubs to hinder him. Like the rest of the ground, though, it was full of treacherous drifts that he had to break through or jump.

The wolf's paws would be faster than his clumsy human feet that had no claws to dig into the snow. That knowledge burned in the magic in his blood. But he couldn't afford the time it would take him to shift.

Someone from the lodge was running behind him, calling questions. But Adam's wolf had risen in his heart, and he was unable to understand the human words. Adam didn't slow himself down by looking behind him.

As he ran, Adam continued to reach out for Mercy through their mating bond. But none of the tricks he'd learned did anything to let him break through.

His wolf pulled on the pack bonds—which were of more use. From that pathway, he could tell she was in a lot of pain. Not quite enough to register in the pack without someone actively seeking her out. She wasn't dying. Not yet. He didn't kid himself that she was okay.

Something was hurting her.

Everything slowed down, as it did in the middle of battle—as if there were seconds between each of the beats of his heart. Someone had hurt his mate.

He would stop them.

His human body was too slow. He was armed, but that wasn't enough for the wolf inside him. He needed to have access to his teeth and claws.

He needed to not be too late this time—as they had been too late before.

A flash of Mercy's garage as it had been, blood and bits of

flesh that used to be a human man. Mercy had already killed her attacker, and all that Adam could do was tear the body to bits. He had not been fast enough.

And on a barren vineyard just two months ago, he'd writhed in the understanding that if Bonarata had wanted to kill Mercy, there was nothing that Adam could do about that.

Adam knew that he didn't have time to change. Even if his pack had all been present, there wasn't time to change. Changing would make him slower. With the pack so far away, he wasn't even going to be half-shifted by the time he got to the place where he'd seen the creature. Adam could fight as human or wolf—but mid-change, he was clumsy and slow.

He understood that.

But someone was hurting his mate and he *needed* to not be too late. The wolf answered that need and ignored logic—because this was not time for logic, or for human calculations. The wolf was ascendant now and Adam had lost his chance to stop it—if he had ever had one.

He shed his clothing as quickly as he could, with no thought of wearing any of it again—including his boots. He didn't even notice when the climbing harness was ripped to pieces. He retained enough presence of mind to throw his gun at the lake.

He threw it like he'd have thrown a baseball. It broke through the ice and fell into the water—where it was less likely it could be used by his enemies. He quit fighting then, and gave himself over to the wolf.

But Adam despaired, even as the wolf pulled on the pack ties. He felt the strain of harvesting the pack's strength from such a distance, but anything that sped up his change might be the difference between life and death. As Alpha, he asked and they gave—and then there was a sudden hard surge of power, different from the pack magic, that brought Adam down to the ground in a spectacular tumbling fall.

Sherwood's wild magic freely sent.

He thrust himself to his feet again, needing to run as long as he could. As he did, he howled through his still mostly human throat with the agony of that burning power that neither Adam nor the wolf had the ability to use. This was wild magic, unfettered power that didn't come willingly to his call the way the pack magic came.

But there was a part of him that could use it. The part that had allowed him to break Mary Jo free of Ymir.

Let me, suggested the Beast that lived inside him.

Neither Adam nor his wolf trusted that creature. This wasn't their pack home, where he could count on others to help if the Beast was freed.

The creature a witch had cursed Adam with was horrific, swift, and deadly. But when it was in charge, it fought only by instinct—and instinct had not been enough to win against Bonarata.

Brute strength had not kept Mercy safe then. Adam didn't think it would be enough now. Worse, he didn't know if the Beast would even pick the right target.

He still had nightmares about the time when it had nearly killed Mercy.

But the Beast didn't require Adam's consent. It fed from the power Sherwood gave them and used it to peel off Adam's human body with the same ease and care that Adam had used to shed his shredded coat—and in about the same amount of time.

There was a moment that Adam felt himself slipping under the rage—but before the Beast could force its form on Adam, the wolf seized control, driving the Beast under with the ruthless efficiency of the Alpha of the Columbia Basin Pack.

And the Beast understood and let itself be thrust to the background.

Adam decided he would worry about what that meant later. Now he rolled out of the snow and onto his feet, four feet that belonged to the wolf. Adam and his wolf fell into the one-in-purpose compromise that they had fought for together and achieved with the help of fifty-odd years of moon hunts.

The change had been at the swifter cursed-by-a-witch speed that brought the Beast out, and not the usual quarter of an hour or so that Adam would have managed instead. It wasn't Mercy's in-a-blink change, but it had been fast. Thirty seconds, maybe, between his fall and rising to run as the wolf.

Four clawed paws meant that he could increase his speed because there was no chance of slipping. While Adam had been down, the one who had been following him from the lodge, running flat-out with inhuman speed, had sped past without pausing. Some part of Adam understood it was Liam, but the wolf only understood the green man as someone who had yet to prove himself an ally.

But now, in wolf shape, the fae was no match for Adam's speed. Far in the lead, Adam crested the rise of ground that hid what proved to be a small depression where he'd first seen the monster in the woods. But he wasn't thinking about the green man except as a possible future threat because, finally, he saw Mercy.

In that odd place where time was plentiful, Adam took in the scene before him as he gathered himself to attack.

Mercy lay naked on the ground, curled on her side. Her body

was wrapped around the walking stick as if to protect it—or the opposite. The old fae artifact was in its battle form, the sharp head of the spear just visible in the snow under her chin.

Crouched over her, the creature had enveloped Mercy's shoulder in its enormous mouth—Adam caught a glimpse of the yellowish fangs buried deep. Mercy's body moved as the beast's jaws flexed. Adam's sudden intrusion didn't distract it from what it was doing. Feeding.

Even as he considered his best attack, Adam noted that he could smell wet dog and a scent that he recognized. But although he could see the fangs buried in Mercy's shoulder, there wasn't enough blood. He caught a faint metallic odor, but not as strongly as he should have for the apparent injury. What he smelled was indicative of scrapes, not wounds. No blood stained the snow.

The creature was immense. It had a bearlike body the size of a horse. The fighter in Adam categorized the fangs as commensurate with its size, but the claws were blunt and short. The rest of him noted absently that it was vaguely canid, from a more distant point of the canid tree than Adam's own werewolf was.

And it had withstood Mercy, even armed with her guardian fae artifact. He tucked that back in his battle plans along with the green man who would be along shortly.

Now, though, now was the time for his fangs to bite deep and his claws to rend. No one was allowed to hurt his mate.

Mouth wide, he leapt upon the beast's back. The best attack, he knew, would have been to go for the creature's flanks. It moved enough like a normal animal that he felt comfortable assuming that its hind legs worked the same as the hind legs of most other mammals on the planet. Hamstringing was unlikely, given the size of the creature, but he could still do enough muscle damage to cripple it. He knew he could have dragged it off its prey—but that would further damage Mercy.

Instead, he aimed himself at the creature's back, as if he were a cougar instead of a wolf—because werewolves had front paws and claws that were more cougarlike than wolflike. Once on the creature's back, he could go for the side of its neck.

Only the landing went as planned.

There was a strange moment where Adam hung suspended on something that felt nothing like flesh and blood. He had already dived for its neck, and his mouth filled with something cool and tasteless that evaporated before he could puzzle out what it was. He was dropped to the ground on the far side of the creature, sliding awkwardly with the leftover force that should have been driving his claws and teeth deep into the enemy.

Somehow, it was like the hungry ghost—not quite in this world. He filed that information away and adjusted his plans again. Any soldier knows plans have to be flexible in the field of battle.

For all that the creature had the apparent consistency of pudding, Adam had managed to knock it off Mercy. But now it stood between Adam and his mate—which was unacceptable.

If he read the signs correctly from the tableau snapshot in his head of his initial sight of Mercy and this thing, Mercy had decided her best defense against this creature was Lugh's spear—and it had not worked. Her first defense, when she was alone, was always to run. Running had not worked.

There were other possibilities, but his instincts and a preponderance of evidence told him that this creature had come specifically to attack Mercy. It had been feeding on her—and not her flesh and blood. The spider had told Mercy just this morning that the damage she'd suffered from the Soul Taker would attract things like the hungry ghost. It could be one of those.

Or.

Here before Adam was a giant doglike being, caught between life and death. How many of those could there be in a winter-torn corner of Montana? One. Garmr.

Lugh's spear had done nothing to it. *Lugh's* spear. If a weapon made by someone as close to a god as any of the fae had ever been was not able to hurt the creature, he didn't know what could.

The creature lunged toward Mercy, and Adam lunged faster, landing between it and his mate. He got his shoulder in its way and shoved.

He couldn't hurt it, but it held enough of some kind of mass that he could move it back. He forced it away from Mercy, throwing his weight against it, savaging it with fangs and claws.

Now he expected the lack of resistance and he followed it. It was like pushing mud. With that thought, he jumped back on top of it and dug at its whatever-it-had instead of flesh and blood as if he were digging a hole into the earth. That was more effective than he'd expected.

It broke away. Adam didn't follow it.

Figure out your main objective, and don't let your enemy distract you.

He couldn't remember just now, in the heat of battle, if that was his old drill sergeant's voice or Zee's.

His main objective was to keep this thing away from Mercy. Because it wasn't hurting him, but it had been able to hurt her. He stood foursquare against it. Against *him*, Garmr. Adam might have reservations about his identification, but his wolf *knew*. Patiently, Adam waited for the guardian of Hel to attack again.

Which he did.

Once more Adam managed to drive him back. This time Garmr jumped away half a dozen yards. Adam thought it might be a retreat, but his wolf wasn't so sure. Garmr let out a hoarse, voiceless something that was not sound, but it shook the snow out of the trees anyway, snapping his vicious-looking fangs in frustration.

The green man was approaching—Adam heard his running feet on the snow. Friend or foe? The wolf moved his position so that, though he was still between Mercy and Garmr, he was also between Mercy and the place where the sound of the fae's footfalls would take him.

With some distance giving him more time to observe, Adam noticed that Garmr was significantly smaller than he had been when Adam first attacked. It was still the size of a big grizzly, but the first time Adam had landed on its back, it had been larger than a polar bear.

Maybe his attacks were doing some kind of damage to it, enough to make it wary of him. He hoped it was true, because that would mean he could win. But it was too early to assume anything so optimistic.

Garmr abruptly turned his head in the direction of Liam's footsteps, then, possibly driven by the knowledge that the green man was coming, it turned to run. It took two loping strides away from Mercy and away from the lodge, and stopped. Its long tail lowered and it dropped its head defensively, focused not on Liam's approach but on something crashing through the underbrush.

The wolf was certain that there had been nothing approaching them from that direction before the noise started. He coiled his muscles, the better to defend Mercy from anyone or anything.

From the woods in front of Garmr, a huge stag broke out of the underbrush. Adam had the impression it had been moving at great speed, but it dropped to a stately walk as it emerged.

It wasn't a real deer. Real deer weren't larger than moose. They weren't white with silver antlers that reached upward and outward in a testament of power.

The liquid-blue eyes of the stag took in Adam and Mercy in a quick glance. It snorted, the mist of its breath in the icy air rising to disappear in the shadow of the glittering antlers.

Its ribs rose and fell like an animal that had been engaged in a mad run through the forest. But there was nothing frantic about the slow strides that brought it closer to the creature that had attacked Mercy.

Without warning, the deer jumped forward, head lowered. Garmr tried to dodge, but the sharp tines buried themselves in the great hound's side. It lifted Garmr off the ground and shook him.

Liam burst over the hill and stopped. Chest heaving, he held a long knife in one hand. Adam would have laid out money that it wasn't a mundane weapon. Like Adam, he made no move toward the combatants.

Out of the wounds and around the horns of the stag a substance flowed from the hound. It was clear and it evaporated into nothingness almost as it hit the air. The hound's body deflated gradually. The stag quit moving, letting the hound waste away to a mist that dripped off the antlers and dissipated before it touched the snow.

It did not feel like a death.

Adam thought about turning to check on Mercy, but the stag's blue eyes focused on Adam. *The enemy of my enemy is not my friend.* Adam bared his teeth and didn't fight the growl that rose from his Alpha heart.

"No," said Liam, striding rapidly between the two of them, staying closer to the stag than to Adam—which was prudent of him, because the wolf still wasn't sure he was an ally.

Unexpectedly, Liam turned his back to Adam and dropped to one knee before the stag.

"My lord," he said. "Thank fate that you are here. I had despaired."

Like Mercy's, the stag's transformation was instantaneous. If Adam had not been watching him, he'd have missed it.

While a part of him might have expected to see a fae lord straight out of fairy tales, dressed in fashions of centuries ago, what stood in the footprints of the white stag was a young-looking man in black jeans that were wet up to his knees and a T-shirt covered in rips, as if he'd been running through a blackberry thicket. He ran his hands through dark hair that was too short to catch his fingers.

He looked tired. Deep circles of sleeplessness ringed his eyes, and it had been a few days since he'd shaved.

"The hound is loosed?" he said, voice hoarse. "I am too late."

"No, my lord," Liam said without rising to his feet. "Just restless, as he gets when the time nears. Especially when it looked as though the marriage and the rebinding were doomed."

"Is there a reason there's a naked woman lying in the snow and we're not doing anything about it? And is the werewolf a friend or enemy?"

Unlike the stag he'd been, Zane Heddar carefully kept his eyes away from Adam's as he spoke. Adam wouldn't have needed introductions if he had met the man at a grocery store—he was a male, dark-haired version of his mother. But his dramatic entrance and the reaction of the green man removed any doubt Adam might have retained.

"Friend—or ally, at the very least." Liam rose to his feet with grace, turning to face Adam.

"Leave off, do," Liam said, his tone making it a very polite request, not an order.

Adam realized he was still growling.

"This is my lord upon whose arrival all things are made right," Liam informed him. "Let us help you bring your Mercy out of the storm."

Zane moved toward Mercy. Adam didn't think the man was a threat, but he would have put himself between Mercy and a stranger even if his wolf hadn't been fresh off the battlefield.

"Let me try," Liam told his lord and master. He unzipped his parka and took it off.

When he approached Mercy, Adam shook with the effort it took to keep his wolf at bay. But he, wolf and man alike, knew how important it was to get Mercy warm, so they allowed it.

With a careful attention to Adam's growling presence, Liam wrapped Mercy in his own coat, setting the spear-headed walking stick aside. As soon as he had her out of the snow, Liam broke into a swift trot back toward the lodge. Zane made as if to gather up the spear—but the walking stick had disappeared while everyone's attention had been turned toward Mercy. Zane gave the snow where the weapon had lain a brief puzzled look. With a shrug, he set off after Liam and Mercy.

Adam brought up the rear—the better to watch the others. To keep Mercy safe.

INTERLUDE

WARREN

WARREN WAS FUELING UP HIS CAR WHEN HE GOT THE call from Sherwood.

"Warren here," he answered, trying to remember if Sherwood had ever called him before. He thought not.

"Car wreck," said Sherwood in a low growl.

He paused and Warren heard in the background a woman sobbing hysterically, a man's angry deep bass, and the howl of the wind.

"Are you hurt?" Warren asked, calming his voice instinctively— as if one of the less dominant wolves had called him for help. He hoped Sherwood wouldn't think he was patronizing him. Upset dominant wolves tended to get thin-skinned. "What do you need?"

Why did you call me? But he didn't say that one.

Sherwood took a deep breath, and when he spoke again, he sounded calmer. "Warren, I need backup, stat. Hurt not-serious but . . . control issue. Too loud, and the storm. And I—"

He was evidently having trouble putting words together, not a good sign. Sherwood was not a big talker at the best of times, but he usually could finish a sentence when he started one.

"Where are you?" Warren said, replacing the nozzle at the pump, though his car wasn't full.

In halting words, Sherwood described where he was. The bass voice Warren had heard blustering earlier evidently figured out what Sherwood was doing, and called out a pair of streets Warren knew. Distantly, Warren heard sirens. That was quick—Warren would have expected the police to take a while, given the storm. Maybe they'd been in the area—or the wreck was bad.

"Got it," Warren said, not waiting for Sherwood to confirm the address. "I'm in Pasco, but only about ten minutes away. I'll call Tony"—who was their unofficial liaison with the Kennewick PD based largely on his friendship with Mercy. They had an official liaison, but Tony was better because the rest of the police were half-afraid of the werewolves. "Hang tight."

"No other good choice," said Sherwood as Warren started his car and switched the phone to the car's Bluetooth. "My car is totaled and I can't walk."

Sherwood hung up without waiting for Warren's reply.

It should have been a fifteen-minute trip, with the cable bridge gone and freezing sleet making the streets as slick as a greased pig. But Warren's boyfriend, Kyle, had bought him an Outback under the pretext that it was a work expense. Warren worked as a PI for Kyle's law firm, which sometimes meant tailing or watching people. Kyle said his old truck was too memorable and the Subaru would blend in. He'd been right. Kyle usually was.

The Subaru also handled the icy roads a fair bit better than Warren's truck did. Warren suspected that it handled the roads better than even an all-wheel-drive with the traction-what-have-you and automatic-make-it-not-slide that it was equipped with should. His Subaru had an odd magical tweak.

It took him eight minutes, most of which he'd spent talking to Tony, who was headed this way as soon as possible. He pulled over into a parking spot well back and on the far side of the road from the wreck.

From his vantage point, he took a quick inventory. Three vehicles. The first two were skewed sideways in the road, a foot or so from the train tracks. The back bumper of the front car, a Mercedes, was intertwined with the front bumper of a battered green Toyota Corolla that he knew was Sherwood's car. If he'd been in doubt, Sherwood himself was leaning against the driver's-side door.

The front car had a piece of the broken crossing gate arm on the hood.

A third vehicle—an aging SUV with a caved-in front end to match the newly shortened back end of Sherwood's car—was stopped a few feet back and still in its lane. The other two cars were skewed so that they blocked all of their lane and half of the oncoming lane. Someone had set out cones and flares, as if the flashing lights of the police cars weren't warning enough that there was trouble.

He got out of his car and came close to landing on his keister. It was merciful slick. He gave the melded, road-blocking cars a more thoughtful look.

Sherwood had clearly sequestered himself away from the other people. He leaned, arms folded and head down in apparent thought. Unusually, he had a crutch beside him, positioned for easy reach. He couldn't have missed the sound of Warren's car—

or the gentle tug on the pack bonds that was felt when one pack member came near another—but he didn't look up.

No one was paying attention to Warren yet, and that was fine with him.

Warren passed by the police officers and accident victims without stopping to talk, taking in the group dynamics as he strolled. One driver, a sobbing girl, her face battered by an exploding airbag, was all but leaning on the broad shoulder of the very young policeman who had put himself between her and a middle-aged red-faced man who was shouting at the cop. Never a good policy, but people tended to get the sense knocked out of them after a bad scare.

"My dad's going to kill me," sobbed the girl, and other such words that amounted to pretty much the same thing, mostly, he thought, designed to elicit sympathy from the young cop.

"You damned near killed *me*," snapped the man. "And you would have if the werewolf here hadn't been able to move our cars before the train came. I can smell the alcohol on you from all the way over—"

"If you don't calm down," warned the officer, sounding less like a calm official and more like a defensive boyfriend, "I'm going to arrest you—"

It was a good thing, Warren decided, that Sherwood had taken himself out of that situation.

One of the officers stood to the side, looking uncomfortable. He appeared vaguely familiar, and when he saw Warren, relief dawned on his face. He tipped his chin toward Sherwood's last stand as if Warren might have missed him.

Or, Warren thought, as if the cop thought it might be a good idea for Warren to be here. Because of his work for his boyfriend's law firm, a number of the police officers were familiar with Warren and might recognize him by sight and know that he was a werewolf.

He picked up his pace a bit, and as he approached the battered Toyota, he saw why Sherwood had his crutch out. One jean-covered leg ended in a boot, and the other ended in an empty space. The prosthesis that gave Sherwood the ability to walk like everyone else was missing.

Like the girl, Sherwood's face was battered. There was a lot of blood on the front of his shirt where his jacket was open. Warren was pretty sure that some of the stains on Sherwood's pants were blood, too.

Sherwood raised his head, and his wolf stared at Warren. Before Warren could figure out whether to meet his gaze—Sherwood had called him for help—or to look away, Sherwood closed his eyes.

Freed from that dilemma, Warren looked away and saw something odd with the tracks on the ground next to the Mercedes. He dropped to one knee so he could get a better look at the marks in the snow where someone had pulled—not pushed—the two interlocked cars off the track.

He'd grown up in a time and place when tracking was part of a survival skill set. The marks told him a story as clearly as if he'd been here to see it. The places where Sherwood's good foot had slipped, unable to gain purchase on the icy ground. The round mark made by something like a pipe that had no trouble breaking through the ice to the ground beneath it.

"Break your prosthesis in the accident, or did you do it deliberately so you could get the cars off the track?"

"Deliberately," Sherwood said tightly.

"Hey, you, werewolf!"

Both Warren and Sherwood looked over to see the young officer striding toward them.

Warren fished his key fob out of his back pocket and tossed it at Sherwood.

"Why don't you go sit in my car and warm up," Warren said, walking toward the cop to intercept him.

Warren didn't mind facing off with the angry cop, especially when the other officer was an ally of sorts. Tony was on his way—and if all else failed, he could threaten them with Kyle. Kyle's specialty was family law, but that didn't hurt his reputation as a shark at all.

Moreover, Warren hadn't been injured in a car accident and forced to expose his greatest weakness in front of an enemy. He had a lot better chance of holding on to his temper than Sherwood did.

Sherwood caught the fob and carefully started to cross the icy road using his crutch. It wasn't graceful.

With another pack member, Warren would have carried them over to the car—or given them his arm or escort. Sherwood wouldn't be able to accept that right now. Warren wasn't worried about Sherwood—much—but his wolf was old and dangerous. The last thing that their pack needed was for him and Sherwood to get in a real fight out where a scared cop and some people with cell phones could watch.

The cop tried to angle after Sherwood, but Warren got in the way.

"I'm Warren Smith," he drawled with a big old friendly smile. "My friend Sherwood is hurt, and he's going to take a time-out over there in my car. He ain't gonna take off. What did ya need him for?"

The cop wasn't completely stupid. He stopped well short of Warren and regarded him with suspicion. "I need his license, registration, and insurance, and his story about what happened."

Warren looked at him. "I hope that you ain't plannin' on giving tickets to two drivers who were stopped at an active railroad cross'n. Because even a stupid hick like me knows that it's the lady who hits the stopped cars who gets the ticket."

"Hey, Warren," said the other officer before the angry one had a chance to respond. "Good to see you. That lawyer of yours did some righteous maneuvers for my friend whose ex tried to take his kids back. I understand that it was some of your work that made that case go the way it should."

Hell, he'd almost forgotten that he had a little more pull with the KPD this week than he'd had before. In his defense, most of his work on that case had been completed a couple of months ago. "Your cop friend needs to have better taste in his next wife," he said.

"That's what I told him." The friendly officer stepped casually in front of his angry coworker and held out his hand. "We never met officially." Which explained why Warren couldn't come up with his name. "I'm Trent Oliver."

Warren shook it. "Good to meet you, Trent."

Across the street, Warren's Subaru started up.

"He's getting away," said the other cop, turning as if he planned on running in front of the car to stop it.

Trent caught his arm and said, "Stand down," at the same time that Warren said, "No such thing, Officer."

To be sure he was speaking the truth, Warren looked at Sherwood, who was sitting in the driver's seat—which he had to, in order to start the car. Warren couldn't quite read the expression on the old wolf's face, but it wasn't the expression of someone who was about to drive away. Sherwood saw Warren watching him, and grinned.

"He's been sitting out in the cold for a while," Warren continued warily. He'd never seen that exact expression on Sherwood's face before. "I told him to go get warm."

Apparently satisfied that his charge wasn't going to go do something dumb, Trent released the other cop. Warren firmly turned his attention back to where it belonged.

"Warren, this officer is Cam Hochstetler. He's new to Kennewick and doesn't know how we do things here. Cam, Warren Smith is the best private detective in the Tri-Cities and third in our local wolf pack. What he's trying to tell you is that he has the right and obligation to step in when he thinks that someone is getting into trouble with one of his wolves."

Everything calmed down quite a bit after that. Warren collected Sherwood's insurance and registration from the Toyota's jockey box—and Sherwood's license, too. Apparently, he kept it in his car.

Tony arrived. The drunk girl was properly cited and sent home with the aid of Officer Hochstetler—who Warren could tell was going to give the pack some trouble down the road. The driver of the first car asked Warren to thank Sherwood for saving his life because he'd still been sitting stunned in the front seat when Sherwood pulled them out of danger. The train had been going past his window by the time he'd had the presence of mind to get out of his car.

Warren tucked the accident report number in his back pocket and strolled to his car.

Sherwood saw him coming and opened his door.

And that was when Warren realized that he'd been close enough that the car's audio had paired with his phone and started the audiobook he'd been listening to. He had a tendency to turn them off when the sex scenes started because having some stranger read about sex to him was just . . . uncomfortable. This was the first time it occurred to him that maybe that wasn't the wisest thing to do.

He was today-years-old when he realized that he could still blush like a schoolgirl.

"Ah, damn it all," he said.

"Are you embarrassed that your audiobook started in the middle of a very hot sex scene between three men in a swimming pool?" asked Sherwood politely. "There's no reason to be embarrassed about that."

"Get out of the driver's seat," said Warren. "I'm taking you home."

Getting Sherwood into the passenger seat took a while longer than it normally would have. Between the crutch and his laughing fits, Sherwood had some trouble on the ice.

The first thing Warren did when he got behind the steering wheel was turn the sound system off.

"Saddest thing in the world is listening to nineteen minutes of a twenty-minute sex scene," said Sherwood in a mock-mournful voice.

"They all die horribly in five more minutes, their efforts unfulfilled," said Warren, "victims of the shapeshifting shark lurking in the deep end."

"Really?" asked Sherwood in polite disbelief.

"I had the audio app on my phone off," Warren interrupted

him. "I have no idea why the car decided to connect to my phone and pull up a book."

Sherwood's eyebrows climbed up his face. "That, my friend, is a lie," he said, sounding delighted.

Warren sighed. "Let me tell you about my car."

13

MERCY

THE FIRST TIME I WOKE UP, I WAS SO COLD MY WHOLE body felt as though I was burning—a feeling that originated at my shoulder and boiled through my body down to my toes. My head hurt so much I wouldn't have been surprised to find I was bleeding out of my ears.

But that wasn't the worst of it.

When the Soul Taker had altered me in October, all that I had to do was look at someone and I saw . . . everything, I suppose, if I'd been fool to look long enough. That had been terrible and frightening, but it had gone away when Zee had destroyed the artifact.

I knew that the creature (Garmr—I knew it was Garmr) was not feeding upon my physical body. He was reopening the channel the Soul Taker had woven using my magic—magic that was divine in nature because my father was Coyote—and my soul to force my mind to do something that it was not made to do.

In my hands, the magic of the walking stick tried to save me. But it was not a thing of soul, like Garmr was. It was not able to do much more than keep my hands warm. But that might be enough to keep Garmr from killing me.

He wanted to kill me—but help was coming.

I could *feel* them.

THE SECOND TIME I WOKE UP, I WAS STILL COLD. SOME-one was carrying me. I ignored that, because it wasn't the most important thing—and if I thought about the stranger carrying me, I would get distracted. I couldn't afford to get distracted.

This was important.

What had the frost giant promised me as we groomed the horses?

Doing the right thing doesn't mean no one gets hurt. I understood, now, that he hadn't been speaking about my brother, or not only about my brother. He'd been speaking about what he intended to do to me after it had been clear to him that I was not going to find the artifact before the solstice with the tools I had available to me.

I will do anything in my power to help you find it.

Hrímnir had known what the Soul Taker had done to me. He knew that the ability was still inside me, despite all that I had done to close it off. And he'd had the perfect tool to rip it open again.

Because he'd turned Garmr into something very like the hungry ghost—a creature of soul, spirit, and magic—while Garmr's physicality was otherwise engaged.

And I knew all that because Hrímnir was watching us. And I could *see*—

I shivered and the motion was enough to distract me, and I could no longer hold on to the flood of information rolling by me too fast to catch or make sense of. I understood why the Soul Taker's priest in Hrímnir's story had gouged out his eyes in an attempt to stop this.

I don't think it could have helped much, because my eyes were shut.

THE THIRD TIME I WOKE UP, I WAS WARM. MY HEAD STILL hurt, but I was getting used to that. The air I breathed in smelled like Adam, and the frost giant's overwhelming presence was gone. It didn't help as much as I might have hoped.

I was on a bed wrapped in a blanket. My face was buried against Adam's hip, one arm wrapped around his leg, the other around his back. He was sitting mostly upright, pillows at his back and his shoulders against the headboard. Adam wouldn't lie down with me vulnerable and a stranger in the room.

And there were strangers in the room.

I used the familiar scent of my mate to anchor myself, focusing on Adam and using him as a barrier to hide behind. When that worked, more or less, I seized the ties between my mate and me— pack and mate bonds.

I kept those bonds tightly shut. I didn't want the information that was flooding my head to also flood the channels between us. I didn't know what it would do to my mate and the pack. But I held on to them tightly, wrapping them metaphorically—and that was how my magic worked best—around my wrists as an anchor.

My head felt like a calculator that someone had managed to

download the entire Internet onto. I might have managed to survive with the damage the Soul Taker had done—but I didn't think that I could function like this for long. Something was going to give out—my heart, my head.

But Hrímnir had given this to me as a gift—and it was a gift, no matter the cost to me.

Without Hrímnir's gift, I would not have been able to find the artifact—*and I knew where it was.* But I don't think the frost giant had meant me to be this helpless—I couldn't even bear to open my eyes for fear of what I might see.

I had this one chance to save the world. I breathed a little deeper, taking my mate's scent into my body. I had this one chance to save Adam.

I would have to be very careful to make use of this gift. To do that—I needed to hide what had been done to me. For just a little while, I had to pretend to be normal.

"I left my rental and luggage at a gas station in Bonners Ferry," said an unfamiliar male voice. "When it became obvious the roads were impassable, I came the rest of the way as the stag."

"Dangerous to travel that far," Liam said, with what sounded like disapproval.

Liam was old. He'd done a lot of things I didn't want to know about. His devotion to Zane was fed by his ties to the Great Spell in a way that made him a servant, exactly as a vampire's sheep are servants of the vampire they feed. But a vampire's sheep weren't usually powerful fae lords. The twist that made Liam serve rather than host felt like a punishment, like he'd done something to merit his fate.

I didn't want to know what he'd done or what had been done to him—though it involved screaming. Happily, before I was drawn further into who and what Liam was, the stranger spoke again.

"I didn't have much choice," countered the first man. He didn't sound defensive. "It wasn't likely I'd meet anyone in this storm."

The groom was here. Zane Heddar.

I didn't need to look at him to know him.

Zane's self didn't hurt me as much as Liam's. Zane had never been a mass murderer or a torturer. Or even a killer. But he was painful in another way.

Zane held his ancestors inside him, bearing the burden of the memories of every man in his family who had been one of the grooms for the Great Spell over the centuries. He knew their names, had access to their memories. If I wasn't careful, I might get lost in those memories.

Zane understood the nature of the Great Spell in a way necessary to its survival. He'd been born with the understanding of his destiny, and it had shaped his life. There were so many people in his head, I wondered that he could function at all.

I had a vision of a five-year-old Zane standing on the railing of a balcony that was on some sort of skyscraper. I could see the other tall buildings around him; a few were higher, but he could look down on most of the city. I knew that he was deciding if he should jump or not. If he jumped, would his parents be forced to have another child? Someone else who would have to bear the weight of their ancestors? Then that chance was over, his nanny wrapping her arms around him and pulling him off the railing. She was shaking and crying.

"Meeting someone would be dangerous?" someone asked— and I realized it was me. And that I was asking why Zane and

Liam both thought that him running around in the storm was dangerous for other people.

"Hello, there," Adam murmured. "Welcome back to the land of the living."

"That's pretty optimistic," I muttered. If I spoke any louder, my head would explode. "Let's say conscious."

"I could be satisfied with conscious," he admitted.

"Hello, Mercy Hauptman," said the stranger. "I'm Zane Heddar."

"The groom," I said—which was better than "Yes, I know." As soon as I spoke, I realized I'd almost forgotten that we needed to do more than just get the artifact. There had to be a marriage. "You made it. Congratulations."

There was a pause. I think they were waiting for me to pull my head away from Adam so I could see the person I was greeting. I didn't know if looking would make my understanding of him deeper—and I had no desire to find out.

"Zane came in to save the day when Garmr—the hound—proved resistant to my attempt to destroy him," Adam said.

And I felt Zane's puzzlement, because he knew Garmr. The creature he'd driven off hadn't been the way he remembered Garmr.

I knew that. Because I knew what Hrímnir had given Garmr. Receiving gifts from Hrímnir was apparently worse than receiving a gift from one of the fae. Dangerous gifts.

"Mercy?" Adam said, and I felt him tug at our bond.

I tightened my fingers—and tightened my hold keeping the tie between us closed. "Headache," I told him. Truth. "I don't want to make you hurt." Also the truth—even if I wasn't going to be able to avoid that.

"To your question about why my encountering anyone while I was running here—"

—*a long, cold run, longer than he'd ever done before. The consequences of failure were so high that he fought past exhaustion into a white space where magic supplied his muscles*—

"As a white stag," I said, comprehending the problem.

There was a surprised silence.

Pretend to be normal, I chided myself. White stags. I remembered a couple of stories about white stags. "Any human who sees the white stag will hunt it until they die."

"I was beginning to wonder if I was the one doomed to run around until I died," said Zane—and I realized he was talking to the whole room, not just me. This wasn't a repeat of a story. "I got stuck trekking fruitlessly around the mountains. It was frustrating as hell. I knew where the hot springs were." There was a hollow sound as he hit something—his chest, maybe. "But I kept getting turned around—and then, about twenty minutes before I ran into you, I was allowed in."

"Hrímnir?" asked Liam.

Oh yes, I thought dreamily. Because Garmr could have killed me—*would* have killed me if he'd been allowed to.

I knew that without the artifact, the frost giant's control of his dog was not without limits. He would not have been able to stop Garmr from killing me. Hrímnir would have known that. He must have timed Zane's arrival. But the frost giant didn't know exactly why Garmr would want me dead, because Hrímnir didn't understand what he'd done to Garmr. I did. I understood because no matter what form I wore—I could die.

Timor mortis conturbat me, I thought muzzily, unsure where I was getting the phrase from, my memories or the memories of someone in the room—but I knew what it meant. Hrímnir did not.

Zane, not a participant in my inner dialogue, said, "I can only suppose."

I didn't remember what question he was answering.

He added, "But just because I'm here in time doesn't mean we're in the clear."

He was the groom, and he was here. Necessary. Right. My efforts to appear normal were doomed to failure. I needed a plan B and I couldn't think.

"We need the lyre," said Liam.

"Yes," I said, my voice sounding oddly muffled. I realized my face was *still* pressed into Adam. His hands were threaded through my hair in a way I'd usually have noticed earlier. "Or harp. Depending apparently on which side of the wedding we're talking about. If Hrímnir doesn't have the lyre in his hands during your marriage, then Garmr is freed and the world ends." I paused. "Poor Garmr. It's tough being a good dog."

"Who have you been talking to?" Adam asked, sounding concerned. I definitely wasn't doing a good job of acting normal.

"I saw a frost giant about a couple of horses," I tried. I had a sudden thought. "The eggs didn't make it, did they?"

His warm hand resumed petting me, and his voice was definite when he said, "Mercy, no one is ever sending you to get eggs again if I have anything to say about it."

Something happened upstairs—I felt it before I heard anything, but the soft cry caught Adam's attention. I heard Liam's indrawn breath before a woman's voice called his name. The stairs were a ways away from this room, but I heard Emily's footsteps as she ran down them.

Liam got up and strode to the door, throwing it open.

"Emily," he said in a voice that would carry without being a shout. "Here. What's wrong?"

"Liam, Liam." Emily's steps, already rapid, changed to a full-out run toward our room. But it wasn't until she burst through the open doorway and Liam caught her by the shoulders that she said, "Victoria and Able are dead."

The goblins, I thought. I'd all but forgotten about the goblins.

Of course the goblins had figured it out—because we'd never gotten around to asking Dylis about the music in the wall. Liam knew the lodge like a chef knows his kitchen. Therefore, I knew where Dylis's room was, and what the outside wall butted up against.

Because of that, I knew why Dylis had heard music. The goblins had known it, too. They hadn't needed to walk through Liam's understanding, they only had to listen to Dylis and know the layout of the lodge.

They'd stolen the artifact—and paid the price of their theft.

"Able and Victoria?" asked Zane.

Emily asked, "Who are you?"

Liam said, "I'll explain, but first, what happened to our guests? *How* did something happen to them?"

A green man couldn't prevent harm from happening to his guests—he just took it personally when it did. He should have known when it happened . . . but he hadn't known about the hungry ghost, either.

But the spirit of the lake was different, and with Liam's knowledge, I understood why she was different. She should have been able to protect the goblins who were refugees from the storm. She should have protected them.

"*How did something happen to them?*" was indeed the right question, I thought. But no one in this room had the answer.

"Shot," Emily said, sounding as if the questions were helping her regain her poise. "Both of them. Right in the middle of their foreheads."

Goblins were fast. I could see someone shooting one before they understood what was happening, but to shoot the second one—

Adam thought, *Elyna*. And then he thought, *Is it dark enough for her to be about?*

But it hadn't been the vampire who killed the goblins.

Emily couldn't answer Liam's real question, either.

That was okay. Liam was thinking what I was thinking. If the spirit of Looking Glass had not saved them, it was because they had never been refugees at all. Predators, not prey. Then, usefully, Liam showed me how the lake spirit defined the status of refugee. The goblins could have defended themselves. But it did not mean they could kill as they willed.

Timor mortis conturbat me, I thought. The fear of death disquiets me. And I knew where I'd heard it, too: English Lit 201, the fifteenth-century poet William Dunbar. My roommate had spent a week trying to memorize "The Lament for the Makaris." But the phrase was older than that. I shivered. As old as mortalkind, I thought.

"Let's go up," said Zane.

Adam said, "I'm staying here."

That wouldn't work. I needed him to go with Liam and Zane. I needed to be alone because I was in no shape to hunt down my prey. If Adam stayed . . . that would leave too many things beyond my control. I thought that I might have this one chance only.

"Go," I told Adam, brushing my hand over the carry gun he had in the small of his back. It didn't feel like his usual HK. "You'll be useful. None of them can scent a trail."

I wasn't wrong. But I didn't know that for sure until after I'd said it and the thoughts of the others confirmed it. I needed them all out of the room.

I didn't have much time, I thought with black humor.

Adam stiffened—he knew I was planning something. He hesitated.

"Go," I told him. "Please." Oh, dear God, I prayed, let this work. One chance.

"I can stay," Adam said, and I *knew* he'd caught my fear and misread it. I wasn't worried about me; I was worried about him. About what would happen to him if I failed.

"Go," I said, willing him to continue to believe that what I was afraid of was being left alone. "You need to go."

He heard the utter truth in my words, because he left, shutting the door and locking it behind him. As soon as they were all gone, I sat up. Then I pulled a pillow over my lap and curled over it, resting my forehead on the cool linen. I waited for the coolness to make my head stop hurting so much, but that didn't happen.

The door opened again. Soft, hesitant footsteps approached the bed. A gentle hand touched my head. I didn't open my eyes, but I knew who it was. I hadn't met him—but Liam knew him, a gentle man who was good with flowers.

"Hello, Hugo," I said, and speaking out loud helped. Not with the pain, but with the confusion that tried to take over my thoughts. Maybe talking it through would help everything make sense. "Can I tell you a story?"

He hesitated. I wasn't doing what he thought I would do. But he hadn't had his magic torn open and his soul exposed to the world, so he couldn't understand me.

"I would like to tell you a story," I said, almost sick with fear of failure—and sadness. "Please, have a seat and listen." I tried to infuse that last sentence with a bit of force—Adam to his pack, giving a polite order.

I didn't need to open my eyes to know that my visitor had moved to sit on the chair in front of the window where someone else had just been sitting. I couldn't remember if it had been Liam or Zane. Then I remembered the reason I hadn't known which one of them had been sitting there was because I hadn't opened my eyes once since I'd woken up. The idea of adding light to my headache still had no appeal at all.

I couldn't read Hugo like I had Liam and Zane. Those two were old, even Zane. Maybe especially Zane.

My visitor was, in all the ways that counted just now, not old at all. I felt him as I expected a child would have felt—a rich *present*, here and now, but not deep or complex.

"Simple," Liam had called Hugo once—I couldn't remember when. The green man hadn't been wrong about the heart of this man, who, obedient for now, walked around the bed and sat down on the chair in front of the window. Though my eyes were shut still, the dimming light told me it was already getting dark. Tomorrow would be the shortest day of the year. Solstice.

Liam was worried because the marriage should take place as dawn replaced the darkness. Not much time at all now. And I was tired, so tired of fighting to find a path through all the information bombarding my head from connections that I hadn't quite gotten rid of when they left the room.

"I am telling the story for me, too," I told him. "So I don't get any of it wrong, or miss something important."

I hoped I got some of it wrong.

My visitor made a soft noise.

"Victoria and Able are thieves," I said. "Were thieves. Very good thieves. They were hired to steal the lyre from Hrímnir." I paused. "Hired by Ymir, I think—but it could have been—"

"Ymir." Hugo's voice was toneless—something had happened to it, Liam had told us. Cancer. Something like that.

Magic, I thought tiredly.

"I was almost sure it was Ymir," I told him. "But when the goblins went to steal the artifact, it was already gone. The storm was building and they . . ."

I paused. "No. I need to start with the marriage—I keep forgetting about the marriage."

"I remember," said my visitor darkly. "Hrímnir could, too, but he chooses to forget."

The sudden burning rage that seared in my head wasn't mine. I couldn't help making a sound.

"Are you all right?" Hugo somehow managed to convey concern in his toneless voice. I had no doubt it was real concern.

Ironic, that, considering everything.

But I reminded myself who I was talking to. None of this was his fault. Most of it wasn't his fault. He'd been facing uphill on skis without realizing it, too.

"No. But there's nothing to be done about that." I felt like I was in a Hans Christian Andersen fairy tale, where there were no happily-ever-after endings.

Now, what had we been talking about?

"Hrímnir." I thought about Hrímnir. "Very old powers are complicated," I said. "They compartmentalize in order to function."

Their minds might be like mine was now, all the time. I shuddered at the thought. Even if they only had their own memories, not those of everyone around them, that was thousands of years of memories. No wonder Zee played the part of a grumpy old mechanic so intently. If he existed like this—

I dragged my straying thoughts back. It was getting harder.

"The part that you see—" I thought of the various Hrímnirs I'd seen. The gryphon. The frost giant in the wolfskin cloak. The quiet man taking care of the draft horses because he'd taken away their caretaker. The one who had engineered Garmr's attack so that I would become what I was right now. So I could assume my role in Hrímnir's play.

"The part you see is real and true," I said. "But it's not the whole truth."

Hrímnir had sacrificed for this spell, too. I had a visceral understanding of how Great Spells worked and I didn't know where I'd picked that up. There had to be sacrifices—and Hrímnir paid that cost willingly. Instead of a Power who could change the world, make it a better place—because that was the kind of Power Hrímnir was—he lived alone except for his good dog and an artifact, the embodiment of his Great Spell.

"He has to forget to protect the spell," I said, understanding why that was. It was the same reason I couldn't pay too much attention to ghosts without making them more real. Hrímnir's knowledge of the Great Spell might make everyone remember. He held that kind of power.

"Victoria and Able," said Hugo deliberately. He didn't want to talk about Hrímnir. Their relationship was complicated and painful. "You were going to explain what their role was."

"You know what role they played," I told him involuntarily. "But this story is mostly for me, anyway."

"I am not sure of that," he said. "I . . . I don't always remember, either. 'Compartmentalize,' you said." He laughed then; it sounded awfully close to a sob. "Compartmentalize. So talk. For both of us. Explain it to me."

"Right," I said. "As the shortest day of the year approaches, the stronger the call." I'd gotten that from Liam, I thought, but I wasn't sure anymore. "People who are needed for the marriage remember, then they come. Or they come and remember. But the Great Spell is not sentient. Not quite. It runs more like an if-then conditional on a computer program. If you know about the spell—and the artifact, the harp, is the embodiment of the spell—then you are called here. You are *invited* to the wedding.

"Victoria and Able didn't know about the wedding or the Great Spell or anything like that," I said. "But they were sent to steal the artifact. They knew about it. When they abandoned their unsuccessful mission, they were called like everyone else."

"Yes," agreed my guest. "Yes."

"Ymir hired them to steal the artifact and bring it to him, so that Ragnarok"—I was having trouble enough with English sounds, I couldn't be bothered to pronounce "Ragnarok" the way Zee would have wanted me to—"so that Ragnarok would begin and he could break free and bathe in the blood of his enemies. You know what I don't understand?"

"What?"

"How did Ymir know about the Great Spell?"

"I told him about it," my visitor said. "I called him on the telephone a couple of months ago, when I understood what was going to happen. I called him and told him how to bring about the end of the world."

Timor mortis conturbat me.

"Okay," I said. "That explains Ymir."

I'd never have figured out that one without help.

"Anyway, Able and Victoria were called to Looking Glass," I said. "So they weren't truly refugees of the storm."

I clutched my pillow to my face and dried the pain-driven tears leaking out of my eyes. Hrímnir was right when he said there wasn't much time.

"The goblins were guests," my visitor said, sounding a little impatient. "But not refugees."

I nodded my head into my pillow. "Victoria and Able, right." I wondered how long I'd been sitting without speaking.

"This place is a refuge," I said. "And people who come here in need, people like you, are protected."

Instead of agreeing with me, Hugo said, "You aren't a refugee, either."

I took a breath.

"Not a refugee," I agreed, then changed the subject. It wasn't time for that yet. "But Victoria and Able didn't know about the wedding, they only knew about the lyre—"

"The harp."

"They didn't understand why they were here. But they thought they figured it out when I told them that the artifact they were supposed to steal, the one someone else had stolen, had been brought here. Ymir, the power they served, would have been capable of herding them here—or they thought so. Dylis heard the lyre—"

"Harp," said Hugo firmly.

"In the walls. Your room—a room in the back of the greenhouse where you sleep when you stay at the lodge—shares the back wall with Dylis's room."

"Yes," he said.

"The goblins waited until everyone was out shoveling snow. They broke into the greenhouse and stole the lyre."

"Yes," he said. "I was asleep."

I opened my eyes to see an older man sitting on the chair by the window. He was a little stooped and his eyes were red-rimmed, as though he'd been crying. He sat a little sideways, so I only had a clear view of the side of his body facing me.

"I have another story to tell you," I said, "if you can bear with me just a few minutes more."

He gave me a faint nod. He didn't want to come to the end of our conversation any more than I did.

"My father is Coyote," I said. "Once upon a time, he was wandering in the world and grew bored. So he put on a mortal body and lived as a young rodeo cowboy, Joe Old Coyote. Joe was a bull rider and amateur vampire killer. He didn't remember that he used to be Coyote. He met my mother, conceived me, and then died under the fangs of some vampires he was hunting. Joe was dead, but Coyote? Death doesn't hold any surprises—or permanence—for him. He dusted off his jeans and went back to wandering around the world. He remembered being Joe the cowboy and he remembered my mom. But he wasn't Joe Old Coyote. My father—with all of his hopes and dreams, his love of my mother—that man was dead." I paused. "I told my brother that story. I think he must have told it to Hrímnir."

"I have a story, too," Hugo said.

I had to squint, because I'd been right: keeping my eyes open made my head hurt worse.

"Once upon a time," he said, "there was a good dog who was bored. And his master said, 'I will give you a body, and you can go live in the world for a while as a human. Until winter solstice, when I shall take back the gift.'" His voice broke and he continued in a whisper. "I learned that I liked to grow plants and be useful. I liked to meet new people." He stumbled to a halt. Then he said, "If the wedding doesn't happen, maybe Hugo can live."

"You became Hugo," I said. "And you knew that Hrímnir couldn't come here. When my brother stole the artifact, he brought it here and left it with you. Where he thought it would be safe. Why did he go back to talk to Hrímnir?"

Hugo shook his head. "I don't know," he said.

"I don't think that preventing the renewal of the spell will save you," I told him gently.

He looked down. "You don't know that. Ymir said . . ."

"Ymir lies," I told him. "You know that."

"Maybe so," he said. "Probably. But at least Garmr will be free. I . . . I will be free. And there will be no more lies."

I was ready when he pulled out the revolver. I'd smelled the peculiar combination of gun oil, gunpowder, and char that is the scent of a recently fired gun when he'd come into the room.

Still, I waited until I saw his finger twitch before I shot him through the pillow I held in my lap. Adam's gun, the one I'd liberated with his permission, given with a nod because Zane and

Liam and Emily had been watching, wasn't the HK I was familiar with. But Hugo was less than six feet away.

He will die there, Hrímnir had told me the first time I'd met him. I'd thought he'd been speaking of Gary. I knew now that he had not been.

Hugo's body hit the floor, and a few seconds later, the giant beast that had ripped my mind open stood over it. He was still not quite real. His lips drew back in a snarl.

"You've done your job," I told Garmr. My head hurt too much—and I was too sad—to be afraid of him. "I played my part in this farce. If you had left me alone, I'd never have figured everything out before Hugo killed me, too. Save your snarls for your master." I put the safety back on Adam's gun. "Hugo was always fated to die."

The words tasted like ashes and truth on my tongue.

Adam would be here soon, drawn by the sound of his gun being fired. Zane was with him, and apparently Zane had been able to drive off Garmr. I wasn't surprised when the door flew open with enough force to hit the wall.

But it wasn't Adam who came in.

An elderly Native woman entered the room, clothed in a white deerskin elk-tooth dress and white leggings, her long hair a shade of gray that looked metallic silver, plaited into two braids that draped over her shoulders and down her chest, ending at her waist.

Her feet were bare and thick-soled, as if she spent most of her days without shoes. Her strong, fine-boned hands bore long, thin calluses, as if one of her usual tasks wore her skin.

Her attention was not on me but on Garmr.

"Poor boy," she said. "Poor, dear boy. It was not her fault. She only had her part to play, and she played it. Come here."

Garmr closed his lips over his teeth and quit growling at me. He carefully stepped over the body, around the bed, and sat at the old woman's heel. His attention focused on her face.

She set a hand on his head, unbothered by the not-quite-realness of it. "This has been difficult for you, and your tasks are not done, poor boy. Fetch the harp for me, if you would. We have need of it tonight."

He whined softly.

"Hugo doesn't need it anymore," she said. "He never did. You know that. Be a good boy and fetch it."

He chuffed and padded out the door—giving me a baleful look over his shoulder when the old woman couldn't see him. Then all that was left was the soft clicking of his toenails on the floor outside as he went about his task.

She surveyed the room and sighed. "Poor thing."

I couldn't tell if she was talking about the dog, the dead man, or me. I was feeling sorry enough for myself that I didn't need anyone else's sympathy.

"I don't know why they put locks on the doors in this place," I complained mildly.

"Locks only ever keep out people who aren't determined to come in," she said.

She sat down on the bed beside me. Without asking, she took the gun from my hand. I looked at it, too. It was Adam's 1911, his spare carry gun. I had killed someone with it. I had known I would use it to kill when I took it from Adam's holster.

After a brief examination, she set it on the bed. She put her hands on my face and looked into my eyes.

And all the pain in my head fled at her touch. The only thoughts running through my head belonged to me. I could *think*.

I could wonder who this woman was. The spirit of Looking Glass Lake, maybe? That didn't seem right.

"I didn't fix you," said the old woman. "I isolated us—gave us a pocket of time to solve our problems."

I blinked at her. With the pain gone, I recognized her voice. "You're the spider. The silver one."

"Call me Asibikaashi," she invited with a grin that briefly displayed her teeth. "Grandmother Spider. Or just Grandmother."

"Oh, Grandmother, what big teeth you have," I murmured, realizing only after I spoke that I was still a little woozy.

She grinned again. "Oh, no. I am no wolf. The big bad wolf is your mate." She made a sound of appreciation, and I remembered she'd seen him naked when she had destroyed the hungry ghost. It hadn't bothered me at the time. "A fine mate for Coyote's daughter."

She frowned a little and shook her head. "Such a smart boy."

"Adam?" I asked.

"Him, too," she said. "But I am thinking of that trouble-maker, my old friend, your papa. I did not see his hand in this— and I should have. I *knew* you were one of his the first time I saw you."

She perceived my confusion, because she laughed. "Oh, I have no doubt that you and I are both here for reasons that have nothing to do with putting off Ragnarok." She gave me a sharp look, shook her head, and said, "All right. I am here for reasons that have nothing to do with that. You are pinch-hitting for your brother."

"Did you just use a baseball analogy?" I asked.

She tapped her cheek just below her eye and said, "These old eyes see, these old ears hear."

She stood up, taking a firm grip on my arm—much firmer than anyone of her apparent age should have been capable of. With a tug, she had me scrambling off the bed.

"Come now, child," she said. "We have much to discuss." She glanced at the dead body on the floor. "And better places to discuss it."

She let me go and urged me out of the room.

"Clothes?" I suggested.

Grandmother Spider made a dismissive noise. "No one will see. We are still in our pocket outside of time."

I might have argued with her, but I didn't see any of our luggage lying around. Probably it was still in our original room. Being a shapeshifter meant I didn't really care about being fully dressed anyway.

I trotted after Grandmother Spider as she made a straight line through the main hall of the lodge, the big windows framing the darkness outside. For a small old person, she was quick.

I wasn't really surprised when she led us outside and down the path to the lake and the hot tubs. That's when I decided I did care about being naked.

"I thought we were in a pocket out of time," I said, my bare feet sliding on the icy path. "Shouldn't that mean we don't have to put up with wind and snow? Doesn't this stupid blizzard need time for it to move?"

She laughed, a warm, youthful sound, and took my arm again. Nothing magical happened except that I didn't fall on my butt when my foot slipped on my next step. I don't know whether she knew I was about to fall and stopped it—or if my start when she touched me made me slip in the first place.

"The frost giant's touch is more difficult to evade than that," she said. "It's a pocket, not a slice. If we can move, so also can the storm."

She paused, closed her eyes, and lifted her face to the wind with evident enjoyment. "Ah, one doesn't encounter a storm like this every day."

I knew what she meant. Part of me gloried in the power of the wind and snow—I thought of Adam's wolf dancing in the snow before he ran off to play guide for me driving the SUV.

The rest of me was tired, naked, and cold.

"Come on," I said grumpily. "Let's get in a hot tub before my toes turn black and fall off."

This time there were no lights, no fire, just the steam rising from the water and the filled tubs and the snow blowing over the lake. Grandmother Spider led me past the modern tubs to the far corner where a short set of stone stairs led down to the surface of the lake.

Native stone had been used to lay out a pool in the corner of the lake. It felt like a secret, tucked to the side of the platform where the lodge amenities held court. Grandmother Spider put a bare foot in the water, took it out again, and said something in a Native tongue that I did not understand, though I felt like my skin might pick out the meaning had I been less tired.

A faint, cool white plane of light traveled from one side of the little pond, reminding me of nothing so much as the light beam from a photocopier as it reads a paper. Grandmother Spider put her foot in again, then nodded her head and stepped aside.

"Get in, get in. You're making me cold just looking at you," she scolded.

As I waded into the waist-high water, she took off her clothing and set it aside, well out of reach of the water, though the snow blowing past began accumulating as soon as she turned her back.

"Tell me," she said, finding a seat along the edge that allowed the water to cover her up to her chin, "about how you ended up this damaged. There are not many things that can rip open both your soul and your magic."

She frowned at me. "That's not really the right word for it, either, is it? Not magic—but the source of your magic."

She grew still and her eyes were full of starlight—though between the mist and the storm, there were no stars visible above us. "You must be precious to him for him to go to all this trouble."

Coyote.

"But we'll talk of him later," she said, closing those strange eyes and snuggling down in the water. "Tell me about the thing that hurt you."

"It was an artifact," I said, "called the Soul Taker."

Unlike Hrímnir, she didn't appear to know about it. She was a good audience and she hummed a little as I talked, weaving her hands through the water. I couldn't see exactly what she was doing. It was dark, and the water from the lake made a small waterfall into the pond, keeping the surface rippled. But I could feel her power fizz against my skin where it touched the water.

When I'd finished my story, we sat in silence for a space.

"Now tell me," she said slowly, "how Coyote poked his nose into the frost giant's business."

"I think he convinced my brother to steal Hr—" I stopped at her hiss.

"Let's not name him now," she said, "in his storm. He can't come here, but still . . ."

I nodded. "My father convinced my brother to come and steal the frost giant's harp."

How had Coyote found out about it? How did he find out about anything?

"Possibly the wind told him," Grandmother Spider said, as if I'd spoken aloud. "The wind likes to flirt with Coyote." She nodded gravely. "Go on."

"I think my brother was supposed to steal it so that Victoria and Able, the goblins, couldn't steal it and take it to Ymir."

"He couldn't be bothered to just drop in with a warning," she muttered, her attention firmly on what her hands were doing under the water. I caught a glimpse of light playing along one of her fingers, but it was gone before I could be sure I'd actually seen anything.

"Hey, look, frost giant. Your brother is sending thieves to steal that artifact you need to keep the world from ending," I said in a cartoon Coyote voice, before dropping into my own. "Not his style. But my brother stole the artifact. I think something about the situation tipped Gary off that our father was playing a game, though. I think he went back to check with a source he could trust. So he went to talk to H— to the frost giant, who, instead of discussing matters, hit my brother with a spell that made communication impossible."

"By then your father knew what the Soul Taker had done to you," Grandmother Spider said comfortably. "He had this plot going already and saw an opportunity. A unique opportunity, in fact. So he saw to it that one sibling was replaced with the other. The one who needed to be here, in this place, at this time."

Yep. That's what I'd thought. Coyote had played my brother not once but twice.

"To what end?" I asked.

"Hmm," she said, bending down a bit and bringing her hands up to the surface. I saw light then, like a red thread in her hands. She lowered them again, and the water was all darkness once more. "Let me tell you how I was brought here, to this pond, to tell stories with you." She paused and smiled. "The night before the shortest night of the year is a good time for stories. For *remembering*."

The water tingled a little against my skin.

"Do you know Baba Yaga?" she asked me.

"Do you know," I said seriously, "that is the last question I expected you to ask me tonight. Yes. Or at least I have met her. And she has taken an interest in me a time or two."

"Ah, that might explain things," she said. "Baba Yaga told me that she had a decoration job in Uncle Mike's pub, and would I do her a favor?" She paused. "I owed her a small favor. And a Christmas tree in a fae pub sounded amusing—at least in theory. In practice . . . let us just say that I was looking for something interesting when you wandered in. Soul damage is unusual by itself. But there was more to it. And your power tasted . . . There are not many of Coyote's descendants running around anymore. He doesn't bestir himself to flirtation as much as he used to and—" She gave me a rueful look. "They do tend to die young, child."

"Mmm," I said.

"He and I are . . . well, not friends exactly, but we are friendly, and I decided to follow you a bit and see if I might mend what was broken."

"Heal me?" I said.

"I am not a great healer," she offered. "But I do weave, and sometimes that will substitute."

"You came here to help me?" I said slowly. "But what about Jack? Why did you attack Jack?"

"Jack?" She paused and gave me a faintly bewildered look before comprehension dawned. "Ah, the vampire's true love."

I think it was supposed to sound ironic, but it sounded a little tender to me. Maybe I was projecting.

"You'd mucked about trying to heal your damage," she said. "And it looked like you had some help, but you might tell the Dark Smith to stick to metalwork next time you see him. Clumsy repairs are guaranteed to make things worse eventually. I needed to see the actual wounding—and it was better for you to rip that patchwork off than for me to do it."

"You can fix me?" I said.

She nodded, then said, "With help. I can fix the damage to your soul, Mercy, but it takes a holy being to fix the damage to the spark of divine that your father bequeathed you."

She stood up. In her hands was a . . . a something. It looked like a piece of cloth maybe two feet by three feet, but it was made of deep red light that flickered and sparkled in turn.

Grandmother Spider walked to the edge of the pond, the one nearest the lake, and held her work over the surface.

I was somehow not surprised to see a woman rise from the steaming depths a few feet from our pond. Like Grandmother Spider she was Native, but her skin was smooth with youth and her braided hair—one long braid down her back—was pitch-black.

"She killed one who took refuge here," she said, her voice so soft I almost could not hear her. I could feel her anger, though.

"Did she?" Grandmother Spider said.

As if her voice called him, I heard the tapping of short claws on the stone where the warmth of the lake kept the snow at bay.

"Ah," she said, not moving from where she stood, holding the cloth of light. "Good dog. Thank you."

I backed up so I could see the spirit of the lake, Grandmother Spider, and Garmr at the same time.

In his mouth, the great dog carried a silver lyre whose blue stones leaked light into the darkness, illuminating the woman's face on the bottom of the lower curve of the instrument.

I took a good look at it, then took a better look at the woman who rose from the lake. It was as like her as her image in a mirror.

Grandmother Spider waved her hand at Garmr, summoning him to her. He set the lyre down and stepped into the water—which lit the submerged bits of his body with gold and red as if his coat were made of fire instead of fur. Maybe it was, just then.

He heaved his front paws to the edge of our pond, extending his nose out toward the spirit. She moved toward him and touched his muzzle.

"Hugo," she whispered.

"Hugo never was," Grandmother Spider told her gently. "He was an idea born in the heart of this one. This good dog who serves so that the world is not engulfed in madness. Mercy didn't kill Hugo—he was created to live briefly and had to die this night so that Garmr could serve as he should. She did him a kindness."

Had I? It didn't feel like a kindness.

As if he'd heard my thoughts—and maybe he had—Garmr turned his head toward me. His tail wagged gently, splashing water on my face.

Yes, said Garmr, his voice a deep bass purr. *A kindness. Though I think you would have saved him if you could have.*

"He was fated to die," I said.

From the moment he was created, Garmr agreed.

"Because of Mercy," Grandmother Spider said, "he did not take the world with him when he went."

He wouldn't have wanted that, Garmr said.

I wasn't as sure as Garmr was about Hugo's wants, but I didn't think this was the time to argue with him.

"Mercy has served us all," Grandmother Spider said. "We should help her in return."

The spirit gave the dog a thoughtful look. But when Garmr nodded, she took the cloth from Grandmother Spider's fingers and disappeared under the water with it. For a moment I could see a faint glow, and then it was gone.

Garmr waded back out of the pond and shook himself dry—or made the motions, anyway. No water splashed around him, but his drenched fur appeared to absorb the water. In a handful of seconds, he was dry.

"Good boy," Grandmother Spider said. "Take the harp that will be to your master, would you?"

Yes, he said. Taking the instrument in his mouth once more, he bounded over the wall and into the storm.

"There," said Grandmother Spider in satisfaction. "That's one thing done." Her bright smile lit the night. "And here's the other."

She reached into the bottom of the pool and pulled. The cloth that emerged this time was still made of light, but now there were threads of white intermingled with the red. She held out the cloth in both hands and then wrapped it around me.

I WOKE UP, WET AND NAKED, SITTING IN THE BED NEXT to Adam's gun. I didn't even have time to look for a towel before Adam burst into the room—tearing the door off its hinges.

"I see Grandmother Spider was right," I told him ruefully. "Locks only ever keep out people who aren't determined to come in."

INTERLUDE

ASIBIKAASHI
(GRANDMOTHER SPIDER)

ASIBIKAASHI RELAXED INTO THE HOT STEAM AND closed her eyes. It would be a while now before the mortal children came to perform their ceremony here. Hours.

She was more tired than she'd thought, but the satisfaction of a job well done warmed her more thoroughly than the water. It had been interesting walking in the world again. Possibly she should leave her cabin more often.

She slid lower until the water touched her chin. She could teach some of the young people a thing or two, maybe.

The spirit of the lake had lingered for a while, but she wasn't one to talk. She'd just needed more reassurance that she'd done right by Hugo.

That had been an odd thing, giving a dog—no matter how intelligent and ancient—a human life. Of course, the poor dear had been terrified of death. Immortal things should not try to be mortal.

As if called by her thoughts, someone got into the hot water beside her with a happy sigh.

She didn't bother to open her eyes to look at Coyote.

"You took some chances there," she said. "What if we hadn't been able to fix her? For that matter, what if your interference had caused the end of the world instead of the saving of it?"

He waved an airy hand and made a noise. "I never intended to save the world—why would I? True that I had no intention of causing the end, either. I had intended to twit that idiot Ymir."

She did look at him then.

He laughed. "You should see your face, old woman. That was the expression on Ymir's face when I told him about the Great Spell."

"Hugo told him about the Great Spell, too," she said.

"Yup," he agreed. "That was unexpected. Not that it mattered." He dipped under the water. When he popped up again, he spat water out in a small fountain, grinning as she sputtered at him.

"I told Ymir the whole thing months earlier," Coyote said. "That's why he had time to hire thieves—and I sent Gary to make nice with John Hunter." He smiled slyly. "Hrímnir."

"You set up an interesting game," agreed Grandmother Spider. She could spin webs, too. "Wasn't your son clever enough to play it out?"

"Gary would have managed," Coyote said. "My boy is good in a rough situation."

"But you found out Mercy needed help," said Asibikaashi in a soft voice. "And you changed the game for her."

He gave her a look she couldn't read.

14

~~~

MERCY

"WHAT DID YOU SHOOT AT?" ASKED ADAM, HANDS ON
my shoulders, body tense. He looked at me as if he expected me
to sprout wounds at any time.

In fact, I didn't hurt anywhere. My headache was gone for the
first time in a very long time. I must still be a bit muzzy, though,
because I thought he asked me what I shot at when—

The room smelled of cordite, but it didn't smell of blood anymore. I leaned over the bed to where Hugo's body should have
been—shot in the forehead like the goblins—but there was no
body to be seen.

I pulled free of Adam's light hold and climbed off the bed, my
legs oddly wobbly—to kneel on the ground where the body had
been. A pile of clothing, unbloodied—and also smelling of nothing except laundry soap—lay where Hugo's body had been.

When I moved the clothes, I found Hugo's revolver. There was
a clunk—and I found the lead bullet from Adam's gun that should

have been rattling around inside Hugo's skull. If Hugo's body had still been where it belonged.

I was dimly aware that people came to the doorway while I tried to figure out what might have happened.

Adam, after a glance at me, shooed them all away, promising them a meeting by the fireplace. A meeting where everyone would tell everything they knew about what had been going on. Zane lingered until the rest were routed.

"The storm is abating," he said. "Can you feel it?"

"Hrímnir has the artifact," I mumbled. "Good. That's good."

Gary would be okay now, because unlike his brother, Hrímnir would keep his word.

I felt Adam's gaze on the back of my neck, felt all the questions he didn't ask me.

Finally, he said, "If she knows anything, we'll tell you about it in a bit." There was a growl in his voice, but it didn't seem to bother Zane.

"This should be interesting," Zane said. "I'll see you in front of the fireplace." He knocked lightly on the doorframe and strolled away.

When the others were gone, Adam knelt beside me. "Who did you shoot, Mercy?"

"Hugo," I said. "He killed the goblins who stole the lyre—" My whole body shuddered, and I stumbled to a halt.

"Worry about that in a minute," Adam said. "Come on, get up. You need to warm up."

He wasn't wrong. He took a moment to holster his 1911, then he saw me to the shower. When he was sure I was okay, he left to retrieve our luggage from our first room, so I could get dressed.

"Bless you," I told him when he returned and handed me a

battered pair of jeans and one of his sweatshirts. The sweatshirt was warm and soft, and I could have crawled into it and slept for a week. The jeans were icy and four inches too long. He must have gone out to the SUV and found them in the box of spare clothes.

"Hugo?" Adam asked, helping me to roll up the bottom of the jeans.

I stifled a huge yawn and said, "Tell me what happened to you first. I need a moment to string everything together in my brain so it sounds logical."

He gave me an odd look and said, "We ran up the stairs. Emily was right, both goblins were dead with a shot to the head—looked like a larger-caliber bullet. We looked around. Then I heard a gunshot and ran back down. Ten minutes, maybe. Tell me about your ten minutes. They sound more interesting."

"It would have been loud," I said. Then clarified: "When the goblins were killed, it would have been loud. I'm surprised no one heard it."

"We decided they were probably shot between the time Garmr attacked you and when we got you back to the room," Adam said. "When no one else was in the lodge."

"Hugo said he was sleeping when they stole the artifact from him," I said. "I think that was when the frost giant called Garmr to attack me. He couldn't be both Hugo and Garmr at the same time. Hugo woke up after Zane exorcised Garmr—I don't know if that's the right word for it. I imagine that he tracked the thieves down like you and I would." I tapped my nose with my hand. "It wouldn't have taken long. I wonder where he got the gun." I paused. "Oh dear, I wonder if my brother gave it to him."

"So Hugo was Garmr?" Adam grimaced at my nod but didn't

otherwise react. "I'll secure the gun and we can ask Gary about it later." He unloaded the revolver and put the bullets in his pocket and the gun in his duffel.

"I killed Hugo," I told him. "It wasn't murder." It felt like it had been. I'd planned to kill him—hadn't been able to see a way out of it. But if I'd murdered him, the spirit of the lake would have stopped me—or so Liam thought. "Self-defense."

Adam said, "Hugo had the artifact—"

I waved my hands at him to stop his questions, gave another jaw-cracking yawn, and said, "Let me tell my part. I think if you start asking questions, I'll start answering, and you'll get the whole story sideways." I yawned again.

Adam frowned at me, and I felt the tug of our mating bond and realized I still had it locked down tight so he couldn't tell that I was just tired. I opened it—and Adam froze.

He inhaled sharply, once. Then he took two quick steps until he was standing in front of me. He put both of his hands on the sides of my face and looked into my eyes.

"Lord have mercy," he said. His mouth opened as if he were going to say something further, but nothing came out. He closed his eyes, rested his forehead on mine—and dropped to his knees until his face was resting on my belly and his arms were tight around my hips. He was shaking.

"Adam?" I asked, more than somewhat alarmed. "Adam?"

"Zee said he'd done what he could," Adam told me, "but he didn't think it could be healed. He thought one day it would—all of the repairs he'd managed would just rip away." He paused and his arms tightened. "That's what happened, when Garmr attacked you, isn't it? You were hurting so badly I could feel it even though you'd ratcheted down our bonds like tourniquets."

"Sort of," I allowed.

"And now?"

"My father is a sneaky rat bastard," I told him. "He risked the end of the world to get my head fixed."

Adam laughed without lifting his head. It was a soggy sort of laugh.

There was a knock at the door, and I looked up to see Elyna, her eyes soft. When she saw she had my attention, she said, "You're having a moment. I'll let everyone else know it will be another . . ." She lifted an eyebrow.

I thought of all that I had to tell Adam and said, "Ten minutes more. Maybe Liam could serve wine on our tab?"

She nodded. "I'll tell him." And then she strolled away.

When she was gone, Adam rose to his feet, kissed me like he meant it, and took a deep breath.

"You are fixed?"

I nodded. "Let's sit on the bed and I'll tell you all about my interesting day. I think I have to start with my visit with the frost giant."

I fell asleep before I was finished with everything. Adam woke me up briefly.

"You're fine because the spider and the spirit of the lake fixed you," he said. "Hugo was Garmr wrapped in a human suit who thought he was real and knew he would die when the marriage took place because the Great Spell requires Garmr in a physical form. Just checking to make sure I have the whole story."

I yawned and nodded. His version was shorter and better worded than mine was. "Been ten minutes," I mumbled. "I'd better get up—"

He kissed me and tucked the covers around me. "Nope. Sleep. I'll be your proxy."

WE GATHERED FOR THE WEDDING JUST BEFORE DAWN. There were still clouds in the sky, but they were softer clouds, lit by the glow of the moon. The wind was light and the snow had stopped entirely.

The bride's dress was white trimmed in silvery lace. Rather than play down her firm muscles, the gown's bare-shoulder-tight-to-the-waist silhouette showed off her strength. I could tell it was expensive because it also made her look delicate. And Tammy was tough because, although the storm was over, it was December in Montana and we were all outside standing beside the hot tubs. She had gooseflesh on her gooseflesh.

I'd assumed that we'd hold the wedding in front of the fireplace, where backless gowns would have been more comfortable. But the divine spirit of the lake was an important part of the magic, and no one could converse with her to make sure she could come inside the building. Liam assured us that it would be enough to hold the ceremony by the side of her lake, because that was holy ground.

In solidarity, the groom did not wear a jacket over his silver silk shirt. All of his clothes were borrowed from Liam, so the shirt was tight in the shoulders and the pants were about six inches too long. Zane was my height, a couple of inches shorter than Tammy. I hadn't noticed it until they stood together.

The storm had gone, but it had left feet of snow everywhere as a calling card. We had decorated around the snow with fairy lights (the mundane kind) and set floating candles in the hot tubs.

The bride's father and his pack wore their dress uniforms. In the light of the lodge, the police uniforms were deep blue, but out here beside the lake they looked black. Elyna had chosen a dress of the same navy blue with gold trim. The cold bothered her not at all. Jack wore a suit that looked black—but was probably the same deep blue that all of the bride's family wore. He carried his gun in a shoulder holster under the jacket—I could see the outline when he moved. Chicago in the 1920s had been a haven to gangsters and whatnot, but I hadn't thought an architect would feel the need to carry a gun.

I had thanked Jack as soon as he showed up a few hours ago. Adam told me that Jack was the one who'd made sure Adam had seen Garmr attacking me in the woods. Elyna's dead husband had given me a grin, told me that turnabout was fair play, and brushed it off.

I thought that I was the only one who could see him until I saw that Peter, talking quietly with Elyna, kept giving Jack a side-eye glance. As if he couldn't quite see that there was someone standing behind her, but kept getting glimpses out of the corner of his eye. I wondered, not for the first time or the twentieth time, exactly what I'd done to Jack.

The blues of Tammy's people might look black in the predawn darkness, but the same was not true of the groom's family. Standing on the groom's side, Dylis wore a long ethereal dress that was the exact color of her eyes—and her son's eyes. The brighter blue caught the reflection of the tiny lights in the tub, giving the dress an ombré effect. Andrew's suit was a gray pinstripe.

The rest of us, Adam, Emily, and I, wore blue, too. Blue jeans.

Emily paired hers with a creamy white sweater that glowed against her skin and looked thick enough to keep her warm even in the subfreezing temperatures. Her eyes were a bit red and puffy. I'm not sure she had believed my explanation of exactly what Hugo was, even with Liam's corroboration that such a thing was possible. She'd been stiff and uncomfortable with me when I'd pitched in to help decorate for the wedding.

But it wouldn't matter what she thought in the end. After a few days she would forget. Because Hugo was Garmr, and Garmr was the center of the Great Spell, even if he wasn't the heart of the wedding.

Like Emily, Adam and I wore our blue jeans, because we didn't have anything else to wear. His shirt was a deep green button-down that dressed up his jeans almost enough for a wedding.

I, on the other hand, did not look like a wedding guest in my overly long jeans and Adam's sweatshirt. I hadn't been able to find anything better in the box of spare clothes because I hadn't had time to restock it after the last moon hunt. I covered myself up as best I could with Adam's coat, my own having been shredded with my last pair of jeans in the fight with Garmr.

"We have the bride and the groom," Liam said. "The bride's family and the groom's family. We need witnesses. The first is the spirit of this lake, who is part of the holy ground we stand upon. We need two other witnesses."

Zane said, "I left my handpicked men behind rather than risking their deaths in the storm. I need a caretaker. The caretaker is usually a healer, one who has made sacrifices for their families, their friends, and complete strangers. Empathetic and kind."

Liam smiled. "The Great Spell provides. Emily, whose people have visited this place since time immemorial, whose chosen field is healing. Would you stand as witness?"

She looked startled—and not a little hesitant. Tammy put a

hand on her shoulder and whispered something I wasn't supposed to hear. Emily nodded carefully, took a step forward. "I will."

And something happened. I'm not sure exactly what, but I felt magic move and concentrate on her. My vision blurred a bit, and when I could see Emily again, she was dressed in a white doeskin tunic and leggings. She carried authority in her straight back and raised chin.

"The spirits of those who bore witness in the past have accepted you," said Liam. "Come and stand here." He directed her to a place behind him and on his right.

Zane said, "The third witness is the avenger. Fighter for justice. There is blood on his hands and fire in his heart. He brings the deaths of his prey without guilt, for his causes are righteous."

Zane looked at Peter and his men. Peter, in turn, a thoughtful look on his face, turned to Elyna.

"I believe," Peter said, "he is talking about you."

She looked more like a high school prom queen than an avenger. Elyna raised an eyebrow at Peter. He took her hand and kissed it.

She freed herself, rolled her eyes, and looked at Zane—then hesitated, her eyes finding the faint light rising in the east.

"For this day," Liam said, "the sun will not burn you, nightwalker though you are."

She stared at him, lips parted. Then she shook her head slightly and turned to Zane. "I accept."

For her, the magic found armor. Not parade armor with gilt and silver links, but the battered kind that had served useful purpose in battle. It looked medieval to me, and Eastern European, but historical battle armor wasn't a specialty of mine. She, too, took her place behind Liam, on the opposite side from Emily.

IN HIS CABIN, THE FROST GIANT PATTED HIS DOG, SAT down on an old leather footstool, and took up the instrument that was, for this last day, a lyre. He closed his eyes and played.

It did not matter that he was not a musician. It didn't matter that he did not know how to play the lyre. Because what he played was magic, and he would continue to play from the edge of dawn until the fall of night on this day that marked the zenith of his power—the beginning of winter, for he was the Winter King.

LIAM RAISED HIS HANDS, AND THE WHOLE WORLD changed.

Behind him and to his left and his right stood witnesses, but they weren't the spirit of the lake, Emily, and Elyna. They were the embodiment of all the witnesses who had stood in their place in centuries past.

Tammy, now clothed in silver from her headpiece—a fantastical creation of tiny flowers and silver branches with silver leaves—to her metallic silver dress embroidered with tiny white stags and black pearls, stepped forward to stand before Liam. Her dress ended at her calves and exposed her strong bare feet. When she stopped, though, her face became a wilder version of itself. White lines of paint or ink drew themselves over her cheekbones and around her eyes in ancient runes. As each one completed itself, I could feel the power rise around us.

Peter stepped forward to stand behind and to the side of his daughter, his men in formation behind him. They could have stepped out of a Viking longship with their full beards and long hair braided in warrior locks. One carried a spear, another a seax, the third a bow, the fourth and last a sling—and my instincts told me that the weapons were important.

Peter's elaborate sword felt like an artifact. I thought of Liam's careful words when we'd asked him if he could sense artifacts in the lodge. I wondered if the sword had been here. I wondered if it was one of the swords the Dark Smith of Drontheim had made.

Dylis and Andrew stepped forward. Dylis looked like a fairy queen, her gauntness elevated to elegance and her dark blue eyes jewels set off by the silver-blue gown that flowed off her shoulder in the kind of simple lines that only magic could attain. A silver-and-diamond net encased her hair, each diamond as large as my thumb. The gems were not clear but subtly blue in color. Andrew wore fae armor, white etched in silver, and there was a silver crown on his head encrusted with blue diamonds. He held a sword, longer and finer than the one Peter held—and it, too, was an artifact.

I had intended to stay in the background with Adam, but I found myself stepping forward as well. My battered garments traded themselves for a doeskin tunic and leggings very like Emily's, but mine were trimmed in white coyote fur. And I thought if I looked at myself in the mirror, I might not look entirely human myself.

At my side, his hand in mine, stalked Adam. He wore black armor and a cloak of black wolfskin. His eyes were yellow wolf's eyes.

The groom was dressed in a tunic and trousers that would have been plain if they had not been made of silver. His feet, like Tammy's, were bare. Upon his head he wore the horns of a great stag, and those, too, were silver. I couldn't tell if it was a head-piece or not.

And there, beside the hot springs, standing on holy ground, Liam spoke the words that would bind the fate of the world for another cycle. As he spoke, music flowed around us and between us, re-creating the Great Spell of binding with bits of power it borrowed from all of us. It wove those little sparks of mortal and immortal with the vast power of the frost giant who played the harp.

It felt as though it took only a moment, but when the power dissipated, leaving us in our before-the-spell selves, the sun was setting again.

INTERLUDE

After the Storm

GARY

GARY PARKED BY THE RANCH ENTRANCE. WHOEVER had run the snowplow—or more probably the resort's backhoe—had stopped clearing there. This left a huge berm of snow blocking the ranch's driveway, but also a pretty good parking place where the big machine had turned around.

Gary had planned on making the trip in one day, but the bone-deep weariness that persisted in hitting him at odd moments since he'd recovered from the confusion spell had forced him to stop in Coeur d'Alene and spend the night. Maybe it was for the best that he'd arrived in the daylight after a good rest, anyway.

From the vantage point of the truck bed, he could see that someone had cleared out the round pen next to the barn and put the Belgians out for their breakfast. There was even a stock tank in the pen that he was prepared to believe held water. Mickey was head down chasing scraps. But Finn, ever the more alert, had his head and ears up and pointing at Gary. Gary waved at him, which caused the big gelding to step forward suspiciously.

Smiling to himself, Gary stripped off his clothes. He'd intended to check on the geldings first off, but they didn't need him just yet. That moved up his other task to first place.

As a coyote, he leapt out of the truck bed and headed into the mountains. Running in the mountains was as close to the Christian idea of heaven that he thought he would ever get. And running in the snow was better.

Skimming the top of snow that was feet deep felt like a superpower that had nothing to do with anything except being nature's most persistent survivalist. The storm was over, but it was December in Montana and the air was crisp and clean.

It felt like home.

Eventually he came to a cabin that looked like the original that the ranch buildings had been modeled on. The logs had been hand-hewn, and the stairs were a series of logs piled atop each other and lashed. The rather crude-looking door had a dog door on one side, and it gave when Gary pushed his nose into the bottom corner—the wards here still welcomed him as a friend.

Maybe Hrímnir had forgotten to reset them.

Gary took his human shape as soon as he was inside. He was unsurprised to find the cabin uninhabited. The snowmobile that was usually parked beside the porch was gone.

The robe that Hrímnir kept for him was still hanging beside the door. Gary wrapped himself in it and tied the belt. Nakedness didn't bother him much, but there was no denying that clothing made for better conversations. And he needed to have a conversation.

His eyes fell upon a harp sitting on the floor beside the only chair in the small living room. It was a Celtic harp, graceful and well-made. Silver and turquoise inlay managed to evoke Native art without actually looking like any traditional art that Gary was familiar with.

It was a knee harp, nearly three feet tall rather than the tidy little instrument the lyre had been. It was properly conformed, too, as if, this time, someone had studied what an actual harp should look like. When he touched it, it knew him.

He picked up the instrument and sat in the chair that was too big for him but still managed to be comfortable. He began tuning the harp, recalling a conversation he'd once had.

HE'D PICKED UP THE LYRE AND EXPERIMENTALLY RUN *his fingers over the strings.*

"You play?" Hrímnir had asked, almost plaintively.

"You don't?"

The frost giant shook his big head. "No. I had a—"

"Lover?" asked Gary, surprised at the gentleness in his own voice. Gary was not a gentle man, but Hrímnir was one of the loneliest beings he'd ever met.

"Yes." Hrímnir touched the silver face on the lyre. "She was fated for other things, though." Then, in an obvious desire to change the subject, he asked again, "Do you play?"

"NO," GARY SAID, HIS SOFT VOICE FEELING LIKE AN INtrusion in this quiet room as he answered in the same words he'd given Hrímnir. "Now, if it were a harp—a Celtic harp, not one of those big orchestral things—I could have played one of those."

He'd had a lover in Europe who played the harp and taught him a little. A small skill that Gary had pursued whenever the whim took him. As his father said of one of Gary's half brothers, "Of course he's an extraordinary idiot. Take any skill and add years of practice and you get extraordinary." Modesty not being one of Gary's virtues, he knew he was a good harpist. He enjoyed it all the more because he didn't look like someone who would play a harp. Guitar, maybe, but not a harp.

It amused him that the harp, which all but vibrated with the magic it held, took so much tuning, as if it were an ordinary harp with new strings. But eventually he was satisfied.

He put his fingers to the strings and started to play.

Fiddly to tune it might have been, but the sound it made was extraordinary. Eventually, he lost himself to the music.

He didn't even hear the snowmobile. The first hint that the owner of the cabin was back was Garmr's cold nose on his bare foot. Without slowing his fingers, Gary smiled at the dog, who wagged his tail happily in return.

When the door opened and Hrímnir stepped inside in a wave of cold air, Gary did cease playing, stopping the strings with a careful hand.

"I didn't expect to see you back here," said the frost giant, closing the door.

Gary didn't know if he was happy to see that Hrímnir was in his most human shape or not. The frost giant was smarter and more rational like this than in any other of his many forms, but Gary wasn't sure that would work in his favor.

"I came to apologize," Gary said. "I feel I owe you that."

"Sorry you stole the harp?"

"The lyre," Gary said. "I'm not sure I could have sneaked out with something this big. But no. I'm not sorry I stole it. My father didn't tell me everything, but he does not lie to me. It was necessary for me to steal the lyre."

"Then what are you sorry for?"

Gary couldn't read Hrímnir's tone or expression, but Garmr, with his nose resting firmly on Gary's left foot, wasn't alarmed.

"I'm sorry I hurt you," he said. He stood up and set the harp gently on the floor. Then he took two steps forward, rose on his toes, and kissed Hrímnir lightly.

Big arms closed around him, and Gary felt a wave of relief. He was forgiven, it seemed.

"I am leaving soon," the frost giant told him. "It is time for me to find a new place."

"I will not stay," Gary said, thinking of Honey. Then, choosing words the frost giant would understand, words Hrímnir himself had given him, Gary said, "I am fated for other things. Another person."

Hrímnir nodded. "But not today."

"Until you have to leave," Gary said solemnly.

"Yes," agreed the frost giant in a voice like the wind in the trees. "Until I leave."

EPILOGUE

MERCY

WE HEADED HOME TWO DAYS LATER—AS SOON AS the roads looked passable. We had to guess because neither the Internet nor any of the cell phones, sat phone or not, were working yet. Probably some lingering effect of the storm or the marriage interfering. The lodge's landline hadn't worked in years.

As we drove through Libby, its citizens in the process of digging themselves out, Adam asked, "When do you think we'll start forgetting the wedding?"

"I don't think we will," I told him. "I talked to Liam about it before the wedding." I'd told him what Hrímnir had told me in the barn. "He thinks that because of the spark of divinity I carry because of who my father is, the forgetting part of the spell won't affect me. He was pretty sure that our bond would keep you from forgetting, too."

Adam's shoulders relaxed a little. "Good. Having Sherwood

in the pack makes the thought of someone altering my memories unwelcome."

"Doesn't it," I agreed.

It wasn't until we came down from the mountains at Bonners Ferry that our phones started working. We took turns returning calls.

I wasn't surprised to hear that my brother had recovered just fine. He'd headed out as soon as they opened the interstate, and we'd probably pass him at some point. Mary Jo was still fighting with Renny, but Honey thought that relationship might still go somewhere, because people like Renny weren't quitters. In New Mexico, Darryl and Auriele had killed the bad guys in a way that wouldn't get anyone in trouble and were headed home.

"The upshot," I said when we were done making calls, "is that the pack, your business, my business, and the Tri-Cities all survived us being away. It's kind of lowering finding out we aren't as important as I thought we were."

Adam laughed. The winter sun struggled through the frost-edged windshield to love my husband's face. I really didn't care that he was beautiful—but I wasn't blind.

"I love that dimple," I told him, reaching out to touch his face.

His laughter quieted, his lovely eyes focused on the road ahead. He leaned his face into my hand, but I knew that he didn't really enjoy compliments on his appearance—which, he observed now and then, was an accident of birth and nothing to do with him. He used his looks as he used every talent, every bit of knowledge, and all of his strength and cunning: to keep the pack—and me—safe.

"Ask me why," I said.

"Why?" His voice was a little dry.

"Because it only comes out when you are happy," I told him. "I like it when you're happy."

He glanced at me and away—but the dimple deepened.

My phone rang and I answered it. Silence drifted through the SUV's speakers, and the dimple disappeared as if it had never been.

Its disappearance made me angry.

"Hi," I said in a fake Southern accent. "Thank you so much for takin' my call. Do you have a few minutes? I'd like to talk to you."

Adam gave me a look, but the roads were still not good. He couldn't take his eyes off them for long.

I didn't pause long enough for the vampire on the other end of the phone connection to say anything.

"Life is short," I said, "and we're not getting any younger. What would you give if you could look ten years younger and increase your energy at the same time? Here at Intrasity Living, we are so proud of our products and the help they provide to people who are tired and beaten down by life."

And I spent about five minutes doing my best imitation of Jesse's best friend's mother's multilevel marketing speech—surprised at how much of it I remembered. I was waxing poetic about how our Good Vibrations essential oil blend not only had proven effective in fighting male-pattern baldness but also lowered blood pressure when Bonarata disconnected without ever having said a word.

"Take that, you bastard," I said, still clinging to my fake accent. "Bless your heart."

Adam cracked up. I was fiercely proud that it took him a good few minutes before he calmed down enough to talk.

"Where did that come from?" he asked.

"Did I mention that Grandmother Spider was urged to decorate Uncle Mike's pub by her good friend Baba Yaga?" I said.

Intrasity Living was owned and operated by the witch Tracy LaBella—otherwise known as Baba Yaga. I had the impression that she was both amused by and passionate about her business.

"Ah," Adam said, obviously making the connection.

I leaned over and put my forehead on his arm. "This didn't solve anything," I said.

"I know," he agreed.

We traveled maybe twenty miles in silence. Bonarata wasn't the kind of problem I could fight with essential oils, not even oils blessed by Baba Yaga for general public consumption.

Finally, Adam—still keeping his eyes on the road—raised my hand to his mouth and kissed the back of it. I sighed and kissed the closest part of his body, which happened to be the top of his shoulder.

"I kept waiting, but you didn't tell him that the orange essential oil raises the humble brownie to ambrosia level," Adam said.

"He doesn't deserve good brownies," I told him.

ACKNOWLEDGMENTS

Sincere thanks to the people who helped me get this book in its proper shape: Collin Briggs, Linda Campbell, Dave Carson, Katharine Carson, Dan dos Santos, Ann "My Trusty Assistant" Peters, Kaye Roberson, and Anne Sowards. Michael and Susann Bock made sure that Zee's German is correct, for which he thanks them. Also a shout-out to Jolene and Bob Briggs, who helped me get a phrase just right.

And thanks to my team at Ace: the art director, Judith Lagerman; the eagle-eyed production editor, Michelle Kasper; my marketing and publicity team, Jessica Plummer, Danielle Keir, and Stephanie Felty; and my editor Anne's assistants, Gabbie Pachon and Annie Odders. It truly takes a village.

ABOUT THE AUTHOR

Patricia Briggs graduated from Montana State University with degrees in history and German. She worked for a while as a substitute teacher but now writes full time. Patricia Briggs lives in the Pacific Northwest.

Find out more about Patricia Biggs and other Orbit authors by registering for the free monthly newsletter at orbit-books.co.uk.